THE BARGAIN

"For every penny you repay, I shall kiss you once in the center of the bailey before whoever might chance to be there. Agreed?"

Her mouth dropped open. He placed his fingertips under her chin and closed her mouth. "Is that a bargain you can make?"

She licked her lips. He felt a sharp punch of desire. In truth, he wanted to kiss her now, draw her to his bed, slide his hands across the shimmery fabric over her breasts, kiss them as well.

Abruptly, she leapt to her feet. "I-I, that is—"

He stood up slowly and closed the small distance between them. A kind of hot madness possessed him and his throat felt tight. "I want you to understand the kind of kiss you will get for your penny."

He wrapped his arms around her and brought his mouth to hers. It took her a moment to kiss him back, a few more moments to bring up her hand and rest it on his thundering heart. . . .

ANN LAWRENCE

Lord of the Hunt

LEISURE BOOKS NEW YORK CITY

In memory of my sister Helen, who loved to read.

A LEISURE BOOK®

January 2003

Published by

Dorchester Publishing Co., Inc.
276 Fifth Avenue
New York, NY 10001

ISBN 0-8439-5139-7

Printed in the United States of America.

Visit us on the web at www.dorchesterpub.com.

Lord of the Hunt

"A multitude of rulers is not a good thing."
                              The Iliad, Homer

Prologue

England, 1217

A row of monks filed into Winchester Cathedral on their way to celebrate the midnight office. Night cloaked the city, clouds the moon. Only the bobbing candles of the brothers marked their passage.

Adam Quintin, garbed in unadorned black to help him blend with the shadows, fell into step behind them. Candles flickered in niches. Wall torches smoked. Still, the nave was as dark as a witch's heart.

He slipped down the south aisle and into the Lady Chapel, avoiding the notice of a few stray parishioners. A monk prayed before the serene Madonna. Glancing about, Adam knelt beside the man, whose face was concealed by the deep hood of his robe.

They knelt in prayer for more than a quarter of an hour. The cold stone bit into Adam's knees. Finally, the man spoke. "Are you willing to accept a task for your king?"

1

Adam recognized the voice. This was no ordinary messenger. This was William Marshal's trusted squire, John d'Erley.

Adam stared at the steady flame of the candles at the Madonna's feet. He felt the thrill of anticipation. "I am always at the king's service as William Marshal knows—"

"Please. Speak softly. Walls have ears these days," John d'Erley whispered.

Duly chastised, Adam started over. "I am always at your master's service."

"My lord much admired the way you handled the trouble for him at Dover."

Adam shrugged. He'd learned long ago to ignore flattery. It usually masked some bitter brew. " 'Twas luck," he said.

"We do not believe in luck. We believe in results. And rewards. Will you pledge yourself to a mission on behalf of our lord and our king?"

A small sigh escaped Adam, setting a flame dancing. He must appear reluctant. Rewards were meant to be negotiated.

The moment stretched. D'Erley hastened to fill the silence. "The reward will be worthy of the deed. You may name your price."

He had waited thirteen long years for this.

"Have you aught in mind?" d'Erley asked.

The air was icy on Adam's bare throat, but a flush of heat swept over him. "I will think of something," he finally managed.

What must he do to remove a banishment? Redeem a father?

William Marshal's squire covered Adam's hand with his. "It is our lord's desire you be well compensated. He wishes you to understand the reward must meet the measure of the duty performed. In truth, you may die if it is discovered what you are about." The man idly patted Adam's hand as if he were a child. "In addition, it is our wish no man, no woman, shall know for whom you labor."

For the first time, Adam turned his head and stared directly into the other man's eyes. "As you wish," he said.

"Will you swear to it? Forgive me, but mercenaries are not known for their discretion."

"I may have joined King John's Flemish mercenaries to catch our lord's eye, but he knighted me and would not have done so had he not believed in my honor."

D'Erley cleared his throat and glanced about. Shadows flickered across the bare chapel walls as he twisted and turned to see who might lurk nearby. Adam waited patiently.

The man's breath smelled of onions and wine as he murmured near Adam's ear. "You know that even before King John's death, the barons were deserting to Philip Augustus of France through his son, Louis. Fortunately, our lord was capable of defeating the rebellious ones this past May at Lincoln."

"I fought with our lord at Lincoln." Adam's interest was greatly piqued.

John dropped his voice to so low a whisper, Adam needed to strain to hear his words. "King Henry may be a child, but he has offended no one, broken no promises *yet*."

"It is our lord the barons rally to."

"Granted, but still, he is acting in the king's name."

"You tell me nothing new."

"Our lord has discovered a viper in our royal nest."

Adam raised a brow.

"There is a bishop who believed the papal legate, Gualo, might wield more influence as the king's guardian than our lord."

"Gualo is but a pale light to Marshal."

"As the moon compares to the sun, aye, but this bishop held hopes of gaining power through Gualo. They are great friends. I suppose this bishop hoped he might ascend

3

to the same power as the Bishop of Winchester, but alas, the opposite has been true."

"And who is more apt to favor an overthrow of power than a malcontent?" Adam said.

"Our informer states that Prince Louis will try again to gather power for another assault on England's throne. This time, Louis will use not only the discontent of the barons, but also of this bishop, who is in a position to take one of the most important castles in England."

Adam smiled. "A bishop take a castle? With what army? No one may gather more than a score of men in any one place without suspicion, and bishops have no armies."

"They do if they can persuade a powerful baron to lend his. Therein lies our difficulty; we know who the bishop is, but not the baron. It is our lord's wish you ferret out this traitor, reveal him for what he is. Unmask him that we might foil this plot before it gathers momentum. At the least we can force the baron to give hostages to his good behavior."

Adam remembered well being a political hostage in his youth.

He placed a hand on his sword hilt and traced the cold, smooth metal. The weapon was out of place in this hall of reverence and prayer, but a man went nowhere unarmed these days.

"It seems an unlikely mission for someone such as myself. I am a warrior, not a thinker."

"We have confidence you will succeed."

"Or perish in the effort."

John d'Erley gave a slight shrug of his shoulders. Adam looked up at the Madonna with her outstretched hands. He sent her a silent prayer.

Make me worthy of my reward.

"So," Adam said, "a bishop will seduce a baron, who will lend an army, which will secure a castle for Prince Louis."

"As you say." D'Erley smiled.

"Have you any suggestions as to where I should start my hunt for this viper? I must assume our lord doesn't intend I blunder about England peering under beds."

"Oh, we can help you there," d'Erley whispered, his face hidden again in the deep hood. "Our lord knows the castle to be taken."

"Surely, the army will be very visible?" Adam could not resist the jest. "As will be the siege machines?"

A small smile played at the corners of d'Erley's mouth. "This baron will take the castle from within. He'll have no need of an army or trebuchet. Remember, a siege is visible. It stirs up others to take sides."

And kills commoners, and destroys farmland, Adam thought.

"Nay, a siege is to be avoided at all costs," d'Erley continued.

"As I said, I am a warrior, not a thinker. You'd do better to send me to fight a more visible army somewhere else. Send my friend Hugh de Coleville in my stead. He's as loyal to our lord as I am. He can outmaneuver me at chess and pose a riddle to test the best of scholars."

"De Coleville's family is far too powerful. The reward he might demand would test the power balance."

Ruefully, Adam realized he was probably not William Marshal's first choice. "And I'll be more modest in my demands?"

William Marshal's squire blinked. "Of course."

Of course. I have no powerful family, no name to tip some invisible scales.

"You will gain access to this castle through the front gates in the guise of a suitor to one of England's most coveted heiresses. Once inside, we expect you to discover who the traitor is and foil his efforts to take control of the castle."

"Without anyone knowing what I'm about."

"Aye. Place your hand here." John d'Erley touched the

small foot of the Virgin where it peeked from beneath her marble robes. Adam placed his fingers there and d'Erley covered them with his. "Now, make an oath you will keep your mission a secret. Swear it now."

"I so swear," Adam said.

"Well done." D'Erley turned over Adam's hand and dropped two sapphires into his palm. "Just to start you out."

Adam closed his hand over the jewels. "So, which castle is our traitor after?"

With another quick glance about, the squire said, "Ravenswood. If it falls, so could Porchester Castle and Portsmouth Harbor with it."

Ravenswood. A heart-stopping pain like liquid metal ran through Adam's veins. For an instant, the flames at the Virgin's feet seemed to flare bright.

The need, the desire to shout the name and hear it echo about the stone walls almost overwhelmed him. He clamped his lips against the impulse.

"Is something wrong?" D'Erley shot him a wary look.

Adam took control of his face and voice. "Is Ravenswood not held for the heirs of Guy de Poitiers?"

The old man crossed himself. "Therein lies the difficulty. Only Mathilda de Poitiers survives. Her father and brother are both dead. Her guardian is our traitorous bishop, Bishop Gravant."

"Ah, I see. If our lord sends a force to hold Ravenswood, the church will object that one of its most illustrious bishops has been insulted, his loyalty impugned."

William Marshal's squire nodded. "Our lord must win the support of the church, not its enmity. We must hold Ravenswood and do so without injury to the church—without siege. What you need to know is written here." He dug into the folds of his robe and drew out a folded sheet of parchment sealed with a familiar mark. "Read it and burn it before you leave."

William Marshal's squire rose with a groan to his feet. Adam stood as well. "How will we communicate?"

"A go-between, by name of Christopher, will seek you out when you arrive at the castle. He's been installed for weeks. It is through him we first gleaned some rumor that all was not as it should be at Ravenswood."

"How will I know him?"

"Christopher's a minstrel much favored by Lady Mathilda."

Adam followed John d'Erley to the chapel entrance and saw the holy office had ended.

The squire joined the long line of monks as they moved up the nave in a whisper of wool and scuff of feet on smooth stone. The heavy double doors thudded closed behind them, the sound echoing down the high-arched cathedral.

Adam saw no other living soul. He was alone.

He turned back to the dozens of candles dripping at the Blessed Mother's feet and knelt. For a moment, he studied the wax seal of William Marshal on the sheet of paper. Once he broke the seal, he was committed.

Nay . . . he had committed himself upon his oath. He drew his dagger and slit the packet open. He unfolded the fine vellum and one word leapt off the page.

Ravenswood.

There were other words, many lines of closely written script on the paper, but he saw only one. Ravenswood.

He could see the castle walls now as they looked in darkest night, the towers touched with moonlight and wreathed in mist. He could see the rolling hills and the deep, silent woods. Smell the water. Taste it even.

For Ravenswood he would attempt anything.

Adam took a deep breath. It was an omen. A sign from God. He raised his gaze to the ivory visage of the Madonna and sent her another prayer, one of thanks.

It was the first time in his life a woman had proved of use to him.

Chapter One

Ravenswood Manor, 1217

Joan Swan followed a well-worn deer trail through the trees near Ravenswood Castle. Her pack of hounds kept pace like a phalanx of the king's men. They did not roam, nor step beyond the length of her stride.

The hound near her right hand whined. She paused and listened. The hounds fell still in a ripple of sleek gray and brown muscle.

At first, she heard nothing. Then she heard the distant neigh of a horse. If she remained still, the rider might pass her by unseen.

The horse drew closer. From her right there was the sudden tearing sound of an animal forcing its way through underbrush.

With practiced ease, she drew her bow from her shoulder, then stepped from a pool of golden sunlight into a pool of soft green shadow.

The thrashing sound grew louder. A horse snorted, whinnied, and she heard the thunder of its hooves as it broke into a gallop, crashing through the underbrush. It was a wild sound, the sound of a horse out of control.

The hound at her side whimpered again.

Through the trees she saw the reason for the animal's fear. A boar. Her arrows were useless against such a beast.

She shouldered the bow. Her heart thumped in her chest. They must get away before it scented them. She lifted her right hand at the wrist so it was parallel to the ground. The hounds crouched. With a sharp gesture, she dipped her fingertips and the hounds went down on their bellies, preparing to slide through the brush like snakes in the grass.

Then she saw the man. He lay on his back, half supported on one elbow. His skin was stark white in contrast to his black hair and beard.

The boar clashed its tusks, lowered its head. Thank God she and her hounds were downwind.

The man was not.

Fear caused her stomach to churn.

Were the dogs ready? Was she?

The man moved. The boar charged.

She swept her hand out in a quick, sharp gesture.

Her dogs leapt in a monstrous, snarling maelstrom of teeth and sound.

The man scrabbled back and rose. He drew his sword. He did not run as she expected. Instead, he faced the swirling mass of animals who held the great boar at bay. In a motion as planned as if he and the dogs were one, they parted and he thrust the blade deep into the boar's neck.

It swung its monstrous head, eyes rolling. The dogs brought it down.

Then all was silent.

She closed her eyes, bent her head, and offered thanksgiving for the man's life. She knew the terrible sounds of the kill would remain in her head. At least none were human, none that of a man being torn apart by razor-sharp tusks.

A hand touched her shoulder and she opened her eyes. Dazed from her deep concentration, she was startled to find the man so close.

"Are you hurt?" he asked.

His vivid blue eyes were grave. His skin, no longer white, was suffused with high color. The close-cropped beard did not conceal his well-formed mouth. His high cheekbones betrayed his Norman ancestry.

Though uncommon in appearance, still, he was common enough. He wore a simple V-shaped iron pin to hold his mantle at one shoulder. Red streaked the humble wool. *Blood.*

"Are you hurt?" he asked again.

He had a low voice with a touch of an accent she could not place. A man-at-arms to one of the visiting nobles at Ravenswood, she decided.

"Me?" she managed, not sure if she could stomach the sight that surely lay over his shoulder. The man looked down and she did too. Blood splotched her gown. She shook off her squeamishness. She had witnessed the end of a hunt often enough, watched the butchering of the quarry. Why did she feel so dizzy?

"It's not my blood," she said. "Are you hurt?" She touched his mantle with her fingertips, briefly, lightly.

He shook his head. "I'm well, thanks to your hounds. They are your hounds, are they not? Well trained, they are, not to feast," he said.

They faced the wide clearing. Her dogs stood like sentinels over the carnage. In truth, the hounds awaited her next signal. They had killed and now wanted their reward. But not here. Not yet. There would be no traditional unmaking of the beast here, no blood of the beast for them this time.

11

What distraction should she offer this man so she might exercise her power over the animals unseen?

A crashing of branches and the sound of several horses coming at speed made the man swing about, his back to her.

"God's throat. They would appear now when I'm un-horsed," he said under his breath. "I've never been un-horsed."

Joan lifted her left hand and cupped her fingers into her palm. The dogs bounded to her, passed her, and disappeared into the thick forest.

A knight on a mud-splattered destrier burst through the trees into the clearing. He drew to a halt by the boar. "By the rood. What happened? Your horse passed us in a frenzy."

The knight's face was hidden by his helm, but when he wheeled his horse, she saw the device on his shield. A blue field with a wolf rampant. The house of de Harcourt. It was suddenly cold in the clearing—icy cold.

The knight slid his helm and mail coif off his head. 'Twas Brian, the youngest de Harcourt son.

Brian de Harcourt's gaze moved slowly over her. He gave her an almost imperceptible nod.

She swallowed hard and backed closer to the safety of the trees, but the man she'd rescued took her arm. His grip was gentle, but yet too firm for her to break away.

"You did not kill this beast on your own, did you, Adam?" Brian asked, swinging his attention to her again.

Adam. A simple name for a simple man. Then she realized the rest of Brian's men would be right behind him.

She must go. *Now*.

"In a manner of speaking. I took the beast with one lucky stroke, but it would have had my entrails for supper if not for this kind woman's hounds. They saved my skin."

Joan tried to tug away from him as three more men and horses pushed their way through the trees. She trusted a pack of hounds far more than a pack of men.

Adam still held her imprisoned, his gloved fingers almost encircling her upper arm. He sketched a quick bow. "Mistress? How may I reward you?"

More men surged into the clearing, their horses shying from the sweet stink of the boar's blood. Soon the clearing was crowded with men. She looked from one face to the other. Most were hidden by their helms as de Harcourt's had been.

The forest shrank around the men and scores of iron-shod hooves. The scent of greenery was overwhelmed by that of horses and men.

"Please, I must go," she said softly, urgently, loath to draw anyone's attention but he who held her.

"This is quite a trophy." Brian dismounted and approached the dead boar. He measured the tusks against his forearm.

Others did as he, touching the beast and prodding it with their feet. A woman was not safe with so many men—with these men in particular. Her heart beat more quickly. Her hands began to sweat.

Brian drew a short sword and hacked a tusk from the felled beast. "Here, Adam, have it carved into dice. They would surely be imbued with your good luck." He tossed the tusk to Adam in a spray of blood.

He let her go to catch the trophy. More blood dotted his mantle and hers. He frowned. "Brian, you've insulted this young woman."

"Joan's not easily insulted, are you?" Brian inclined his head to her. He had hair the color of chestnuts.

Joan made a deep curtsy to him, but bit her lip on any retort. Brian's father held an adjoining manor, had hunted with Lord Guy the day of the man's death, though Brian had not deigned to visit Ravenswood for nearly two years.

Heat ran over her cheeks. Brian could be at Ravenswood for only one purpose—the Harvest Hunt and Tournament at which the lady of Ravenswood was set to

13

choose a husband. The suitors, ten in all, were all due to arrive before nightfall.

Joan carefully turned to Adam, a man more of her station—a man who, by the lack of ornamentation or trim on his black garb, was the only man here she might comfortably speak to or acknowledge with any propriety. "You owe me nothing. Now, I must go."

"Surely you could use a few pennies?" Brian's words held her in place. "After all," he continued, "you saved Adam's life. He can spare the silver, I assure you."

How dare Brian imply she was needy? Her father was Master of the Hunt, not some lowly kennel man. She fought to keep her voice mild. "I ask no reward, my lord."

There were some quips about Adam's unhorsing from the newly arrived men; then a voice penetrated the banter. It was as hard and harsh as the winter wind that would come in a few weeks.

"Ah, Adam Quintin and a wench. A dog and a bitch will always end up in the grass together."

Joan pulled against Adam Quintin's hold. His fingers tightened on her arm, then relaxed and slid down to take her hand. The sensation was soothing, but nothing he could do would make her feel at ease, unless he would release her—and she could flee.

"I can only assume, my lord Roger," Adam said, "that you've spent so much time with your men, you've forgotten how to conduct yourself before a woman. Lady Mathilda will be tossing you in the moat where you'll stink as much as your manners."

There was a beat of silence. Then the men laughed and the baron reddened. Joan was a bit shocked a lord would tolerate so tart a response from a mere swordsman.

The baron jerked his reins and retorted, "I've no time for such nonsense. Fetch someone to butcher this animal and see that the best of the beast gets to the bishop's table." With a kick of his mount, he and half the party cantered off. The ground trembled at their departure.

"Forgive Lord Roger's churlish manners," Adam said to her.

Joan's heart slowed, her stomach eased. "It is nothing."

She squared her shoulders, prayed the man would release her hand. His glove was frayed, but of fine, well-tanned leather. It made her uneasy to stand with her fingers in his.

Just as the thought entered her head, he dropped her hand and made her a more proper bow. "A few hours in the saddle and Lord Roger is as prickly as that boar's snout."

Then Adam smiled and Lord Roger and Brian de Harcourt fled her thoughts. She could but stare at his eyes. They were blue as a field of harebells and framed with thick black lashes.

"Now," he said. "Your name is—?"

"Plain Joan," interjected Brian.

She wanted to put an arrow right through his throat. She almost reached for the bow slung at her back.

Adam raised a black, straight brow. He cocked his head and considered her. "Plain Joan?"

She ducked her head. "Aye. So I am called."

His voice dropped even lower. It coiled about her like a silken thread. "Lord Brian is right. I must reward you in some manner, Plain Joan."

Now. I must go now. She turned. Her path was blocked by a small, wiry man on a dun-brown mare coming straight toward her. He led a gray horse as huge as any she'd ever seen. Its hooves were the size of meat platters, its black mane plaited in a fanciful manner with leather thongs. The horse danced and pawed as it neared the dead boar.

"Yer mount," the little man said to Adam. "Ye rightly named him when ye called him Sinner."

Adam grinned and looked sheepishly in Joan's direction.

15

"He should be called Lady. He's as spoiled as any of those fine creatures." Then he took the reins and patted the destrier's heaving side. "And he dumped me like an inconvenient suitor the instant he saw that boar. Never take a nervous horse on a hunt." The horse bumped his shoulder.

Slung across the battle charger's saddle was his shield. Adam was no common man-at-arms, for the shield bore his personal device. It echoed the simple shape of his mantle pin. But painted on the leather cover of the shield, she saw it more clearly. It was a gold V rendered as if by an illuminator of fine manuscripts. The Roman numeral five—five for a man whose name meant fifth son.

Men with their own devices were not simple. That she'd mistaken him so staggered her.

"I have to forgive him, though, as he's not a hunter," Adam said, pulling himself slowly into a sleek saddle of Spanish leather. "Now, in battle, there's no finer horse in all—"

Joan darted into the trees.

He was a knight. Mayhap a lord. That meant he, too, was here for one purpose only—marriage to the most beautiful woman in Christendom. Lady Mathilda.

Joan heard Adam Quintin shout after her, but she ignored him. She would save a beggar with her hounds if he had been one so cornered. And in truth, 'twas the dogs, not she, who'd done the work. She paused a moment, hand to her breast, and took a deep breath. The boar had almost killed the man, but the dogs had performed as she'd directed.

Her hand signals had worked.

The dogs were waiting on the bank of the river that wound from Winchester to Portsmouth Harbor, passing Ravenswood Castle on its way. They had run through the shallows, romped on the banks, cleaning themselves.

She hugged them one by one, stroking velvety ears and rubbing smooth bellies. "I am sorry you cannot have your just reward, but I could not remain for the butchering. You made me proud, my loves. You rescued a man of worth for Lady Mathilda."

She remembered how he'd been addressed with familiar ease by the other men. It took little effort to imagine the carnage to the men's friendship as they vied for Lady Mathilda's hand.

Plain Joan, Brian had called her. His tongue was as quick as ever. Her cheeks heated that Adam Quintin should be introduced to her in such a manner. Now, Brian's opinion would be Adam's. It was an uneasy thought and she thrust it aside.

Her passage through the woods was no longer a joy, the dogs frolicking ahead of her no longer the pleasure of the day.

At a barely perceptible crossing of one deer path with another, she turned to the west. She would come up to Ravenswood Castle from that direction lest she meet any more men who might be rushing to fall at Lady Mathilda's feet.

But as she walked, she found her thoughts on fields of harebells. Harebells as blue as the new gown Lady Mathilda had worn this morning at chapel.

Adam Quintin was as fine in appearance as Brian de Harcourt, mayhap finer. Lady Mathilda would have great difficulty choosing between them. She discounted Lord Roger altogether. He looked like a starved crane. She hoped Brian fell in the foul water of the moat along with the rude Roger.

"Adam Quintin." She said the name aloud without thought. One dog lifted his head and whined. "Aye, Paul. You're right. I will not think of him." The young hound she'd named after her favorite saint barked. She patted his head. "Nay. I mean it. He's forgotten already."

Chapter Two

Adam Quintin rode a pace or two ahead of his men and friends. He wanted to see Ravenswood Castle alone. He stared straight ahead and as they came around the bend in the road, he saw it up ahead. The massive walls seemed to burst from the earth itself. The ramparts were touched with the gold of a setting sun. Banners flew from each of the four towers.

The banners were not his, or rather, not his father's. They belonged, instead, to Lady Mathilda's guardian, Bishop Gravant.

They would come down soon, to be replaced by the device of whoever won Lady Mathilda's hand in marriage. They would fall just as his father's had when King John had replaced him at Ravenswood with Guy de Poitiers, Lady Mathilda's father.

But de Poitiers was dead and Bishop Gravant ruled here now.

Behind Adam, someone called out his name. Adam

18

knew he would not make it over the drawbridge unscathed, and the barbs were as sharp as he'd expected.

Brian started it. "Shall I tie you to Sinner's saddle lest you fall off again? We would not want you to shame yourself when you greet Lady Mathilda."

His close friend, Hugh de Coleville, took it up, damn him.

"Sorry I am to have missed your unhorsing, Adam. I'd have given my best mare to have seen it. But surely, this bodes well for you, Brian? You may spare your lance and arm in the tournament if Sinner tosses him again."

With a grin, Brian nodded. "Aye. I swear 'tis Adam's mount that causes him to win so often."

"Shall we tie you to the saddle?" Hugh continued despite the scowl Adam shot in his direction. "Aye, Adam, let us tie you on. You cannot afford to injure yourself. Bruises will not turn the lady's head, you know. I'd best do it now before you get into more trouble. Toss me some rope, Brian."

Adam shot Hugh a rude gesture and galloped forward, ignoring the pain in his spine from the fall.

Sinner crossed the drawbridge. Elation rose in Adam's throat as the horse's hooves sounded on the wooden planks, then struck the stone that paved the outer bailey. He wanted to shout his exultation.

He was inside. Inside Ravenswood for the first time in over a decade. Inside for the first time since his father had been banished and lost all to the unworthy de Poitiers.

Adam found himself smiling, nay, grinning. The insults and barbs from Hugh and Brian mattered not at all. He rounded on the men, standing a bit in his stirrups to relieve the ache in his back.

"Are you saying Lady Mathilda will be seeing my bruises so soon? On my ass, they are. Will she choose me that quickly? If so, you both might as well give up the hunt now."

Hugh's grin turned to a frown as he maneuvered his mount next to Adam's. The frown only intensified the deep lines about his mouth. He had tawny-colored hair and a ruddy complexion, now even redder as his thoughts turned sour. "Make no mistake, Adam. I have no designs on the lady. You forget I've met her—several times. I'm here to watch you rout these other suitors in the tournament, nothing more."

"And glad I am you've come." Adam dismounted. The outer bailey was as unrecognizable as the village had been when he'd ridden through an hour ago. With a tournament but a week away, every possible merchant and craftsman in the area had come to set up a stall in the outer bailey. The village was filled with them as well.

A horde of grooms rushed forward to grab the reins of the many horses now milling about before the long row of Ravenswood's stables.

Brian de Harcourt addressed himself to Adam as he dismounted. "I haven't seen Lady Mathilda in two years, but if she's grown so shallow your bruised ass is enough to snare her, I've little interest in her myself."

Adam shrugged. "Who cares if she's shallow? She's a woman, after all. And I intend to be first and foremost in her mind from the instant we meet."

Adam wanted Brian to know he would not be an easy opponent. He intended to excel at both the tournament and the hunt—the hunt for William Marshal's traitor, that is.

And he intended to ask a high reward—his father's banishment lifted, and Ravenswood returned to the de Marle family. He would insist on command of the strategic manor and raise a different banner over its walls. His own.

Joan walked over the drawbridge, the hounds a few paces behind her. Thickening dusk muddied the bright colors of the banners that flew from the tents set out for the Harvest

Hunt and Tournament. They ranged in size from small dun tents that housed the pages and squires of lords and knights to the more elaborate pavilions for the wellborn.

The most important lords or knights would be within the keep. The status of a man would be clear from where he laid his head—from the highest honors of a chamber within the keep to the tents in the cold bailey.

She passed through the gate that separated the outer bailey from the inner. This area surrounded the great stone keep. It was filled with the bustle of servants running from bake house to hall. Here stood the tents of the most important knights. Around the tents were the usual accompaniment of cooking fires and men.

One pavilion with a high-peaked roof stood a bit apart from the others. It was stark black. No pennant flew from its peak. Two men strolled back and forth before it and Joan knew they must be guards.

There was something sinister about the way the tent began to disappear into the shadows as night fell. Then the entrance flap lifted, revealing a quick glimpse of a candle's glow. A small man burst out and hastened away, calling a greeting to the two guards.

It was the man who'd brought Adam Quintin his war horse. Joan's step slowed. She watched a moment, then shook off her reverie. The men who flocked to Ravenswood held no interest for her save as people to be avoided.

The black pavilion remained in her line of vision as she entered the kennels. They were new, expanded within the last twelve-month to half again their original size. The building was circular, made of well-seasoned timber, with a thatched upper story. She entered at the end of the run, greeting the dogs who roamed the space, petting each hound, praising their coats and their lineage.

A feeling came over her that she was being watched. She glanced around. There was no one loitering about. The knights and their men were making their places, marking out their areas with banners thrust into the dirt. Servants ran back and forth with water and trays of meat.

Once in the warm shelter of the kennels, Joan lost the sense of unease. She gave orders to the kennel lads on the strewing of fresh straw, then ran the few steps to her father's cottage.

Built against the castle wall behind the kennels, the three-room stone cottage was a luxury designating her father's lofty status in Ravenswood's hierarchy of servants. The great front room had a hearth at one end, a couch covered in furs along one wall, and an oak table polished smooth by years of scrubbing in the center. Her father sat in the gathering gloom at the table, idly stroking a spotted hound's ear.

Nat Swan looked up and smiled. "Ah, Joan. Back finally. We've had a busy day—we're hungry, girl."

A bowl and spoon sat by his elbow. Joan stirred it once and frowned. "Papa, you've let the potage grow cold."

"Eh?" He stared at the bowl as if he'd only just noticed it. "Did I?"

Then he laughed and wrapped an arm about her waist and squeezed. He was still strong, although he was more than six decades old. It was a bone-crushing hug.

"You're a good girl, Joan. I'm sorry I wasted the food. Give it to Jupiter, here."

Jupiter. A hound dead at least ten years. Most of the hounds of today bore saints' names.

Joan moved about the cottage lighting wicks in small dishes of oil to chase away the gloom. She cleared her throat. "Papa, Brian de Harcourt is here. Come for the tournament."

His gray brows knitted into a frown. The hand he used to rub his temple was gnarled and trembled a bit with age. "Brian de Harcourt? Do I know him?"

"Nay, Papa, do not fret on it. You don't know him." Joan discarded the cold potage. She put a bowl of bread soaked in broth on the floor for the spotted lymer, Matthew, not Jupiter.

Matthew, and the other lymers, dogs slightly larger than a greyhound, would be busy with Nat this week as it was the lymer who went out in advance with the Master of the Hunt when he tracked important game. Finding the quarry depended on the scenting abilities of the lymers.

She gave Matthew a rub behind his ears and a sign that he might eat.

"Explain to me again why they've all come, sweetling."

"Bishop Gravant is honoring Lord Guy's dying wish that Lady Mathilda might choose her own husband."

"Then let the lady choose, eh?" Nat addressed the dog. "Though 'tis a folly, isn't it, young fellow, to allow a lady such an important decision?"

Taking another wooden bowl from a shelf over the low door, Joan ladled a fresh bowl of potage for her father.

"Eat." She placed the spoon directly into his hand this time and stroked his gray head. "And the bishop agrees with you. He has grown impatient with Lady Mathilda. 'Tis why he's holding these festivities. He has gathered England's finest and at the end of the week, Lady Mathilda must choose her husband or the bishop swears he'll choose for her."

Nat looked up at Joan. "Festivities, you say? We'll be busy, then?"

There had been orders on a daily basis from the bishop about hunting. How could her father be so vague? "Aye. Very busy. Now eat before your supper gets cold."

He nodded and bent over his bowl.

She would not tell him about the boar. He would want to know why she'd had the dogs out in the forest without him. She had not the energy to talk around the truth.

She plucked up one of Nat's tunics and began to stitch a small rent. Then she saw the dried blood on her skirt. He'd not noticed it. She rose and hurried into the chamber where she slept. It had a wide window facing the kennels. She pulled the shutters closed and took off her soiled clothes. The air was cold as she stood in her linen shift and looked over the gowns hanging on a row of pegs. She ignored those cast off by Lady Mathilda. They were far too fine for wandering in the woods with a pack of dogs.

Instead, she pulled down a worn gown of deep russet wool with an overgown to match. Hastily, ere Nat remarked on her absence, she dressed. She plaited her hair, tied it with a thin leather thong, then gathered up her bloodstained gown into a bundle, which she set by the door. Edwina, the woman who commanded the wash house, would see to it.

Joan sat by the hearth fire to finish her mending as Nat nodded over his meal, but she could barely see to set her stitches straight.

How could Nat forget Brian de Harcourt? He had figured largely in their lives once. There was so much that Nat forgot these days. Then she chastised herself. Nat was always more forgetful of an evening. He would be fine in the morning sunshine.

Something warm dropped on the back of her hand. A tear. Others spilled down her cheeks. Angry with herself for such weakness, she dashed them away. Then, unable to stem their flow, she rose and escaped the cottage.

The kennel was warm and scented with the dogs and freshly cut wood. She told the lads to have a wander around the village if they'd like. When they scurried away to enjoy a few moments of unexpected leisure, she leaned on one of the dividing walls that separated the alaunts from the mastiffs, the greyhounds from the running hounds.

It was the running hounds she'd taken to the forest that day. Unlike the greyhounds and the more reckless alaunts, running hounds were not bred to pull down prey. So

Adam Quintin had been blessed that they'd done so. They were bred, instead, to run all day long in pursuit of the quarry and lead the hunter to the kill.

She sank to her knees, gathered a favorite hound in, and buried her face in his silky coat.

A dog and a bitch will always end up in the grass together, Lord Roger had said. How could she endure such a man's contempt? How could she escape his notice? She must accompany her father when the hounds were brought out, and surely Lord Roger would be at every hunt.

She allowed herself only a few moments more of self-pity; then she stood and shook out her skirts. Glancing outside the kennel to be sure no lads lingered nearby, she climbed a ladder to the second floor.

The upper story was quiet and dim, the torches on the lower level not lighting the space well. In summer, the lads might sleep up here away from the heat of the hounds, but now, with the crisp autumnal weather, no pallets lay about. The floor was swept clean of straw. At one end stood several locked coffers that held the more valuable collars and leashes. The mundane ones hung on hooks below.

She unlocked one chest and withdrew a small store of hard nuggets. She had baked them herself from honey and crusty bread. Meat and blood were given to the hounds only at the kill.

As she climbed down the ladder, the hounds rose and as one, wagged their tails. They knew what came next.

"You're anxious for our lessons, aren't you?" she whispered to the pack. "Well, if you attend, you shall have your reward. And we have little time before the lads return."

With that, she moved from stall to stall, teaching the hounds desperate lessons needed to survive her father's descent into some world she could not visit. Lessons that

25

commanded the dogs by silent hand signals. Hand signals they would obey no matter what confused order her father uttered. Silent and subtle signals lest Bishop Gravant notice it was she who commanded them, not her father.

Chapter Three

Adam jammed another thick candle onto an iron spike. His squire, Douglas, grunted and fumed behind him. It was difficult to conceal a grin as Douglas insulted first the slotted wooden bed frame, then the bedding.

"Ye cultivate a hard air, ye do, but I know ye sleep on a soft mattress. Feathers indeed! Linen and furs!" He sniffed. "Why ye cannot sleep on a straw pallet like the rest o' us I'll never know."

"You claim contempt for all trappings of wealth when you're at the alehouse, but I've caught you napping on the very mattress and furs you so soundly curse, so you don't fool me."

Douglas sniffed again and tossed a fur across the bed.

Adam gave the man a clap on the back, then a nudge toward the tent's flap. "See to Sinner and then hie yourself to the alehouse. I want to know what brews."

Douglas touched his forelock and bobbed his head. "Oh, aye. We'll see what brews. Ha, ha. Good one, sir."

No sooner had Adam tugged off his boots and fallen with a groan on his soft mattress than Hugh came through from the front section of the pavilion to the back sleeping space. He sat on one of the two folding stools near a trestle table on which a page would soon lay out the evening repast.

"So, you persist in this nonsense?" Hugh swept out his hand to indicate the luxurious pavilion. "Why not share my chamber?"

"It is not nonsense. You may sleep in the keep, but I will not. Not until I can assume my rightful place."

"And if you don't win Lady Mathilda?"

"Then I will never sleep there." He grinned at his friend. "But I do not intend to lose."

It pained him he could not tell Hugh the true reason he was at Ravenswood. He would miss his friend's counsel. Adam shifted his backside on the mattress. "I feel as if I've been beaten with a stick."

Hugh dragged his stool close to the camp bed and dropped his voice to a whisper. "Have you no fear someone will recognize you?"

"Mayhap someone will find me somewhat familiar. But I visited Ravenswood only three times between my ninth birthday and my fifteenth. Twice at Christmas and once to see my mother buried. Who will remember a child from so long ago? I'm a man rising three decades. I've nothing in common with that boy."

Hugh grunted. "Marriage is no way to get Ravenswood back. You have to take the lady with it." He shuddered.

The tent flap opened and Adam's page entered with a tray of stewed lampreys.

Adam swung his feet off the bed with an oath, then shuffled over to the table. "Thank God it's not boar."

He patted the page on the shoulder. "See to my sword. It may have sustained some damage today." The boy bobbed his head with every order.

When he was gone, Adam settled at the table and sliced the lampreys. "Would you like some of this?" he asked his friend, but Hugh refused with a grimace.

Adam shrugged. Eels were his favorite dish, but after one taste he said, "The cook will not recognize me. Whoever made this was not here in my mother's time. She'd have sent him to feed the dogs, after she threw the dish in his face." With a shake of his head, he poked an eel with the point of his dagger. "Tasteless. In need of some spice or other."

Hugh cleared his throat. "Adrian."

Adam lifted a staying hand. "Do not start. And do not slip and call me Adrian again. You do not appreciate what troubles you could cause me. I've not the power to test a king's banishment—or not yet."

"As you wish, *Adam*. But I think you're foolish to persist in this endeavor."

"We had this discussion in Winchester. I cannot acknowledge that I am Adrian de Marle. King John might be dead, but my father isn't cleared of his crimes. He's still banished, and I'm still a banished lord's son. Had we not been fostered together at de Warre's castle, you'd not even know I was . . . who I am."

He covered his emotion by attacking the eels.

Hugh touched Adam's arm. "I recognized you. Others might."

"Not by my face." Adam pulled away. "If I'd not whistled, you'd never have recognized me either."

"Aye. You've changed, I'll grant you that. You're a hand taller than you were at ten and five. You've a beard, you've that scar through your eyebrow, but still, you have your father's mien. 'Tis that which might give you away."

Adam shrugged.

"If you shaved, you'd have better luck with the lady. As it is, you look like a tuppence-a-day mercenary."

Mayhap it was fatigue that made Adam turn from the

table and stab the air with his dagger. "I am a mercenary."

"You cannot change what you are. You were born a baron's son and banished or not, you remain one."

"No longer. Forget who I once was. I am Adam Quintin now and no one else. Adam because I have no history. I can claim nothing. I am no one." He thrust the dagger into the table.

Hugh shook his head. "You may still be recognized. You risk hanging for entering England under banishment."

"I've been here more than ten years. You're the only person who's recognized me in all that time."

"But I'll wager you've not been in company with so many of England's highborn in one place at one time."

Adam withdrew his dagger from the table. "Bishop Gravant will not know me. He was fawning over the pope when my father was banished."

"It is said he will choose for Lady Mathilda if the week ends and she's not made her own choice."

"The lady will choose me," Adam said. "I was to have been the fifth lord of Ravenswood and nothing will stop me. Did you know the first de Marle gained this manor through his prowess as a warrior with William the Conqueror?"

"Ah, then if there are any Saxon folk here, they would dispute your claim."

Hugh grinned, but Adam could not join in his amusement. "He wed the Saxon lord's daughter. That should satisfy those who want a lineage from before William's time. I grew up on stories of this place and my right to rule it."

Hugh shook his head. "You're setting yourself up for pain. You're placing your future in the hands of a feckless female and the power of your face to lure her to your bed."

Nay, he was placing his future in his ability to ferret out a traitor.

Adam rose, ignoring the pain in his spine. "You, who can have anything, do not know what it is to lose everything. You only grant me your time because you know who I am. If not for our mutual suffering under de Warre's tutelage, you'd not sit within ten feet of me at this table. A mercenary? A man with no lineage? A man with nothing but what he's seized with his own two hands?"

"That's not true." Hugh shot to his feet. "Do you think so little of me? Am I not here to cheer you and your men in the tournament when I could be currying favor with William Marshal?"

Adam instantly regretted his harsh words. He lifted his hands palms up in peace. "That was ill considered. I must have jarred my head when I fell off Sinner." He extended his hand to his friend.

Hugh stared at it a moment, then took it. "You're a right knave when you want to be. If you'd not saved me from de Warre's fist a dozen times, I'd toss you like Sinner did—over my head and into that dish of eels."

Adam stabbed a lamprey and wiggled it in Hugh's face, splattering him with the wine sauce. "I saved you a thousand times. And what of de Warre's fat daughter? Did I not protect you when she tried to get under your tunic? Now, sit."

The two men sat, but not in their usual comfortable silence. It pained Adam to be at odds with his friend, the only man before whom he usually need have no pretense. He wished he could tell Hugh he was here to pull the mask from a traitor, not court a fine lady.

He could have Ravenswood, but only as a temporary owner through the rights of marriage to the lady. If no son was born of a union with Mathilda before he died, the manor would go to one of her relatives, not his.

Instead, he would have Ravenswood through a worthy

deed for King Henry, granted to him and his heirs for all time as it should have been. And his first act as lord would be to send Lady Mathilda away to a convent somewhere.

But sometimes, when he lay on his bed at night and tried to sleep, he doubted his ability to find William Marshal's traitor. So far, and he'd joined up with most of the suitors in Winchester, they seemed to be only what they were—men who wanted to lay claim to a valuable manor through marriage. It did not make them traitors, it made them ambitious. His inadequacies as William's arm taunted him.

"So what were you doing alone in the forest today?" Hugh asked.

Adam was grateful for the switch to a neutral subject. "I thought to visit a few childhood haunts. I've never encountered a boar so close to the castle."

"Mayhap 'twas enchanted. Mayhap Mathilda turned one of her cast-off lovers into the beast and he could but linger near for a glimpse of her."

Adam laughed. "If she has such power, she could conjure up a mate without resort to a tournament and hunt."

Hugh stood up. "If you win Lady Mathilda, and I have little doubt you'll fail, you're setting yourself up for misery. I've met her half a dozen times. She's vain. Vain women think only of themselves and their own wants. She'll take lovers. Or, if she does not, you'll need to fight off those who aspire to be her lover."

"I'm not afraid to fight."

"You'd fare better with a woman like that huntress you met today."

"Huntress?" Adam frowned. "When did you see her?"

"I saw her for a moment in the forest, running away; then I saw her again at the kennels." Hugh pointed in the direction of the west wall of the castle. "She's more your sort. Invite her here and end your monkish ways. She looks a tasty morsel, and it might soften your manner to the fair Mathilda."

"I don't think the huntress is a whore." Adam had seen Joan at the kennels as well. He'd not thought her an easy mark as he'd watched her lead her dogs inside.

Nay, he'd thought of how the fair huntress, far from plain by any but a blind man's standards, might appear in bright sunshine. Would her brown hair glitter with the golden strands that wove in profusion through its mass? Would her skin feel as soft as it looked? And what would her doe-dark eyes look like in sunshine? Or moonlight?

"I should have bedded that wench at Winchester," he muttered. To Hugh he said, "The men may say what they wish about her, but the huntress saved my life. I owe her more than a tumble in the hay." He picked up the boar's tusk that Brian de Harcourt had sliced from the great beast and slid his hand along its length. "It was uncanny, Hugh. The boar had me. I was stone-cold dead. Then she and her dogs appeared. I owe her a debt I can never repay."

Night cloaked the bailey in its protective embrace. Joan loved this time of day. Work was done and it was time for one's own concerns. The soft light of torches gleamed in every arrow slit and at the open doors of Ravenswood's hall. It had not been illuminated in such a grand manner since King John's visit a few years before his death. What must it be like to be Lady Mathilda and look out over this sea of tents and know 'twas all for her?

Two men, knights by their garb, hurried by on their way to the hall and swept her with admiring glances. One of these men would win the lady's hand. Unbidden, Joan's eyes went to the black pavilion close by the chapel.

A truly highborn man would not be sleeping in a tent in the bailey. He'd be given an honored place within Ravenswood's keep. She knew from the preparations there that every spare chamber and space had been cleaned and readied, and pallets stuffed with straw and sweet herbs to receive some noble head.

Joan watched her feet and quickened her pace that she might not attract the attention of the many strangers about. She headed for the wash house and her good friend, Edwina.

Edwina was not to be seen. The moist heat from the many boiling pots made sweat break out on Joan's brow.

"Where is Edwina?" she asked Del, the young man who kept the wood fires going. He was tall, strong, blond, and good-natured.

"Come for some gossip, have ye?" he asked with a grin. "Folks have been in and out all day after 'er. She knows everythin' about everybody out there." Del pointed with a length of wood to the many tents. "Edwina's eyes are as sharp as 'er nose. She'll know what ye want about yon suitors."

Joan's cheeks heated. "I've just brought a gown that has blood on the skirt."

Del took it, but his grin remained in place. "Aye, well, ever'one else just has somethin' they need washed, too. If ye want her, she's out there. Some squire, Douglas by name, methinks, had some bloody garments as needs cleaning. As if a body needs no sleep." Del shook his head with disgust.

Joan thanked Del and turned away. The air in the bailey felt cold after the wash house, but her cheeks still burned. She headed toward home.

Joan and the mice had the dark perimeter of the castle wall to themselves save for the sentries who stood high overhead on the ramparts. The evening air was almost balmy.

She heard Edwina's voice before she saw her. The tiny woman stood at the magnificent black pavilion, her hands on her hips. She was as round as she was tall. Her full cheeks were permanently red from her years bent over boiling pots. Her graying hair was hidden under her linen headcovering. Joan's step slowed, and she peered from behind the low branches of an old chestnut tree.

Edwina looked like a child next to the taller figure of Adam Quintin.

"Ye'll hand that bloody tunic over as well, sir," the laundress said. "I've seen the likes o' ye before, and will no' blush at the sight, so give it here."

Edwina shook her finger in Adam Quintin's face. Joan took a quick step forward to interfere, should the warrior take umbrage.

Instead, he smiled. "I'll wager you can do nothing about this blood, mistress. But as you're so sure of yourself, I'll give you ten pence if you're right and I'm wrong."

Edwina wriggled like one of Nat's pups. "Ten pence! 'Twould pay a laundress for weeks of service. I'll see it perfect, sir, doubt it not. Now off with yon tunic. I've work to do."

Joan stood in place, one hand to her throat as he complied with Edwina's tart order and pulled his tunic over his head. He tossed it into Edwina's waiting arms. Next, he peeled off the long black linen shirt he wore beneath it.

Joan sucked in her breath. The knight was nearly naked in the light of the two torches that flanked his tent. The flickering flames gleamed on the long, lean muscles of his torso and arms. It was a body whose perfection was marred with scars and abrasions—the marks of a warrior. Heat, like that of the fires in the wash house, ran over her skin.

"And yer braies," Edwina ordered.

The rush of heat became a flush of something else, something that snatched her breath.

The man spread his arms wide, displaying the length of his grasp and the wings of black hair that stretched out across his chest. This man could swing the heavy battle ax that hung beside the keep's hearth, said to have been captured during a Viking raid.

"You would take my braies and leave me naked?" Adam Quintin teased the laundress.

Edwina sniffed. "I'm sure I've seen better—and bigger—before. Give 'em over. And if yer so poor ye've but one pair o' braies, ye'll no have my ten pence, now, will ye?" She snapped her fingers in his face.

He tipped his head back and laughed. It was a low and joyful sound. It also attracted the attention of men at nearby fires. Joan pulled back closer to the wall.

The knight turned away and entered his tent. A moment later, his braies flew out the flap and landed at Edwina's feet.

"Thank you, sir," Edwina shouted as she stooped to scoop up the linen undergarment. "Ye count out those pennies now. I'll be here at dawn to collect 'em."

Joan hastened away before Edwina saw her in the shadows. The woman would think nothing of calling out her name, and everyone who heard—Adam Quintin included—would know she'd watched the knight strip off his bloody garments.

Once Joan had hoped that Nat and Edwina would marry. Though they never had, Edwina often served up advice like a mother would and watched over her.

She stopped at the cottage. "Papa, I'm going to take Matthew for a run." She did not tell him she wanted to teach the lymer a new hand signal. Matthew spent so much time with Nat, she had little opportunity to keep his training apace of his fellows.

Nat stood up and stretched. "I'll be off to bed then. I've got to be up before the sun."

She kissed his cheek and left the cottage. She made a light clucking sound with her tongue to bring Matthew to her heel. They passed the kennel and she leashed an older, more experienced lymer named Basil. The three of them walked through the many stalls and tents in the bailey. Men did not bother her with two sizable dogs at her side.

Some newly arrived merchants were erecting their make-shift stalls for the week. Servants stood about talking to the visitors, sharing gossip.

At the gate, Joan nodded to Thomas, the gatehouse guard. "I want to run the lymers along the river."

Thomas frowned. "You shouldn't be out so late. I've orders from the bishop that any who wish to come or go may, but I think he had yon suitors in mind."

"I'll not be long." She hastened on as she spoke, lest the man try to detain her.

Matthew raced away from the village and toward the river though the older dog remained at her side. "So, you're of the same mind as I," she said when Matthew circled back. "There's naught in the village we care to see, is there?"

She ruffled the hound's ears. He made a happy, snuffling sound, then bounded off toward the muddy riverbank.

After he'd had a short run, she called him back for training. She held her hand by her side, her fingers together. The older lymer, Basil, immediately sat. Matthew followed suit, still as a statue. When she spread her fingers, both dogs rose, but crouched low on their haunches, bodies tense, ready to spring. She closed her fingers and without hesitation, both sat again. She rewarded them with fine words of praise and her baked nuggets.

Then she worked on another signal, her hands crossed on her breast, one she thought she might need with so many men on the castle grounds. The signal would cause the dogs to hold a man in position. Guarding, she called it. And if the man tried to pass the dogs, they would menace him until he stopped.

It was not a skill needed for hunting. It was a skill she had taught each dog for her own protection.

"Is Matthew not a canny student?" she asked Basil. "You are both wonderful," she said when they were done. "Now play." She snapped her fingers. Matthew bounded off. The older lymer remained at her side, never moving more than a foot away.

She followed Matthew at her own pace, keeping the castle walls on her right. The dog wandered, nose to the ground, occasionally pausing to look back at her, then offering a muffled woof to let her know she moved too slowly to suit him. With a sigh, she looked back at the castle.

The moon rose from behind the walls to illuminate her path and silver Matthew's sleek coat. He looked like he might be the ghost of the long-dead Jupiter as he slipped and slid from shadow to shadow.

Chapter Four

Adam and Hugh crossed the bailey to Ravenswood's great hall, lighted with dozens of smoking torches. They climbed a high wooden staircase meant to be withdrawn in times of siege. The iron-strapped doors at the top of the steps opened and noise spilled out into the night.

Emotion choked Adam's throat as a guard flung the door wide. Adam's last visit here was to see his mother laid to rest. He thrust the thought aside.

In the brightly lighted hall, he had a sudden qualm that someone might recognize him. He ran his hand over his jaw. He'd only grown the beard in the last few weeks and it still surprised him when he touched his face.

No one paid him any heed as Hugh led the way past ranks of tables toward the great hearth. The company was too busy fawning on the more important Hugh de Coleville to see a mere knight.

"Is it much changed?" Hugh asked when they'd reached the fore of the hall and a dais upon which sat a draped table for the bishop's most illustrious guests.

"There's little familiar here. There were not so many benches. Or embroidered cushions." He leaned close to Hugh's ear. "There are far too many cushions, if I might venture an opinion. I do hope Lady Mathilda can do more than stitch a pillow cover."

"She'll have other things to do with her hands if she weds you."

Adam smiled. "There were paintings by the hearth, but I think I like this better."

The huge paintings that had flanked the hearth were now replaced on the left with a fine tapestry and on the right with ranks of weapons.

"Quite a collection. I see a Viking ax and isn't that a Saracen blade?"

Adam nodded, then froze in place. There, amidst a starburst of weapons, was his grandfather's sword. He opened his mouth to tell Hugh the sword had once cut down a score of men at one battle when he became aware of the scent of flowers. He turned from Hugh to the woman who stood with one foot poised on the edge of the dais.

She was a vision of beauty. He belatedly bowed. It would not do to be more interested in the weapons than the object of the matrimonial hunt.

"My lady," he managed when Hugh nudged him sharply in the back. Hugh introduced him.

Lady Mathilda tipped her head to the side. "Adam Quintin? I believe I know your name."

The lady's golden circlet made a halo about her lovely blond head. Her face was as serene as any angel's worthy of a halo, her lips and cheeks as pink as rose petals.

"I would not know in what capacity, my lady." Her hand in his was delicate, made for stitching useless things. No freckles marred her skin. She had a ring on every finger. He touched his lips to her hand, then turned it and kissed her palm. She wore another ring on her middle finger, turned palm in. Her skin was scented with almond. She was perfection.

"I am sure I know who you are." She raised her eyes to the lofty ceiling overhead with its smoke-blackened beams and sighed. "Ah. I have it. You're the mysterious knight who is undefeated in tournament play. It's an honor to meet you."

Lady Mathilda dropped into a deep curtsy that belled her golden skirts, trimmed at the hem with six inches of embroidery. He feared she might not rise under the weight of the many gold chains about her neck.

Hugh grunted and stepped forward. "He's the undefeated Quintin. The best with a sword in all of Christendom."

Adam coughed. Hugh usually only made the sword reference when referring to his prowess between a woman's thighs.

Lady Mathilda turned to Hugh. He took her hand in a perfunctory way, lifted it, and with barely a touch of his lips, dropped it. The perfect line of her brows was ruined when she pulled them together in a frown.

"Lord Hugh," she said, "it has been a long time since we've seen each other."

Adam wished there was some way to excuse Hugh's lack of manners, but the man still smarted from the barbs of Cupid's arrow and treated women with either bland indifference or outright contempt. His usually formidable features were rendered even more so when he frowned as he did right now.

"Hugh is also a fine swordsman," Adam ventured.

Hugh rounded on him. "Nay. Flatter me not. 'Tis your sword famous in poem and song. I'm sure Lady Mathilda would wish to see you ply it."

"*Mon Dieu,*" Adam muttered.

"I look forward to seeing you on the tournament field, then, Sir Adam." She turned to Hugh. "And you, as well.

41

I have long wished for the pleasure of seeing your sword."

Adam almost choked.

"I do not intend to enter the fray, my lady," Hugh said, his face blandly indifferent. "I am here to watch Adam Quintin take all honors."

Brian de Harcourt approached. He whispered in Adam's ear, "Do you see why Joan is called plain?"

Adam ignored him, grabbed Hugh's arm, and marched him away.

"Was that necessary?" he asked. "I'll have your tongue stewed by the cook for that."

"I don't see what I've done to warrant such punishment," Hugh said with mock solemnity, his hand on his breast. "I merely wished the lovely lady to know that you're a master swordsman."

Lady Mathilda clapped and the hall fell silent. A boy held her arm as she climbed onto a stool and then onto a chair that she might be visible to all who gathered in the hall.

"I wish to welcome my illustrious guests to Ravenswood Manor. I have many festivities planned to entertain you who have come to our Harvest Hunt and Tournament."

A cacophony of cheering and shouting burst from the gathering. She held up one delicate hand and again the hall fell silent. "Each night, as we gather here for supper, I will assess the day and award a kiss and a token to the man who has afforded the most pleasure to one and all."

"What is this?" Adam asked Hugh.

"A woman making fools of men. If you want her, this is what you must bear."

Adam headed away from the dais and the small, perfect woman who ruled there.

"Do you think it was wise to abandon the field to Brian?"

"Why not? I'm as sore as a virgin on her wedding night and have no wish to sit down right now. I want to do nothing more than rest my bones. And the bishop's no-where about."

Hugh stepped in front of him. "Adam, you are here for one purpose and one only. As is every other man you see." Hugh swept out his hand to the crowded hall. "How can you win the woman if you allow such a man as Brian to occupy her attentions?"

Adam glanced over his shoulder to where Brian was seated at Lady Mathilda's feet. The lady was smiling and giggling in a manner that set Adam's teeth on edge. He realized he must pretend to care about her. No one must know the true reason he was at Ravenswood. Yet he had other matters to attend to this night.

"I cannot turn about now," he said to Hugh. "I'll unseat Brian when the time comes as surely as the boar unseated me today. And why are you leaving?"

Hugh shrugged. "I'm not after the lady. I thought I'd do my hunting over at the kennels; perhaps see if the hunt-ress is lonely."

Adam frowned. Hugh's tawny hair was unruly and his face a hard collection of lines, but he'd not failed with many women, save the one who'd just broken his heart. Was it because, for once, Hugh's name and wealth had been of no use to him? The lady had been seduced by a man with greater power—a brother to the king of Spain.

A knot of minstrels began to strum their lutes and sing of a knight's bold and brave deed. The refrain emphasized the size of the knight's heart in comparison to the size of a boar's great tusks.

Adam's frown was transformed into a wide grin. "You need not fear Mathilda will forget me. Listen and hear how my single sword blow killed a boar this very day."

He bowed to Hugh and strode through the keep doors. The air was warm for the time of year. The scent of burn-ing torches filled the night as did the rich scent of roasting meat. Dozens of fires were lighted about the bailey where servants and men-at-arms fed themselves while their masters courted the lady of the keep.

Adam did not go to his tent as he had told Hugh he wished to do. Instead, Adam passed it and entered the castle chapel.

He took a seat on a bench along the wall and waited. An old woman came to light candles, eyeing him with obvious displeasure, but Adam remained in place. Air stirred against the back of his neck and told him another had entered the chapel. A young man of about a score sat beside him. It was one of the minstrels from the hall.

When the old woman had shuffled off, the young man held out his hand. "I'm Christopher," he said.

Adam examined the young man's night-black hair and beard. He grinned. "You look enough like me to be my brother."

Christopher grinned back. "I warrant I'll not get as much attention as you, though."

"Thank you for the song," Adam said.

The minstrel shrugged. "You did the deed, I but set it to music."

"You left out the hounds." *And the huntress.*

"Lady Mathilda will not be enchanted by a hound."

Adam sobered at the reminder of his task. "What news have you for me?"

"Nothing much, I fear. Just that Prince Louis will try again, and this time he'll have Bishop Gravant to smooth his way with the church and whoever weds Mathilda to gather support among the barons."

"What of the lady? Where do her loyalties lie?"

"With herself. It's believed that no matter what Lady Mathilda thinks, it will not be she who chooses the next lord of Ravenswood, but the bishop."

"Which man does the bishop favor?"

"I've heard naught to lead me to one man over another."

"And you get this from gossip?"

"Nay, more a chance word here or there."

"In truth, the traitor need not be here. A baron may send his son to take Ravenswood without stirring from his own keep."

Christopher shook his head. "Nay. Barons are far too arrogant to allow their sons to see to this deed. It's too capricious a way to secure the place. That's not my thought, but our lord's. Nay, the son will be used to secure the lady, but the father will ride in after to take the keep.

"And with Marshal's edict that no man may gather more than a score of men in any one place—well, what can a man do with only a score of men? The castle must be taken by marriage."

"Why doesn't the bishop open the doors?" Adam asked.

"The Church cannot afford a rift with the king any more than the king can afford a rift with the Church. But you may be sure at week's end, the bishop will have chosen Mathilda's husband and it will be our traitor. By then it will be too late. By right of marriage, the traitor will possess this castle. A siege would be needed to wrest it back. The Church would be offended."

"And what if the lady wishes to choose me?" Adam grinned at Christopher.

"Forgive me, but if William Marshal is right, you will not be chosen." The minstrel shook his head. "The lady may want you, but she'll not have her way."

"But this edict also demands I have but a score of men with me. There's little I can do with so few."

"Do you have men elsewhere?"

"A score here and a score there," Adam said vaguely.

Christopher lowered his voice. "Others may have done the same. I'll try to find out. We must arrange a signal of sorts when we need each other, something we can use no matter whether we're in the hall or in the fields."

"What do you suggest?"

"Can you sing?"

Adam grimaced. "Not to speak of. I can but whistle."

"That will serve." The minstrel pursed his lips. The small chapel was filled with a familiar strain heard at any hunt.

"A fitting choice." Adam followed the minstrel's effort, trilling the notes.

They talked for another quarter of an hour, divided the suitors between them, and made plans to search each man's belongings for evidence he might connive with Prince Louis. Last, they arranged for daily meetings.

Adam remained behind on his knees, but only for a few moments. He left the stone church, dwarfed by Ravenswood's towers, and walked around the east side. There, he approached the entrance to the crypt. The door was not visible to any other building, nor to the towers themselves. A pavilion concealed its view from the bailey as well. His pavilion.

Adam entered the rib-vaulted crypt. He felt along the top of the door, but encountered only dust. He searched farther back where the mortar had begun to crumble and smiled when his fingers encountered a key. The last time he'd held this key, he'd been at Ravenswood to see his mother laid to rest.

He groped about on a stone ledge and found a stub of candle and a flint. He lighted the candle, closed the crypt door, and took the five steps down to where his mother lay at rest.

After a brief prayer for her soul, he passed a hand over the chiseled letters of her name. He had never believed the essence of a person remained behind to watch over, or torment, the living.

Just past the rows of burial niches, he set his candle down. It flickered in the draft caused by a slit between the fitted stones of the crypt wall and the painted wooden floor. He inserted the key in what looked like a knothole in the wood. A section of the floor lifted away.

Before him lay a rough-hewn staircase. He retrieved his candle, pulled the section of floor back over his head, plugged the keyhole with a scrap of linen he'd brought along for the purpose, and hurried down the steps.

With each step, the air grew cooler. At the bottom a corridor veered right. He examined the stone floor. A fine dusting of dirt covered the square-cut blocks. He made the only impressions as he walked quickly down the corridor that followed the outer wall of the castle until it reached the river.

Cobwebs, another indication that no one had discovered the passage in the many years of his absence, draped the ceiling. As children he and his brother, Robert, had delighted in their secret knowledge of this place.

A series of arches decorated in colored tiles marked other corridors and empty chambers off the main path. They, too, remained unchanged. Robert and he had hidden their boyhood treasures down here and practiced combat, playing at Roman gladiators, shouting and racing about, sure no one could hear them and order them back to their lessons.

Finally, Adam reached his destination. He passed through an arch and entered a round, domed chamber. He lifted his candle and surveyed the space, turning in a circle.

The chamber was as it always had been.

It was covered in a delicate mosaic tile. The dome was blue as if 'twere the sky. The walls depicted the forest rendered in fine detail. The floor was likewise tiled, but with flowers and butterflies on a field of green broken by a path in mottled brown. The design led the person who entered the room to walk to the opposite wall.

Adam followed the path and set his candle on a marble slab that might have served as an altar in ancient days. Idly, he drew his fingertips through the thick dust collected there and looked up. The altar served an ancient goddess.

Diana the Huntress.

She was a beauty, standing with her bow in one hand, the other on the horns of a stag who bowed his great antlered head in homage. Diana's hair tumbled about her shoulders and breasts. She was naked. The artist, who'd rendered her in tiny tiles of multicolored stone, had been a man of great talent.

She looked as if she might step down from the wall and put out her hand to him. Adam remembered offering a prayer that such a thing might happen when he and his brother were boys. As a child, he'd place a hand on the smooth, cold tile of her breast and wish to know the soft flesh of the real woman. He stood back this time and simply looked. He was no longer a boy to make such a wish.

The flickering light of the candle flames ran over the mosaic. Suddenly, his Diana looked like the woman Hugh had styled the huntress. *Joan.*

A bolt of lust ran through Adam's body as if shot from Diana's bow. It coursed through him from his groin to the soles of his feet. He put a hand out toward the wall, then drew it sharply back. He waited for the sensation to recede.

Instead, as he looked up at the goddess, the desire intensified. He wanted to see the real huntress posed as this Diana was, with her hair in a tumble about her bare shoulders, the tips of her breasts showing swollen and ripe between the strands of gold and brown.

He knew in that moment he wanted the huntress in his bed. He wanted to watch her dark eyes as she found her pleasure.

"Enough," he chastised himself. "I do not need the distraction of one woman whilst I'm courting another."

He swept up the candle and left the chamber for the short length of corridor that opened to the right. The tiles and arches gave way to rough stone again, and he ducked the intrusion of tree roots where the vaulting had fallen away through the centuries. Corridors gave way to simple caves, caves within caves, a confusing labyrinth, yet he wandered them as if 'twere yesterday when Robert had scratched the small telltale marks to guide their path through what they called the Roman Way.

At last, Adam saw a glimmer of moonlight. He pushed aside a tangle of matted roots that masked the back of a damp cave and slid behind a slab of rock dropped by some ancient god's hand. He emerged to stand on a tumble of boulders high over the river that passed by Ravenswood Castle.

Adam looked out over the countryside. Ravenswood's towers were concealed by a wreath of mist in the moonlight.

All this should have been his.

He'd walked at least a mile in the Roman caverns. He imagined the advantage to Marshal's traitor should he learn of the Roman Way. As of yet, no man had disturbed what he always considered his private place—and Diana his private goddess.

He knew his mind should be on traitors and fine ladies in search of worthy husbands, but as he looked across the river, his thoughts returned to the huntress.

In his mind's eye he saw her as she had been in the forest, head bowed, the boar dead, her dogs waiting as if carved in marble. A sound, the baying of a hound, echoed across the cultivated fields to mock him.

"I am mad. Marble indeed," he said to the distant moon.

He climbed down the steep bank to the river's edge. It wound like a silver ribbon through the manor lands. He stripped off his clothing and plunged into the icy water to exorcise the huntress from his mind.

Just as he rose from the water, a heavy body dropped on him, plunging him beneath the surface. He flailed about, seeking some hold on the sleek skin of the hound who licked his face and pawed his chest.

He wrestled the beast to arm's length and stood up in the shallows. "Come, boy, you'll drown me."

The dog broke from his embrace. The hound swam to the bank and scrambled up to shake himself off at his mistress's side.

Adam rose, water swirling about his thighs, arrested by the sight of the huntress on the riverbank. She was molten copper and ivory in the moonlight, but her face was hidden in deep shadow. He could not breathe.

Then she turned and disappeared between the trees.

Had he imagined her? Conjured her out of desire?

He put a hand to a trio of scratches along his shoulder. He'd not dreamed the hound.

Chapter Five

Adam walked his stolid hunting mare, a horse not likely to dump him on his ass, through the milling party of men and women who gathered for the day's hunt outside the castle walls.

Today's fare was tame park hunting. It allowed the ladies to participate and others to watch from the castle walls. There would soon be little point in the hunt as morning waned. Lady Mathilda had yet to appear. She was more than an hour late.

She had not attended the breakfast at which the hunt strategy was outlined and the stag droppings displayed among the bread and cheese to be examined for age and size by the hunters. He smiled at the unlikely image of the dainty Mathilda poring over the excreta of a stag. No wonder the lady lingered in bed.

Joan had not been present either.

Few huntsmen or hounds remained near this sweep of castle green. Most had gone out in relays to confine the stag in a convenient area. From his years at Ravenswood, Adam knew the hunting area would be the defile, for it could be seen from the castle ramparts. The defile was formed of two hills separated by a rushing stream. He knew the area as well as he knew the lines on his hand.

The relays of huntsmen along the defile ensured the joy of hunting without the loss of the quarry. They would drive the stag toward the hunting party.

A few feet away from Adam, Ravenswood's Master of the Hunt, Nat Swan, marshaled the remaining men and dogs who would ride along with the hunting party. It was no easy task as Roger Artois, along with several other suitors, had brought his own hounds to add to the confusion.

Amidst it all, Joan Swan moved about with a regal grace. Adam admired her tall, fine figure. She was garbed in deep green as were the other huntsmen.

Her hair was not loose to glitter in the morning sun as it had been on the previous day, but was hidden beneath a head covering.

She smiled and rubbed the ears of two coupled hounds. He enjoyed the way her breasts moved against her gown.

Roger Artois's hunt master, a gangly redhead, chastised Joan's father for getting in his way, though Adam thought 'twas more the other way around.

A blast from a huntsman's horn turned his attention. Lady Mathilda and Bishop Gravant rode from the castle gates.

She was garbed in white from her veil edged in gold to her leather boots. Her horse was snow-white with a braided mane.

Beside her, Bishop Gravant looked like night to her day. His rich black surcoat and mantle had the look of ecclesiastic robes though they were not. His concession to religion lay on his chest, a gold cross heavy with rubies. The ruby in one of his rings was the size of a plover's egg. The bishop's long face had the jowls and flush of a man who dined well. His head was fringed with wiry black hair now beginning to gray.

Gravant made the sign of the cross over the hunting party and they moved down the greensward toward the defile.

"Look at Randy Roger pushing his way to Mathilda's side," Hugh said. "That should be you."

Adam smiled. "You're as bad as a mother trying to make a match for an ugly daughter. Leave off. I've little fear Roger will have the lady. He's as appealing as a starved fox."

"Did you not notice the way Gravant fawned on him? And look"—Hugh nudged Adam's knee with his—"Roger's hunt master is filling the bishop's ear with some nonsense about his dogs."

Adam looked for the redhead. Indeed, the man was flailing his arms and pointing about. "Aye, but he's doing more harm than good; he has agitated the lady's mount."

There was little time to think of a retort as the hunt began. Adam had to lie back and hide his knowledge of the ground and forest. The hounds who hunted by scent raced ahead, encouraged by the music of the horn and the sharp cries of the huntsmen.

As the stag passed the relays, the huntsmen uncoupled their hounds, and their voices were added to the mix.

Adam knew the stag could not win. He and Hugh kicked their horses to a quicker pace as the beast was driven down the defile, chased by the running hounds.

Adam enjoyed the wind in his face, the skill of the hounds, the horse moving beneath him. He also enjoyed maneuvering his horse so Joan remained in view.

Mathilda rode badly, swerving in front of Hugh's horse on several occasions so he barely missed riding up her mount's hocks. The speed of the hunt deteriorated to accommodate Mathilda's pace. In the end, the stag was brought down by a pair of Lord Roger's alaunts.

Adam worked his way to Mathilda's side at the curée, the unmaking of the stag, the time when the best of the beast was set aside for the bishop's table, the dogs rewarded with their own portion, and the rest sent back to the castle kitchen.

The bishop performed the unmaking with great skill, not wearing a drop of blood, nor even rolling back his sleeves.

The party formed a procession, led by the bishop and a servant bearing the stag's head mounted on a staff. The suitors maneuvered for a position by Mathilda, and Adam swallowed a grin when a boy suitor, not more than five and ten, named Francis de Coucy, outplayed them all, nudging his horse close to the lady.

They wended their way back down the valley to the greensward in view of the castle walls. There they found a pavilion with pastries, pyramids of fruit, and pitchers of ale. Adam drew his horse alongside Hugh's. They watched Roger Artois elbow Francis de Coucy aside and help Mathilda dismount.

Adam shook his head over the duo. "Do you think the lady has a black gown for a black horse?"

But it was Brian de Harcourt who answered him, not Hugh. "Or a blue horse for a blue gown?"

Adam smiled and acknowledged the jest with a bow. "Do you think she feels hunted like the deer?"

"Mathilda? Nay. She's used to such adoration."

"You've known the lady for years, have you not?" Adam dismounted, stifling a groan at the ache in his spine after several hours in the saddle.

"I was fostered with Lady Mathilda's brother, Richard, and spent my summers here until about two years ago." Brian dismounted. Along with Hugh, they led their mounts to a patch of shade as had others who rested from the hunt.

"Then you have an advantage over Lady Mathilda's

other suitors," Hugh said, beckoning a servant strolling about with tankards of ale.

Brian shook his head. "I must confess I was much occupied with Richard and paid her little notice."

"You must have been blind," Adam said, draining his cup. A servant rushed forward with a pitcher to refill it.

Brian colored. "Richard was an avid hunter and often at odds with his father. He rebuilt an old verderer's hut into a fine hunting lodge, and we spent most of our time there." He grinned. "Drinking ourselves senseless and swiving the serving maids."

"What became of Richard?" Adam asked, though he knew.

"He died of a fever. Lord Guy was a broken man after that. Richard would have made a fine lord here."

Nay, Adam thought, the de Poitiers family were interlopers. Usurpers of his father's rights and honors.

Hugh pointed to where Joan Swan stood in the field, her hounds in a circle about her feet. "She's quite lovely, in her own way, is she not?"

"Plain Joan? Aye," Brian said. "In truth, I found her much more to my taste than Mathilda."

Adam swung his attention to Brian, but found the man's face unreadable.

Hugh crossed his arms on his chest. "Plain Joan," he mused. "There's nothing plain about her lush ass. I'd like to get on all fours behind her."

There was no mistaking the quick shift of Brian's shoulders. Adam thought it likely Brian knew the huntress quite well. It explained their manner to each other in the forest the previous day. Jealousy, an unreasonable emotion, surged through Adam like a fierce alaunt after a stag.

To exorcise the vision Hugh had conjured, Adam turned toward Mathilda's ivory perfection.

But Joan walked in their direction, and he found he could not concentrate on Mathilda—nor call this other woman plain. The huntress looked at everyone but him. That, and her high color, told him she had seen him quite well swimming the night before.

"My lords." She curtsied, including him in her address. "Lady Mathilda wishes to return to the castle and bids me inquire if you are finished for the day."

Brian said to Adam, "We might as well retire with the quarry gone from the field."

Adam gave Brian a mock salute.

Plain Joan was but a few paces off, and when Brian turned to speak to Hugh, Adam hurried to catch up with her. He walked at her side toward the dogs being coupled and put into carts.

"I pray you will forgive Matthew's lapse last evening, sir." Her voice was low, meant only for his ears. "Matthew is spirited and loyal, but ofttimes lacking in manners."

Adam rubbed his shoulder. "I can hardly fault the hound but a few hours after I've had my life saved by his fellows."

She took a deep breath, and said, "You are good to be so generous."

"I would still like to offer you some recompense for—"

"Nay, please, say nothing more." She looked not at him, nor at the men who followed a pace or two behind, but at her father. "I should not have had the dogs out. I would rather—"

"I understand." He searched for an opening to further conversation. She looked ready to run, the high color back in her cheeks.

"I much admire the way you handle the hounds," he said.

She smiled. "Nat taught me all I know. He's a true master with the hunting hounds."

Adam could not help smiling back. Her brown eyes

were flecked with gold. Freckles were scattered across her nose and cheeks like sand over a silken cloth. He imagined Lady Mathilda would weep an hour for each one if 'twere her face so marked.

"Has your father been master long?" Adam remembered Nat but not because of his hounds. Nat had meted out discipline to his kennel lads—and the lord's sons—in equal measure.

"For over three decades." Her voice was filled with pride.

Adam wondered why he did not remember Joan as a child here at Ravenswood. Surely, she should have made an impression on him, although she was probably five or six years younger than he. The females of the keep had always flocked around him, no matter their age—much like men flocked about Mathilda, he thought, ruefully.

Hugh and Brian gained on them. Adam found himself outflanked by Hugh, who shouldered his way next to Joan.

"Has your father any pups to sell, mistress?" Hugh asked her. "I'd like to have one as canny as that spotted hound."

"I'm sorry, my lord, not now, but we would be most honored to give you the pick of the next litter."

Brian and Hugh engaged her in a long discussion on the spotted bitch's lineage while Adam listened.

Why did he not remember this forest sylph? He'd have surely called her Dog Wench or some other derisive name. It was what boys did to female servants, especially young ones.

Nat Swan kept glancing over at them, and Adam turned away with a sudden apprehension the hunt master might recognize his former lord's son.

"I must go, my lords, sir." She curtsied, then turned to Hugh. "I'll tell my father you would like one of the pups."

She walked away with a sleek grace that matched that

of her hounds. As Adam watched, she fisted her hands. Two dogs rose from where they lay in the grass and flanked her. The way the dogs moved with her smacked of some magical communication. He smiled. Maybe she was a forest deity after all.

"Plain Joan little resembles her father," Hugh said. "Her mother must have been a beauty."

"Actually," Brian said, "Nat is not her father."

Adam swung his attention from Joan to Nat Swan, who called out orders to his huntsmen, setting the carts of dogs in motion. "How so?"

"If I have the story right, Nat was sent by the former lord, Durand de Marle, to purchase hounds in Chichester. Upon Nat's return he came upon Joan's family. They'd been traveling to Winchester Cathedral. She could not have been much more than ten at the time. I believe her father was a scholar of some note and wanted to consult the books there."

"A scholar? How curious," Hugh said.

"Go on," Adam said, impatient with Hugh's interruption. "What happened?"

"As I said, Nat came upon her family. Joan's mother was being raped by three men. Her father and brother had been butchered by the trio and lay there beside the mother in a pool of blood, or so the story goes. Nat set his dogs on the men, but he was too late to save the mother."

"And Joan?" Adam watched her touch Nat's sleeve and smile up at him. He now saw how dissimilar they were. Joan's features were fine and elegant. Nat's revealed peasant ancestry, and Adam remembered that the man had risen to his rank as Master of the Hunt, not through noble birth, but from the ranks of the huntsmen.

"Nat found Joan hiding in some brush. Or rather the dogs found her. He might have left her at the Convent of St. Agnes; it was nearby, I understand, but instead, he brought her to Ravenswood. He just . . . added her to his pack, so to speak. And she's been at his side ever since. I believe Lord Guy formalized the adoption in some writ or other."

Adam took his reins from a groom who led their horses forward. So, that was why he didn't remember her. She must have come shortly before his family had been banished, during his fostering with de Warre.

"Was it ever discovered why Joan's family was murdered? Was it thievery?" Adam asked.

Brian shrugged. "I cannot remember. Mathilda can give you more details should you wish them."

Nat Swan handed Joan up onto her mount. She swept her long skirts aside and took up her reins, then guided her horse aside so Lady Mathilda might pass. Roger worked his way between the lady and Bishop Gravant.

Hugh rolled his eyes and maneuvered his horse so Adam's was forced into line with Brian's. They followed Mathilda's entourage back to the castle.

Brian leaned near Adam. "I do remember something more of Joan's story. The men who killed her family were some of King John's Flemish mercenaries. There was quite a furor about it at the time."

Adam jerked on his reins. His horse shied. He controlled his mount and his voice. "Flemish mercenaries?"

"Aye. It is said Joan Swan has but one passion—the hatred of mercenaries."

Chapter Six

Douglas shook Adam from sleep and handed him a tankard of cool, fresh ale. Adam's head felt stuffed with wool after a night of drinking and feasting, and not one step forward in William Marshal's mission. Adam had managed to search only one chamber, Lord Roger's.

The man was slovenly. He hid his documents and money purse under his mattress where any servant might find them. In addition, the man had naught incriminating save a list of properties, bolts of cloth, spices, and jewelry for the lady.

As a bribe to a bishop, it was mediocre. Surely, Roger, rising forty years, could do better. His father, an earl, might be as old as the Roman Way, but he was rich as Croesus.

The sun painted a bronze gleam on the tent.

"I was having a wonderful dream, Douglas. In it, you allowed me to sleep until supper and instead of your ugly face, I was awakened by a sweet young maid wearing naught but her hair."

"Happens she was here, but ye chased 'er off with yer snoring."

"Would that it were true." Adam handed back the empty tankard and washed his face and hands in a basin of hot water Douglas set out on the table.

"Ye've some nasty bruises on yer arse," Douglas said, handing Adam the linen shirt he would wear beneath his tunic.

"Aye. I feel like I took two fingers off my height with that fall from Sinner."

"Can ye manage the brute in the tournament?"

"Don't look so downcast. I'll excel and nurse my aching body after. You'll not be shamed by my performance."

"At least the tournament is a few days off. Ye'll heal some in that time. Find a bath and soak a bit—none o' that swimming yer so fond of. Evil poisons in river water, ye know."

"Aye, my physician. Any other advice?"

Douglas shook his head and held out three belts.

"This one." Adam buckled on the belt he liked best, one studded with smoky topaz, a gift from a fine French woman who'd ordered one topaz for each night of passion they'd shared. "What has the bishop planned for our day?"

"*My* day is set. Burnishing harness and weapons, oiling leather. Ye're to grapple for the lady's attentions. Half naked. It isna decent." Douglas gave a loud sniff.

Adam shook his head and thrust a topaz-embellished dagger into his belt sheath. "So the lady lied. It is not we who will enjoy the festivities, but we who will provide them.

"What happened to skewering each other with swords and daggers, and the last man standing wins the lady's

61

hand? We'll not likely eliminate any candidates with such tame amusements."

"Bloodletting being more sure? But it will not amuse the ladies quite as well," Douglas said.

Adam plucked a pair of braies from his bed and stuck his finger through a rent in the linen. "You'll need to stitch this then, or I'll shame myself."

He headed for the armory to see about his sword. When he entered the hot space, the armorer looked up, his hammer raised over the tip of a lance.

"I sent my sword over last evening."

"Don't have yer sword." The man returned to his hammering.

"A page brought it. It has my V incised in the hilt."

The man's eyes shifted left, but he shook his head. "Never seen it."

Adam turned and examined the ranks of weapons. There were far too many for peacetime. And just the right number for war. He plucked his sword from the group. "This is it."

He examined the hilt. It bore a mark along the cross guard as if a chisel had been hammered against where it joined the blade. "What have you done here? It's worse now."

The man shrugged, but he lifted his hammer and hefted it in his hand. The action was less threat than nervousness, Adam decided.

Adam examined the sword from one end to the other. "I'll give you twice what you were offered to damage this hilt if you will tell me who hired you to do it."

"It were given to me that way." The man licked his lips.

Adam spun and pressed the point of the sword under the man's chin. "This hilt will last but one thrust, I imagine. Enough to cut your throat. His name."

Sweat ran down the man's temples. He licked his lips. "I ne'er seen 'im."

62

"Then I suppose you'll die."

"Nay," the man croaked. "I know only he were alone. He came up behind me, offered me three marks to fix a sword. He said I were not to turn, I'd find it in the straw."

"In what manner did he want it fixed?"

The man blinked as sweat ran in his eyes. "He just said, 'Fix it so 'e willna last more than a thrust er two.'"

"You knew it was my sword."

"Ever'one knows ye wear the—" He stroked the air with a quick, slashing V.

"Do they?"

"Aye. Some say as ye've carved it into the breast of every one o' yer lovers."

How reputations were made. "I'll give you six marks to repair my sword—properly this time. Ten marks if you can discover the name of the man who plots my fall."

The man stared. "Ye're not goin' to kill me?"

Adam smiled. "Oh, I'll kill you. I'll carve my V in your chest so deep you'll be dead before you fall"—the man's face paled—"*if* my sword fails in the tournament."

He tossed the weapon through the air. The armorer caught it and clasped it to his chest like a cross on which he would pledge his eternal soul.

Once in the bailey, Adam found his page. He hooked the lad by the neck of his tunic and dragged him aside. "To whom did you give my sword?"

The boy met his gaze with a guileless stare that told Adam the lad was innocent as a virgin bride. "I give it o'er to one o' yer men. He were waiting outside, he were."

"Which one?"

The boy's face screwed up in thought. "I canna say."

"And what did he look like?"

" 'E wore a helm, and it were dark. 'E had a mark 'ere." The boy touched the back of his hand.

Adam gave the boy a shake. "Next time, give nothing of mine into any hand but the one to whom I direct you.

63

Now find Douglas and seek a worthy punishment for such stupidity."

Joan and Edwina followed Del up the outer steps to the wall walk. He elbowed aside a few lads from the wash house to make space and set an empty nail keg down for Edwina to stand upon.

"This will do," Edwina said. She patted Del's beefy arm.

Joan propped her arms on the stone ledge of the wall and looked across the crowded bailey. "I've not seen such finery since last King John visited."

Below, a seating area ringed an open patch of clipped grass, like a bed of lush summer flowers. Flowers formed of the bright colors of the ladies' gowns and men's tunics.

Next to Joan, Del wagered with a few spectators. Edwina nudged Joan's ribs. "Step aside, I'd like some of that play."

Joan curtsied, smiled, and stepped back so Edwina could join in the wagering. When Edwina resumed her position, Joan searched the spectators for Nat, but did not see him.

"I hope Nat's not making wagers," she said.

"He's no sense to 'im. He'll wager on a man 'e likes rather than on one with the strength to win."

"Or worse, on the advice of others who know as little as he. Do you see him? Should I look for him?"

Edwina held Joan's arm. "Leave the man be. He's probably with the hounds. He has little interest in wrestling."

"I have little interest in it either. How watching sweaty men grapple will help decide whether a man will make a good husband, I cannot say."

"And I suppose ye think she should judge him on his kindness?" Edwina grinned.

"And why not?"

"A kind man is most likely a weak man. Our lady would be just as happy picking the finest-looking man. He, at least, might please in bed."

The wagering men laughed and Joan looked away. "Edwina—"

"Hush." The laundress pointed down at the circle of grass marked off with ropes. The bishop took his seat in the tiers of benches constructed for favored spectators. All others must watch from where they could. Mathilda sat between the bishop and the wife of one of Ravenswood's knights.

An expectant hush fell on the crowd when two men walked to the center of the grass. They wore only their braies. They were barefoot and weaponless.

The bishop outlined the rules. The winner must throw his opponent to the ground such that he hit on at least three points. The bishop, alone, would determine the winner.

Gravant called out for the contest to begin and the two men circled each other, arms extended. Along with the start came a swell of shouting for one man or the other.

Joan tore her gaze from the bishop. Her hatred of him surely meant a long stint in purgatory.

"What do you know of this pair?" a woman near Edwina asked.

Edwina gave the lineage of each man. "They've a poor chance o' winning the lady. They may be finer of face than Roger Artois, but they haven't his wealth or influence. De Harcourt has my money. He'll make a fine match there"— she nodded at the small arena—"as well as for the lady—" Edwina broke off.

One of the wrestlers put the other on his back.

Shouts of derision accompanied the winner and the loser as they left the circle. Edwina sighed and handed a penny to Del.

The bishop raised two fingers. The bishop's silent signals to his minions had given Joan the idea for taking control of the hounds. It had been watching the scurrying to please Gravant that made Joan realize she might be able to save

65

Nat from the man's unkindness—nay, the word was too mild.

The bishop had no kindness. Or patience. He begrudged the smallest compliment to the servants. Over the past month, he'd evicted any number of tenants for petty reasons so he might set his own men in their places. The manor was in an uproar. These festivities mocked the people's mood.

And Nat wandered vaguely through his tasks, accomplishing all of them, but not always in as timely a manner as he once had.

Fear of the bishop's wrath, his quick dismissal of men and women no matter how long they'd served the manor, gave her sleepless nights. Now, the anxieties were drawing to a close.

Mathilda would choose her husband and the bishop would return to his palace. If the hounds obeyed Joan's signals over Nat's increasingly vague orders, all might be well.

A man by the bake house, his arms crossed on his chest, drew Joan's eye away from the bishop. It was Adam Quintin.

He wore his black mantle flung back over his shoulders. He no longer looked common. The pin holding the mantle might be simple, but the ivory tunic and jeweled belt were not.

"Is Quintin not wrestling?" Joan felt an unaccountable disappointment.

"Aye, he will. Mathilda said every man, no exceptions."

Joan forced herself to shift her attention from Adam Quintin to Lady Mathilda.

"Aye, look at her and dream." Edwina gave her a sharp elbow. "Ye should be sitting down there."

Joan examined the women who filled the seats near Mathilda. Not all were noble, but those who could not claim such high birth were worthy wives of the castle's knights.

"That day is done. Only you miss it," Joan said.

"If Richard hadn't wanted ye, Lord Guy would have been content with your friendship with Mathilda."

With a glance about to see who might be listening, Joan shrugged. "Richard was a wonderful man, God rest his soul."

"And mad with love for ye."

"He'd have forgotten me soon enough if Lord Guy had not taken on about it. It was a boy's love, not a man's."

"He loved ye. He left here and swore he'd never return until Lord Guy agreed he could offer for ye."

"It was defying his father he was in love with, not me."

"If any good come of 'is death, it were Lord Guy's vow to leave Mathilda to make her own choice."

"Aye. He did blame himself for Richard's death."

"And rightly so. He drove the man out. And poor Richard dead within a twelve-month."

Joan said a short prayer for Richard's soul. He would have forgotten her, but still, he had risked much for his boyish love—or his stubborn ways.

"I spoke with Mathilda today."

"Why? Did she ask you to fetch something for her?" Edwina wrinkled her nose.

"She asked after a huntsman who's ailing. She specifically asked that I bring the reply, so she did wish to speak to me."

"What else did she say?"

Joan made a wry face. "She asked about Brian de Harcourt."

"Ah, ha! She cared naught for you—or the huntsman. She wanted information on a suitor. That is all." Edwina spat on the wooden floor of the wall walk. "Don't ye be drawn into fetching for her. Yer not her servant."

Joan tried to attend to the wrestling, but found little to

hold her interest. She looked over the spectators, assessing gowns and the features of suitors who awaited their bouts. Unable to resist, she turned toward the buttery and Adam Quintin. He was gone.

Chapter Seven

Adam ignored the many stalls and the importuning of several merchants, skirted the buildings crouched at the base of the castle wall, and strode through the inner bailey to the outer ward.

An old man, Ivo, one of his father's clerks, hurried by, looking straight through him. The man's lack of greeting reminded Adam he was a stranger in his father's castle. Euphoria warred with a deep sadness. He needed anonymity to accomplish his mission for William Marshal, but once, he'd been an honored heir here.

He looked up at the tall towers touched with a patina of age and knew it was not because of the stone edifice that he must have Ravenswood. Nay, it was what the towers represented. The first lord of Ravenswood had not built this fortress to have it fall into the hands of any but his own kin.

His father's banishment must be lifted. The de Marle name, as venerable as these walls, must be restored.

Adam knew his first action as lord of Ravenswood Castle would be to take his grandfather's sword down from the wall. He would clean it and hone it. *And wear it.*

It was for the de Marle honor he labored. A rueful smile overspread his face. To regain his honor he must leave it behind and skulk about like a common thief. The irony amused him . . . when it did not pain him.

Eventually, and circuitously, he ended his wanderings at de Harcourt's tent. The man had a chamber in the hall, but Adam also knew by Douglas's gossip that Brian came here to dress. To garb oneself as finely as de Harcourt did, he must have at least one sizable coffer. Within, Adam hoped to find evidence de Harcourt either connived with a foreign king or did not.

With a glance about to be sure no one observed him, Adam entered the tent. It was empty and filled with a dim morning light. Outside, the sounds of merrymaking would mark his time. He could count by the jeers and cheers how long he had until his bout, second to last, and if anyone challenged his right to be here, he would simply say he wanted to talk to Brian in privacy.

The accoutrements of Brian's tent did not compare to his own. The tent held little but a simple pallet with furs for a servant, Adam assumed, since Brian slept in the keep. Luckily, there was one chest.

It was not locked as was his own. Adam lifted the lid. The scent of oiled metal, leather, and wool wafted up to him. Atop the well-filled chest was a neatly folded gambeson. The padded leather garment, meant to be worn beneath armor, was old. A fine, well-oiled hauberk was next to it. His own mail coat was not quite as well maintained, and he made a silent vow to take Douglas to task when he returned. It would not do to be shown in a poor light next to Brian.

As Adam searched deeper, he found other clothing worthy of a man courting a fine lady. Several documents and five linen-wrapped packages lay at the very bottom of the chest.

His heart thundered. To be found reading Brian's papers was to be caught out. What excuse had he? None.

Quickly, standing as near as he dared to the tent flap to keep watch for anyone approaching, he unrolled and scanned the first document. It was a directive from Brian's father to his son, admonishing him to secure Ravenswood at all costs. Brian was bidden to spare no expense, do his duty, show his manly strengths, excel in every test, and extend the family holdings as every de Harcourt before him had done.

Roger's father had merely listed the bribes he should offer. No long, strident sentences, no terse admonishments, just a dry list.

Adam imagined the missive *his* father would write. It would say something like follow your heart or that Ravenswood bought through wedded slavery was not worth the price.

His father did not understand the burn Adam felt inside to regain what King John had snatched away. Adam knew he was capable and worthy of the trust in arms that rule of Ravenswood Castle required.

It was this battle of wits, a hidden battle, he felt inadequate to win.

Adam rolled de Harcourt's letter and dropped it into the coffer. The second was an accounting of gifts Brian was to offer the bishop if he was chosen by Mathilda. The list was about equal to Lord Roger's, but Adam knew he could match them both possession for possession.

He opened a third document. It held close writing in a careless hand, much blotted.

"*Jesu.* Greek. I'm sunk." He stuffed the letter into his tunic, retied the other two, and turned his attentions to the five bundles on the floor. Each proved to be a piece of jewelry, a portion of those detailed on the parchment from de Harcourt. A sample of riches to come.

Adam replaced the bundles and reached for the clothing. A laugh outside drew his attention. *Brian's*.

Heart racing, Adam hastily folded away the clothing and had just shut the lid and sat upon it when Brian entered his tent.

"Adam!" Brian started back. "What the devil are you doing here?"

"Waiting for you." Adam praised himself for the calmness of his voice and God for the dimness of the tent. He knew his cheeks to be as red as a king's robe.

Adam's heartbeat stilled a bit from a thunder to a horse's gallop. He wrapped his arms about one knee in negligent ease.

"So, what is it you want?" Brian asked. "More information?"

"What?" Adam said sharply. Had Brian seen through him so easily?

"Aye. About Joan Swan. Come, do not tell me you are not interested. You watched her at the hunt like one of the hawks might watch a sparrow." Brian took three strides toward him. He placed his hand on his sword hilt. "Joan is not some bitch in heat to be chased. Leave her alone or you'll answer to me."

"And what is she to you?" Adam's disbelief felt as tangible as a punch in the chest.

"I have a duty to protect her in my friend's memory who loved her. She may be as plain as a simple sparrow, but she is not prey."

Adam shot to his feet, then forced himself to stand still, hands at his sides. The sharp edge of the parchment he'd purloined from de Harcourt's coffer reminded him he must not offend, but leave with dignity, giving no hint of his sins here.

"Richard loved her, I assume?" Adam knew he must

ignore the insults, the ludicrous accusation that Joan was plain.

Or prey.

"Aye," Brian said. "Richard wanted her badly, but Lord Guy would have none of it. Richard thought he could bring his father around if he left for a bit, gave the old man time to reconcile himself to the idea. Instead, Richard died."

"Did Joan love him?"

Brian paced around the tent, fingertips skimming over surfaces. "I think she was dazzled, as one is when looking at sunlight reflected on snow." He faced Adam. "She needed comforting not only for the loss of Richard, but for Lord Guy's treatment of her both before Richard left and after. She has been forbidden the hall until these festivities for Mathilda."

"You must watch her as much as I do," Adam said.

They stood toe to toe.

Brian spoke first. "Do not be another who heedlessly harms her. If Richard dazzled, you, who are akin to the sun itself, will blind her. And if you do aught to hurt her, you will answer to me."

Adam now knew who had comforted the huntress.

The muted sound of the crowd's congratulatory cheers reminded them both that their turn was nigh.

"These are heated words for a man courting another woman. Is it Joan you fear I'll dazzle or our lady?" Adam turned and left the tent.

Joan stifled a yawn, then swallowed it. Adam Quintin was walking with long, hurried strides toward the tent where the wrestlers disrobed. He had a deep furrow between his brows. Several steps behind him followed Brian de Harcourt. He wore the same frown.

"Forget yon knights. They'll be on soon enough," Edwina said. With as much grace as possible, Joan slowly turned her gaze from Quintin to the greensward. She feigned an interest she could not feel.

One of the wrestlers was unexceptional—Yves of York, Edwina called him. The other, half his size, with a face marked by angry pimples, darted around his opponent to the great amusement of the crowd. He looked like one of Nat's puppies challenging the leader of the pack.

"That boy is far too young to be a serious candidate for Lady Mathilda. I wonder who he is," Joan said.

Edwina gave his name as Francis de Coucy. "He's but ten and five. It is his father, Lord Charles, who makes him a strong candidate." Edwina shuddered. "But 'e's an ugly brute."

"I cannot wait for that Adam Quintin to wrestle," a nearby woman said. "Now there's a fair face."

"Oh?" Joan hoped her voice sounded disinterested. "Is he expected to win his bout?"

"Quintin?" the woman said. "I imagine he will win any bout he fights. Have you seen his men? A man who can control those mercenaries must be strong, else they would not respect him."

"He's not one of them, though," Joan said.

"Aye, he is. He rose from the ranks of King John's Flemish mercenaries. They're not as bad as the Bretons, but still, they're all brutes, I say."

Joan gripped the stone ledge of the wall. "F-Flemish mercenaries?"

"Aye. Led them, bested their commander, saved William Marshal's life at least once, and was knighted for his valor in the field, by Marshal himself."

Joan looked up at the sun. She used the light as an excuse to shield her eyes and turn aside.

A Flemish mercenary.

All around her wagers flew, men laughed, women flirted, children ran back and forth. But Joan felt none of the joy.

"Edwina, I think I'll go look for Nat."

But Edwina took her hand. She raised it, kissed it, then held it tightly. "I heard what she said. So, he's a mercenary. He's too young to have been one of *your* mercenaries. I'll not let you run away and hide in the kennels."

"Thank you, you're right. It is nonsense."

As Joan stood there beside her friend, her hand held by that woman's square, strong fingers, she felt strength returning. It was thirteen years ago. It was long over. Adam Quintin must have been all of ten and seven or ten and eight at the time. *Her* mercenaries had been older men. Ancient they'd looked to her ten-year-old eyes, though they might have been any age from thirty to forty.

She'd only seen them afterward. *After the dogs had finished with them.*

Edwina slid an arm around her waist and hugged her closer still. "They're not all bad, ye know. Some are just men earning a wage."

"They kill for a purse," Joan said softly.

"And they'll leave here soon enough, so you may put them from your mind."

"But should Quintin win our lady's hand, they'll stay," Joan said. The sound of her voice shamed her, for it was a stew of jealousy and fear.

"Then go yourself. Now hush."

Joan stared at the chinks of mortar between the wall stones, mortar beginning to crumble as was her fortitude.

Go herself. So easily said. So impossible to do.

Below, the man and boy displayed their strength before Lady Mathilda, though the lady looked bored. The man named Yves slipped on ground made muddy by combat. He did not rise.

As they watched, the man's squire ran out to him while the bishop declared his opponent the winner. The boy capered about, his arms raised in victory.

"He's broken 'is arm, the wretch." Edwina slapped a

75

penny in Del's hand. "Now he won't be in the throwing competition either, and I did much hold hope for him there."

The crowd taunted the man, his wrist cradled against his chest, as he left the circle. The boy received the same treatment despite being declared the victor.

A murmur went up from the crowd. Brian de Harcourt and Adam Quintin had entered the grass circle. The two men made their obeisance to the bishop and a hush fell across the spectators. No pair of combatants had commanded such attention from the crowd.

Heat washed down Joan's body when she saw the long, red trio of scratches on Adam Quintin's bare shoulder. They disappeared in the thatch of hair on his chest. He was better garbed than he had been in the river shallows, for then he had been naked.

A cloud crossed the men, draping them in shadow, and for a moment, Joan was back on the riverbank, staring at the knight as he rose from the water like a water deity, laughing, thrusting Matthew aside, the water washing across his honed muscles. He had appeared forged in metal like the sword he had used to kill the boar.

As it had by the river, a liquid sting of desire joined the heat already kindled within her middle.

The men met in a smack of flesh. In moments, their bodies were slick with mud as one after the other they put each other on their backs, but never on three points. Each time, they leapt apart to circle each other anew.

"They might as well be naked," Edwina said with a nudge in Joan's side. "Romans wrestled naked hereabouts, ye know."

The stirring in Joan's loins intensified. Edwina was right. Sweat streaked the mud on their torsos; their wet braies clung to their thighs and buttocks.

As the bout continued, the crowd grew frantic. The shouts of encouragement or derision seemed to echo from one end of the stone-walled bailey to the other. Quintin shook mud and sweat from his eyes. His body was as supple as the hounds she ran, and yet he reminded her more of one of the huge stags that locked antlers in the forest in battle over the hind.

And Lady Mathilda was the prize to be won or lost in these mock combats. Joan watched Lady Mathilda slip to the edge of her seat, then rise on tiptoe. Her eyes were round as coins and she held her hands clasped to her chest. Which man did Mathilda most desire?

Then, like a man who's been toying with his opponent, Quintin smiled and jerked Brian off his feet.

A servant stepped up to the bishop and whispered in his ear, handing him a rolled parchment. The bishop nodded, opened the small scroll, and with barely a glance at it, stood up, and clapped his hands just as Quintin flung Brian to his back.

"A draw," Bishop Gravant called in his deep, sonorous voice. "Well done."

Quintin stood over de Harcourt, still as stone.

"This has been a fine display of strength, but the field is muddy and we endanger our fine warriors," Gravant said. He held out his arm to Mathilda. Confusion was evident on her face as she placed her hand on his sleeve. They left the grounds, their entourage in a long line behind them.

The crowd roared its disappointment when Quintin held out one hand to de Harcourt and hauled him to his feet. The opponents looked as puzzled as the crowd, but bowed to each other and walked off the greensward.

"A draw! The field too muddy? They are not women to be coddled. What nonsense." Edwina thumped her fist on the wall. " 'Tis likely that old bird Roger did not wish to be seen as less than these. He would have been next. With Edgar of Wareham. Now, I've lost more than I've gained."

With a sigh of disappointment, Edwina turned around

and jumped off the small barrel. "Back to work," she said.

Joan picked up the barrel and headed down the steps in the laundress's wake. When they reached the bottom, Joan almost ran up Edwina's heels. Blocking their path was the bishop's party. Mathilda and her ladies stood but a few paces away like a row of colorful birds perched on a fence.

Before the bishop was an old man in a monk's robe. It was Ivo, one of the clerics who'd been at Ravenswood when Joan had come to live here. The bishop shook a small scroll in Ivo's face.

"Oh dear," Joan said.

"I have had enough of your incompetence, old man," the bishop said. "You'll pay for this paper and ink you've wasted, do you hear?"

"But, my lord, I do not understand," Ivo said.

"I have never seen such an ill-written page. I have a dozen men who can do better, and I intend they shall."

"B-but, my lord—"

"Silence, old man. You try my patience. Hie yourself off to some abbey somewhere and bedevil them. If I see you in the hall again, you'll be copying in a dungeon."

Joan's heart beat like a hound's after racing across a field. She ached to intervene, for Ivo looked ready to weep. When the bishop swept off, Lady Mathilda and her party in close file after him, Joan hurried to Ivo just as he sank to his knees on the grass. Several of the bishop's servants brushed past them heedless of the old man's misery.

"Come, Ivo," she said. "Let me help you."

She pulled the man to his feet. "What happened?" She touched the brown-spotted skin on the back of Ivo's hand. He turned his palm over and grasped her fingers.

"Lord Roger asked me to pen the bishop a note. He said it must be done with all speed. It was just a few words. It may have been a mite hastily done, but Lord Roger was snapping his fingers, telling me to hurry. I did just as he said, wrote word for word what he asked. Nothing more." Ivo's head bowed. His lips quivered. "There was one small splash of ink in the corner. But I could not trim it off as Lord Roger snatched the note away. He rolled it before 'twas dry. It was not my fault. What am I to do?" He sniffed. "And just this morning, there was a document on the bishop's table that Lord Roger was signing. I merely thought to move it out of the way once they were done. I simply touched it, nothing more. But our lord bishop snatched it away." Ivo's voice quivered. "He called me a fool. I merely wanted to make more space on the table. I should not be treated in such a manner."

"I know," Joan said.

"And Lord Roger smirked at me. Smirked at his elder. These young people have no respect."

Joan thought that Lord Roger was likely older than the bishop, but she held her tongue.

"Where will I go?" Ivo wailed. "Why wouldn't the bishop listen?"

"Why indeed?" Joan patted Ivo's hand. His fingers were covered by paper-thin skin. "What did Lord Roger ask you to write?"

Ivo stared at her. "Oh, I could not tell you. 'Twould be a violation of my trust."

"I understand. It does not signify. I imagine Lord Roger did not wish to be seen in a poor light before our lady after the magnificent display of strength by Quintin and de Harcourt. He thought of some excuse to end the matches."

Ivo didn't answer; he only repeated, "Where am I to go?"

"You can stay right here."

"Nay, I cannot be found here. The bishop is an avid hunter. He'll see me. Nay."

"The bishop said only you were not to show your face in the keep."

"Do not quibble about details," Ivo said. He wiped his

79

nose and shook his head. "He's been looking for an excuse to dismiss me since first he came. Nothing I do pleases him. My writing is not so steady as it used to be, I grant you, but still, I am careful of details. His clerks cannot touch my translations; they are flawless. I am the only one with Greek and Latin!" He began to sniff and shake.

Joan patted Ivo's hand. "I have an idea, Ivo, but you must come with me to the village."

Chapter Eight

Adam walked at Brian's side through the tent where they'd waited and wagered on the wrestling bouts, through to the area behind it—his mother's garden.

Her ornate gate was gone, as was the orderly concentric circles of flowers and herbs. Now, it was merely a pleasant place of shade and grass for a lady to wander away from the scrutiny of the lesser folk who inhabited the manor.

He took a deep breath. The air was redolent with the scent of apple trees, though little fruit remained.

Wooden walkways had been set out for the men to stand on while they waited for the castle servants to haul out buckets of hot water with which to rinse off the mud.

Adam and Brian stripped out of their wet braies as did the other wrestlers. Suddenly, there was a clamor and calling out from spectators on the high wall overlooking the garden. A hunting hound had gotten loose and run at one of the wrestlers, shoving its muzzle into the man's groin.

Adam's skin heated, not because he was naked under

the scrutiny of a score of people—almost all women. Nay, the racing hound had reminded him of a time when he'd been little more than Francis de Coucy's age and had been deflowering a kitchen maid in a garden corner when one of Nat's hounds had bounded over and jumped around them.

Nat's voice had cracked the silent pleasure garden with anger and condemnation. Luckily, it was to his mother Nat reported him and not his father.

His mother had merely reminded him that bastards cost heavily and kitchen maids could be tiresome, might even put something in the food if displeased. She had turned away without another word.

It was Nat he had respected more than his mother that day. It had been Nat who had talked of his honor and how his behavior reflected on his father and all those who dwelt at Ravenswood. Since that time, Adam had tried to measure his actions against those expectations.

Brian broke into Adam's thoughts. *"Jesu,"* Brian said. "Is every maid and lady up there?"

The man had lost the rancor from his voice—had perhaps worked it out in the bout. "It looks as if you're right," Adam said.

Women leaned over the parapet, waved ribbons, and called out to the naked men. Some of the suitors pranced and paraded around. Some washed hastily and pulled on their clothes.

Brian was one of those who grinned and waved.

"Is Lady Mathilda among them?" asked Francis de Coucy.

It was the first time Adam had seen aught but a haughty expression on his face. The boy covered his groin with his cupped hands.

One of the men said, "She'd not be seen indulging her curiosity in such a way. 'Tis not fitting in one of her station."

"But you can be sure her maid is there to tell her whose cock is biggest," Brian said, then stared at Francis. "Or smallest."

Francis stepped off the wooden walkway and scooped up some mud. In moments Adam was dodging flying clots of sludge.

Though Adam found the ensuing battle annoying and reminiscent of boyhood pranks, the ladies and maids loved it. They screamed their approbation, calling out wagers on their favorites. Adam stepped off onto the grass verge and waved to Douglas. "Bring my mantle."

When Douglas put the black woolen cloak over his shoulders, Adam bowed to Brian and the others. "The maid's seen my cock, and my ass, so I'll be bathing in my tent."

He followed Douglas. The water in his tent was cold, but he didn't want to wait for more to be heated. He washed hastily, and thought of how wonderful a swim in the river would feel. Of course, there would be no alluring woman waiting on the bank today when he was done— or dog to scratch him, either.

Joan could report to Lady Mathilda on the size of his attributes as well.

Douglas offered him a block of soap.

"This isn't my soap," Adam said. "From which woman did you steal it?" The smell carried him back to his mother's chamber again. She had prized exotic scents, potpourri, sachets. She had bathed in milk and perfumed her skin. This soap reminded him of her bedchamber, redolent as the garden she'd created in the midst of his father's military stronghold.

"I gave it to him," said a voice from the front of his tent.

Douglas tossed him a length of linen just in time. A woman, followed by two maids, shoved back the hanging divider that separated the two sections of his tent and smiled at him.

"Adam Quintin?" the woman said.

"You're Lady Claris, Francis de Coucy's mother, are you not?" Adam asked. Cold water dripped from his hair to run down his back and chest. The other two women watched the drops and one licked her lips. He felt like a roast of mutton on a spit.

Francis's mother gave him an inviting smile. He met it with a bland mask. He did not need this woman, the mother of one of his rivals, attempting a seduction.

"Lady Mathilda craves a meat pie for her dinner and bids you to provide a brace of hares." Lady Claris raked her gaze down Adam's body as Matthew had raked him with his claws.

With that the lady and her maids left his tent. The maids looked over their shoulders and one waved.

"Watch the short one," Douglas cautioned. "She's a jolly one, she is."

"And you know . . . how?" Adam asked with a grin.

"Oh, she's of a mind that lying with the squire will get her closer to the knight."

Adam frowned. "I'll not tell you how to spend your nights, Douglas, but do not make trouble for me. I cannot afford it."

Douglas laughed. "I'm not sharing her pallet. She just comes around. I fancy she wants me to let her into yer bed one night when yer sleeping."

"And you'll be sure it doesn't happen, right?"

"Oh, right. She hasn't a chance of getting by me. You'll gain no ill will from her. It'll be me she'll run against, not you. Ye needn't fear she'll complain to her lady about ye, but ye better watch de Coucy's mother. She'll have yer braies about yer knees ere ye can say 'God love me.' And Lady Mathilda will not want ye after that one's had ye."

Adam clapped Douglas on the shoulder. "You'll guard my honor, won't you?"

"Every moment."

"You're worth your weight in gold—have I said that?"

"Many a time. If only ye'd make good on yer word." Douglas sighed and picked up the block of soap. He wrapped it in cloth and tucked it into Adam's wet mantle.

Adam pulled on his clothing.

"Ye'll need to see Nat Swan," Douglas said. "He'll have a harrier to lend ye, I'm sure."

And a huntress to direct me, if I'm lucky, Adam thought.

It was a mark of Ivo's despair that he did not even inquire into Joan's plan. He followed her like an obedient dog into the village, cowering away from the crowds in the street. She imagined Ivo rarely attended a market day or a fair.

She intended to settle Ivo with the baker's wife. Smells of roasting meat and smoking fires filled the air when she reached the circle of ovens. Here, the yeasty scent of baking bread overpowered everything else. Aelwig, the baker, sat on a bench by one of his ovens, gnawing on a partridge wing.

He grunted a greeting while Joan tugged Ivo toward the low cottage that stood before the ovens.

"Estrild?" she called in the open doorway. "It's Joan."

Estrild, surely of Norse extraction, burst from the portal and enveloped Joan in a bone-crushing hug.

"Yer so thin," Estrild said to Joan, drawing the two of them inside. She slathered the end of a cut loaf with a thick layer of butter and then cut off the slice. "Here, eat. Both of you." She repeated the buttering and slicing and handed the next piece to Ivo.

"Thank you, but I must speak to you first." Joan tugged Ivo to a stool by the large open hearth and pushed him down. She set her bread and his on Ivo's lap. He lifted one slice and pecked around the edges like a bird.

She beckoned Estrild to follow her into the yard. Chickens scattered from their feet as they walked arm in arm toward the river.

"Ivo has been dismissed by the bishop. He has lived at Ravenswood since . . . well, I don't know how long, but he has certainly been here since I arrived. He drew up the request to the king for my adoption."

Estrild said, "And you'd like me to keep him."

"Aye, and bless you. What would he owe you?" Joan held her breath and prayed it would not be too much.

"Tuppence a week should do it."

Joan's stomach flipped. "So much?"

"Aye. Sorry, but I cannot take less. The bishop has demanded another ten pence a week in rent from us."

Joan knew she had at least forty pennies. Nat would understand that this was a good use of their money.

"The bishop won't endear himself to anyone if he dismisses such a one as Ivo without thought for his welfare. And he a man of God," Estrild continued.

Joan nodded. She thought of her father. Nat would be before the bishop all week with the hounds. If Nat made a mistake and angered the bishop, he, too, would be dismissed.

Twice Joan had overridden Nat's vague orders at this morning's hunt. Neither incident would have created any disaster, but with Oswald, Lord Roger's hunt master, ready to criticize any lapse and preen over his own prowess, she could not take chances.

If Lord Roger won Mathilda's hand, it would be Oswald at Ravenswood, and she and Nat who needed the pennies and a place to stay.

She shivered. Nat would die without his dogs. Although Nat thought of each pup as his, they really belonged to the manor and whoever was lord there.

Had she been foolish to offer her precious pennies for

Ivo's care? She and Nat might need them one day. Nay. It was never wrong to help someone in need, or so her mother had taught her. "If you don't mind, Estrild, I'll tell Ivo of our arrangement myself. And I'll stop by as often as I can to see how he fares."

Joan hurried back to the castle. The sun streamed down on the many colorful banners in the bailey. When she reached the cottage, Nat stood in the doorway, a frown on his face.

"Where've you been, child?" he asked. "Something terrible's happened."

"What's wrong? Is one of the dogs hurt?"

"Nay, why do you ask?"

"You just said something terrible had happened."

"Did I?" He shook his head and scratched his chin. "Oh. I must have meant the purse."

"What purse?"

"Our purse," he said softly. His gaze went to the hearth. "I lost it."

Joan snatched up a knife and wedged the tip into a crack between two hearth stones. She levered up a block of stone, slightly smaller than the others, and stared at the recess beneath it. She shifted a wooden box that held a few treasures from her mother: a comb, a needle case, a faded ribbon. The purse was gone.

"Papa, what did you do with our money?"

"Oswald said 'twould be a good wager."

"Oswald? Lord Roger's hunt master?"

"Aye. He said he'd double my money if Quintin won. He said de Harcourt always loses to Quintin." Nat fisted his hand and smote the wooden door panel. "When is a wrestling match ever a draw? I thought my money was safe. He and the bishop were in it together, I'll wager."

She sat back on her heels and looked up at him. So strong, so upright, so easily led astray these days. "You

87

promised, no more wagers." Joan curled her fingers on the cold edge of the stones.

"Oswald assured me Quintin always wins. How could I know 'twould end in a draw?"

"This certainly is something terrible. What will we do for money?"

He smiled. "Ah. We have few needs. Bread for the hounds comes from the castle. If we need new leashes, we've but to ask."

Joan could not help smiling back at him. "You only think of the hounds, Papa. What if *you* have some need? Fall ill? Are injured?"

"Tush! I'm never sick. 'Tis the hounds who take all we have, and I'll earn the pennies back soon enough if the hunt goes well."

If the hunt goes well.

The harshness with which the bishop had dismissed Ivo for blotting his copy made her shiver. Her smile felt false and stiff.

"Did someone mention a hunt?"

Joan hastily shoved the stone back into place and stood up, wiping her fingers on a cloth. Adam Quintin stood just outside the cottage.

"We're to hunt on the morrow, sir. Is there aught I may do for you until then?" Nat asked.

"I've been charged with a quest by our lady. She craves a meat pie and I'm to provide the hares. Can you spare the time?"

"I've naught but time for you suitors. I'll fetch one of the dogs."

Adam remained in the doorway. He was relieved Nat showed no signs of recognition even when standing this close. Adam waited outside the cottage, unsure whether he should enter or not.

Joan set a bowl of apples on the table.

"If you don't mind, I'd like a word with you," he said.

"I've work to do."

"I'm sure your father will only be gone a few moments." He boldly stepped over the threshold but was pained to see Joan put the table between them.

"I've come from the castle. There, Oswald—you know him—Lord Roger's hunt master, was regaling the company with his luck wagering on the wrestling. He bragged that he'd probably taken Nat's whole fortune over my bout. Did he?"

Joan nodded. Her throat felt tight.

"Was it all you had?"

"It would not matter but—" She broke off. What would this man care about Ivo?

"But?" He plucked an apple from the bowl and bit into it.

She shook her head. "Oswald told Nat you never lose."

Adam ate the apple, watching her. Never had she cared overmuch about her appearance, but with this man's gaze on her, she wished for her comb.

"It was a cheat," he agreed.

"But Nat should know better. He thought to make some easy money. It's happened before." Then she could not hold back the words. They tumbled out. "But, you see, I needed those pennies. I'm paying the rent for an old cleric from the castle—a man the bishop dismissed today—Ivo by name."

Anger coursed through Adam like lightning in a storm. How dare the bishop put castle folk in need? Especially one who'd served Ravenswood all his life? He clenched his fist. How many others were in need thanks to Gravant?

Nat's whistle could be heard and in moments, he was back, a harrier, Peter, at his side.

"Shall we go, sir?" Nat asked.

"Could Joan accompany us? 'Tis said the ladies much enjoy hunting a hare."

"Aye. Joan would love a meat pie, wouldn't you?"

"I needn't join the hunt to have the pie, though, Papa."

"Nonsense. Come along," Adam said.

Moments later, he was handing her into the saddle. To Adam, it seemed Joan did not enjoy the hunt.

She spoke not at all and he gave up trying to draw her out. Nat was efficient and they were not out more than an hour before his bag was full.

They rode back through the castle gates with Joan as silent as when they'd left. Nat filled the gaps with tales of former hunts. It gave Adam time to think about Roger and his huntsman.

At the kennels, Nat lingered, telling Adam a legend about a great stag reputed to have antlers with more than twenty tines—some said as many as thirty. The animal had roamed the hills around Ravenswood since ancient times. It was said that if one saw the beast it brought great good luck. To hunt the beast brought ill fortune.

Joan smiled at Adam's enjoyment of the tale and his promise never to lift his bow if he saw the stag. The tale was an old favorite of Nat's. She wished it were true so she could search out the animal and glean some good luck to ward off the bad she sensed had come to Ravenswood with Bishop Gravant.

Nat took the dog into the kennels, but Adam did not walk off as Joan expected. He took up his reins and hers and accompanied her to the ranks of stables. When he'd handed off their mounts to a groom, he took her elbow and escorted her to the cottage.

"Now, we've had a fine hunt, you've a brace of hares for a pie as does our lady, and yet, you're silent, and you have not unfurrowed your brow all afternoon. What may I do to bring a smile to your face?" he asked.

It was not possible to deny him. She smiled. "I have my concerns," she said.

"The purse Oswald won from your father being first?"

She looked at the kennels. "I'll not deny I'm worried.

Nat used to have difficulty with wagering, but I thought he had put it aside."

Adam propped his foot on the bench by the cottage door. He leaned his forearm on his thigh. "I feel responsible for your father's loss."

"Why? You did not make the wager."

"I was in the bout."

"You did not call the bout a draw, sir."

"I suspect there was something more to the matter than we know. The bishop's excuse that the ground was muddy seems mighty thin."

"Perhaps Lady Mathilda was bored."

Adam grinned. "No one is bored when I wrestle."

Joan smiled. "You're very sure of yourself."

"I've wrestled de Harcourt several times. He always loses."

"So Oswald says." Then she frowned and looked at Nat, who was bandying words with Edwina and Del. "Nat lost everything we had," she said softly.

Adam pulled his purse from his belt and held it out to her. She took a step away.

He was on her in one stride. He snatched up her hand and pressed the purse into her palm. "You must take it. It was Roger's man who cheated your father. It's the least I can do, after you saved my life, and this is Roger's silver, won honestly by my own wagers during the bouts. I'd prefer to handle the matter in another way, but I cannot risk the bishop's displeasure. This is not the most satisfying end to the matter, but the most politic."

Joan kneaded the leather purse between her palms. When she looked up, guilt swept over him at the sheen in her eyes.

None of these people would be suffering if his father had not been banished.

"How can I thank you?" she asked. She kissed the purse. Then, she rose on tiptoe and kissed his lips. It was naught but an impulse, he was sure, and the kiss naught but a whisper of touch so fleeting it might have been the kiss of a butterfly, or the brush of a cobweb across his skin.

She turned and ran into the cottage.

Adam touched his lips. A kiss on the mouth was a kiss of equals. Did she see him as her equal, not much more than a servant ordered to fetch meat on Mathilda's whim? Or did she see herself as higher than that?

After all, according to the gossip Douglas had gleaned from the alehouse, Joan Swan had been more than Richard de Poitiers's friend, she had been his lover.

Chapter Nine

Joan skinned the rabbits for Nat's supper. She made a stew as she hadn't the patience for a pie. Her heart thumped wildly each time she thought of her impulsive act of kissing Adam Quintin.

She closed her eyes and touched her mouth with the back of her hand. Her body felt weak and her legs unsure. She knelt at the hearth and pulled out his purse. It was of fine leather. Painted on it in gold was the V found on his shield. She smoothed her thumb over the letter, well worn from much handling, then tipped out a stream of silver pennies. She counted one hundred before stopping. More than twice what Nat had lost. She separated forty of the pennies and wrapped them in a linen square. The remainder she put back into the purse. When next she had an opportunity, she would return every penny over the forty.

She took up the purse and linen-wrapped bundle of coins and shoved them up into a space where the thatching met the wall stones, a place Nat would never look. A few moments later, she also tucked away her box of treasures. She would take no more chances.

Adam sat gingerly on his bed. His back was getting worse. Wrestling had made it worse. Wrestling brought his thoughts to Joan Swan's kiss.

Why had the bishop called his match a draw? There was little to suggest the paper the bishop held was very important. The bishop had left the field, but according to Douglas, not gone into his chamber or consulted with any of his clerics. Instead, the man had called for meat and wine, then settled down to eat with his ward and those suitors not flinging mud like children in the garden.

Had the bishop made his own wagers? Perhaps on de Harcourt? And when he had seen that de Harcourt could not win, had he manufactured an excuse to end the match and save his money?

It amused Adam to give Roger's pennies to Joan. Although there was little luxury in the cottage, it was warm and inviting, with a fine stone hearth and a couch of furs along one wall. He would not want to think of his huntress deprived of that warmth or of the furs.

His huntress. Nay, not his, but still, he would like to see her on that couch. He would kneel over her, draw up the furs about her throat, and kiss her as she needed to be kissed.

Was the gossip true? Had Joan enjoyed Richard's kisses? And what of Brian's display of jealousy? Had Brian kissed her?

Adam forced himself from his soft bed. He struck a flint to a candle. He drew out paper and pen. Without allowing Joan to intrude again on his thoughts, he made a list of tasks he needed to do to accomplish William Marshal's goal—unmask the traitor: Look through Francis de Coucy's belongings, follow the most likely candidates, spend more time wooing the lady.

He examined the list and drew a line through the last item. He then rewrote it at the top of the list. If he failed William Marshal, perhaps he could win the lady. At least that would ensure the prosperity of the tenants and eliminate the frown on Joan Swan's face.

"Adam? I saw your light." Hugh swept into the tent and stood there, half in shadow.

Adam rose and set his list to the candle flame.

"A lover's note?"

"Aye. Her husband would have my balls if he read it." Adam held the burning paper until it was naught but ash and one smooth, ivory corner. He dropped that to the dirt floor.

"We need to get across to the hall before Roger has snared the quarry."

Adam lifted a pitcher to pour his friend some ale, but found it empty. "What do you think of Roger, beyond the obvious conclusion that he's a lickspit?" Adam asked. "I think he tried to cheat Nat Swan over the wrestling."

"Roger's a man who will align himself with whatever breeze blows the most glory his way. He's one of those who will equivocate until the last moment, until he is sure of a winner, and then he will cast his men that way."

"I agree. He's like the wrack floating on the tide. Until he's washed onto a rock, he'll not cling."

"Did you see the huntress on the wall?"

"Were not all the women on the walls? I felt as a horse must at auction. Thank God the women were not allowed in the ring to examine our teeth."

"Or peer into your braies."

Adam grinned. "They had no need. We took them off most willingly after the bouts."

"Roger, too? He bared that tiny eel?"

"Eel? You insult my favorite dish. Worm."

"A lickspit, sycophant worm?" Hugh stood up. "Let us get to the hall and drink some of the bishop's fine wine."

The two friends entered the hall. While Hugh walked to the high table and took a seat a few places from Lady Mathilda, a seat closer to the lady than Brian de Harcourt, but one farther than Roger Artois, Adam headed to where several knights sat at a far lesser position.

Laden trays with roast boar and poached pears made the rounds. Wheels of cheese and mounds of honey pastries followed the meat and fruit. Adam noted a large meat pie in front of Lady Mathilda, and when she looked his way, he bowed and raised his goblet of wine. She lifted hers and smiled back.

Adam ate absentmindedly. He fixed his attention as he should on Lady Mathilda. She giggled into her napkin every time Hugh opened his mouth. Adam could almost hear Hugh grind his teeth.

A man tapped him on the shoulder. "You made a fine showing today, Quintin. I lost a few marks on you, but still, if the bishop had not called the match, you had de Harcourt cold."

They discussed the wrestling. "Come," Adam said. "The matches and all other contests serve no purpose but to please the lady. She's seen us all in the flesh now, and it is my hope her decision is made."

"We've not seen her in the flesh, though," one knight sighed.

"I can tell you what you're missing," Brian said, sitting at Adam's side.

The pair opposite stared openmouthed at de Harcourt.

Adam sliced some cheese and ate it off the tip of his eating dagger. "You must go on after that provocative statement."

Brian also speared some of the well-aged cheese. "She will look like any other woman. Plump in the right places, spare in others. It is not her form one should care about, it is this place. The lady could be shaped like that wheel of cheese or a cask of ale and it would matter not a whit."

Brian was right. It was Ravenswood everyone here really craved.

"Well, enjoy your visit, Brian," said Adam. "It'll be your last . . . unless I invite you back after the wedding."

The men around them laughed.

"We will see about that—" Francis de Coucy's words cut across Brian's. "And if gossip has it right, you've been hunting other quarry, Quintin—female quarry."

Adam forced himself not to react to the comment. Who else had observed him with Joan Swan? Mathilda? Her ladies? The bishop? Should he shove Francis's teeth down his scrawny throat? He chose, instead, to lift his cup and take a long, cool drink.

Another man across from them said, "You must be fairly confident, de Harcourt, to leave our lady to Roger."

"Roger can do naught but fawn on the bishop. You would think 'twas the bishop he wished to wed, not Mathilda," said Brian.

"Is it not the bishop we must please, perhaps more than the lady?" Adam asked. "If she cannot choose by the week's end, it is he who will."

Brian shrugged. "I believe he has already chosen. Who here would mostly willingly kiss his ecclesiastic ass?"

"I would if 'twould decide the matter," the suitor with the broken arm said.

Adam looked at Roger, who was telling Mathilda and the bishop a story replete with gestures, then sighed. "I was prepared to offer many kisses in this effort, but none in that direction."

"Then get in practice," Brian said, rising. He set his hand on Adam's shoulder. "Or should I say . . . practice your kissing in more productive places?"

Adam was saved a response when the bishop rose. He banged his dagger hilt on the edge of a pewter goblet and commanded everyone's attention.

"Let us drink to King Henry's health," the bishop said.

He drank. "And to our great regent. The finest knight who ever took sword in hand—William Marshal." This second toast brought every man to his feet.

When the noise subsided, the bishop held out his hand. "Lady Mathilda, will you honor our guests?"

Mathilda rose and bowed to the bishop, who kissed her hand. She wore her hair plaited and coiled into a crown about her head. Pearls were stitched on her ivory gown. A queen could not command greater attention or interest.

"It is time to honor those men who tested their mettle against one another in the wrestling bouts," Mathilda said. "For each man who won his match, I salute you."

She raised her cup and drank. The minstrels, Christopher among them, strummed their instruments with frantic energy for every moment she held the cup to her lips. When she lowered the cup, they ceased on a single note, and she laughed. "Now, a kiss and a token for the best display of manly strength and courtly behavior. Step forward, Brian de Harcourt and Adam Quintin."

A frown creased Roger's face. As Adam walked at Brian's side to the dais, he saw Roger lean toward the bishop. The bishop held up a hand and Roger fell silent.

"Most noble knights," Mathilda said. "Accept these tokens and know that I could not choose between you." She rose on tiptoe and kissed Brian on the lips. She sheared a ribbon from her gown with a small silver-handled dagger.

Brian's men rose and stomped their feet, clapping and cheering their master.

Adam bent a bit to accept the lady's kiss. It was a very proper, simple kiss. She pressed a silky ribbon into his palm. His men, not to be outdone by Brian's, raised a tumult of whistles and cheers.

The minstrels took up the business, Christopher's voice rich and pure over the others, as he led his company into the song he'd composed on Adam's boar.

When Adam turned from the lady to take his seat, he

caught Lady Claris's eye. She licked her lips and lifted a brow.

Adam kept his expression neutral. He held his ribbon aloft, then knotted it about the hilt of his dagger, a reminder to all he was now favored. Brian grinned and tied his on his belt.

Mathilda commanded everyone's attention again when the men had taken their seats. "On the morrow, after chapel, we'll have another competition. Those who feel so inclined are invited to test Brian de Harcourt's mighty throwing record, marked in the outer bailey. Who wishes to take the challenge and toss the stone?"

Adam grinned as every suitor leapt to his feet, himself included. "Why not?" he said to his neighbor. "What else have we to do but *pleasure* the lady?"

Adam lighted a brace of candles in his tent. He stripped to his linen shirt and sat on his camp bed, painted with ravens in flight. Not that many would interpret his V as a bird's wings, spread.

Despite the lure of his bed, Adam knew he could not sleep yet. He took out the parchment he'd purloined from de Harcourt.

Why would de Harcourt have a document written in Greek? It made a fairly secure way of passing information that few common men, and not even many learned men, could read, he thought. Yet Adam found it hard to believe Brian had the skill.

He needed someone to translate the page. Whom could he trust to do the task and not share its contents after? Possibly, Ivo? Nay, too many years had passed to trust the old man. Who knew where his loyalties now lay? The page must be sent to John d'Erley at Winchester.

Adam also knew the paper was too valuable to trust out of his sight. He sighed with resignation, sharpened a quill, and set about copying the page. He wished for a clerk he could trust, frowned over the poor representation he was making, and knew dawn would break before he finished.

Hugh heard the light tapping on his bedchamber door. He ignored it. A moment later, the door opened with a small creak. He slid his hand under his pillow for the dagger he kept there. Then he sat up, eyes wide. "Mathilda? What are you doing here?"

He saw she wore a dark robe as she climbed onto the end of his bed. Her hair was down, her feet bare.

"I must speak with you."

By the meager light of the dying fire in his hearth, her eyes looked huge and grave.

"Speak." He yawned to hide his complete consternation that she sat perched on his bed like a bird who'd escaped her cage.

"I must have your advice about these suitors."

He looped his arms about his knees. "What the devil can I tell you?"

"You're so much wiser than I. And you don't want me."

"*Mon Dieu,* that's the truth," he said.

She sat in silence for a moment, plucking at the coverlet. "We've known each other for several years, Hugh. I think a lot of your opinion, so help me make a choice."

"Adam Quintin." He flopped back on the pillows and turned to his side. "Be sure to latch the door on your way out."

She slapped the bedcovers. "That's it? One name?"

He closed his eyes. Her hair dragged across his hip as she climbed up closer to him.

"Aye. One name. One man most worthy. Now, may I sleep?"

He heard her sharp intake of breath, then only measured silence. Had he done Adam a disservice by touting him?

"Give me reasons."

Hugh sighed and rolled to his back. She was on her

knees, so close, he could smell her. Flowers. Woman smells. "Adam Quintin has what a woman needs and wants most in a mate."

"Hah. You think a woman wants naught but a pretty face!"

She slapped the bedcovers again with the flat of her hand, hit his hip and just missed his genitals.

He sat up and snatched her hand that the next blow might not be more accurately placed. "You misunderstand. Adam Quintin has *honor*. He will never play you false. He will guard and protect you all your days."

"Is that so rare? Would you not do the same?"

"It's very rare. I know few men of whom I could say the same. As to me? I'd play you false with the first serving woman who bared her breasts."

He nodded to her chest and flung her hand away.

She hopped off the bed and ran to the door. She did not slam it. She left as quietly as she'd entered.

Adam looked over his copy and though 'twas a pathetic effort, he thought it was readable. He wrapped and sealed the paper, then hid the original in a shallow hole he dug beneath his bed. He flopped back onto his mattress, with naught but an hour until he must rise.

Yet sleep eluded him. He tried to concentrate on Mathilda. She seemed incapable of any conversation beyond remarks on the minstrels or the heat of the hall. Hugh's riddles, favorites in most gatherings, drew naught but blank looks from the lady.

Would Joan Swan have understood them? He conjured Joan's face. Had she freckles elsewhere? He'd like to hunt beneath her habit and know the answer.

He heard the stirring of men in the bailey. Servants clanked pails of water down outside tents.

Who connived with the bishop? Roger? Francis? What proof should he look for?

101

With a sinking heart, he knew he must search the bishop's belongings. How? Even during a holy office, someone lurked about the steps leading up to the man's bedchamber.

A dog barked.

Joan's sweet face supplanted every other thought. Why did the huntress's kiss so disturb him? He'd been kissed by many women. He closed his eyes, and conjured her dark eyes. She'd closed them just as she'd kissed him. What would it be like to hold her and look into her eyes as he kissed her? Next time, he would demand she keep her canny eyes open.

Next time. How would Joan's body feel against his?

Hugh's words about her lush ass heated Adam's body. As he waited for sleep, he reveled in thoughts of kneeling behind her, his hands spread on the rounded flesh of her bottom, leaning forward to kiss each dimple he imagined he'd find. Abruptly, he returned to the simplicity of her kiss. His lips almost itched with the sensation lingering there.

He fell into a restless doze. Then Brian's words at the hunt jolted him awake and cooled his ardor.

Joan Swan's passions were not directed at lovemaking. They were guided by hate. A hate for mercenaries.

"And that is what you are, Adam. A mercenary. Flemish and despised," he said aloud.

"Are ye speaking to me?" Douglas asked, flinging back the tent partition.

"To myself." Adam stood up and stretched, then pulled on a mantle. "I'll sleep next month. Now, come, I want you to find me some throwing stones."

"Stones? Not before we break our fast!" But Douglas trotted after him despite his protests.

At the riverbank, as the sky lightened, and the trees shone as if touched with ice, Adam threw stone after stone, each retrieved by Douglas and dropped with great sighs at his feet.

"That will do it," Adam finally said. He'd banished the huntress from his mind . . . and his body. He stripped and plunged into the river, now deep green and cold as melted ice.

When his feet and hands grew numb, he climbed out and dried himself in the first rays of the sun. Douglas handed him his shirt.

A movement in the far field drew Adam's gaze. A greyhound raced across the grass. Behind him, a woman ran, her hair loose, whipping out behind her in a wild tangle.

"So much for banished thoughts."

Chapter Ten

Joan smiled at the dog who ran before her with the joy of a pup, though he was long past his prime. They hastened back to the castle as the sky brightened. She put up her hair before she entered the kennels. There she greeted each hound. She examined a mastiff's paw and made up a poultice of vinegar and soot to treat a bad scrape. As she sat cross-legged and tended the wound, she eavesdropped on several of the boys who cleaned the kennels and kept the dogs from quarreling.

"Ever' one knows a black dog is bad," one said.

"Aye. Black is evil. Did ye ev'r see a black tent like the one there?"

Joan resisted an urge to interrupt their gossip.

"Evil doin's in there, sure as a black dog do evil. And 'is 'air is dark as sin. So's 'is armor, though I ain't seed it. Black 'air, black clothes."

" 'Tis said 'e carved 'is mark on a woman's teat. Marked

'er so's no other man would 'ave her. John Armorer tol' me."

"Wish I could see a woman's teat."

Joan rubbed the mastiff's ears and praised his patience for sitting so still for her ministrations, then she stood up and walked to the two boys. "If you wish to keep your position, you will not spread gossip. Do you understand?"

The boys bobbed their heads, eyes round with dismay. They hastened away to spread fresh straw on the bed racks.

She heard a yelp, then the sharp-pitched cry of a dog in pain. Someone was abusing an animal. She ran along the partitions housing the visiting hounds. Oswald Red-hair raised an iron bar over a cowering greyhound.

"What are you doing?" she demanded, snatching at his arm.

Oswald pulled away. "A dog must know who is leader of the pack."

Joan threw herself between the dog and Oswald. "There will be no beatings here." She saw scars across the greyhound's flanks. "If this animal will not obey, I will take him off your hands."

"I do not believe you can afford his price."

The bar in Oswald's hand was lined with thin ridges. He tapped it against his leg.

"You're Nat Swan's wife, aren't you?" he asked.

"I'm Nat's daughter." She traced a row of scars along the dog's flanks, old scars, new ones, made by the bar in the man's hand. A glance at the animals resting on the bed racks revealed similar marks of abuse. She shivered at the cruelty.

Oswald rocked on his heels. "You coddle your dogs."

He cleared his throat and kicked at the straw in the manner of a child. It was an act. Any man who would beat his dogs as these had been was a devil. She gathered the hound into her arms.

"I must be blunt," Oswald said. "Nat wagered my master quite a sum on the wrestling, you know."

"I thought he wagered with you." The dog buried his head against her breast.

"With my master, through me. You need to know Lord Roger charged me with the debt's collection. Fifty pence, it is." He slid his hand back and forth along the bar.

"Nat said forty." Joan involuntarily tightened her arms. The injured greyhound whined and nuzzled her cheek. She took a deep, steadying breath and relaxed her hold. "He also said he had paid you."

He smiled. His pale, watery blue eyes roamed over her.

"Oh, he paid me forty pence, 'tis true, but he owes another fifty. And my master would like it soon."

"It's not possible. Nat wouldn't wager ninety pence on anything!"

Oswald pressed a finger to his lips and glanced about the kennel. "Forgive me, mistress, if I've distressed you, but you can ask any number of folks to confirm it. My lord Roger specifically directed me to say, 'Forty-five on Quintin, double if a draw.' Nat agreed."

Joan felt acid seethe in her belly. "I wish the name of these witnesses."

The smile left his face. "Are you saying I am lying?"

Joan tempered her tone, though she wanted to shout that anyone who beat animals with a bar was surely also a liar. "Not at all, but I don't know you. I must hear it from someone else. 'Tis a fortune you're asking me to turn over."

"My master is well respected. Your suspicions of me are suspicions of him. It is he who sent me to collect the money. If you will not accept *my* word, then you must accept his." With a sniff, Oswald turned and left the kennels, the bar still gripped in his hand.

Joan cursed his skinny form. What was she going to do? She gave the injured dog to one of the kennel lads and asked him to treat the animal's wounds.

She told several huntsmen of Oswald's iron bar and asked them to prowl the kennels in hopes their presence might deter the man from further abuse of his dogs. Then she took up her brushes and called Matthew to her. The usual soothing balm of her work, the rhythmic stroke of the brush over the dog's coat did naught to still a rising fear for Nat, for the kennels, for their future—for herself.

Mathilda's maid came to the kennels. Joan put aside her grooming brushes and met her near the fencing.

"Is there aught I may do for you?" Joan asked.

"My lady requests your presence at this morning's games."

"My presence?" Joan looked down at her dirty hands. "I'm not fit to appear—"

"Immediately, my lady says."

Joan frowned, but could not refuse. She went to the cottage and hastily washed. She jerked her comb through her hair, each stroke fueling her fear and anger. This was what Edwina had spoken of, Mathilda commanding her like a servant.

She plaited her hair and donned a fresh gown the color of the leaves cast off in autumn by the tall oak trees, cast off as was the gown. Its beauty lay in the fine sheen of the linen and the matching overgown stitched with a bordering motif in red and green. It became her well, though the hem had needed letting down and the line showed if one wanted to see it.

She looped her plaits and put on a headcovering, securing it with a circlet of braided red cording. With quick, long strides, she headed for the games. If she must face disaster, at least she would do so with her head held high.

Everyone was in attendance. The throwing field had

been marked out so the castle ramparts could again serve as a viewing stand.

Hugh de Coleville, unshaven, his eyes bloodshot, a frown on his face, came toward her. "Ah," he said. "The worthy huntress."

She gave him a polite curtsy. "Have you seen my lady?"

He stiffened. "Why?"

"Her maid summoned me, but I cannot find her."

His mouth twisted into an odd expression, half smile, half grimace. "She's in the center of it all. I'll take you."

He put out his arm. She placed her hand on his sleeve and smiled. To be summoned like a servant was one thing, to arrive with a fine lord was quite another. He led her through the crowd, which stepped aside easily to his simple order, "Make room." The company parted and Joan saw the field.

On one side stood the company of suitors, all half naked again. Adam and Brian stood side by side, both with arms crossed on their broad chests.

Mathilda graced a semicircle of women at the end of a long open space. She held a tall, beribboned crook. The ribbons matched her scarlet gown. She looked like a wild poppy standing in the field, albeit a poppy decorated with many gold chains.

"See Lord Roger," Hugh said, and Joan looked for the older man. "He sets himself to a better advantage over there with Francis, a mere boy, rather than stand beside the likes of Quintin and de Harcourt."

Joan wanted to smile, but Hugh wore such a fierce expression, she swallowed it and instead asked, "Is there something wrong, my lord?"

"Nothing," he said. "Come."

"I cannot go out there." Joan pulled on his arm.

He looked down at her, covering her fingers with his large, rough hand. "Why not? You are fairer than all but one, and she grows less lovely as you come to know her.

Walk with me, your head high, and put them all to shame."

Without another word, he strode down the center of the greensward. She felt heat sweep up her cheeks as the chattering crowd watched them. Her heart thudded in her chest. If Mathilda asked her to fetch a footstool or a pitcher of wine, Joan knew she would sink into the earth in shame.

De Coleville reached Mathilda and bowed with a flourish. "My lady, I have brought the fair Joan."

Mathilda smiled. "Thank you, my lord. Joan?" Mathilda held out her hand. She wore a ring on every finger, her thumb included. Amid her chains dangled a fine gold cross decorated with pieces of jet—a gift from a suitor, Joan imagined.

"You wished to see me?" Joan said, putting her work-roughened hand in Mathilda's smooth, soft one.

"I want you to join me here. You remember how you and I used to watch Richard and Brian toss the stones? I believe you are the one who suggested the marker." Mathilda tapped a stone set in the field with her staff.

Joan remembered. The stone had only a few words scratched on its surface. *De Harcourt—25 feet.*

The bishop stood up and one of Lord Roger's huntsmen blew a long salute on his hunting horn to alert the crowd. Everyone fell silent. The bishop consulted a roll of vellum a cleric held—a young cleric, upright and tall. The sight of the man brought tears to Joan's eyes at the thought that Ivo had been dismissed without pension or consideration.

The bishop called Francis de Coucy to throw first. Francis's mother, standing in Mathilda's bevy of women, elbowed her way to Mathilda's side. "My son would be honored if you would give him some token of good luck."

Mathilda smiled and floated down the field toward Francis. He looked no more than a boy, his chest and arms spotted with the same sores that disfigured his face. But it was not for his sorry skin that Joan did not like him. It was the way he looked at Mathilda. It was the look of a fox before he stole a hen.

Mathilda held her staff in one hand, and placed her fingertips lightly on the boy's bare shoulder. "For luck," she said. The crowd made a collective sound, half sigh, half gasp, as she touched her lips to the boy's.

Then Mathilda turned away and walked back along the throwing field to stand ready to mark the distance Francis threw.

The boy hefted the stone to his shoulder. Joan did not see his throw. Nay, she looked at Adam Quintin, but he was not watching Francis. She saw him slip through a gap in the crowd and disappear.

A burst of jeers and screams of laughter turned Joan's attention back to the field. Francis's throw had gone into the spectators. A woman lay on the ground, blood on her temple, his stone by her side.

Lady Claris broke from the crowd and ran to where he stood. She screamed invectives in his face as the crowd enfolded the injured woman.

"A sorry beginning," Joan said.

Mathilda nodded. She directed a servant to see to the woman, while the bishop called the next name.

Joan realized there was one woman on the field for each man who threw the stone. As Mathilda marked the spots with her staff, she called one of her women to stand on the edge of the field, a bright, smiling marker.

With great impatience, Joan realized this game might take all day because of Mathilda's insistence on giving every man a token kiss. Each suitor must watch her walk the length of the throwing field and enjoy the touch of her lips on his. They must also watch her walk slowly back. The crowd loved it.

Joan looked in vain for Adam Quintin. Why did he not appear? Her hand went to her breast when she thought of

the kennel lads' words. What a terrible rumor to spread—
that he'd marked a woman. For the first time, she examined his men.

Hard men. Mercenaries. A dependable force—for as
long as you paid, they fought. They cared little if William
Marshal ruled through the child king, or Prince Louis of
France.

She forced herself to watch the competition, to concentrate on every toss, to smile when spoken to.

Roger Artois's toss landed with a thud, the best in the
field. He preened at the wealth of cheers that greeted his
fine throw. To Joan's dismay, Mathilda called her to mark
Lord Roger's distance. He scowled at her with narrowed
eyes.

Adam Quintin's name was called. To Joan's surprise he
stepped onto the field. Now, where had he hidden himself?

When he walked to the foot of the throwing field, Joan
saw one of the long scratches on his shoulder looked a bit
inflamed.

Why did she care?

Mathilda headed for Adam to give him the lucky kiss.
With a stab of jealousy, Joan realized she cared whom
Adam Quintin kissed. She cared very much—but without
any right to do so.

Mathilda stood on tiptoe before him. He reached out
and swept an arm about Mathilda's waist. He pulled her
against him and set his lips on hers.

The crowd burst into a thunderclap of approval. It was
just a kiss, Joan said to herself. A mockery of the competitions. *Meaningless.*

Hugh de Coleville made a sound like a growl in his
throat, caught Joan's eye, and said. "She's easy with her
kisses."

"She's playing a part."

He shrugged, pushed through the crowd, and headed for
the inner bailey.

Adam set Mathilda aside. He bowed, brought the stone to his shoulder, spun, and threw it. It landed with a thud and buried itself half into the dirt just past Roger's mark. Another of Mathilda's ladies, Lady Isabelle, stood at the spot.

Brian took his place, last to throw. He did not wait for a kiss. He had a grace and strength that made him as beautiful to watch as Adam. With what looked like little effort, he spun and heaved the missile.

It seemed to hang in the air, then fell with a loud smack. He grinned and shrugged. Quintin's distance prevailed.

"A new record. Adam Quintin by a hand," Mathilda declared.

"She moved," a voice said from the edge of the crowd.

Roger elbowed his way to Mathilda. "I saw Lady Isabelle step aside. She added at least a hand to Quintin's distance."

Adam opened his mouth, but Mathilda held up her staff. "I feared some might think such a thing, so I dropped a penny in Quintin's divot. We shall use that as the marker, shall we?"

Lord Roger's cheeks blotched. "Of course, my lady. How canny that you should think of such a thing."

Everyone stepped forward. Even the bishop, who'd been chatting with his cleric and paying little, if any, attention to the competition beyond calling out names, stood up.

"Joan. Find my penny, please," Mathilda said.

Joan felt every eye on her as she walked across the width of the grassy plot. She stood in line with Lady Isabelle and looked around. There, even with the place where Lady Isabelle stood, was a shiny silver penny. The win was legitimate. Joan placed her toe near the spot. "It is here, my lady."

Mathilda looked at Roger. He bowed. "I stand corrected, my lady. Forgive my error."

She giggled. "Oh, my lord, everyone makes mistakes."

She swatted his arm with her crook. "But see you do not make too many or you'll be leaving."

She walked to Adam Quintin. She extended her staff. This touch was not the cuff Roger had received. This was a slow drag of the ribbons across Adam's honed shoulder and against the strong line of his throat.

"You were gone a very long time during our games, sir. Where were you?" She shook her beribboned staff in his face.

Joan watched a touch of color rise in Adam's cheeks. He said, "Delicacy prevents my saying, my lady."

"Delicacy? From a warrior?" Mathilda smiled.

"If you must know," Adam said with a grin, "I was not far away. I was in the privy." He lifted his hands and shrugged.

The crowd broke into laughter. Mathilda clapped her hands over her face and giggled. Then she sobered and lifted her crook. "I declare you the winner. We shall have a new marker set to honor your toss. What reward do you claim?"

Joan did not wish to hear what Adam wanted. 'Twas obvious. He wanted what they all wanted. The lady of the keep.

Joan walked away, but not in time to miss Adam's words.

"I claim the privilege of watching you plant the marker, my lady, after a small, private supper, perhaps along the river."

Chapter Eleven

Adam found his way to the river through the Roman Way. He carried only a small rushlight. At the shrine to Diana, he stopped a moment to look at the beauty, but his Diana only served to remind him of Joan. Kissing Mathilda had not exorcised the feel of Joan's lips from his mind.

He placed a hand on Diana's knee. "I want the huntress, but not yet. I shall wait until I secure Ravenswood and send Mathilda away." He patted the mosaic knee and admitted he no longer thought in terms of *if* he bedded the huntress. It had become *when*.

Adam extinguished his flame as he neared the dappled light that poured through the tangled roots. No one observed his exit. About a league along the riverbank, he hunkered down in the shadows of a huge stump, mossy and crumbling from years of insect work. He heard footsteps from his left and remained hidden until Christopher came into sight.

The minstrel lifted his tunic and urinated into the reeds.

When he finished, he pursed his lips and whistled.

Adam returned the sound. Christopher did not immediately come to him, but wandered about, plucking a few river reeds and plaiting them quickly into a cord. He whistled as he worked lest anyone interpret the earlier notes as a message of sorts.

Finally, he sat by the stump and leaned back, hands busy on the cordage. "So," Christopher said, "you spent an hour in the privy. Food too rich for you?"

Adam grinned. "It was all I could think of. I thought no one was paying me any attention, so I slipped away and searched tents. Pathetic quarters all and not one piece of paper to be found. So far, this is all I've found of any note." He handed his copy of Brian's letter over. "I found it in de Harcourt's chest. Can you take it to one of our lord's clerics, someone trusted, for interpretation? It's in Greek."

Christopher took the sealed letter. "Done."

"How long will it take?"

"Oh, a day, no more. I've only to go to Winchester. There's a man there in our lord's employ who'll make short work of this."

"I feel I've made little headway, beyond finding that paper. And it could be a list of dirty laundry—or quotes from Sophocles. I cannot see how I'll uncover this traitor in just one week. They all seem—"

"Ill suited to rule Ravenswood?"

"Aye, except for de Harcourt."

"I agree. Between us we've searched ten suitors who have little in common save they are younger sons whose lot will be greatly enhanced by marriage to a wealthy heiress."

"Agreed."

"If you've no confessions duly signed and sealed by week's end, you had better wed the lady."

"Sealed . . . hmmm. Why did I not think of that? To act

for Louis, the bishop or this traitor will need to show he has Louis's authority. He'll need a ring. A seal, or some token to show his authority."

"Aye. Have you seen aught that would serve?"

Adam remembered the ring turned palm to that Mathilda wore. "Only on the lady. And she's an unlikely candidate. She already possesses the castle. If the ring was given her to hold, however, by someone . . . Nay, it does not make sense that she would hold a king's seal. What would it serve? And why wear it for everyone to see?"

"Is there aught else I should find out in Winchester?" Christopher stood up and looked cautiously about.

"I want to know why Francis's father has sent his lady here. Francis is naught but a boy and the mother a harpy. What is the man thinking?"

"Consider the question asked. Where shall we meet?"

"How about the village well, after dawn on the day after tomorrow?"

Christopher agreed and Adam watched the minstrel fade into the foliage before heading down to the river.

The sun had not yet fallen behind the treetops, but he saw Mathilda and a servant walking along the bank. The man's back was bowed under the weight of a huge pack. They were early. "How very flattering," he mused.

Adam sat on a flat rock, one knee raised, an elbow thrown around it as if he'd been waiting there for hours. He watched her progress. She had the air of making an entrance though there were no doors or arches to pass through.

He jumped to his feet and swept her a bow when she drew near. "Welcome, my lady, I'm pleased you chose to sup with me."

She curtsied. "It is I who am pleased to grant your small wish. Would that each desire presented to me were so easily met."

The servant set out a blanket and cushions for the lady

and unpacked cold meat and cheese, wine and fruit.

"Heron," Mathilda said, offering him a meaty leg of fowl. "I'm particularly fond of it."

"A noble bird." Adam accepted the offering.

She took a leg for herself. Adam hid a smile over the way she nibbled up and down the bone. If Hugh saw this, he would have many quips and jests to make about cocks and feasts.

The servant removed himself a few paces and sat with his back to them.

Mathilda had garbed herself in rich cream from head to toe. Pearls graced her throat, wrists, and breast. She looked ready for a king's banquet, not a riverside supper. A flash of movement over her shoulder caught his eye.

Mon Dieu. Joan walked across the distant field with her dogs. He forced himself to look at Mathilda's sparkling splendor.

Silence fell. Adam searched for something to say. "I thank you for handling Roger this morning."

"Do not thank me. I put a penny in each place for just such an eventuality."

"It was well thought out, then."

Mathilda arched her back and leaned on her hands. The posture thrust her bosom at him. The offering did little for Adam save make him think that she must be very uncomfortable.

"I cannot take the credit," she said. "It is what Joan used to do when Brian and my brother competed. They argued so that she finally settled it one day. A penny in each toss as a marker. She's clever."

"Aye." Adam drank from his goblet of wine. He would not discuss Joan.

Over Mathilda's shoulder, Joan's hounds sat in a neat row like students before a master. Suddenly the dogs burst past their mistress, circled, returned, and seated themselves.

117

It was magical.

Mathilda offered him an apple. "I'm glad Joan attended the competition. She spends too much time with the dogs or Nat. He's not her father, you know."

"Brian told me."

Mathilda patted his thigh. "She's terribly afraid of mercenaries. You should watch your men around her."

"I shall." He must watch Mathilda's hand as well.

"I believe Joan has been cheated in this life. I don't know what she'll do when Nat dies. No one would accept a female Master of the Hunt and she's almost too old to marry. There are many younger women about who need a husband."

"Perhaps she is content as she is."

"Nonsense. She needs to put ribbons in her hair and wear pretty gowns, amuse herself."

He bit into the apple.

"Do you not agree?" she asked.

"All women like to wear pretty clothes and deck themselves with ribbons and jewels. Why would she be any different?"

"Because she has been denied. My brother professed to love her. It infuriated my father—her so low, and Richard so high. My father ordered her from the hall. She was to hide herself away lest he see her and spend his anger on her."

"So, she cowered in the kennels. Not very admirable."

Joan's dogs slunk low on their bellies, disappeared in the grass, then bounded up to return to their mistress. She lifted her hands and turned. The dogs swirled around her, then ran in all directions. He imagined the joy of her laughter at the animals' antics.

Mathilda sat up straight and pointed a beringed finger at him. "Joan *never* cowered. She merely donned hunting clothes and went about her work. She never once complained or wept. I would have wept to be treated so."

118

"And what did you do to alleviate the woman's suffering?"

"I am sorry to say I did naught. I'm the coward. I had not courage to question my father's decisions or orders." She brought her arms forward and clasped her hands in her lap. Every finger bore a ring.

"I question mine all the time." Adam held out his goblet to be filled. The servant withdrew again to a discreet distance.

"Tell me of your father." Her face was as smooth as fine marble in the late afternoon sunlight. She looked like an angel carved for some cathedral monument.

"My father is ruled by his heart, not his head."

"Ah. And you hold contempt for such beliefs."

Adam stood up. "My father gave all he had to the woman he loves. He took off the mantle of his authority and stepped to her level."

It occurred to him that Richard had been willing to do just that for Joan. "My father and my stepmother care for naught but my brother and a quintet of sisters I barely know."

"A quintet. An omen. Five sisters."

"Four of the girls are orphans my father and my stepmother gathered in over the years. Imps all, I understand from my brother."

Mathilda rose and stood by his side. She asked the servant to go to the river and remain there until she called him.

"You must make a point of seeing your sisters," she said, linking her arm through his. "They may need you one day and you will be a stranger to them. They may hesitate to call upon you when they might desperately need your help."

"Is that how you feel? You've no one to ask for help?"

She nodded and looked off across the fields where the dogs ran about with wild abandon. "Aye. My brother is

119

gone. My father, too. Would that I had another brother."

"What of Bishop Gravant?"

"He'll do what's best for the Church. If I had a brother, I'd ask him to choose my husband."

Under the guise of comforting her, Adam took her hand. "If you cannot choose, my lady, then all hell will reign here. The country and the king cannot have it so. You must know your mind. It will take courage. Look not to the man who can toss a stone the farthest. Look for a man who can hold this place and serve it with honor."

"And are you that man of honor?"

"I believe I am. Tell me how I may succeed with you."

She smiled. "Begin by paying less attention to Joan Swan." She swept out her hand to the fields.

He bent his head, his skin as hot as if she'd held a brand to it. He raised her hand, turned it, and gently kissed the soft skin of her palm, noting again the ring turned palm in. "This is an interesting ring," he said.

"This?" She plucked the ring off. It was bound with thread to fit her finger. It had been lodged beneath a cabochon ruby much like the one the bishop wore. The ruby swung toward her palm when she drew the other from beneath it.

Adam's fingers almost trembled when he took the seal ring and slid it on his hand. Without the thread it might fit his smallest finger. "Where did you get it?"

"I found it. Is the marking French?" Her head was very close to his as he examined the fleur-de-lis.

"Aye. French. May I keep it?"

"Throw it in the river, if you like."

Chapter Twelve

Joan fussed for over an hour with her hair, cursing its wild ripples and sun-tainted streaks. She scrubbed her face until it hurt, then put on a bronze-colored gown she'd not worn in over two years.

Nat entered the cottage as she picked up her mantle. "Where are you off to?"

"The same place as you—the hall. I was just coming to fetch you. Mathilda has ordered us to sup with the company. Now wash your face and hands and put on a clean tunic."

He put his fingers under her chin. "I'll not see you unhappy. Isn't de Harcourt here? Didn't Lord Guy banish you from the hall?"

"Lord Guy is dead, Papa. This is Mathilda's wish and we must obey."

"Dead?" He shook his head. "I'd forgotten. Do you remember the time he set the hounds on Richard's and

121

Brian's trail and found them in the forest lodge with those two strumpets—"

"I do not need to hear that tale, Papa. It is not for my ears. Now, no more stories. Wash up."

When Joan entered the hall on Nat's arm, she was pleased to see it crowded with strangers. No one would note their presence. They sat with many of Nat's men and their wives, with one of whom she shared a trencher of rich venison stew spiced with pepper and cloves.

Joan kept her mantle on until the hall grew so warm she had to shed it. Nat helped her lay it across the bench before she sat on it.

"I remember that gown," he said. "Did you not stitch it for . . ." He frowned. "The last time you wore it, I had to go to the tavern, did I not?"

The rich sauce bubbled in Joan's belly. She pressed a finger to her lips and nodded to the high table and Mathilda in hope of distracting him, though he often could not be deflected from a course by a simple gesture.

Mathilda tapped gently on her goblet.

Nat subsided but continued to watch Joan. She tried to distract him by linking her arm through his and whispering. "Mathilda is very lovely tonight. See, she wears her mother's rubies. They match her gown."

Nat swung his attention to the lady and Joan took a deep breath. Why had she worn this particular gown? To draw someone's attention? What folly.

"We have reached that happy time for the giving of tokens. Adam Quintin?" Mathilda said.

Adam wore a blue tunic trimmed in black fur. He walked toward Mathilda without looking right or left, though several ladies and men snatched at his hem as he went by.

On the dais, Mathilda clipped a ribbon from her sleeve. A scarlet ribbon. He knotted it alongside the one already on his dagger hilt.

A hush fell over the hall. The air felt as heavy as it did before a storm broke. She knew what would happen, tried to look away, but failed.

Mathilda placed her hand flat on Adam's chest. She rose on tiptoe at the same time he bent his dark head.

A fiery pain coursed through Joan's middle as their lips met. It was a longer kiss this time, less a touch of lips to lips and more a joining or pledge of some kind. Every moment of it hurt Joan's skin, her throat, her middle. And worst of all, she didn't know why.

The minstrel company beat on drums and the crowd cheered.

Not everyone. She did not. Nor Roger, nor Francis de Coucy.

"Come, Nat. 'Tis time for bed. You'll want to be out early and look for another stag," she said.

"Nay. Stay. See, the bishop is going to speak. To leave now may offend him."

Joan subsided to her seat, folded her hands in her lap, and admitted defeat.

The bishop smiled and bowed to Adam and Mathilda. "I believe we should make room for Quintin here at our table to save him this lengthy walk."

Laughter broke out across the hall and Adam bowed, his fingers now linked in Mathilda's. She smiled as a servant rushed forward to slide a stool next to her chair.

The bishop waited for the noise to abate before speaking.

"As everyone knows, we will hold a fair on the morrow—a special fair to honor our suitors and please the ladies who accompany their men. But beware, suitors, even the market will be a test."

Adam shifted uncomfortably on his stool despite its thick embroidered cushion. A test at a fair? *Mon Dieu*. What could that encompass? What did he know about the price of goods?

Mathilda joined the minstrels and took up one of their lyres. She strummed along while Christopher sang about Adam's boar kill.

Hugh topped off Adam's cup of wine.

"Did you drink sour milk?" Adam asked his friend.

Hugh's scowl deepened. "Worse. I've been asked to escort Lady Mathilda to the fair on the morrow. I'm not even vying for her hand, yet I cannot refuse her."

"Why would she ask you? I should be insulted."

"I think Mathilda needs a respite from those who curry her favor. You must help me slip the duty. Why don't you deliver my excuses and offer to act in my place?"

Hugh's face flushed a bright red. Blotches of color stained his neck.

"Let me see . . . an excuse . . . How about, you become ill when asked to bargain for ribbons and thread?"

Hugh grunted and frowned.

"Or, you could say you injured yourself falling off your horse and cannot ride or walk."

"But then I could not attend the hunting. And that would deprive me of the huntress."

Adam shot to his feet. "Think up your own damned excuse. I'll offer myself as escort in your place, but I'll not be party to your lies."

Joan saw Nat settled for the night. She paced in front of the cottage, waiting for Adam Quintin to return to his quarters in the bailey. When she saw him, alone fortunately, she said a small prayer for strength, then headed for his tent. She knew the color was meant to intimidate his opponents, but she found it worked on her senses just as it would on any man. Her heart began to beat faster, her palms broke out in sweat.

The guard was not the amiable Douglas. This man

stared at her from beneath a ridge of bushy brown eyebrows. She asked him if Adam would see her. The man disappeared into the tent, then returned, and held the entryway open for her.

Adam's tent was divided into two parts, the fore of which he used for conducting business or entertaining. It held a folding table and several camp chairs. Everything looked worthy of a king, from the wax candles to the chair carved with Adam's V. She was glad she'd not changed her gown to something more serviceable.

He sat at the table, a brace of candles near his hand. Beside the candles lay a whetstone and a long dagger decorated with topaz. He stood up, one eyebrow raised in question.

She curtsied but turned her gaze to her toes. "I have made a most unfortunate discovery."

He brought one of the chairs forward. When she remained standing he said, "Please. I'm too weary to stare up at you. Sit. Now, what is this unfortunate discovery?"

She sat on the edge of the chair, still unable to meet his gaze. She cleared her throat. "I've been trying all day to find a way to solve my problem without involving you, but I fear it cannot be done."

"This sounds ominous."

His tone was light, and she looked up to see if he mocked her. His gaze was steady and even . . . kind?

"Nat wagered far more than I thought," she said.

"How do you know?"

"Oswald, Lord Roger's hunt master, informed me of the misfortune this morning."

Adam went to a coffer. He opened it and pulled out a small cask. He picked up a key from the table, inserted it into the lock, and the lid fell back. It was full of pennies. "How much do you need?"

"Nay. I did not come here to ask you for more money. It is just I have discovered . . . that is . . . I do not know

125

how I can ever repay what you have already lent me."

Her fingers hurt from gripping them together. He reached forward and took her hands in his. He ran his thumbs over her knuckles.

"You have no need to repay me. It was not a loan, but recompense. As I told you, I thought Roger and Oswald had cheated Nat. And as you can see, I can spare the money, so please, forget 'twas I who gave it."

"I wish I could."

Her eyes gleamed in the candles' glow. They were wide and as dark as the water in a mountain tarn. He could drown in them. Her bronze gown shimmered with each movement of her body. He cleared his throat. "I suspect Oswald's claim is but another cheat. Do not worry about returning my money. It was a gift, not a loan, do you understand?"

She shook her head.

He stared up at the peak of the tent for a moment, then took her hands again. He rubbed his thumbs across the backs, enjoyed the softness of her skin, the heat of it, the sprinkling of tawny freckles there.

"If it would make you more comfortable, let us make our own bargain. You shall repay me one penny at a time, to be given whenever you are able."

Her gown shimmered almost gold as she bobbed her head in agreement.

"And for every penny you repay, I shall kiss you once in the center of the bailey before whoever might chance to be there. Agreed?"

Her mouth dropped open. He placed his fingertips under her chin and closed her mouth. "Is that a bargain you can make? Every penny you give me, I shall give you a kiss in the center of the bailey."

She licked her lips. He felt a sharp punch of desire. In truth, he wanted to kiss her now, draw her to his bed, slide his hands across the shimmery fabric over her breasts, kiss them as well.

Abruptly, she leapt to her feet. "I—I, that is—"

He stood up slowly and closed the small distance between them. A kind of hot madness possessed him and his throat felt tight. "I want you to understand the kind of kiss you will get for your penny."

He wrapped his arms around her and brought his mouth to hers. It took her a moment to kiss him back, a few more moments to bring up her hand and rest it on his thundering heart. He covered her hand, drew her even closer, and in doing so, felt the press of her soft breast on the back of his fingers.

He wrapped her tightly against his body, sealed his mouth on hers, and drank in the small cry she made. Her lips were soft and full, her tongue warm and slick across his.

Her breast filled his hand and he slid his fingertips on the smooth material, learning her shape as his tongue learned the rich, sweet taste of her mouth.

Her breath became his, her taste his—a mix of the wine he'd drunk and an apple she'd eaten. It was heady, the mingling of the tastes on his tongue and lips, a potion more intoxicating than any brew of man.

When he plucked her nipple between his fingertips, her gasp sucked his breath from his mouth and sent a rush of blood to his groin. He plucked her again as if taking a small berry from a bush. She moaned.

He abruptly released her, setting her aside.

As if a wind blew through the tent she swayed in place. "Remember, Joan. For every penny, a kiss."

He hooked her arm and led her to the tent entrance, handed her out. "Please escort Mistress Joan to her cottage. Be sure she gets there without harm."

Joan followed the guard, blind and deaf to her surroundings. The air was heavy and at the same time misty; all sound was muffled.

When the guard had bowed and turned away, she raced to the kennels and, heedless of the boys who slept on the straw or the fineness of her gown, she clambered over the wooden barricade that kept the dogs in separate stalls. She threw herself into the center of the running hounds and buried her face against Paul's warm coat.

He nuzzled her hair and whimpered, but she just held him tightly and closed her eyes.

But as she knelt there, she still felt Quintin's palm on her breast, could taste him, feel his heartbeat. "Oh, Paul, this will never do. He's destined for Mathilda. And what man courts one woman whilst kissing another?"

Chapter Thirteen

Garlands of vines looped the stone archway of the bridge over the river, marking the way to the village. Their leaves were glossy green in the autumn sunlight. Torches were set at intervals along the road, though they would not be lighted until night. Music and laughter drew one to the colorful stalls even if one was feeling as morose and heavy headed as Hugh was.

The air was balmy, the sky bright blue as carts carried ladies and men from the keep to the fair—but not Mathilda.

She rode at his side, her yellow gown slapping his legs. Every time he edged away, she maneuvered her horse closer.

A groom ran to take their reins when they reached the fair grounds, on the outskirts of the village. Mathilda immediately looped her arm in his and smiled up at him.

He glared at her. "Do not ask my opinion on anything."

"What of my gown?" She smoothed a wrinkle only she could see.

"Yellow makes you look . . . yellowish."

She frowned. "Then I shall look for new material to make a better one. Have you a color you prefer?"

Hugh pursed his lips. "I like brown. Mud brown."

Two hours later, they had two servants trailing them with armloads of fabric and trim. None of it was brown.

"What do you think of—" she asked for the twelfth time.

"I have no opinion on thread, my lady." Hugh yawned, scratched his chin, and studied the stalls of the Ravenswood fair. There were far too many, all stuffed with goods to appeal to ladies or wealthy suitors.

Mathilda held a small wooden stick with thread wrapped around it against her breast. "I think this one will look well on this gown—perhaps some trim will make me look less jaundiced. Send all of it to the keep." She made a sign to the woman who managed the stall, and tugged Hugh along. "You need to be more conversant of a woman's needs."

"Adam Quintin would know about such matters."

"Would he? I shall have to remember to invite *him* next time." She looked up at him. "Tell me, Hugh, why aren't you a candidate for my hand?"

"Good Lord, a man can only have so many castles. The de Colevilles have an even dozen. One more would be excessive, wouldn't it? Like taking more deer than one needs to stave off hunger. Anything beyond that is gluttony."

"I see. Is that your opinion or the king's?"

"The king's. I believe William Marshal said to steer clear of you the last time I saw him." It was always nice to have someone on whom to blame one's actions, Hugh thought.

"And you agreed without a fight?"

"Fight? Why would I fight over something with which I am in complete agreement. A man, if he is canny, knows how far he can extend himself. The de Colevilles are on the verge of overextending themselves."

"I see."

She smiled and for a moment, he could only stare. Then he frowned. She was naught but a combination of pleasing features. A gift from her ancestors.

Their progress through the fair was interrupted often by men who vied for her attention. They gave her gifts. They offered her sweetmeats, spices, drinks.

More servants trailed them with useless fripperies.

Hugh steered her toward their horses. "May I suggest a short rest? You must be exhausted as am I."

To his utter surprise, she made no demur. He helped her up into the saddle and would have turned away, but she extended her foot and prodded him in the shoulder. "I'm not done with you, Hugh de Coleville, man with too many castles."

"Not done with me?" He rubbed the spot she'd tapped.

"Follow, please." She kicked her palfrey and in a swirl of flowing yellow skirts, cantered up the path.

Hugh mounted up and followed at a more leisurely pace, his stomach unsettled. "I must have eaten something that disagreed with me," he said to his horse, patting his neck. "I'll be in the privy as much as Adam if I don't watch it."

Near the stable, Hugh dismounted and tossed the reins to a groom. He jerked his gloves off; his hands were suddenly sweaty.

Mathilda stood on the bottom step of the keep, a smile on her face. "Come, Hugh." She clapped her hands and then turned away.

He followed. She dashed up the steps, across the hall, and through an arch. No suitors turned to watch her progress, for most were still in the village, unaware the quarry had escaped.

The arch led to the lower levels. They were dark, chilly,

131

and silent. They smelled of harvest, sacks of grain, racks of apples, and bunches of hanging herbs.

Where had she gone? His mouth was dry. He licked his lips. "My lady?" he said softly.

"Hugh." He heard her whisper from his right.

He entered a storage room filled with sacks of grain. She was a swirl of sunlight in the dim chamber. He feigned a yawn.

"You are bored, my lord?" She pulled off her headcovering and slowly shook out her hair. The gauzy veil drifted to the ground. She put her hands to her laces.

"What are you doing?" He took a step back, suddenly feeling as if he were a stag being forced down a path to his doom.

Her laces made a hissing sound as she whipped them open. "I'm seducing you."

"Why?" He licked his lips again as she peeled her overgown off her shoulders, then down her hips to pool at her feet. She stepped daintily out of the golden pile as if stepping from her bath. The vision caused his whole body to clench. His palms were sweaty again. "Why?" he repeated.

She sighed and bent down. She lifted her hem and drew her loose linen gown up her body, revealing her legs, hips, belly, and breasts in a slow journey that boiled his blood.

"You are very stupid, Hugh, if you cannot figure it out. Think of me as one of your clever riddles."

He clenched and unclenched his fists. She dropped the gown to the floor.

"Do you like what you see?" she asked, hands at her sides.

He shrugged. "You're a bit plump in the middle."

She skimmed her fingers across her smooth belly and laughed. It was a sound that ran like a whip across his senses. "Yellowish and fat?"

"This is madness," he said. But in three strides he was

on her. He scooped her into his arms and thrust her back onto the feed sacks. "No one seduces me."

He covered her face with kisses, finally claimed her mouth, while he held her captive against the rough grain sacks. She held his head and moaned, arching against him.

He kissed down the center of her body, learned the valley of her breasts, the mound of her belly, the silky hair and skin between her thighs. She gripped his hair and cried out as he kissed her most intimate places. Then she planted her feet on his shoulders and arched again and again to his ministrations, finally crying out in ecstasy.

Just as suddenly, she fell still. Her arms dropped away, her eyes closed. Hugh backed up, gently placing her legs down over the edge of the sacks. He ran a hand over his face and took several deep breaths. She was a golden angel.

"What have I done?" he said.

Her eyes opened. She smiled at him. "You have granted my second deepest desire."

A blade of hot lust twisted his insides. "Second?"

Then she sat up and put out her arms. "Come to me, Hugh."

His legs seemed to belong to someone else as he granted her wish. She embraced him, stroking her hands up and down his back. Then she tugged up his tunic and reached beneath the cloth for the lacings at his waist. Her fingertips skimmed his hard cock. "This is the first," she whispered.

He gripped her wrists and shook his head. "We cannot do this. I'm Adam Quintin's friend. I'll have trouble enough facing him with what little—"

"Little?" She flexed her wrists and tried to jerk from his hold.

"Aye. We cannot compound what has surely been naught but a momentary madness."

She stared at him, her eyes great luminous pools in the half-light. "It is madness to think we can forget this moment. I have wanted this since last we met at court. It is madness to think we can go back to what was."

He pulled away from her and adjusted his clothing. "I can go back. When I walk away. It is forgotten. *You* are forgotten."

She slipped off the grain sacks. She walked past him to her clothing. "Then walk away, Hugh de Coleville, walk away."

The air seemed heavy and close as he strode back through the storerooms toward the steps up to the hall. He prayed no one had seen them descend here. With luck he could put these moments from his mind.

He hadn't really cheated his friend of anything. After all, they'd not had intercourse. What they'd done didn't really count.

Adam did as the other suitors did, watched Mathilda wander the fair with Hugh. When she rode off with him, Adam heaved a sigh of relief that he need not worry another would woo her away.

He circled the fair grounds. At one wooden board, several of his men drank with Roger's. They looked reasonably companionable. He passed a string of horses.

Francis de Coucy was leaving the temporary stable, but did not ride for the castle. He wheeled his horse and in moments, had entered the forest by a deer path.

"Now where the devil is he going?" Adam grabbed his reins and tossed a coin to the man who watched the beasts.

He followed Francis along the cool, leafy path. He knew it from boyhood. Francis proved easy to follow.

Eventually, to Adam's consternation, Francis circled back to an old verderer's cottage, now rebuilt into a more substantial building. The lodge was within the trees, not a stone's throw from the village. Francis could have walked here in but a few minutes. Why the evasion?

Adam pulled up his horse and looped the reins over a

low branch. He continued to the cottage on foot. He circled the building, keeping to the trees. Francis's mount stood tethered behind the lodge. Adam dropped to a crouch and used a deadfall to move to a shuttered window in the front.

A murmur of voices told him Francis had met someone. Adam searched around for cover so he could get close enough to hear the conversation.

There was nothing.

Joan folded the rich bronze gown into a small bundle and took it to Edwina at the wash house. She saw her friend laboring under a great armload of wood. "Edwina! You'll hurt yourself. Let me." She cast her bundle to the floor and took the wood. "Where's Del?"

Edwina puffed out a long breath and dusted off her hands. "I cannot find the man. He must be at the fair and the devil take him for leaving me with this." She shot out a hand to the mounds of linens to be washed. Many women stirred boiling pots and the shed was thick with steam, but there was only one man to keep the fires burning. "I'll not ask the women to carry wood if I'm not willin' to do so myself."

Without a word, Joan fed the fires beneath several pots, nodding to each of the laundresses. When the fuel pile was exhausted, she went with Edwina to the mountain of wood behind the shed. As she picked up a piece of wood it slipped from her fingers, scraping the skin and leaving a sliver protruding from her palm.

Edwina pulled her to the wood pile and propped her ample buttocks on a stump, while Joan sat on another beside her. They had often sat thusly on a fine evening, enjoying the ambient warmth of the laundry shed and talking of the day. As Edwina worked at the sliver, Joan's eyes welled with tears.

One dropped on her skirt.

"Joan! Ye're crying! What ails ye?" Edwina hugged her hard to her soft bosom.

"I'm not crying." Joan dashed away a tear. "My hand hurts."

"Ye've been bitten by dogs, fallen out of trees, skinned yer knees on yonder bailey cobbles, and ne'er shed a tear. Now, what is it?"

Joan watched her friend probe the remaining specks from her palm. Had she come to this place to ask Edwina's advice? Or had she come for the comfort of Edwina's simple presence whilst more complicated personages roamed the fair?

"It seems I've made a confusion of my life," Joan finally said. "And if I weep, it is in want of a friend."

Edwina picked out the last speck of the sliver and patted Joan's hand. "Ye'll always have a friend here. There's those who love ye right under yer nose. They're not in the keep, I fear, only here."

Joan looked up at the great towers of Ravenswood. "She was my friend at one time, was she not?"

"She was only eight when ye arrived. She followed ye ever'where like a pup. 'Twas she who worshipped ye then. She's just grown enamored of her own importance. And it may be she is a touch jealous of ye."

"Jealous?"

"Aye." Edwina stood up and plucked her sweat-dampened gown from her breasts, fanning herself in the mild autumn air. "Ye took the young lord's attentions. Ye drew that other one . . . the one that wrestled Quintin."

"De Harcourt," Joan said softly.

"Aye. And spineless she was to let her father banish ye from the hall. We all expected she would make Lord Guy see reason, but she dint."

The hurt of Mathilda's rejection felt like a sliver in her heart. "I cannot sit here wallowing in self-pity. Let me fetch some more wood for you."

"I'll see to it," said the man who worked with Del.

"Aye, be off and buy yerself a few ribbons at the fair."

"I've no desire for ribbons. I have one."

"One! Our lady must 'ave a dozen, a score, even." Edwina dug in her bosom and pulled out a small purse suspended about her neck. She shook out a penny. "Buy yerself a scarlet ribbon."

Joan smiled. "I'll buy us each a scarlet ribbon." She kissed the laundress on her round cheeks. "And I'll see if Ivo has aught he needs whilst I'm about it."

Adam waited less than a quarter of an hour before the lodge door banged open. He flattened himself in the grass. The red-haired Oswald strode out of the cottage, trailed by Francis. For one brief moment, Adam thought Oswald's gaze drifted over him, and he sucked in his breath and willed himself as still as a hare gone to ground.

But Oswald parted with de Coucy without a word. Each took a different direction, neither heading for the castle.

"Devil take it," Adam swore. "I cannot follow two of them. Where is a wandering minstrel when I need him?"

He headed after Oswald, but could not say why he chose him over Francis. The man headed along toward the defile the stag had followed on the hunt; then to Adam's consternation, he disappeared.

Adam used what he knew of tracking game to search for a sign of the man, but he seemed to have vanished—or become aware someone was on his trail.

The day was waning. Adam realized he was miles from the keep and needed to make an appearance or he would be missed. It would not do to have his absence noted again—especially by Mathilda, who might decide he'd spent the day gaming or whoring rather than in a privy.

He found the narrow stream that coursed the defile and followed it. Robert and he had once become lost in these woods. Adam whistled just as he had in those days to cheer his brother.

"Adrian!"

Adam started and wheeled around. Nat Swan stood at a ford, a lymer at his side.

"Nat?"

"Adrian? Is it not you?" Nat pursed his lips and finished the ditty Adam had whistled.

Adam stepped into deeper shadow. "I am Adam Quintin. You mistake me."

A confused look crossed Nat's face, and he tugged on the dog's leash. The lymer whined. "A boy once whistled just so. Adrian. Adrian de Marle."

"You've made a mistake." Adam turned, and with rapid strides, headed up the narrow gully.

The sun was low in the sky when Adam stabled his mount. He cursed his ill luck and Nat's memory. Resigned to meeting any suggestion he was any man but Adam Quintin square in the face, he walked boldly from the bailey and down the hill toward the colorful stalls and throngs of people.

A man walked from torch to torch, lighting them for those who would remain at the fair after night fell.

Adam practiced possible responses if Nat called him Adrian again. He recognized a figure hurrying up the hill at a run. Her hair was down, her skirts about her knees. *Joan.*

She ran straight into his arms. Her gown was damp with sweat, her hair in wild disarray. He held her for a moment. Her fingers clutched his tunic, and her body quivered against his. He ran a hand over her cheek.

"Please. Can you come with me? Ivo is missing."

"Ivo? The old man who used to be a cleric in the castle?"

"Aye. Dismissed by the bishop. A cleric. I've come from

the baker's where he was lodged, and they said he ran out very suddenly and has not come back."

"Perhaps he had business to attend to."

She shook her head. "He said to Estrild, the baker's wife, that he must see me. That was hours ago. He has missed his supper."

"Perhaps he's at the fair and you've missed him."

"Nay. He told Estrild he hated all the bustle. The noise. Nay. He said he must see me. He said he regretted not telling me something. He said perhaps it would help him get his position back."

"Could he have gone to your cottage? Does Nat know where you are? Surely he'll direct this Ivo that you have gone to the village after him?"

"I've been home, and back to the baker's, and home again and even—" She broke off.

"Even?"

"To the hall. To inquire after him. No one has seen him. He's a very frail old man—ten years Nat's senior."

"Then, by all means, let us find him." There was no denying her. No denying the urgency or concern in her voice.

She took his hand and tugged him along the path, back to the village, and the baker's. He remembered the place, though he doubted the same man ran the ovens. The baker of his time had been a bluff, leathery man, baked as dry as an old crust.

They questioned Estrild a moment, a woman who immediately fell to bowing and scraping when he arrived. She repeated what Joan had said and added that Ivo had been muttering and rocking over his pot of ale before rising and running out.

"Which way did he go?"

"I canna say. Just out."

Adam took Joan's elbow and led her toward the village well. There, a group of seven small boys were crouched, tossing pebbles and shoving each other back and forth.

"How would you boys like to earn a few pennies?"

Their eyes went round, and they nodded in mute agreement. "We're looking for an old man. He is . . ." He glanced at Joan, who took over.

"He's this tall." She held her hand at her shoulder height. "He has white hair and is very old. He is—was the bishop's clerk, so he will be wearing a priest's robe."

"He may be somewhere in the village still, or even at the fair. The first one to find him will earn an extra penny." Adam placed a hand to the purse suspended at his waist.

The boys exchanged looks, then dashed off, each in a different direction. Adam took Joan's arm. "They'll not be long at the game. While they are gone, we will think of other places he could be."

"I've looked everywhere."

"Could he have walked to a monastery?"

"He has not the stamina."

"But would he attempt the journey?"

He slid his hand down her arm to take her hand as he had in the forest. She did not stand at ease.

A shriek drew them at a run toward the baker's cottage. One of the boys stood there, his hand outstretched toward the ovens, his face so white he looked ghostly.

Adam set the boy aside and strode into the baker's yard, to the three ovens that, even now, were steaming a bit as the air cooled around them.

Behind him, Joan's gasp told him she had seen what the boy had. A foot protruded from between two ovens.

She rushed forward, then whirled around and crashed into Adam's chest. She buried her face in the wool of his tunic.

Adam took her by the upper arms and held her away. "I'll see to this. Take the boy off and give him and his friends their reward." He folded her hands around his purse.

Her eyes were huge, dark, glistening with tears for the old man who lay so crumpled and shrunken in death.

"Are you able?" he asked.

She nodded and hiccupped. He skimmed her cheek with the back of his fingers, wiped the tears away. Then he touched her lips briefly, gently with his fingertips, and turned her. He pointed her toward the gaping boys.

When he saw she was handling the children, he returned to the ovens. Ivo lay behind one oven. Except for the incongruous place of his demise, the man looked peacefully asleep. Upon closer examination, Adam saw a dark patch of blood in the old man's white hair. The skull beneath the spot felt spongy. He'd not died naturally.

With a prayer for Ivo's soul, Adam rose and found Joan alone at the well, the boys run off he was sure, to spread the grisly news.

She came into his embrace as if she belonged there.

"He was so kind. A gentle soul."

"Shhh," he said. "He's with God."

"Do you think he became confused?" she asked. "I don't understand how he could come to be—"

"We'll take him back to the keep. There are two physicians there—for those who might be injured in the tournament. They'll look after him. I want you to remain here until I see the sheriff."

She nodded against his chest, then took a deep, shuddering breath. Inside the baker's cottage, her hands shook when she tried to light a wick in a dish of oil.

"What was he to you?" he asked.

"He was Nat's friend. He clerked here for at least thirty years. The bishop dismissed him."

She swayed. He came around the table and held her shoulders. He combed his fingers slowly through the silky mass of her hair. He smoothed it from her brow, her neck, and down her back.

She shivered. Her damp gown clung to her body, molded her breasts. He chafed her arms by running his palms up and down her sleeves. Without thought he drew her in again. She pressed against him. He felt her breasts on his chest, her thighs against his. It seemed natural and right to comfort her. The sound of voices in the lane forced their situation upon him.

"You're to wait here until I return for you."

He left the baker's cottage and walked quickly through the village to the stone manor house of the sheriff and his wife. The sheriff was at the fair. It took another quarter of an hour to locate the man. In a few terse words, he informed the sheriff of Ivo's death and that he was taking the body back to the castle.

The sheriff provided a cart and a donkey to pull it. With as much respect as possible, Adam lifted the old man into the back of the cart, then he returned for Joan.

She walked at his side toward the castle. The fair, still busy though the hour of darkness was nigh, mocked their task.

Halfway up the castle road, their fingers brushed, and she took his hand as if he'd offered it. There, between two torches, in the shadows, no man or beast save the donkey to see them, they stood, fingers entwined.

He lifted her hand and kissed her fingers. He kept his mouth there, breathing in the scent of her skin. Heat and desire for her warred with a need to comfort her and yet, he must keep his distance.

Shouting turned his attention. He urged her behind the cart. "Remain here."

The shouting men came to them. He saw who it was, three of his company, in their cups, shoving each other. Lambert, Claude, Eilart. A woman, a whore by the look of her, screamed when Lambert drew his dagger.

More daggers appeared as the other two prepared to challenge Lambert for the woman. Adam swept his sword from its scabbard and in three long strides reached them.

Two of the men backed off, sheathing their daggers, but Lambert clutched the woman and shook his head. "She's mine. Bought and paid for."

"You were under orders, were you not? Another drunken incident and you would be dismissed?" Adam spoke mildly, aware of Joan only a few feet away.

Lambert spat on the ground.

Adam slashed his blade across the man's hand, who shrieked and dropped his dagger. The man's cry of pain pierced the drunkenness of the others. They froze, eyes rolling from their friend's bloody hand to him.

"You are gone, Lambert. You know I tolerate only one lapse and you had it in Lincoln. Get your wound stitched, then take yourself from Ravenswood. Do not wait for the light. If I find you anywhere on the manor, you'll find my blade less merciful."

Joan sagged against the cart. She looked as hunted as any doe held at bay.

He gave his men more orders. "Pay off this woman for her trouble, take Lambert for stitching, then find your beds. At dawn, report to the stables and exercise the horses, and there you will remain until you find my favor again."

Eilart placed his hand on his sword hilt. Adam lifted his and approached within thrusting distance. He was aware that every word he said reached Joan's ears.

"If you wish to protest, do it now," he told Eilart. "You are one of my company or you are not."

The man withdrew his hand. He tossed a purse to the woman and put his arm about Lambert's shoulder.

Adam sheathed his sword. The whore gripped his sleeve. "They was set on cheatin' me," she said. "Yer a brave man to go one agin' three."

"They're my men, and I owe you an apology for their behavior. How they act reflects on me."

The woman ran off, purse clutched to her chest, and his men lurched up the castle road. He realized he was now one man short to take the tournament field. He must find a replacement immediately or forfeit.

Joan looked as if a high wind had buffeted her. He read her thoughts. He touched the small, pathetic shape of Ivo. "They did not do this."

He tried to take her arm, but she shook him off.

"My men may drink too much and fight over women, but they do not hit scholarly men over the head."

It was an oblique reference to her own father's death and he regretted reminding her. She smoothed the covering over Ivo's body.

"My men did not do this," he repeated.

She turned around and looked at him. The wind whipped her skirt against her body, her hair across her cheeks.

"You are one of them—a mercenary—are you not?" Her voice was barely audible. A whisper on the wind.

What would it serve to try to justify the manner he'd used to rise or the men he chose as his companions on the way? There were good men in all companies. And ill.

"I am," he said.

Chapter Fourteen

This time, as Adam and Joan walked the final half league up to the castle gates, they did not touch, not the hem of her skirt against his boot, nor the brush of her shoulder against his.

The gatekeeper summoned the bishop's dean, who made a face of irritation, then left to fetch the priest. Joan stood watch over the cart until finally, the priest came from the chapel. Within moments, Ivo was gone.

Adam stood awkwardly by the empty cart.

Joan spoke to him in the same level tone she had used with the priest. "Thank you for your care of Ivo. He was a good man. Now, I must tell Nat what happened."

"Joan."

"It is best we not—"

"Say any more?"

She nodded and in a moment was absorbed into the last rays of the sunlight, a slender sylph of green against the harsh gray of stone walls.

*   *   *

Joan broke her fast after chapel the next morning with an apple and a cup of warm wine. She forced herself to think of her duties. Nat had already received his orders from the bishop. Despite a torrential rain, a score of deer must be taken to feed the men who accompanied the suitors as well as the many merchants and craftsmen drawn to the castle for the fair.

The suitors would not dine on venison. They were to have roasted swan with apples and pears stewed in spiced wine.

Joan combed her hair. The comb, made of horn and delicately etched with flowers, had been her mother's. It, and the other treasures, a faded blue ribbon, a needle case made of ivory from the holy land, were all she had as mementos.

Like the ribbon, the faces of her parents were faded in her mind, overlaid with the image of them lying in blood, faces contorted in pain and death. Time had not faded those images a whit.

"It was more than ten years ago," she said to the lymer curled under the table. "And yet, I blamed Adam for his men's behavior and them for that deed done to my family so long ago."

She set out a trencher for Nat along with a cup for his warm wine. He would need it. A drip drew her attention. Repairing the thatch would be another chore for when the suitors left. How many pennies would that take?

Rain hissed in upon the hearth to sizzle on the roaring fire.

Adam Quintin would leave with the others. Why did it matter? Why was she so confused? One moment she hated all he stood for. The next . . . It did not bear thinking of.

Could a man be faulted for making his way as best he could?

The door opened with a bang.

"Mars is missing," Nat said. The rain ran off his mantle and hair.

"Mars? Do you mean Matthew?" She pushed the door closed against the wind.

"Nay, did I say Matthew? I mean Basil."

"How? When?"

"Since we went out to set the hunt. I fear the worst."

Joan handed Nat a drying cloth and took his mantle. "He can't have gotten out on his own."

Nat rubbed the rain from his face and hands. "Aye, those damned kennel men and the lads were gambling and drinking last night, by the bishop's leave, they say. Now, someone has stolen our best dog. I'd like to toss the lot o' them." He gave a quick glance at the door. "And the bishop. Thank God yon maid will pick a husband and Gravant will go back to his palace."

Joan bit her lip. "Do you think Oswald might have taken Basil? He might want to see the hunt go badly and then put himself forward."

Nat paused in the act of drying his neck. "Oswald? The new alaunt?"

"Nay," she said, handing him a wooden cup of ale. "Oswald Red-hair. Lord Roger's hunt master. If Roger wins Mathilda, we'll have Oswald to deal with."

"He'll want my place." Nat said it as if it had only just occurred to him. His forehead puckered into a frown. "We canna let that happen, child. Is Oswald the one whose dogs shrink when a man raises his voice?"

"Aye."

"Then we've naught to worry about. I've just to tell Mathilda the man's got cruelty in 'im and she'll send him on his way."

Joan knew it would not be so simple. "If it was Oswald that took Basil, he'll not succeed in making trouble. Matthew is ready to stand in Basil's place—"

"He's too young, apt to run off on a diversion."

She had more confidence in the lymer's abilities. Nat had not watched the dog's rapid progress with her hand signals, and only the youngest alaunt, Simon, was fiercer in guarding her.

"We'll find Basil, then. I'll look now."

Nat sank to a stool and cut some of the cold meat pie. "This on top of Ivo. It makes me feel old."

"You're not old, Papa."

"At least we have rain today and Mathilda will not want to ride out, though she wants games and singing in the hall. And Ivo scarce dead a day."

There was naught to be done about Nat's grief over Ivo. The masses they would say for his soul mights ease some of the pain. Basil, however, was another matter.

She touched Nat's shoulder. "All will be well, Papa. I'll find Basil, I know it."

His bowed shoulders rose and fell in a dispirited shrug. "If ye say so, child."

His crisp, curly hair was thinning across the crown, the skin showing through spotted with age.

"Would ye go out and look for him . . . now? I'll take Matthew and see if we've a stag still in the valley."

Joan glanced at Nat's mantle. The cloth steamed gently before the fire, draped on a bench. He should not get wet.

"If Basil's been let loose or gotten out on his own, he might be scavenging in the village." Although she said it, she did not believe it.

The dog was disciplined. He would not wander far or miss his daily bread. She felt a shiver of unease. "If Oswald took him, or one of his men, as he might not risk doing the deed himself, then I will complain to the bishop. Put on dry clothes, Papa."

Nat stood up, his eyes bright. "First I'll see to those idle huntsmen and fewterers who'll do naught but game in the hall if not given some task."

148

She helped him on with his mantle, putting the pin straight, then donned her own.

"I set great store by that dog." Nat shook his head. "I remember when I brought him from Winchester. He was all paws and tail."

It was not so. Basil was born and raised on Ravenswood.

Joan accompanied Nat to the kennel, where he handed out work to the idle men, the kind of work that was saved for just such a day as this: repair of collars and leashes, training of the younger dogs, construction of bed racks.

After casting about the perimeter of the kennel for some sign of Basil, a paw print perhaps, as the dog had a slit across his right fore paw, one that might leave a telltale impression, she walked slowly through the inner and outer bailey.

The air held a tang of wood smoke from the many fires burning about the tents. Their smoke twisted low to the ground. Men huddled inside, or near fires, few doing more than stirring something over their reluctant flames.

She gave a whistle now and again, but no hound crept from behind a building or tent, sheepishly hanging his head for escaping his kennel. As rain filled the impressions left by her pattens, she knew it was useless to search for paw prints.

"I'll see those boys thrashed," she muttered, as she drew her hood close about her cheeks. "Half the night in the village, still half drunk this morn. And with the bishop's say-so. Who is he to interfere in our work? Now, we've lost a valuable animal." As she said it, she knew Basil was just as much a friend to Nat as Ivo had been.

She thought of Oswald making his claims that Nat was incompetent, citing the wagering as evidence along with the missing lymer, and realized they'd lost more than just a dependable dog. Yet she could not quite bring herself to think of the dog as stolen. It meant a deliberate plot.

Should she speak to Mathilda? Had they enough of a connection still for her to do so? And wouldn't Mathilda expect such complaints to come from Nat and go straight to the bishop?

Joan felt no more free to seek Mathilda's help with Basil than she did over the wager.

Joan asked after the lymer at the gate, but the keeper had not seen a hound wandering. No one stirred in the driving rain and she surveyed the long, sloping road through the gate. The village lay about the base of the castle like a fringe of stones cast by a giant hand. Save the nearest, the cottages were barely visible in the mist.

Smoke smudged the air over chimney holes, tearing quickly away or clinging close to the roofs as the wind and rain drove straight into her face. She walked as far as the bridge, its green garlands now drooping in sad disarray across the stones.

"Basil," she called, turning about, crossing the bridge and heading for the eastern fields of the castle.

Though the wind whipped harder now, and she must hold down skirts that snapped with a sharp sting against her legs, 'twas at her back, not in her face.

"Only the mad would be out in this," she said, whistling for the lymer, swallowing dread that the dog might be dead.

The turn east along the spongy, sopping terrain led her to a stream that fed the fish pond. A small channel, man-made, diverted water from the river to feed the ornamental oval fashioned to suit Lord Guy's love of fishing. Reeds and willows had grown up along the pond bank.

Even Mathilda had spent some time here as a child with Richard, casting for pike, squealing, and tossing worms at Joan, who did not like the occupation much and had usually sat upon the bank, watching her friends.

Her friends. That friendship had been illusory, born of close proximity, unable to survive the rise of age and with it importance. She discounted Richard's ardent marriage offer. It had been made out of a youthful need to defy his father.

Water trickled along Joan's cheek, into her mantle to dampen the neck of her gown. She pulled her hood closer about her face.

Her pattens were thick with mud, her shoes also, the wooden forms not protecting them as they'd been designed to do, but rather sucking her deeper as she slogged along.

At the fish pond, she traversed the fringes, inspecting the muddy verge for paw prints. She saw deer tracks, deep ones of an animal in at least his fifth year. She also saw the spaced-out impressions of a man's boots, which indicated he'd been running.

Reeds on the pond perimeter protected the prints from obliteration in the rain. The greenery was trampled in places. She followed the markings along the edge of the pond. They ended abruptly—in a chaos of deeply incised marks.

She neared the sluice gate, built to be opened and closed to control the water flow. Against the gate rested debris, attesting to the neglect of Guy de Poitiers's men now he was gone. Decaying branches and leaves clogged the gate in matted confusion.

Then she saw it. Bobbing against the gate.

A form. A swirling drape of sodden cloth.

Black hair floating like seaweed.

White hands reaching out, fingers lax.

"Adam!" she screamed. She cast off her pattens, her mantle, and plunged into the water. Her feet sank into the muddy bottom, shoes lost, water to her knees.

She reached out as far as she could, one hand on the gate. Her foot slid into a void, jerking her off her feet. Her fingers caught in the matted branches.

She went under. Pain stabbed like a dagger through her

arm. Muddy water filled her mouth. She kicked to the surface, gagging.

But he was closer. Within reach.

"Adam!" She regained her feet and edged along the slimy fence, thick with rotted bracken.

Her hand skimmed his hair. It slipped through her fingers.

"Help me, God, help me."

She extended her fingers as far as she could and snatched at his hair. He shifted away, undulating on waves caused by her movements.

Nausea and sobs choked her throat like the weeds on the gate. Fighting the sucking mud, she reached again for that man's hand who had just a day before held and kissed hers.

Chapter Fifteen

Adam walked back through the village and cursed the rain and his folly at suggesting the village well as a place to meet Christopher. Before the storm, it had seemed a brilliant choice. It gave him a chance to speak to a few villagers again whilst waiting for the minstrel. But the villagers had added nothing to his store of information on poor Ivo's death. In fact, they clearly thought Adam witless to stand about in the rain asking questions.

The physicians had confirmed Adam's suspicion that Ivo had died from a blow to the back of the head. Adam wanted to find the culprit for Joan's sake—or for his own, that she might not condemn him as completely brutal.

Worse than the soaking rain, Christopher had not appeared. "Caught in the mud somewhere between here and Winchester," Adam muttered.

All along the roadbed to the castle, the ditches were rushing with water. Years of neglect had rendered them ineffective. When he was lord of Ravenswood, he would see them cleared. As a result of the rushing water, the road was awash and cut with deep ruts. He stepped onto the spongy grass verge.

A shriek cut the air.

He stood where he could see the flat gray twist of the river and the narrow inlet that fed the fish pond.

The shriek came again. He dashed toward the pond, hand on his sword hilt, sinking into the soggy earth with every step.

Something stirred in the pond.

A woman. In the water. It took no more than a moment for him to see she was trying to pull a body to the bank.

He tore off his mantle and shed his sword and belt as he ran.

She went under.

The body spun like a weathercock on a barn where she'd disappeared.

He leapt in after her. Frigid water snatched his breath. The heels of his thigh-high hunting boots sank into the mire, and he gasped with shock as icy water poured down them.

The water churned as the woman sought to rise.

He lunged forward and grasped her arm.

Joan.

He knew her the moment he touched her. His heart, already racing, now stuttered in his chest.

He snatched her into his arms. She fought him as she surfaced, a cry of pain on her lips.

She caught at the cloth of his tunic, and he heaved her away from the floating body.

The soft slimy bottom made it difficult to bring her to shore. Her frantic thrashing hindered his efforts as well.

"Be still, Joan. Be still," he said, muddy water lapping his mouth as she nearly pulled him under.

"Adam?" She quieted in his arms, her body rigid.

She gulped for air, clinging to him now, no longer fighting. He pushed against the mushy bottom and lunged toward the bank. She began to cough. He half dragged, half carried her from the pond, her woolen skirts entwining his legs.

When he deposited her on the bank, she gagged, her face concealed by the ropes of her hair.

He returned for the body. His boots offered him little purchase against the muck of the bottom as he embraced the man and hauled him to the bank through water now brown and thick as stew. He turned the man over.

Christopher.

Rain beat upon Christopher's gray, staring eyes, filled his half-open mouth. Adam's eyes stung with grief for this man he'd known but a few days.

Adam made sure there was naught to be done, not a thread of life to revive. No wish would resurrect him, no hope would add color to the ashen cheeks.

Adam searched the minstrel as he knew he must. There was a gash, the edges white and gaping, on the young man's temple. He had no purse and nothing hidden about his clothing, even in his hems and seams. Whatever message he had carried, it must have been in his head and was now lost.

Adam folded Christopher's arms on his breast, passing a hand over the face, to close the eyes, though he could not effect a change in the staring countenance.

Joan still remained where he'd left her, and although he wanted to go to her, for her own cheeks were pale, her lips almost blue, he forced himself to walk along the edge of the pond for some sign of where Christopher had gone into the water.

Adam inspected a place where the reeds and muck were trampled. More than one man had made the prints, perhaps two or three. He waded in to his thighs and snatched something from the water.

It was a small leather shoe, a sturdy one for a woman

who did not spend her time stitching useless pillows. He went to Joan. "One of your shoes," he said. "Where can I take you?"

His silent "without giving rise to a thousand questions" hung on the air between them.

She did not look at him, but at the corpse. "I can see to myself," she said, her words barely audible.

Her teeth chattered. Her hair was tangled with reeds. She was almost unrecognizable.

"If that were true, you would not be here leaping into fish ponds; you would be sitting by your hearth." The words sounded harsh, as cold as the water from which he'd dragged her, yet neither her eyes nor her voice accused him when she spoke.

"One of our dogs is missing. I must look for him."

"Not until I have you dry."

He knelt at Christopher's side and said a prayer for the young man's soul. He tried to think, to calm his rage; he was assailed by an uncontrollable need to find the men who'd made the prints by the pond so they could pay for Christopher's death. His hands shook with the need. He prayed for control that he might not frighten Joan with the anger boiling in him.

She came to his side and sank to her knees. Her body, encased in wet wool, shook as much as his hands did. She, too, prayed.

Joan touched his arm, but Adam slid from the contact. His anger needed motion.

He strode back to the belongings he'd discarded, belting on his sword. The action, one he performed every day, calmed him.

His mantle was scarcely drier than Joan's clothing but he swathed her in it anyway. She disappeared in the voluminous garment, and he had to fold back the hood to see her pale face.

"Who is he?" she asked. Her eyes were almost black in the pelting rain. Her lips quivered.

He skimmed his thumbs across her wet cheeks.

"His name is Christopher. He sang in the hall." Although Adam felt calmer, outrage and fury still held him in their grip. "If we do not get you dry, you'll take ill."

A tear appeared at the corner of her eye. Or was it rain? The drop ran quickly over her cheek and slipped into the corner of her mouth.

"I am—"

"Hush, Joan, you'll do as I direct."

He pulled her close, pressing her head to his chest, chafing her back, trying to restore some warmth to her. Yet she could not be warmed. He scooped her into his arms.

She gave a small cry of pain.

"What is it?"

"Nothing."

"You've hurt yourself."

"I bumped my arm, 'tis all. Put me down and I shall fetch someone for . . . him." She struggled in his arms, but he held her tightly and she fell silent and still, not at ease, but quiet.

He knew where he must take her.

The walk was torturous for his injured spine. Every footstep needed to be taken with care as the way was slippery, sloping, and running with water. His boots were wet, her skirts slapping the leather with every step.

When he reached Richard de Poitiers's hunting lodge, the ground surrounding it was smooth and unblemished. No one else had sought shelter there.

Adam set Joan down on a broad, stone step at the lodge door. He flung it open to reveal a large, single room, dim from shuttered windows. It smelled clean. The hearth was laid as if Richard might yet appear—or others who wished a private place to rendezvous. Adam made short work of lighting a fire.

157

"We must get you warm," he said to Joan, who had not set foot within the lodge. "Come in."

She shook her head. Her face was almost as white as Christopher's, and her shivers had become deep shudders. She held back the edges of his mantle and he saw what concerned her. Her muddy gown was plastered to her body, water pooled at her feet.

He thought her overly scrupulous of a dead man's floor, but acquiesced when another thought flitted through his head. Before the impulse passed, he reached out and tugged his mantle from her shoulders.

The step was flanked by a bench and a great, stout rain barrel. Water sluiced down from the sloped roof to form a small waterfall enclosing them in a curious privacy.

She made an inarticulate protest, but did not fight him as he pulled off her gown. It fell in a sodden heap at her feet. The shift followed it.

Her skin was icy when he lifted her over the side of the full barrel.

"Consider this your bathtub. I'll give you but a few moments before I come back for you. Call out if you need me."

He searched the interior of the lodge and found several moth-eaten tunics that had probably once belonged to the dead Richard. There were no shoes, hose, or dry mantles. The tunics must serve.

He listened to the splashing sounds of Joan's ablutions and warmed his hands at the fire now blooming into a fine blaze.

"Adam?" she called and he swept a blanket off Richard de Poitiers's fine curtained bed and stepped outside.

She was trying to climb out of the barrel. It was like watching a doe clamber up a steep hill. She was awkward and somehow graceful at the same time. She tipped over the side.

"*Jesu,*" he said, catching her up in his arms. Her skin

158

was slippery, clean, her hair in a wild tangle over her white shoulders, breasts, and back.

He set her on the step and covered her with the blanket. When he tried to help her dry off, she backed away and darted into the lodge.

Adam pulled off his clothing and dropped it beside hers. He stepped to the edge of the eaves and allowed the rush of water to rinse him clean. He was too large to fit in the barrel, so he used a dented copper ladle and his hands to wash the remaining mud from his hair and skin. The barrel water felt almost warm compared to the rain or the fish pond.

He rinsed their clothing and wrung it out. He used the time and task to quell the desire pouring through his veins like the rain pouring from the thatched roof.

Desire ran like a deluge within him, raging along with the anger at Christopher's death, tangled and confused.

Inside, Joan had taken several furs from the bed and made a nest for herself before the hearth. Adam snatched up a blanket and dried himself. He pulled on one of Richard's cast-off tunics and held another out to Joan. While she pulled it on, he gave her privacy by spreading their clothing to dry, draping the garments across two oak chairs near the hearth. The cloth began to steam and the scent of the wet wool filled the room.

He had nothing more to occupy his time. He turned to Joan. She knelt on the nest of furs, her back to him. Her shoulders shook. He did not need to see her face to know she wept.

Adam knelt by her and she whipped around, rising to her knees, a hunted look on her face.

As gently as if she were a frightened doe, he put out his hand. He smoothed back the hair that had begun to curl around her shoulders and brow. He skimmed his fingers across her wet cheeks, lifting her chin. She looked like a wild creature of the forest, untamed.

159

"Forgive me," she said, wiping her cheek with the back of her hand. " 'Tis just . . . Ivo and that man. He was so young. To die that way. It is so—"

"Cruel," he finished for her. His voice sounded overly harsh in the silent lodge—silent save for the rush of the water on the thatch and the whine of wind in the chimney. "You might have drowned," he said.

She would have drowned had he taken the river way instead of the road.

A lump rose in his throat. "Why did you do it? What possessed you?"

"I thought it was you."

Her words smote him like a hammer against an anvil. The lump inside his chest twisted and knotted tighter. He could not breathe, nor control the quick spasm of his arms that pulled her close.

She came easily into his embrace. Her lips were soft against his.

He was ravenous. And lost.

She slipped her hands around his neck and her blanket shifted, fell from her shoulders to pool at her knees. He dropped his alongside it.

They knelt thigh to thigh, breast to chest, separated by only the thin linen fabric of the old tunics. She did not protest when he set his hands on her hips.

"I thought it was you," she said again. Tears ran down her cheeks. "First Ivo. Then you. I—"

He stopped her words with his mouth.

A mix of fear, anger, and lust raced through his vitals. He bore her down before the fire. It flared to life at the very moment he stroked her hair from her face. The flames lighted her eyes so they shone gold.

The tunic she wore rode up her hips, and he felt her soft, cool skin against his—cool because she had gone into a fish pond. For him.

He eased the two tunics up to their waists and moaned as she embraced his hips with her thighs.

Her lips were soft, lush, wet, and he feasted there whilst she ran her hands down his back to draw up his tunic, baring him further. Her fingertips journeyed in the valley of his spine. An unmerciful surge of blood rushed into his manhood, and gripped him like a fist. A groan was torn from deep within him. Her hands flexed in response; her nails bit into his flesh.

He bent his head over her breast, nuzzling aside the loose linen. Her nipple proved as hard as a pebble. He licked it and savored the hiss of her breath and the soft, answering moan when he took the taut peak between his teeth.

She tasted of rain and outdoors.

"Joan," he whispered and put his hand between her thighs.

This part of her burned. She was wet as if he'd just lifted her from the rain barrel.

Slippery with want.

He moved his fingertips over her and felt a shudder run through her body; her legs locked about his hips so he could scarcely move.

Her mouth was as hungry as his. He groaned with every sweep of her tongue.

He caressed her. Readied her. Postponed the taking. Aroused her whilst arousing himself.

All his senses were consumed by her. His head was filled with the scent of her, his mouth with her taste.

"Adam," she whispered at his ear, and he felt a twist of regret that in her passion she did not call for Adrian, but rather for a man who did not exist.

They moved against each other. It was an almost frantic undulation, hips bumping hips, his fingertips stirring her passions and his.

Every fiber of his body went hot along with the rising

161

flames by their heads. From where her hands cupped his buttocks to where her tongue roamed his throat, he broke out in sweat.

She quivered against his fingertips and her hips twisted beneath him. She gave a keening cry, sweeping away any doubts her completion had come.

He rose on his hands to watch as passion and the fire's glow stained her skin scarlet.

He thrust into her.

And tore through her maidenhead.

She choked back a cry; her body went rigid. Her fingers locked on his hips.

Her eyes opened wide and filled with the reflection of the fire. The tide of his desire was tempered, soothed by the knowledge she was innocent. He slowed his thrusts, tried to gentle his touch.

He watched the changing expressions on her face until, at last, need took over and he drove deep inside her.

A surge of emotion constricted his throat, so he closed his eyes lest she see that it was not the smoke that caused the moisture in them.

She wrapped her arms around his chest and arched her body to meet his, saying his name again and again.

With each plunge of his body, he reveled in the slick, hot feel of her and imagined she held a fire inside to lick along his manhood and consume him just as the flames consumed the wood in the hearth.

Chapter Sixteen

Hugh de Coleville considered the driving rain. He frowned. Adam was making himself scarce this morn, and the way to his tent would be a wet business. Hugh thought he'd do better to search out a lightskirt and crawl between her warm thighs.

Mathilda came up behind him as if conjured from his lascivious thoughts.

"Where are you going?" she asked.

"To the privies," he lied.

"They'll be a noisome place on such a day."

He shrugged.

"Come with me. I'll find you better."

"I am a dog trained to her heel," he muttered.

"Did you speak?" she asked, glancing over her shoulder.

"Not me," he said.

They stopped at a chamber he realized must be hers. "I'm not entering your chamber. Have you lost your wits?"

"I'll wait here for you. I cannot be inside with you if I am standing out here, now, can I?" She held open her door. Her voice dropped to a whisper. "I have my own privy behind that curtain. 'Tis sweetly scented and will serve you well."

He stalked across her chamber, leaving some muddy boot prints on the wooden floor, fouling the rushes. It gave him a perverse delight. He pushed aside the curtain that concealed the thunder box.

She had cloths laid out for washing and pots of soap and fresh water. He inspected the amenities, thinking his mother had not been more pampered in the de Coleville manor and regretting he'd already used the cold, dank privies outside and had no real need of her facility.

He strolled about her chamber, finally standing by the bed. "Mathilda," he called.

She opened the door and peeked in. "Did you want me?"

Her words sent a rush of heat through him. "That I want you is not in dispute. That I care no more for you than some tart in a tavern is the real point."

The smile fled her face and he felt a twinge of something akin to guilt.

"We need to speak," she said as if commanding a groom. "But not here. Meet me in the little chamber behind the hall."

Her peremptory tone defied the look of her. Her hair was loose down her back like a child's. Her gown was one she might wear among her family or women, loose and straight without ornament.

"I'm not aware we have anything to say to each other. What little chamber?"

"You'll know it when you find it." The portal stood empty as she flitted away.

*   *   *

The wind died. An uncanny silence fell over the lodge, broken only by the hiss of the fire, and the inarticulate sounds Adam made in his throat.

Joan embraced him tightly with her arms and legs. His skin was hot and wet with sweat.

He groaned from deep in his chest; his movements became quick, short thrusts. She thought 'twas as if a hot blade possessed her, not the flesh and blood of a mortal man.

She rode out the storm that consumed him, awash in her own torrent of sensations.

A sudden cold fear blunted her passion. Would she open her eyes and find this was naught but a dream, a trick of the mind as Nat was wont to have?

A moment later, Adam collapsed to his side, drawing her with him, holding her hips tightly to his.

She placed her palm on his chest. His heart still beat with a frantic pace. Her own had calmed.

Their tunics were damp with sweat where they were bunched between them, high on their ribs.

What should she say? How did women act when they'd lost their virginity in a moment of blinding passion—lost it to a man who would be husband to another?

What had possessed her?

If he asked the same question now, she must say madness.

She wanted to leap up and run away.

He shifted so he could see her face. His vivid blue eyes demanded she meet his gaze.

"You are my Diana," he whispered. "My huntress. I feel like a stag in rut and would take you ten times within this hour if I had the strength."

She said nothing.

He pulled back, gripping her chin and lifting her face.

"What is it, my love?" he said.

She rolled out of his embrace, stood up, and tugged the tunic down her hips. "I must find Basil."

"The dog is an excuse to separate yourself from me. Why?"

How easily he saw within her. She could not get the words, words of Mathilda, past her throat. She just shook her head. The loose mass of hair that swung across her breast merely reminded her of her wanton behavior.

Wanton. It was what Brian had called her and he spoke the truth. Wantons claimed the men of other women.

"You'll not find a dog in this rain," Adam continued. "He'll have taken shelter as have we. Come back."

He had not pulled down his tunic. Desire flicked through her like the crack of a whip on bare skin.

What had she done? She pressed her hand to her stomach and fought a rising panic. All this time, she had sought to protect Nat's place at Ravenswood so he might live out his days here, and in one mad moment, she had ensured that they must leave. How could she ever look Mathilda in the eye?

Adam stood up, the tunic falling to cover him, but it was short and did little to conceal his shape. What a beautiful man he was. Yet there was more to this than physical lust, was there not? There had to be after what she'd done.

"What's wrong?" he asked. "Nay, do not speak. I know what it is. You have remembered who I am. You've been thinking you have given your innocence to a hated mercenary. A man who will not scruple to sell his sword to the highest bidder."

"Adam. Nay. I thought nothing of the sort."

He snatched up the blanket near his feet. "Do not lie."

She caught the corner of the blanket and they held it between them. He was taut with anger.

"I am not lying," she said.

"Then what were you thinking? Not of your missing

Basil. You were not thinking of a dog when you left my arms."

"I thought of Mathilda."

The name stood between them for a dozen heartbeats. "In truth?"

Something in his tone told her she must speak only the truth at this moment. "Aye. I thought of what we had done. And that you want Mathilda. And that she was once my friend."

His shoulders relaxed, and he dropped his end of the blanket. "Grateful I am that it was not my status in the world that turned you cold." He put his hand on his chest. "Feel my heart. It's beating far too quickly. You've done that to me."

Then he groaned and rubbed his lower back.

"What is it?" she asked.

He turned around and lifted the hem of the tunic and she gasped at the ugly bruises overspreading his hips and buttocks.

"How can you bear it?" she asked, placing her palm to the mottled black, purple, and yellowing marks.

"I bear it because I must. And, in truth, it is better each day."

A consciousness that she was touching him most intimately made her withdraw her hand.

And she realized he had not spoken of Mathilda.

How could she justify what she had done?

He had almost drowned. She could not take back the leap into the pond, or the demonstration of her feelings for him. Had she shouted it from Ravenswood's ramparts, she could not have told him more clearly what she thought of him.

Hate him? Nay, 'twas much worse than that. She loved Mathilda's soon-to-be husband. Joan took a step away from him.

Adam caught her hand. He held her fingers for a moment, then lifted them to his lips. "Why are you suddenly wary of me again?"

She felt scrutinized the way a hawk watches its prey.

"If I was wary, I would not have touched you."

"You touched me as you would a wounded animal. One can fear an animal and still offer it succor. What were you thinking?"

This time she lied. "I thought of the drowned man."

"You could have done nothing for him. He had been dead many hours." Then his voice went low and husky. "You leapt into the pond to save me. I am humbled."

An hour ago, by the pond, she had thought of nothing, felt only a screaming pain when she'd seen the black hair floating on the water. That pain had been as raw as if someone had dragged a blade across her breast.

An hour ago she had been a virgin.

She had betrayed a onetime friend. Another kind of pain throbbed in her temples.

He cupped her face and lifted it. "Are you sorry for what we did here?" he asked.

His eyes were so blue, so alive, so seeing.

She bit her lip. "It is just—"

"Just what?"

"Mathilda."

His fierce hug wrenched her arm. She cried out and he lightened his hold.

"Forgive me, I've hurt you again." A smile curved his lips. "I showed you my injuries, now you must show me yours." He eased up the tunic sleeve and gently probed her upper arm. "I may have forgotten your injury, but I have not forgotten Mathilda."

Joan pulled away, going to her gown and spreading the skirt that it might better dry. It was imperative it dry. She must leave this place. Now. Before she gave in to the compulsion to feel his body joined to hers again. Perhaps on Richard's grand bed this time.

"You are here to claim Mathilda—" she said.

"I am here to claim Ravenswood. There is a vast difference."

Something burned in Joan's breast. A coal of misgiving. "How can you have Ravenswood without her?"

"Trust me."

He put out his hand. It was a strong hand. She went to where he stood. And took it.

He tugged her near. His fingers were gentle across her cheek and brow. "You must trust me. I did not take you in idle pleasure."

His forearms were roped with muscle. Veins near his wrist throbbed with blood. And 'twas blood she knew that flooded through her to swell her in places that embarrassed her.

He kissed her forehead and brows. "I know it is hard to trust someone who has served in John's Flemish company. Yet, I ask it of you. Ask, not demand. Will you believe me? I am here for Ravenswood and Ravenswood alone. Trust me."

They did not make love on Richard's bed.

They made love as they had before, on the furs before the fire. This time, Adam stripped off her tunic and his before they began.

As she watched the fierce expressions chase each other across his face during his release, she held herself in check.

One part of her wanted to give everything to him, from the first simple kiss to total submission of her body. Another part of her held back and stood outside to watch over them and say, *It will never be.*

That part of her ruined the rapture.

Chapter Seventeen

It took Hugh less than a quarter of an hour to admit he must find the small chamber or perish of an aching cock. The room proved to have once been used as a private, family chapel, but was now filled to the brim with discarded furniture and crates.

Mathilda waited, perched on a chest. She traced her fingertip through dust. "We must speak of what happened between us at the fair."

Hugh crossed his arms. "I suppose I must apologize for my behavior. Though a woman is wanton by nature . . . or so the philosophers tell us."

She frowned. "Wanton by nature? And that you call an apology?"

"Nay. I said I supposed I should apologize. I have not yet done so."

Her small feet dangled, swinging against the chest with a rhythmic tapping. "I am waiting."

"For what?"

"For your apology, you dolt."

"I apologize."

"I sense a hesitation. Have you more to say?" She mimicked his stance.

The posture pushed up her breasts and drew his gaze. What a lush place to rest one's head.

"Hugh," she said.

He jerked his attention to her face. "If I seem to hesitate, it is because you, my lady, laid hand to me first."

"Oh? Is that a signal you should release your restraints?"

"It is usually so. A woman touches a man in a certain way and he may see it as invitation. You never said 'Stop' or 'Unhand me, you beast.'"

She hopped off the chest and walked toward him. "You are a great beast." There was a smile on her lips, a bright delight in her eyes.

He took a deep breath. She walked toward the door. The back of her gown was dusty where she'd sat on the chest.

"Wait," he said.

Her buttocks were soft and warm through the thin gown as he swept away the dirt. "Anyone would think you were—"

He never finished his sentence. She turned. Somehow, she was in his arms again, her lips on his. He spread his hands across the lush mounds of her buttocks and lifted her. Her legs came around his hips, and he walked her back to the chest, set her down, and threw up her hem.

She was rosy pink flesh, moist and ready, when he laid his hand on her. Her palms were also damp when she slid her hand into his braies. His breath was expelled in a long sigh as she palmed the weight of his stones.

He made short work of his clothing, did not bother to remove hers, merely shoved the loose gown up her body.

As he entered her he discovered she was not a virgin.

171

She was inexperienced, but not pure. The fact chased away his guilt that this should be Adam's moment, not his.

"Hugh," she gasped, a deep flush of red rising on her cheeks. She was slick and hot around him. He could no longer wait. Her head fell back, her hips lifted sharply. He clamped his hand over her mouth as she twisted and arched through her climax. He jerked out of her, groaned through his own finish, then dropped his forehead onto her shoulder.

She combed his hair from his sweaty brow and trailed light kisses along his temples and cheeks.

"How many men have had you?" he asked.

"Why?"

"A man likes to know how many swords have fitted a sheath."

She shoved at his chest. "What does it matter? You were not chaste, were you? I am not your first, so what does it matter if I've had more than one lover? Nay, what does it matter if I've had one hundred lovers? I should ask how many sheaths have held your sword, you hypocrite."

"You do not even know who Hippocrates was. Do not bring him into this discussion."

"Now you call me stupid."

He moved away to pick up his tunic. She remained as she was, legs spread, gown twisted at her waist, golden hair tumbling everywhere.

"I am calling you ignorant. There is a difference."

"I hate you, Hugh de Coleville. I've hated you since I met you when I was twelve and you were a bullying ten and eight."

"Oh, aye, you hate me, you who are wet with my passion and flushed from your release."

He jerked his buckle closed, then went down on his knees between her thighs. She mewed a protest when he set his lips to the delicate skin of her inner thigh just above her knee.

"What are you doing?"

"Marking you so your next lover knows I was here."

She gripped his hair and tugged, but he resisted the pain and her gasps of indignation, gasps that only lasted until he slid his fingertips into her damp curls and massaged the still swollen treasure there.

He suckled her soft skin until a large angry mark appeared. Then he left off the effort, delighting in her confused look.

"My lady." He bowed and left her.

Adam carried Joan back to the castle in his arms. He walked straight through the bailey, ignoring surprised looks and whispers, and set her on her doorstep. There he left her without word or gesture to indicate the passion they'd shared.

His arms felt empty, his mind flooded with thoughts as he strode toward his tent. On the way, he paused to tell Hugh of the minstrel's death, then summoned Douglas and gave orders about Christopher's body.

He felt some guilt that Christopher had lain out in the elements whilst he had warmed himself at a fire with Joan.

But one must tend the living over the dead.

What had Christopher learned in Winchester? Had he died with a translation of Brian de Harcourt's paper in his head? There was nothing for it but to try to find another way to have the paper translated.

Adam tossed on warm clothes, the finest he could find in his coffer. He must make his explanations to Mathilda before the gossip reached her that Joan had come home in his arms. The whole purpose of taking Joan to the lodge, to hide her state until she was dry and warm, had been negated by her insistence they return at a time when many were apt to see them.

He wanted not one speck of dishonor to touch his huntress.

And he wanted her in his bed. Without delay. As soon as Ravenswood was secured for the crown.

He needed to bring his full force from the surrounding countryside and take possession, but now with Christopher dead, Adam realized he had no one to summon his troops.

He could not go himself. Beyond the suspicions his disappearance might provoke, he would forfeit the tournament. Until the very last moment, everyone must think his goal was Mathilda. When his men were in place, he would lay claim to all of this. Mathilda could go to a convent and the bishop to the devil.

Would Mathilda choose a man who involved himself with another woman, a woman he'd been warned to look at less? Never.

Adam smiled as he dashed through the bailey and took the keep steps two at a time. He'd done far more than look at Joan. And more than touch her tawny skin. Thinking of her was like having a fine madness boiling in his blood.

Never had he known such a woman. She had marshaled the hounds to save him against a boar when she could have run. She had cared enough about him to leap into an icy pond.

His last mistress would have stood on the bank, weeping over her muddy slippers and wringing her hands. Mathilda struck him as cut from the same cloth.

The guard opened the great doors to him. The hall was crowded, almost every seat taken, including the one he had been elevated to at the previous supper. Rather than confront the slack-faced suitor who had usurped his place, Adam strolled about the hall, keeping an eye on his men. It pleased him that they behaved with great restraint despite a day indoors. They had separated themselves as well to garner gossip he might find useful.

He paused in midstride and drew in his breath.

Not because Mathilda and her women were arrayed before the fire like gems on a merchant's table.

Nay. A thought hammered him like a blow to the chest.

Joan had leapt into the pond to rescue a man she'd assumed to be him. Had someone else made the same assumption? Had Christopher been struck down by mistake?

Servants filed past him with pitchers and began to fill empty tankards. Others offered loaves of bread and fresh butter. Had one of these suitors wanted him dead? He put his hand to his dagger and found his ribbons gone.

Adam hooked Hugh by the arm. "I must speak with you."

They stood in the arch that led to the storerooms below. Adam crossed his arms on his chest in an effort to look at ease, though inside, his mind was in a turmoil.

"I believe I have made a rather distressing discovery," Adam said.

"I tried to resist her."

Adam stared at Hugh's face. "What?"

"I tried to set her from my mind. I have pretended I do not want her, but, in truth, I met her years ago and twice in Winchester within this past year. She preys on my mind and I've tried to forget her, but I cannot do it."

"Hugh, what are you saying? You knew Joan before—"

"Joan?"

"Her . . . you said her."

"Adam, I'm going to ask you a question, and you had better give me a truthful answer."

"If it's within my power, I will do so." Some truths were not his to give.

"Are you in love with the huntress?"

"*Jesu,* lower your voice."

"Forget I asked. 'Tis none of my business. As to me, I confess to liking the huntress quite a bit. If I ever decide to wed, I'll come back for her."

"The devil you say!" Adam frowned.

Hugh slung an arm around his neck and ruffled his hair, then pushed him away. "I'm just testing you. And the expression on your face says much. If you like the huntress, have at her. She would be perfect for you, as I've said before. Lush ass, worthy breasts, and I would imagine *very* strong thighs to ride you after a hunt."

Adam raked his fingers through his hair to smooth it down. He must not respond to such bait. "Listen, I've had a most disagreeable thought. The young man who drowned . . . he looks much like me."

"What? That's what you wanted to talk to me about? You fear the dead minstrel was mistaken for you?"

"My first thought when I saw Christopher was that he looked more like me than my own brother."

Hugh scratched his chin. "It makes sense someone would kill you. You are the most likely man to win Mathilda."

"So who has the mettle to try it?"

"I'd have to say only de Harcourt has the mettle."

Hugh's answer did not sit well. No matter Brian's hostility toward him, Adam liked the man.

Adam headed for Mathilda, who stood out from her colorfully garbed women by wearing all white. She also wore her hair loose.

He thought of Joan's hair, not smooth and combed like Mathilda's, but wild and curling about her head. And not this yellow either, but the color of ale streaked with gold.

Joan had been a virgin. As a virgin, she was more precious than any gold. It meant she was completely his, untouched.

Richard or Brian might have loved her, wanted her, but they had not had her.

What if she had not been innocent? Would it matter? Not if 'twas Richard who'd loved her. A dead lover was only a threat in the afterlife. But, if it had been Brian . . .

Acid burned up Adam's throat. Brian was a formidable

rival. Mathilda seemed enraptured by his conversation at this very moment.

A woman's first lover must, by rights, remain in her mind and possibly her heart, always. Or so the jongleurs sang. He remembered his first woman. And his second. He frowned.

Although she had not lain with them, had Joan loved both Richard and Brian? And in what order had she loved them?

What ailed him? It only mattered whom she loved *now*.

"My lady," Adam said as he reached the dais. He bowed to Mathilda and gave Brian a curt nod.

The rushes were strewn with sage and lavender, mingling their odors with that of the damp wool and muddy leather of the men. Great logs burned in the mammoth fireplace and a sheen of perspiration glistened on Mathilda's forehead.

"We missed you, Sir Adam," Mathilda said. "Where have you been hiding? In the privy again? And why do you not wear your ribbons?"

Adam propped one foot on the dais and touched his dagger hilt. "I've lost the ribbons, my lady, but not in the privy."

Mathilda giggled and floated like a fairy being to where he stood. "How did you lose your ribbons? Not gaming, I hope. I'll not wed a gamer."

Hugh, who had sat down at a nearby table, shook a dice cup and called out his joy as the dice landed his way on the table.

Adam frowned at his friend's unusual behavior. Hugh hated dicing. "Nay, my lady, I lost them drawing a drowned man from your fish pond."

Silence fell around them; then whispers broke out. Mathilda drew her delicately arched brows together. "A man drowned in my fish pond? What say you? How could this be?"

She looked at the bishop, who waved a negligent hand. "It was one of the minstrel's company, I believe," the bishop said. "He must have taken too much drink at the fair and mistaken his way home."

Mathilda put out her hand to Adam. He took it. So small and free of blemish it was compared to Joan's strong freckled one. Had Mathilda ever done aught but ply a needle and thread?

She squeezed his hand. "I must thank you for caring about the man. If you drew him from the pond yourself, it speaks of a compassion men often lack. I must reward such kindness and regret I have no ribbons on my own gown to give you."

So saying, she pulled the jeweled dagger from his belt—very slowly. She walked along the row of her women, then back again. To gasps of dismay from her ladies and cheers from the men, Mathilda sliced ribbons from their gowns.

Mathilda ignored a sharp reprimand from Lady Claris and with a wide smile, walked back to Adam. Every eye in the hall was on them. She knelt on the dais. Slowly, she slid his dagger back into its sheath and wrapped the ribbons about its hilt.

Adam felt the provocative nature of her actions, yet she looked as innocent as an angel, her expression as guileless as a child's, as she knotted the finery.

When she was done, she surveyed her handiwork. "Ah, there is one more thing to make this complete."

On the dais, she had not to rise so high to reach his mouth. The kiss was short, a brush across his lips. When she stood back, she said in a carrying voice. "Oh, forgive me. It was one kiss for each ribbon, was it not?"

If she wanted a spectacle, he would give her one.

Adam clamped his hands on Mathilda's arms, lifted her into the air, and held her level with his mouth. This kiss he planted himself, bruising the delicate pouting cushions of her lips. He set her down just as quickly, turned, and saluted the crowd, now cheering his efforts.

The hall erupted into disorganized conversations and a resumption of games. Serving maids offered more ale and wine, dodging the roaming hands of the men.

Adam consumed a trencher of jellied eels, then walked about the hall, questioning his men. None of them had seen the minstrel, or for that matter, Joan's missing lymer.

Amidst the clatter of eating and drinking, dicing and bragging, Mathilda banged her eating dagger against her cup. Attuned to her ways, the hall grew quiet.

"The beast that rages without keeps us from hunting other beasts this day. In the place of that dear activity," she said, with a small smile, "I have planned a few games here."

"That word play must be accidental. She's not the wits to think of it on her own." Hugh shook his head. "There is only one thing worse than a dull-witted wife."

"What?" Adam asked.

"A man who wants her anyway."

When Mathilda clapped her hands, two men carried in an arrow butt from the practice field. It was placed at the end of the hall by the door. A few serving women shrieked when men entered, bearing bows and quivers of arrows.

"We'll be putting another body in the graveyard next to that hapless minstrel," Hugh said at Adam's ear.

"I may not be the finest bowman in the land, but I'll wager I can do better than Roger."

"I don't wager."

"What was that you were doing just now?" Adam nodded to the table that still held the discarded dice.

"Making sure Mathilda had someone depraved to compare your compassionate nature to."

"I think the gesture was lost on her."

"She's a cock-tease," Hugh said with some heat.

"She's an innocent child."

"She knelt within kissing distance of your *enfourchure*."

179

Adam stifled a smile. "Then she will know the way there when I am wed to her."

"If you wed her, you'll not wait many months before you find her kissing someone else's *enfourchure*. You'll never know if your child is your own."

"If she is locked in a convent, I need not concern myself with her at all."

The bishop stood up and gestured to the archery butts and said in his usual deep, slow voice, "We have only a small field in which to compete, so we shall make the task more difficult."

One of the bishop's knights held out a length of cloth. "Would each of the suitors please advance."

Nine men, as Yves with his broken wrist must sit out this competition, approached the dais. They tossed dice to choose the order of shooting. Roger was first, Adam eighth.

Mathilda had her stool brought to where Roger stood. She mounted it and the crowd gasped, men shoving each other aside to escape the hall, when she used the length of cloth to bind Roger's eyes.

The bishop's man set the bow and arrow in Roger's hand, turned him three times, and set him straight. Roger wove in place, but kept his feet planted. More spectators fled the hall. It pleased Adam that none were his men. They stood out like pepper in a white sauce, sprinkled throughout the dwindling crowd in their black garb.

Roger, like most well-trained knights, had no need to see to ready the bow. But his aim sawed back and forth before he settled himself and drew the string. The arrow flew. It smacked viciously into the wooden doorpost, ten feet adrift of the butt and inches from the guard who stood there on duty.

Women screamed, more men fled the hall, but Roger's men shouted and whistled for their leader.

One by one each suitor took his turn, submitting to the

blindfold, the turning, the blind aim. The hall, though greatly diminished in company as wild shots drove even more spectators into the rain, nonetheless echoed and rang with cheers and stomping men.

Only one suitor remained before Adam, the youth, de Coucy. The boy's shot went low, skimming the butt to the astonishment of all. The collective gasp made the young man grin when he took off the blindfold. He was the only one so far to touch the target. The boy licked his lips and when he turned his back to Mathilda made a quick graphic thrust of his hips that sent Adam after him.

He snatched the boy up by his tunic and shook him. "You'll not have the lady with crude gestures." He set the boy on his feet and acknowledged the rousing claps from his men.

Mathilda looked puzzled, and he merely bowed to her. But behind her, Lady Claris shot Adam a look so hard, so full of malevolence, he thought she might be a Medusa sent to turn him to stone. Acknowledging he might have made an enemy, Adam took his place.

Adam decided that he must close his eyes behind the blindfold and picture the butt on the practice field, take longer than necessary to aim so his head had time to settle.

He submitted to Mathilda's artful tying of the blindfold. Was he mistaken that she caressed his ears with her fingertips as she knotted the cloth?

His head swam after the three turnabouts. He took his time raising the bow. His eyes, closed all the while, looked inward, but not at an imaginary greensward. Nor did he visualize the narrow alley of space in the hall. Instead, he imagined he was a raven coursing the dawn sky. He heard, without really noticing, the chant of the crowd, who stomped in time to his heart's beat.

With a slow, deliberate motion, he pulled the string by his ear. He saw the arrow fly, rising to join his imaginary raven to ride the golden rays of morning sun.

The smack of the arrow into the butt made him rip the blindfold off. The arrow was embedded in the top edge.

"Not center, but not bad for a blind man," Hugh said, clapping him on the shoulder.

Adam acknowledged his men's cheers with a wave of his arm, then handed off the blindfold to the last contender, Brian.

When Brian stepped up for his turn, there was still only one arrow in the butt. Adam's.

Mathilda blindfolded the only man Adam truly felt could defeat him if manly form and prowess on the battlefield were the means of choosing. The lady did definitely skim her fingers on Brian's ears as she had on Adam's. There was no mistake. It was a favor laid on only for them.

Brian submitted to the turning, then did as Adam had. He waited for his head to right itself, making much ceremony of raising the bow. The arrow whistled through the air and thudded into the target.

A silence swept the hall; then de Harcourt's men leapt onto benches and shouted for their master.

The arrow quivered at almost dead center. Brian walked the length of the hall, arms out, nodding to the delighted crowd. Adam's men hissed and stomped their feet as Brian slowly drew Adam's arrow, casting it to the floor, then knotting the blindfold on the shaft of his.

Mathilda laughed and clapped her hands. It was Brian's turn to receive a ribbon. She blushed a pretty pink as she knotted it to Brian's belt buckle, only a few inches from his *enfourchure*. Ribald comments flew about the room as men nudged each other.

"See," Hugh said, "a wanton."

A few drunken men rose and stood upon the tables. They sang as was their wont. No minstrel company entertained today; instead they kept a vigil over their friend in the chapel.

Adam joined them a few moments later. He knelt and prayed for Christopher's soul, deeply saddened that the young man might lie cold and silent before the altar for no reason beyond the color of his black hair and beard.

Chapter Eighteen

Joan took her time slicing bread for her supper. Nat was not about. It worried her that he might still be out looking for the lymer in the dismal weather. When the rain eased, she would go back out herself, no matter what hour it was.

"Joan?" Oswald stepped into the cottage without waiting for permission. "Are you alone?" Water ran off his mantle to drip on the rushes.

She nodded, stepping closer to the hearth and keeping the knife in her hand.

"Your father asked me to tell you he is going out with some of his men after more venison. The bishop ordered more for the feast after the tournament."

"More?"

"Aye. As if there was not already enough." He sat at the table.

"What do you want?" She placed the knife on the mantle and crossed her arms over her chest. Her nipples felt sore against the linen of her gown. She wanted nothing more than to go lie on her pallet and think of Adam.

Oswald licked his lips and smoothed his hair back. "I saw you with Quintin."

"And?" Had Oswald read her thoughts?

"And our lady might object to what I saw."

Joan took a deep breath. "What is it you want?"

"I want to warn you. I would hate to think our lady would dismiss you for your attentions to one of her suitors."

His words paralleled some of her own thoughts. "Thank you for the warning. Now, I have much to do."

He didn't rise. He gripped his hands tightly together as if praying. "I much admire you," he said softly. "The way you handle the hounds, a hunt."

Her throat went tight.

"I hope you understand this business between my Lord Roger and Nat is just that—their business—not ours."

She waited. Did he want more money?

"We've had the same upbringing, you and I. We'd do well together."

"Together?" She forced the word out.

"I'd like to ask your father for your hand."

Joan felt as if someone had struck her in the stomach. "Don't." The word came out in rush.

Oswald got to his feet and held up one hand. "There's no need for hasty answers. Think on my offer."

"I don't intend to leave Ravenswood or Nat. Ever."

He bobbed his head like a wading bird. "If Lady Mathilda chooses my lord Roger, you won't need to, nor will Nat. He can serve as my right hand. And I've spoken to de Coucy. He's willing to make me his hunt master if favor smiles on him. I'll talk to the other suitors as well, if you like."

"You've discussed this with others?"

"Aye." He smiled. "I want everyone to know how much I think of you." He bowed and went to the door. "Oh,

185

and the bishop heard Nat lost a valuable dog. He's not pleased. It might be best to keep your father out of the bishop's sight."

Joan watched Oswald dart across the slippery cobbles to the hall. The rain pelted the stones at the cottage entrance, splashing her hem and bare feet. Behind her, water from the leak pinged into the metal pot set out to catch it. Each drop seemed to echo in her ears.

Her body ached from making love to Adam and her mind whirled with Oswald's words. How dare he presume to seek Nat's job? She must speak to Nat and Mathilda, lest Oswald get to them first. What if Oswald persuaded them to the match?

Joan changed into a clean gown and plaited her unruly hair—unruly from drying whilst she lay on it before a fire—making love. She tied it with the ribbon she'd bought at the fair.

After pinning on her mantle, she was ready.

When the company grew restless, Roger proposed each suitor entertain the crowd with either a verse or a song.

"What ill conceived notion is this?" Adam asked Brian, sitting at his side, aware Mathilda's attentions had shifted since his time in the chapel.

"Assume he's paid a jongleur to compose something for just such an opportunity," Brian said, draining his tankard. He walked to the table that abutted the front of Mathilda's and leapt boldly up onto it. To Adam's dismay, Brian challenged Roger, and all the other suitors, to a tournament of verse.

"*Mon Dieu.*" He had no skill to stitch words into rhymes.

As Mathilda solicited those who wished to compete, Adam found himself hiding in his ale cup. Roger leapt onto another table opposite Brian's and said he'd pit his verses against those of any man in the room.

Joan Swan walked into the hall. She looked about, then, clinging to the wall as if she feared someone might see her, edged toward the laundress.

Adam lost the thread of Roger's speech. Hugh joined Joan, and the laundress slid down on her bench to give him a seat. He lifted Joan's plait and shook it, making a remark that sent laughter down Edwina's table and color into Joan's cheeks.

A sickening feeling, as if someone had taken his stones in a fist and squeezed, overcame Adam. It was simple jealousy in its rawest, purest form.

Oswald, the red-haired hunt master, detached himself from a company of men and joined Joan's party. With relief, Adam watched Edwina shoo Oswald and Hugh away.

The women were but two among many who had sought the hall as evening waned and the deluge lessened. No room could be brighter than this one now that Joan was in it.

The poetic thought amused him. He caught her eye.

In her glance he saw the remembrance of their time together. Those memories took him from his seat.

He made his way through the throng and sat beside her, near the steps to the lower storerooms. The scent of dampness overpowered the sweet rushes on this side of the hall.

Edwina acknowledged him with no sign of chasing him off. "Ye missed winning a ribbon this morning."

"Did I?" Adam looked at Joan.

"Mathilda gave a test on the fair. It were great good fun. Only Francis de Coucy could answer the questions." Edwina stood up and mimicked the boy. "Ribbon's a farthing a foot. Bread is two a penny." She dropped onto the bench and slapped her knees. "The boy knew the cost of everything. He earned his ribbon."

Indeed, Francis did have one ribbon. He wore it knotted about his wrist.

187

Adam wanted to take Joan's hand and lead her to one of the storerooms below and make love to her until he was drained of seed. And any thoughts of ribbons and fairs.

Edwina interrupted his thoughts.

"Have any of you seen Del?"

No one had. Edwina frowned. "He's given to laziness, but he's never been gone so long."

A man at the table made a remark about the number of loose women about because of the fair and Del's prowess between female thighs. Adam watched Joan's cheeks flush. The conversation was more ribald here away from the high table.

The laundress snapped at the men to mind their tongues, then pointed to Brian and Roger, who stood upon the table. "Is this worth wagering on?" she asked.

"Lord no," Adam said. "It's a combat of words."

"What do you mean?"

Joan wore her hair in one long plait, bound with a scarlet ribbon. It was the only spot of color as her gown was a drab brown. Yet she needed no finery. Her skin was as downy as a peach, her brow smooth and clear.

"It seems we're to entertain Lady Mathilda in verse or song," he said hastily, lest they discern his thoughts.

Tendrils of hair escaped Joan's plait, and he remembered how soft the strands felt to his fingers, his lips. Unbidden, his gaze dropped to her mouth. He also remembered how soft her full lips were. With difficulty, he forced his attention to the tournament of verse and those at the high table.

Mathilda and her ladies giggled. Bishop Gravant leaned toward Lady Claris and said something that made her nod and touch his wrist.

"Those two look cozy," Adam said.

"Oh, aye." Edwina glanced about and then leaned near his ear. " 'Tis said she's been his mistress these twenty years."

Jesu. Twenty years. Adam examined Francis. Was there a resemblance to the bishop? None that he could detect. This added a nasty wrinkle to the question of whom the bishop would select if Mathilda could not choose. Roger Artois could kiss the ecclesiastic ass all he wanted, but if blood would tell . . .

Lady Claris touched the bishop's wrist again. Adam wondered if the traitor might be a woman. Could Lady Claris be working toward more than a powerful manor for her son?

The laundress nudged him in the side. "These verses are magnificent."

Roger posed, one foot before the other, and held out a hand toward Mathilda. "Mathilda, jewel of eternal beauty."

Adam listened, incredulous. Each time Roger paused to begin another verse, Brian broke in with his own lyrical lines.

Adam's stomach knotted. These two were smarter than he. They'd come prepared with praise for the lady, elegant, courtly praise, memorized and flowing from their lips with such ease, one might think they made their living at it.

By the sixth verse, Brian and Roger had come to an understanding that they were most evenly matched. They walked along their respective tables, stepping over trenchers as the diners snatched tankards from their paths.

They stood face-to-face at the distance of only a few feet, the gap between their tables, and said their verses, first one, then the other, heads of spectators bobbing first one way and then the other.

Mathilda sat rapt as her womanly virtues, beauty, and kindness were lauded in metered verse.

Joan said, "I believe they hired the same jongleur."

Adam snapped his attention to her. Her hair was no longer plaited, but fell in glorious disarray about her shoulders.

She touched his sleeve. "She much admires the rose."

He looked down. In her palm lay the scarlet ribbon. As he watched, she folded and knotted it into a credible rosebud. She leaned down and plucked something from the rushes. A bright piece of greenery. She slid it into the back of the knotting.

She held it out. "Richard always gave her roses. He compared her golden hair to the honey she liked to lick from the comb."

She stood up, touched his shoulder lightly, and walked around the room to sit near a man who might be one of the fewterers or huntsmen. From the look of the man's gestures, they talked of dogs, not rosebuds or honey.

Finally, with a flourish of bows, Roger and Brian fell silent. Mathilda jumped up, her hands clasped over her breast, and then sank into a deep curtsy. Roger and Brian were lauded and whistled from the tables.

One by one, the other suitors either declined to compose a verse, or sang some well-known song of love or valor to show the range of their voices. But Roger's and Brian's efforts had eclipsed the sum of their contributions.

Finally, Adam became aware the hall was silent. He realized they waited for him. He got slowly to his feet, his heart thudding. He walked the short distance to Mathilda and stood before her.

"You are golden honey, sweet and pure. A rose may blush to you compare. That is my verse, I am no poet, 'tis sure."

He held out his hand.

Mathilda's shook a bit as she reached for the rose. She skimmed it with her fingertips.

"Richard would have said the same." She took the flower and tucked it into her gown at the breast.

Then she shook herself as if waking from some dream. "Well done, Sir Adam. You have touched my heart, but I fear for all that, you have not won the day."

He offered her his arm. She laid her hand on his sleeve. Thus he usurped Roger's and Brian's moment, escorting her to them. Adam made a great show of slicing the ribbons she indicated from her lady's gowns, one by one, then handing them off to the men. Mathilda never so much as touched their sleeves.

Brian raised his tankard. "Here's to verse, and the lady fair, but who will kiss us? Pray not Quintin there."

The lady and company laughed with him and she ran on light footsteps, skirt raised to show her tiny feet in embroidered shoes, to where each man stood. She kissed them lightly, saluted, and returned to Adam's side.

Adam realized he'd not won a ribbon, but he'd gained the lady's favor anyway. He led her to an oak chair, his step faltering a moment when he realized it was one his mother had used when she sat in this place.

As he seated Mathilda, he laid claim to her hand. "Could you say some praise of Joan Swan—private praise? I do not want her embarrassed here or singled out," he hastened to add, "but she did risk her life to pull the minstrel from the fish pond."

Mathilda studied his face. "I thought it was you who tried to save the minstrel."

"I went in after Joan. She was weighed down by her skirts and not doing very well. But her valor was extraordinary to even attempt the thing. She thought only of saving the man. She might have drowned."

"So, you and Joan both chose to fish this morning? So early?"

It was his cheeks heating this time. "Nay, I was on the way to the village to see if my men had behaved themselves last night when I saw her struggling in the water."

"I see. And what was she doing out and about in such dirty weather, I wonder?"

"Nat's favorite lymer is missing."

Mathilda's gaze sought the old man. "Is Nat here?"

"I've not seen him, only Joan."

"He has always been kind to me."

"Then be kind to the daughter."

"You chastise me?" Mathilda's small chin tipped up.

"Never."

"Then you merely recommend my actions? Not dictate them."

"It is only for a guardian or husband to dictate actions."

"So, you would order me about if you were chosen."

He recognized a sincerity in her tone that warned him he fished in dangerous waters. "Nay, a woman may be offered advice by her mate, but she may not take it if she does not wish to."

"Sit here, Adam, by my feet and tell me more of how a mate should behave."

Realizing he was the favored one for this fleeting moment, he sat down and accepted a cup of wine she passed to him. He hoped Joan was able to trust that his attentions to Mathilda were all part of a game he must play.

"Were your own parents well suited?" Mathilda asked.

Lady Claris interrupted him before he could speak. "It is not a matter of suiting each other. You are very young, my lady, but surely you know a marriage must first be one that extends and enhances one's properties and strength. Therein lies the suitability."

"I must agree with you, my lady." Adam lifted his cup to the older woman. "But there must be some equality in temperament and nature, or some complement at least, else days like this will be weary."

"Aye," Mathilda said. "One may find oneself in one's storeroom performing chores that have no purpose."

Hugh, listening to the conversation, took a step closer. "I would think you have servants enough to tend your needs."

Adam frowned at the abrupt tone of Hugh's voice.

"I think you need to take a turn in the fresh air, my

lord," Mathilda said. "You've been too long confined."

Hugh bowed. "I will do just that now Joan Swan informs me the rain has ended. Perhaps I shall help her search for her missing dog."

"You will miss the love court," Mathilda said.

Adam quailed inside. *Love court?* Then his thoughts scattered. Brian, not Hugh, was escorting Joan from the hall. The rain was done. When the guard flung the two doors wide, Adam looked upon a sky streaked with a fine autumn's sunset.

Joan could not refuse Brian's offer to see her to the kennels. What had possessed her to think she could speak with Mathilda in the hall? And Nat had not appeared.

As they walked, Joan explained about the missing lymer.

"I'll ask my men if they've seen the dog. A well-trained animal is always noticed," Brian said.

"He's the sire of the pup we nursed," she said. "The spring Richard died."

"I remember. You sat up all night with the pathetic thing."

She nodded. "Aye. I was sure he would die, too."

"I remember more of that night." Brian led her away from the kennels toward the stone path through the old garden. "May I be so bold as to give you a warning?"

Everyone had warnings for her, it seemed.

Joan sat on one of the marble benches. The setting sun cast gold lights through his chestnut curls. He was a handsome man—had been two years ago. Now, lines had formed about his mouth. They gave him a melancholy look when he did not smile. He was not smiling now.

"What warning do I need?" she asked.

"That night you nursed the pup, 'twas the same night we learned Richard was dead."

A lump filled her throat. "Aye. Mathilda was frantic— I could hear her wails from here."

"We went too far that night, you and I."

"Brian—"

"Nay, let me finish. You offered me comfort and in the morning, lying in the straw with you, that damned pup between us, I lied to you."

She examined his face for guile.

"I lied when I said you were not good enough to wed, that you were only good enough to be a mistress, and that you were wanton to tempt me with your kisses."

"Stop this." She stood up, her skin suddenly hot.

"Please, sit down." He set his hand on her shoulder. She had no choice but to obey. To try to break from his grip would attract the attention of the sentry who was looking down on them from the ramparts.

"I lied in that I really wanted to wed you, to do as Richard had sworn he would. But unlike Richard, I had not the courage in here"—he touched his chest—"to defy *my* father . . . or hurt my friend."

He held out his hand to her. She ignored it. After a moment, he dropped it to his side and continued. "I had my opportunity with you that night when we nursed the pup and shed our tears over Richard, but I lost it. I hurt you. I've always wanted to tell you I was sorry."

"It was two years ago." She looked off to where the old kennels had stood, swamped by memories, none of them joyous.

"It seems less to me."

"So why now? Why say anything?" She clasped her elbows in her palms to keep from wringing her hands.

"Because I'm determined to be lord here. And if I succeed, we'll see each other daily. I must tell you I did love you then. You are my only regret."

"Regret?" She forced a smile. "Pray put it from your mind. We comforted each other—that is all. I thought no more on our night together past that day."

"You're lying. I saw the way you recoiled from me when we met at Adam's unhorsing."

"I was recoiling from the crowd of men. I do not trust so many men together at a kill."

He acknowledged her lie with a shrug. "If you say so. But I think you were remembering when Nat needed to chastise my men at the tavern for calling you my—"

"Don't say it," she cried. "Stop this. What purpose is gained by talking over times past?"

"I don't want you to be uncomfortable with me or my men if I'm lord here."

She would never be comfortable with his men. They'd called her a bitch in heat, said Brian's pup would be whelped in the kennel with the other dogs come spring. Nat had been enraged enough to threaten one man.

"Nat was hurt by your men's jokes," she said softly. "That was the harm you did. Nat was hurt, Nat who has harmed no one."

"Should I be making my apology to him?"

The door of the keep opened and the sound of singing spilled from the hall. Several men stumbled down the steps, drunken men as those in Brian's company had been.

"I must go," she said.

Brian hooked her arm. "Do not let him hurt you, either."

"Who?" She summoned as much ice in her voice as she could.

"Quintin. No one knows whence he comes. He has risen because William Marshal sees something of himself in the man. He's some baron's by-blow and can offer nothing to this estate save a mercenary attitude and a brutal company at arms. Mercenaries serve no man save themselves."

How could she have forgotten Adam Quintin's men? Had they killed the minstrel? And if 'twas Adam who became lord here, his men would stay, would they not?

"My lord?" One of Brian's men approached, his feet

crunching on the pebble path. "Lady Mathilda summons you to her love court."

It was not to the kennels Joan went, but back to the hall on Brian's arm. But it was not to see how Brian fared in Lady Mathilda's mock court. As Joan stood along the edges of the throng who waited as she did to know just what sins a love court might judge, she knew it was to see Adam again and no other.

Chapter Nineteen

Adam watched Mathilda command the hall's attention with naught but a wave of her small, white hand.

"Eleanor of Aquitaine and her ladies once held a court of love," Mathilda said. "I would like to resurrect that tradition here tonight. If any man feels inadequate to be here judged, speak now."

Silence ruled in the hall. Men looked from one to the other, and Adam knew none of them wanted to be thought inadequate.

A flurry of servants cleared the dais and set up the table much as Adam's father might have when he held a manorial court. Mathilda stood by the principal seat. Her women, among them Francis de Coucy's mother, sat in a line to the right and left. It amused Adam to see proceedings his father conducted with gravity mocked in this manner by the ladies.

Then he started; a servant led Joan to a seat at the end of the table. High color stained her cheeks. He wanted to leap up and say she should not be part of this mummery. She had suffered a grievous experience at the fish pond. She needed quiet and sleep to heal.

Why wasn't she back in her cottage instead of here at the end of this row of women, a wren among peacocks?

Adam thought to protest Lady Claris's place there as well. Surely, the lady could not be impartial with her son one of the suitors? Adam shook off the thought. 'Twas naught but an amusement for ladies just as the poetry and archery had been.

"What's this nonsense?" Hugh asked, sitting at his elbow. "I may have to take myself off to Winchester. The tournament may not be worth this wait."

"I need you at the tournament, I'm a man down. I meant to ask you to stand in Lambert's place, but forgot."

Forgot because I am befuddled with lust.

Hugh clapped him on the back. "With pleasure. I'll put that craven boy, de Coucy, on his back for you." Hugh bumped Adam's arm and raised his cup of wine.

"All are in place, we may begin. Will Yves of York approach," Lady Mathilda said.

The man with the broken wrist stepped forward. He bowed low and grinned.

"You are charged with flagrantly playing false with a womanly heart. How plead you?"

Yves touched his splinted arm. "I am incapable of playing a woman false with this broken wing. I spend my time, when not in your lovely presence, saying my prayers."

Mathilda smiled and the hall burst into laughter. She curtsied and indicated her women. "My ladies, what say you? Is this knight guilty or innocent of playing false? May he remain or shall we cast him out to find his way home?"

The bishop paid little heed to Mathilda's antics, his head close to Roger Artois's. Adam had gone through all of Roger's belongings, questioned his men. If he played William Marshal false, and through him King Henry, it was not to be discovered here and now.

Mathilda and her ladies held a murmured discussion on the suitor's "guilt." Adam noticed Joan said little, her gaze upon her hands, folded in her lap. Her drab gown was unbecoming. Her hair, however, was as untamed as her nature when making love.

His body tightened at the memory of the long, slim column of her spine, the sweet fullness of her buttocks as she tried to climb from the rain barrel.

Mathilda clapped her hands. "We have made a judgment. Yves of York, we find you guilty. We sentence you to hie yourself from this hall and thence from this manor."

An uproar like a tidal surge swept the hall. The bishop clapped his jeweled hands. Silence reigned again and Gravant smiled. "It shall be as our lady requests. You are dismissed."

This time, the silence was ponderous, charged with unspoken words. Yves bowed, albeit with little grace, in Mathilda's direction. His stride, as he headed through the hall, his men falling in behind him, was stiff with anger.

Adam bit his tongue on a question to Hugh. So this love court was not an idle amusement. It served another purpose, Adam suspected—eliminating suitors. Ones displeasing to Mathilda or the bishop?

Did a dismissal mean the suitor was not going to champion Louis's or the bishop's cause? This was a complication Adam needed to think about. This new game might aid him. And was Mathilda part of the bishop's plot? She did wear the fleur-de-lis seal ring.

De Harcourt was called next. The same accusation was made by Mathilda. Had he played false with a womanly heart?

To Adam's amazement, Brian went down on one knee and said, "I plead guilty. I have played a woman false. Two years ago."

The timing, coupled with the sudden jerk of Joan's body, told Adam the woman wronged was she. The blades of jealousy carved his insides.

Mathilda placed a delicate hand on Brian's shoulder. "Have you made amends?"

"I offered my apologies, my lady. Amends are impossible. A hurt is a hurt. It heals with a cicatrix whether dealt with a blade or a tongue."

She nodded and went to her women. Lady Claris's words were inaudible, but she pounded the table with her fist. Mathilda listened with respect to each woman. When it was Joan's turn to speak she looked at Mathilda for a very long moment before shaking her head.

Adam half rose in his seat. Hugh clapped a hand over his on the table. "Do not draw attention to her or yourself."

"What?"

"You know de Harcourt is talking of his love affair with Joan Swan. Do not appear interested. Mathilda will see you."

Adam sat down and propped his chin on his hand, in an effort to feign ignorance. "How do you know this is about Brian and Joan?"

"Oh, I like a good gossip and de Harcourt's men do as well. I drank with a few of them at the alehouse after the fair. It is an accepted fact that de Harcourt had her two years ago the night Richard died. In fact, there are some among his men who believe de Harcourt had her earlier still, under Richard's nose, so to speak."

The impulse to say 'twas all false, that Joan had been innocent until that very morning, was on the tip of Adam's tongue.

But he could not speak of his morning with her. That would only injure Joan and his cause here. "I said it before, I do not believe Joan is free with her favors. It's nonsense."

Join the Historical Romance Book Club — and GET 4 FREE* BOOKS NOW!

A $23.96 Value!

Yes! I want to subscribe to the Historical Romance Book Club.

Please send me my **4 FREE* BOOKS.** I have enclosed $2.00 for shipping/handling. Each month I'll receive the four newest Historical Romance selections to preview for 10 days. If I decide to keep them, I will pay the Special Members Only discounted price of just $4.24 each, a total of $16.96, plus $2.00 shipping/handling ($23.55 US in Canada). This is a **SAVINGS OF AT LEAST $5.00** off the bookstore price. There is no minimum number of books I must buy, and I may cancel the program at any time. In any case, the **4 FREE* BOOKS** are mine to keep.

*In Canada, add $5.00 shipping/handling per order for the first shipment. For all future shipments to Canada, the cost of membership is $23.55 US, which includes shipping and handling. (All payments must be made in US dollars.)

NAME: _____

ADDRESS: _____

CITY: _____ STATE: _____

COUNTRY: _____ ZIP: _____

TELEPHONE: _____

E-MAIL: _____

SIGNATURE: _____

If under 18, Parent or Guardian must sign. Terms, prices, and conditions subject to change. Subscription subject to acceptance. Dorchester Publishing reserves the right to reject any order or cancel any subscription.

Hugh met his gaze. "De Harcourt's men think differently. They say de Harcourt found her to his liking, for she much liked to suck the marrow from the bone."

Adam shot to his feet. Hugh rose and snatched at his tunic. "Sit down. Now. You betray yourself."

Blood surged through Adam's veins. It sang hot like it did when he was deep into a tournament or when he was confronted on two sides in battle. He wanted to flail out in all directions, but only Hugh stood before him. He became aware the hall had exploded in laughter.

"What happened?" Hugh asked the man nearest to them, one of Roger Artois's men-at-arms.

"De Harcourt has been sentenced," the man said.

Hugh let Adam's tunic go. He righted his garb and sat down. "Is he dismissed?" Adam asked Artois's man.

"Ye'll no have such luck. He's still yer competition. He's to give a kiss to every woman in the hall."

Hugh shivered. "*Mon Dieu!* I would dismiss myself if I were so taxed."

The laughter around the table gave Adam time to collect himself. The next man called was Francis de Coucy. He approached the dais with an arrogant swagger.

"Someone needs to polish that rooster's tail," Hugh said.

Adam grinned, but without mirth. "I'll be happy to do so in the tournament. I'll unhorse him within a quarter hour of the opening horns."

De Coucy was questioned. Adam was not surprised the court found Francis "not guilty" of a crime of the heart. His mother sat on the dais, after all. Then Adam smiled whilst the hall erupted in jeers. Mathilda sentenced him to practice his manners on a kitchen wench. De Coucy's face was almost purple with rage. Mathilda called a serving woman forward. She was at least two score, almost a decade older than Lady Claris, and stout as an ale keg.

De Coucy bowed, albeit stiffly, and relinquished his place to the next suitor.

"I must give him credit," Hugh said. "He could have acted the child, but was quite restrained. I elevate him past Roger."

One more suitor was found "guilty" by Mathilda's ladies and summarily dismissed. The others were given penance like Francis's or Brian's. Men moved about the hall, kissing ladies on the hands or cheeks.

Roger's name was called. Mathilda curtsied to him and posed her question.

"I—I, that is. I do not know how to answer, my lady. What constitutes playing a woman false?"

"Have you caused one tear to fall from a woman's eye?"

"Does my mother count?"

The women tittered behind their hands, except for Joan, who sat as if a statue, neither smiling nor frowning. Adam worried she might be suffering still from the shock of finding Christopher.

He drummed his fingers on the table. He was last. How should he answer? Confession had done Brian no harm.

Roger scratched his chin. "I believe I have caused some tears . . . That is . . . perhaps I might have—"

"My lord, you are very unsure of yourself," Mathilda said amidst giggles. Adam found himself grinding his teeth each time he heard the inane sound. Yet Adam enjoyed Lord Roger's discomfort along with the crowd. The bishop, too, watched the proceedings with evident enjoyment, a grin on his face.

Was this not an unseemly occupation for a man of God? The other holy men, clerics and the bishop's dean, had all left the hall long ago. Was Mathilda dismissing the men by the bishop's orders?

Roger whipped around to intimidate the laughing members of the audience. The men in his entourage fell abruptly silent. Others were not cowed at all. Some of the worst offenders were Adam's mercenaries.

"Indeed, my lord. I am quite displeased with you. Have you no answer?" Mathilda tapped her foot.

Roger held his hands out in supplication. "I am prepared to make any apology you deem necessary, pay any penance."

Mathilda smiled to her women. "Let us decide this man's fate."

The women quickly decided Roger's fate. Mathilda returned to the edge of the dais, a length of pale rose cloth in her hands. "My lord Roger, we have found you guilty of a crime of the heart. Your penance is to wear this sash for the remainder of your time here so all might know your sins." She knotted it on his waist.

"At least she didn't kneel to his *enfourchure*," Hugh said.

Roger opened his mouth, then snapped it closed. When Roger turned to go, Mathilda said, "My lord, please remember this sash is a symbol of your ability to practice tolerance and patience with a wife's demands should you become a husband. You have done admirably well, a man willing to accept correction. Wear the sash in good health."

Hugh snorted through his nose.

"Have you something to say to the court, my lord Hugh?" Mathilda asked.

He stood up and gave her a fine but somewhat mocking bow. "I have naught to say, my lady. I am but an observer."

"Might I offer you some advice?"

"My lady?" Hugh said after a pause.

"If you have naught of worth to say, save your tongue for other matters."

Adam watched a flush suffuse his friend's face. Hugh did not sit down; instead he bowed and left the hall. Another man chose that time to exit as well—the bishop. He left with his men behind him, going up the steps to the lord's chamber. Adam watched him until Mathilda called his name.

She gave him a deep curtsy and smiled. Adam decided it would not do to direct even one glance at Joan. He held himself taut for he had not yet decided how to answer the question.

"Adam Quintin, you are charged with playing false with a woman's heart. Are you guilty?"

A few of his men called out bawdy answers for him. He ignored them, suddenly sure how he would reply. He believed one should always use the truth in situations where uncertainty ruled.

He went down on one knee and held out his hand. Lady Mathilda placed hers in his. Her skin was smooth and soft, cared for, made for stitching and soothing a man's brow, or making love. As he took her hand, he did glance at Joan, and knew instantly what he intended to say was the right and proper thing. He might face Mathilda, but he intended to speak to Joan.

"I am guilty, my lady, as is any man who might stand before you. From the great King Arthur, down through time, all men must admit to their guilt if so summoned to a court such as this one. All men play women false.

"We deny our mother's love when we march to war, never looking back or displaying our fear. We deny our sisters when they plead for a suitor who offers no alliance that will fill our coffers or enhance our name.

"We deny our lovers when we set them aside to make an alliance of power. We deny our love to the women we wed in pursuit of that power. We deny our daughters when we bid them wed against their wishes. There is no time, no day, no moment, when men do not play women false."

Chapter Twenty

A hush fell over the hall. Joan let out her breath, unaware she'd been holding it. Every word of Adam's speech lingered in her mind. Did he mean the words?

Mathilda broke Joan's reverie. "My ladies, you have heard this noble knight accept his guilt. As such, we must determine his punishment. And if we accept what he says, then he and the men he represents are guilty indeed. Shall we banish him? Or shall we punish him?"

"Banish him," Lady Claris said, her voice high and shrill.

"Punish him, but keep him," Lady Isabelle said with equal vehemence and a wide smile in Adam's direction.

A babble of voices rose from the tables and Joan had difficulty hearing Adam's fate. She offered no opinion, but it was to her Mathilda finally appealed.

"Joan, we have four who wish the dismissal of this knight from the field of love. We have four who are merciful and wish to give him a punishment. How say you?"

Joan lifted her gaze to Mathilda, then flicked a glance in Adam's direction. What did Mathilda want of her? She understood neither her place at this table, nor the role she must play.

Her fingers hurt from knotting them in her lap. Every eye in the hall was on her. *Adam's as well.*

Joan took a deep breath. "I believe you should decide the matter, my lady. It is you who must choose after the tournament, and so you must know your mind to decide who stays and who does not."

Mathilda tapped a toe on the floor and then walked to where Adam knelt. She circled him, one finger on her cheek. "You are wise, Joan Swan. I shall decide this man's fate myself."

Even Adam's men knew to hold their tongues at this crucial moment. Of course, Joan thought with a bite of cynicism, it was for the ransom of horses and accoutrement that Adam's men had come. If he left, they left.

"Rise, Adam Quintin," Mathilda said. "I find you guilty, but will exact no punishment. Your honesty serves you well."

Joan's legs were wooden as she left the dais. Mathilda caught her sleeve. "The bishop wishes to see you in his quarters now. I'll take you."

Joan felt as if a guard had come to summon her to the dungeon. What could the bishop want of her? Had he a complaint about Nat? Was it about the missing lymer?

As they walked from the dais, Adam turned toward her, one hand pressed against his lower back. Joan missed a step and stumbled on her hem. She knew why he did it. He had deep, painful bruises from his unhorsing. As if taken on wings, she was back in the lodge, watching the light from the hearth play over his body—and face—a beautiful, uncommon face.

She looked down lest she trip again. With each step, she realized an appalling truth. The man with whom she'd lain

206

was no common man. Adam was as handsome as Mathilda was lovely. A man who looked like Adam Quintin did not need the daughter of a hunt master. A snap of the fingers and he could have any woman he desired. Such a man would wed a goddess, not a servant.

"Sir Adam has asked me to offer you thanks for your valor today," Mathilda said as they reached the top of the steps.

"What?" Joan could not concentrate on Mathilda's words. Weariness sapped her strength. She feared the bishop.

"For trying to rescue a man from drowning, Joan. Christopher, our minstrel. Well done."

A guard led them to the bishop's chamber. She barely saw the beautiful hangings on the great bed or the servant who directed her to the bishop, who sat at ease in a chair draped with fur.

He wore no priestly garb, but a gorgeous blue and yellow tunic over a yellow linen shirt. The only signs of his holy stature were his tonsured head and the cross on his chest.

Joan knelt and kissed Gravant's ring, then stood before him, hands folded, and waited patiently for him to speak. He considered her with his chin propped on one hand. It was a long-fingered, leathery hand, very unlike the priest's in the chapel who did little toil. This hand belonged to a man who hunted and rode often.

"I have had an offer of marriage for you," Gravant said.

Joan felt faint. "An offer of marriage?"

"My lady," the bishop said. "Have we not had a very good offer of marriage for Joan?"

Mathilda nodded, but did not speak. Nor did she meet Joan's gaze. Instead, she set to work on a linen square embroidered with harebells.

Joan's heart began to thump slowly, heavily.

"Your parents are dead, are they not?" the bishop

asked. "You have only Nat Swan who took you in, have you not?"

"Aye."

"I do not hold your lack of standing against you," the bishop continued. "Indeed, it makes the man who wants you that much more admirable that he will take you with the little Nat may offer. So, it is settled, then. I give my approval. I think the match a fine one and will bless it myself by officiating at the service." The bishop curved his lips, but the smile did not reach his eyes.

She felt numb.

Mathilda said, "I think the marriage should take place as soon as the tournament is over—if Oswald is agreed, that is."

Mathilda approved.

The room tilted a moment, the bishop's face wavered. A sick dread filled Joan's belly. How could she escape this?

"Call Oswald here, will you?" the bishop said to the hovering servant.

Joan remained rigidly upright, her hands clasped before her, trying desperately to think of how to refuse this offer which had the weight of the bishop and Mathilda behind it.

It was but a moment before Oswald entered the chamber. He knelt and kissed the bishop's ring, his red hair falling across his cheeks. He then rose and bowed to Mathilda.

"Joan," Oswald said and took her arm. "I am pleased that the bishop and Mathilda approve our match."

His fingers locked about her upper arm where she'd bruised it at the fish gate. She pulled away, though the defiant gesture cost her dearly.

"Forgive me, my lord Bishop," she said, going down on her knees before Gravant. "I am honored by this man's kind offer, but must refuse."

The bishop frowned. Mathilda merely looked at her blankly.

"What reason have you for refusing?" Gravant asked.

Oswald shifted at her side. She could only see his shoes, fine leather shoes, stitched with red and yellow thread as if he were a lord.

Joan took a deep breath. "I do not wish to wed, my lord Bishop. I wish only to serve my father in gratitude for his care of me when my parents died."

"Nonsense." Mathilda tossed her head. "Nat can fend for himself."

"You can fend for yourself also, my lady, but you have women devoted to your every need. I wish to devote myself to Nat's needs."

Oswald placed a hand on her shoulder and squeezed. "Perhaps it is Nat we should be speaking to. I shall go and—"

"I would prefer you do not." Joan slipped from under Oswald's fingers and stood up. "He will feel as Lord Guy did about our lady. Nat will want me to choose my own husband."

But would he? Had not Nat said 'twas foolishness to allow a woman to decide such an important matter?

The bishop frowned. "You are very sure of yourself. You will find it is best if a man guides your decisions. And I find no fault with this match. Reconcile yourself to it."

"My lord Bishop," Joan said, "you force me to speak more plainly." She could feel Oswald's gaze upon her, but speak she must lest the bishop prevail on Nat and doom her to a life she would abhor. "I do not need anyone to choose my husband or point out Oswald's advantages. I already know what I need to know to make my decision; I know Oswald treats his dogs ill. How a man treats his animals indicates how he will treat people. I will not have him."

Oswald started. "My lord Bishop, we are speaking of people, not animals."

The bishop nodded. "I find no fault in Oswald's behavior, and I have often hunted with him whilst visiting Lord Roger. You are a proud young woman, Joan Swan. Your father and I shall decide this matter."

Oswald displayed no animosity, but his words chilled her. "When another is lord here, you may not be so haughty, for your father may not be hunt master then."

"Then I shall serve him wherever he goes." She curtsied to the bishop. Mathilda took her from the chamber. In the corridor, Mathilda gave her a pat on the arm and left her.

Oswald caught up with her at the bottom of the steps. He gripped her arm and swung her about. "You insulted me before the bishop and Lady Mathilda. It is not an attractive quality in a wife."

Joan took a deep breath. "I cannot apologize for speaking the truth. To do otherwise might have led you or the bishop to think I might change my mind. I thank you for your offer of marriage, but we would never suit. I am sure we would both be miserable. Now, I must go."

He made a grab for her hand, but she jerked free, pain radiating from her wrist to her shoulder.

She felt another pain when she saw Adam. He was sitting beside Mathilda at the head table. Joan's body, still sore from Adam's lovemaking, mocked her.

He is a beautiful man, she thought with regret.

Nay, he was not really beautiful. His was a hard face. One sculpted on the battlefield. He had high cheekbones, a strong jaw, stubborn in appearance, but his features worked in concert to draw the eye and hold it.

She had lost her virginity to a man she really did not know. If she were honest, she knew naught of him except that she had been drawn to him for all the wrong reasons—physical ones.

The same ones that had drawn her to Brian. Luckily,

Brian had dashed cold water in her face with a few choice words. And his men had completed the drowning of the allure by their mockery of her in the village alehouse so long ago.

Now, in trying to save Adam's life through her precipitous leap into the fish pond, she had proven that the visceral pull of the man was greater than any power Brian had ever exercised.

And like a small cinder, like one that leaps from the hearth and makes a hole in one's gown, every touch of Mathilda's hand on Adam Quintin's sleeve burned a hole in Joan's middle.

Mathilda. Sun to Adam's night. Gold to his ebony.

Mathilda's laughter ran through the hall and straight to Joan's heart.

What ailed me that I thought he might want such a one as I, Joan thought? *A woman not much above a servant? A man this compelling, this powerful, will want his match.*

Chapter Twenty-one

Joan waited until the bishop, his clergy, and a few faithful left the chapel after Matins. A wind fluttered the banners on the many tents, snapping them in a sharp staccato tap, tap. Some men, dicing before a fire by one tent, laughed with a touch of drunkenness that made her hasten her steps.

A woman that Joan occasionally saw in the village left one of the tents clustered by the stables. Now that Joan knew what truly went on between men and women, her cheeks heated.

She lingered in the shadows by the castle wall for the man guarding Adam's tent to walk away. Surely, he must be cold, she thought, and would take advantage of a nearby fire to warm himself. If he did not do so soon, she would have to approach him and seek admittance to Adam's tent on some pretext. That pretext escaped her.

Her wait was long, more than a quarter of an hour, and her hands and feet grew cold. But her patience was rewarded. The guard stepped away, hands to the fire, which put his back to the tent entrance—and her. She slipped behind him and lifted the flap.

Adam turned around. His face evinced no surprise. Nor any welcome. In his hand he held a small package the size of a meat tart. He had just sealed it, if the wax and ring that lay nearby on the table were anything to judge by.

"Joan," he said, "how did you get past my guard?"

"I waited until he went to the fire."

He frowned. "I should take you into my company. You could slip into an enemy camp, take their measure, and none would be the wiser."

"Oh. Will you punish him? I could not bear it if you—"

Adam clasped her outstretched hands between his. "Do not fear I'll draw my sword as I did at the fair. I shall merely remind him to be vigilant. After all, if I told him you were here, it might not be to your advantage."

The heat of his hands warmed her, but his words cast a different chill than that of the outdoors. Of course, this would be her second night visit to his tent. Once did not have much meaning, but twice said far too much. To whoever might have seen her. To him.

"I had to speak to you," she said.

Adam held a finger to his lips, then drew her past the partition to the back section of his tent. This space had only a brazier that warmed the space without giving much light. The darkness added to the sense of privacy. The scent of a man, leather, metal weaponry, and the damp furs that covered the floor made it a foreign place to her.

He drew her close, encircling her waist and bringing his lips to her ear. "What is it you wish to say, Sweet Joan?"

His presence was too alluring for clear thought. She pulled from his arms and went to the foot of his bed, warming her hands at the brazier as his guard had done outside.

"I know you asked me to trust you," she began. His

face was in the deepest of shadow, and she found it easier to speak now she could not see his piercing blue eyes. "It was so easy to ask no questions, express no concerns when we were in each other's arms, but when we were in the hall . . . when you were walking arm in arm with our lady, I could not so easily set aside the fears I have."

"Fears? Of what are you afraid?"

"That you toy with me. And if you do not, that you are misled in thinking there is some way to have this"—she swept her hand out to encompass the castle they could not see, but within whose precincts they stood—"without Lady Mathilda."

He no longer looked at her. He might be in contemplation of his boots . . . or be thinking of some way to explain himself. Or . . . he might be stifling his anger that she did not blindly offer trust.

Then he looked up. "Come," he said softly. He held out his hand. A tempting, strong hand. One she could so easily take and within its grasp, forget her cares. Yet he had held Mathilda's hand in the hall.

She shook her head. He came to her. He locked his fingers in hers and put her hands behind her, making her his prisoner.

His lips moved over hers, warm, firm, commanding though they claimed her with great gentleness.

"I have taken an oath that will not allow me to say more than these two words. Trust me."

"An oath?" she said.

"Aye." His lips traveled along her jawline to her ear. "Would you have me burn in hell for breaking a sacred oath made at the feet of the Virgin?"

Although his words were whispered, his mouth warm at her ear, she shivered. What possible oath could he have made that would have aught to do with Ravenswood or Mathilda?

His fingers released hers, sliding around her waist to draw her tightly against his body.

She could not help encircling his neck. The scratch of his beard on her throat as he kissed down to her shoulder replaced the shivers with a flush of warmth. It sped from her breast to her loins as he moved his body subtly against her. He left her in no doubt of his needs.

His breath had grown short, or was it her panting that filled the tent? A warmth within her became the wet heat of arousal.

She disentangled herself. "I cannot think when you do that," she whispered, afraid the guard might hear her. "I must be able to think."

"Think about what?" He sat down on his bed, fingers curled on the edge of the mattress, legs spread.

She could step between those long, muscled thighs and wrap her arms around his head, bring it to her breast—

"Sweet Mother of God." She swallowed hard, whirling away from him, covering her face with her hands. She heard him stand up behind her. He settled his hands on her shoulders and turned her. Dark as it was in this part of the tent, this close, she could not avoid his eyes.

"What is it, Joan? Is your distress caused by thoughts of Christopher? Of Ivo? Or is it because I am a hated mercenary and you cannot forget it? Cannot trust one such as I? Is this what you must be separate from me to think on?"

How could she tell him that all thoughts of dead men and mercenaries had fled with the ache of desire? How could she tell him Oswald wanted to marry her?

"I thought of none of those things. I thought of how much I wanted you just now, and then, I thought of Mathilda." It was not completely true.

"*Jesu.* I want you, too, Joan. Enough that I would—" He stopped speaking.

"Enough that you would what?"

"Nothing. We speak of you, not me. What can I do, or say, to make you trust me? Ask anything of me, save that I break my oath."

"Tell Mathilda you are no longer a suitor for her hand."

"That I cannot do."

A knife-edge of pain filled Joan's breast. "Then we have naught to say to each other. I must go." The words caught in her throat, they were so hard to say. Nausea almost spilled from her lips with them. "By all the saints, what have I done?"

"Joan, you have done naught that is wrong."

Pain in her middle held her prisoner as much as his hands on her shoulders.

"How can I make you understand that courting Mathilda is part of what I must do? It may appear to be heartless, this seeking her hand, but trust me that no wedding vows will be said between her and me. But I *must* play this game."

Adam drew her back toward the bed, sitting down and setting his hands on her hips, looking up at her. The brazier coals were dying and the shadows cast by their dim glow on his face smoothed some of the hard edges of his jaw and cheekbones.

It was a noble's face she saw. No peasant had forged this man. A baron's by-blow, Brian thought—a man whose face was so fine in this half-light she could so easily see him standing, arms crossed on the dais, dispensing judgment beneath an ancient banner.

Did Adam work to attain the honors of Ravenswood because a father did not acknowledge him? It was common enough. Bastards often envied their legitimate brothers.

"Who are you?" she whispered, doing as desire dictated, stepping within the embrace of his thighs. She slid her fingers into his thick black hair and combed it off his face, traced the lines of his brow, his high cheekbones, the

216

bridge of his nose, the full curve of his lips. "Who are you?" she repeated when he did not answer.

"A man in love." He pressed his mouth hard against her breast.

The flame of desire flared into a conflagration of such need, she fisted her hands in his hair and gave a strangled cry.

Instantly, he set her aside. "We cannot do this here. Come, perhaps if I trust *you* with a secret of mine, you will be able to trust me."

Curiosity warred with a need to flee.

Curiosity won.

She followed him, for he had thrown back the partition curtain and tugged her along by the hand. He set her to one side of the tent flap and pressed his finger to his lips. He took a step outside and she heard him speak to the guard, though his words were indistinguishable.

A few moments later, he was back. He picked up a black mantle lined in black fur, and wrapped her in it. "Hide your face," he cautioned her.

He took her hand and led her out of the tent. The guard stood with his back to them, and she realized Adam must have told him he had a guest he preferred to remain anonymous. She kept the great hood of his mantle close about her face.

To her utter surprise, he took her to the crypt. The low ceilings in the crypt and the many souls resting here caused her to shiver despite the heavy weight of his cloak.

"Adam, what is this?" she asked in disbelief when he lifted a section of the floor.

"A simple key and a canny hinge. Nothing magic, nothing to fear. Follow me."

And she did. She held his sleeve and stumbled after him, tripping on uneven stones in the meager light of the candle, his mantle's hem dragging behind her.

"Stay here." He smiled when she shook her head.

"Nothing will harm you; I just want to close the trapdoor lest anyone see where we've gone."

Reluctantly, she let go of his sleeve. It had been an ordinary key he had held in his hand, one she'd seen about his neck the night Matthew had leapt upon him in the river.

So, he had this key in his possession on the first day at Ravenswood. That meant he had been inside this castle before. Or knew someone who had.

"Follow me," he said. It was less a command than a request, and he waited for her compliance.

"As you wish," she said. "I have come this far—I must confess to a curiosity that will not allow me to turn back."

But she held his arm tightly lest he disappear into one of the dark archways they passed as they walked along a corridor with smooth, rock walls, not made by nature, but hewn by man.

"What is this place?" she asked.

"I believe it was part of an old Roman fortress at one time. There's a honeycomb of corridors down here. Most have collapsed, but this one with its vaulted ceiling seems to have lasted. There is but one chamber I wish you to see, the others being empty and naught but cold cells suitable for storing foodstuff."

"Where does this end? And how did you know this was here? Where did the key come from?"

"It ends at the river. As to how I know of its existence—" He hesitated. "I found the other end—a cave—by the river while exploring the castle's defenses. I could see no man had come through here for many years by the amount of dirt and debris lying about. As for the key, that was hanging on a simple hook on the back of the door to the crypt."

There was a note to his tale that told her it was not all of the story, but all she would get this day.

He led her forward and then stopped at an arched opening not much different from the others they'd passed.

"Take my candle and follow the path," he said.

With only a slight hesitation, she took the candle from his hand, looking down. There she did see a path—a mosaic way crafted untold hundreds of years before. She held the candle aloft, fascinated now. She set foot on the path. Hand at her elbow, he led her forward. She had an impression of walls coated in blues and greens, foliage and animals, but had no time to see much more before they had left the room for another corridor. This one was narrower than the one leading from the crypt, its walls crumbled in places, roots protruding from the ceiling.

He led her along more corridors, each one successively more deteriorated in condition the farther they walked. They passed into a cave. It was concealed by a thick mat of roots that hung like a curtain across its back.

Lifting the roots aside, he lighted another candle he took from a crevasse in the rocks. They passed through three more caves, climbing over rubble and past twisted roots that had come through the earth from above, perhaps over hundreds of years. Finally, she saw a gleam of light and smelled fresh air.

They were high above the river, but under an overhang. One needed to squeeze between two boulders to see the water.

"Oh my," she said softly. "This is where you were swimming that first night."

"Aye." He set his hands on her shoulders and pointed. "There's a shallow spot there, a place where the water is still."

They stood together, looking up at the moon. Its light bathed his upturned face. She was struck again by the certainty he was not of peasant stock.

He led her back through the maze of caves to the brilliantly tiled chamber. This time, he walked her about the perimeter, his candle held aloft, and she gasped with wonder at the lovely mosaic work that made the room feel like a woodland bower.

They stood before a simple altar. There were many candles on it, and he lighted them all. Many were candles marked to tell the passage of time. Who had placed them here?

When the chamber was ablaze, she gazed up at a very realistic-looking, and very naked, woman whose hand was on the shoulder of a bowing stag.

It was the Roman goddess, Diana.

"Does she not look like you?" he asked. "It is how I see you. You are my Diana, my huntress."

He stood but a few feet behind her. As he spoke, he took her candle.

"Your huntress?" she whispered, though no mortal man could hear them.

"Aye." He pulled his mantle from her shoulders and spread it on the floor in the very center of the chamber. "It was your skill with the hunting hounds that saved my life the first day we met."

He undid his cross-garters. She put a hand to her heart. It beat so rapidly, she thought it might leap from her chest.

Next, he drew off his tunic and the long linen shirt he wore beneath it. She took a closer look at Diana so she would not see him strip off the rest of his garments.

The candles sent wisps of smoke to the high blue ceiling. Joan remembered that smoke was supposed to carry the prayers of the faithful to heaven. She sent a prayer to the pagan Diana that she was not making a mistake trusting this man.

And if it was a mistake? Why did she not flee down the corridor and avoid these gut-twisting decisions?

Because she wanted to join him on his mantle and know the touch of his hand again and the taste of his mouth.

"Come lie with me," he said.

She knew what she would see when she turned around,

but the sight of him standing in the center of the chamber, his body lighted by the blaze of candles, was magnificent.

He looked like a statue carved in marble, every muscle delineated by light and shadow. He wanted her.

She drew off her loose overgown and let it fall from her fingers to the floor. Her undergown and shift followed.

"Let down your hair," he said.

She did as bidden. Her hair felt like silk as it slid down her back to brush her buttocks. Never had she been so aware of herself as she was in that moment, the cool air on her skin, the sound of her breathing, the scents of her body.

Anticipation of his touch puckered her nipples and sent moisture to flood her insides. She understood its purpose now.

She stepped on the mantle. The fur lining caressed the soles of her feet.

He settled his warm hands on her hips. "My Diana."

"And who are you?"

Adam wondered how he should answer her question. *I am Adam Quintin, a member of a company of men you hate. Or I am Adrian de Marle, son of a banished baron.* Making love to her felt dishonest under either name.

He cocked his head and looked over at the mosaic. "I must be the stag, for it is only he with whom Diana has spent the centuries."

"And the stag bows down to the goddess," Joan said.

Molten heat cascaded through his body as he knelt before her. He pressed his lips to the soft skin of her belly.

She stroked his hair from his brow and as he made the kiss more intimate, her hips shifted—not away, but closer.

Kneeling as he was before her, aware of her near innocence and how different she was from every woman he'd ever met, he knew he would not trade all the silver pennies in his coffers for this one moment with her, this tiny sliver

221

of time, when he knew by taste, touch, and scent that she wanted him as much as he wanted her.

Joan stood with her fingers entwined in Adam's hair and gasped for air, air scented by the dust of the ages and the heat of their arousal. The touch of his fingertips, his lips, his tongue, drove sense away. She wanted more.

When he urged her down on the mantle, she went willingly.

He entered her. She moved with him as if they had been partners for as many centuries as this chamber had lain hidden.

She kissed his throat, now slick with the sweat of his passion, and then sealed her mouth over his to possess every essence of him from the salty moisture to the very breath of his lungs.

Then, as the stag stands poised before the hunter, he fell still as stone. And like the stag who makes a final leap, the hard muscles of his back, thighs, and arms tensed for the last, deep thrust.

She imagined she could feel every scalding drop of his seed as it flowed into her.

It was not imagination that her body screamed for a repeat of the rippling sensations she had experienced that morning. She thought that like a hunter who has missed the stag with his final arrow, she might cry aloud for wanting it.

He must have heard her silent plea or known all too well a woman's needs. He kissed down the length of her body. He kissed the inside of her knee, and brushed his lips up and down the sensitive skin of her inner thigh. Again and again.

Her body went taut as a drawn bowstring. She arched and moaned—made sounds she could not restrain.

He licked up her inner thigh. She blindly opened to him and accepted the intimate tasting.

Lord of the Hunt

He knew how to draw the bowstring so it must break. He did it with his lips, tongue, and teeth. Though she fought it, sensations whipped her like a severed string might lash whatever lay in its path.

Chapter Twenty-two

Adam stood at the altar and looked from the cold Diana to the warm woman who lay on his mantle, her limbs sprawled, gaze fixed on the blue tiled ceiling. A sense of modesty must have overcome her, for she suddenly drew in her arms and legs and rose.

She was shaky on her legs like a new fawn as she walked around the chamber. She plaited her hair, aware of his gaze on her, he thought, for she hunched her shoulders a bit, protecting her nudity from his view.

Adam went to the mantle and sat down. He could feel the warmth of her body on the soft fur. He looped his arms about his knees and pleasured himself with the look of her, from her slender, delicate ankles, up the slim column of her spine, buttocks still rosy from his hands. His cock stirred again.

When she turned, he was struck, not by her full breasts with their dusky tips, but instead by the glimmer of the candle flames in her eyes.

"Can you see in the dark?" he asked. "If I snuff these candles, can you see like the deer can at night as it ranges the hills? Would you find me if 'twas dark?"

His heart beat faster when she walked slowly along the altar, a small smile curving her lips. At each candle, she licked her fingertips, then pinched out the flame. One by one.

Then it was dark—as black as if someone had drawn a mask over his head. His blood rushed so fast in his veins, he could not hear her steps.

He stood up. "Where are you?" he asked.

"Find me," she whispered from the left. He whipped around and put out his hand, but found nothing.

A tiny sound made him turn again, to the right this time. He slid his foot forward to the edge of the mantle and stretched out his arms. "Come. Do not play."

She gave a low, soft laugh. It seemed to come from in front of him so he slid forward again, hands searching the air.

"Joan."

"Adam." His name came as if from the lips of a phantom. It came from behind him and in front of him at the same time. She had spoken only as loudly as necessary to cause an echo.

He turned. And turned again. His flesh was hot. Arousal surged through him with such intensity, he grew hard enough to come apart without even a touch. Sweat broke out on his back, chest, and thighs. The soles of his feet grew slick, as did his palms.

She set her hands on his hips from behind. The intense arousal grew to almost painful proportions.

He realized he could smell her—musk and outdoors, heat and his seed. She stroked her fingers up and down his hips, skimmed his thighs, his buttocks. His eyes were wide open, but he saw nothing. He could only feel, breath deeply, accept her caresses.

She stepped up against him, touching him with the tips of her breasts, the down of her womanly hair. Her mouth was warm and moist as she kissed his back. Then she was gone.

Loss rippled through him. His body throbbed for an ending.

"Joan." He said her name sharply. "Where are you?"

"Find me."

He whipped toward her voice, took a quick step, and touched naught but air.

She laughed—not with the giggle of a Lady Mathilda, but with a low, seductive sound of joy.

This time, he closed his eyes and remembered how he had shot the arrow whilst blindfolded. And so, he smiled to himself as he envisioned his huntress walking naked in a forest meadow, seeking the stag who would come to her call.

He envisioned the shape of her, the gold-brown tumble of her hair, and when the air stirred he put out his arm and she was there. He encircled her waist, drew her in, her back to him.

How perfectly they fit.

When he opened his eyes, he still saw nothing, but every other sense had ripened to her.

"I am Diana's stag," he whispered at her ear, spreading his hands on her hips as she had on him. Her bones were delicate, her skin warm.

He urged her down to her knees. In his mind, he was the stag and she the one he'd chosen for his mate.

He took her as the stag would his woodland lover.

She moaned his name and within moments he was overcome as she met each of his thrusts with one of her own.

Chapter Twenty-three

"Will your father be looking for you?" he asked.

Joan shook her head. "Nat's wonderfully delicate in his sensibilities and would never look in my chamber after I retire. He might say my name, but if I did not answer, he would not know whether I was missing or merely asleep. And he would not seek the answer."

"Good for me." He kissed her brow.

"I hear a river rushing, but I think 'tis only the blood in my head."

"Can you hear my heart beating?"

They lay entwined on his mantle in the darkness. She placed her hand on his chest. "I can feel it."

She climbed astride his body, settled herself on him, and smiled when he groaned. With a shake of her head, she spread her hair out. Then she took up a handful of it and rubbed it across his chest.

"Joan." He said her name with a quick, sharp gasp.

They bumped noses when he raised his head at the same

time she bent to kiss him. Her laughter and his mingled in the chamber and bounced around them.

He fell still, but his muscles were tense as she stroked her hair back and forth over his nipples. He began to breathe quickly when she ran her hair over his belly to his groin.

It was a heady feeling, Joan realized, controlling a man's pleasure. She licked his skin after her caresses. She tongued his nipples. His throat. His ribs. His belly.

"Mon Dieu," he whispered. His fingers were gentle as they smoothed the hair on her head in a rhythm that matched the strokes of her tongue.

The black chamber broke down restraints she might have felt if he were watching. She kneaded every sensitive inch of him, tasted him, whispered her breath on him as her tongue brought him to the edge of the madness that coursed through her veins.

And she knew he felt as she did, for he moaned with every slide of her tongue and the sound echoed around them.

Adam could not hold the moans inside. He moaned again and again and again until the sound had no end and no beginning.

Joan pulled away. Icy air ran over his skin.

"Joan. Sweet heaven, where are you? Come back." He put his arms out in search of her.

She must have felt the shift in the air. "Put your hands down, Adam. I'm still here."

"Why did you stop?" he asked.

"I don't know."

"Joan?" He knew just where she was by her voice and the heat of her. He swallowed her up in an embrace. Unerringly, he found her lips, kissing her gently, but holding her so tightly she couldn't shift an inch and avoid his questions.

"You are thinking something and it made you wary of me again," he said.

"Not this time. I thought only how kissing you . . . that way, made me feel frantic. Here." She took his hand and pressed it to her belly.

He slid his fingers lower. "No more frantic than it made me."

They knelt knee to knee, every inch of their bodies touching as they had their first moment together, in the lodge.

"Pretend we have never met," she said, covering his hand. "Pretend you do not want Ravenswood and I am not a servant. Pretend you'll not hurt me."

Adam swallowed hard; his throat filled with a lump. "Is that how you feel when you are with me? My inferior? You did once kiss me on the lips before any who might have been in the bailey. Did you not think yourself my equal that day?"

" 'Twas a mad impulse. I forgot myself. I cannot do so again. Now, hush, and indulge me. Forget who we are. Let me forget who I am."

"You are not a servant in my eyes."

"I am a servant to Lady Mathilda."

"But you are not to *me*." He pulled his hand free.

"Just for this night, Adam. Indulge me. Now, when you cannot see me and I might be . . . a lady of the king's court. Perhaps even . . . a Mathilda . . . so lovely every man wants her. Forget that my hands are not very soft and my skin not perfect."

How could he convince her she had naught to fear from Mathilda? "Joan—"

She placed her hand over his lips; his words died in his throat. If it was silence she wanted, then that was what she would get.

He gathered her supple body into his arms and bore her to the floor. He kissed her eyelids, lingered on the cheeks she disdained, paid homage to the golden dusting of marks he could not see, but found he already knew by heart.

As he ran his fingertips after his lips, he thought he must tell her how foolish she was the instant they stood in sunlight—so she could watch his face and know he told the truth.

Her hips lifted against him, her thighs opened. He slid into her with ease, for she was slick with his seed.

In the complete dark, he felt things he'd never felt before—how her muscles tensed on him, how her thighs quivered with each shift of his body.

He used her moans to guide him, to tell him when to move more gently—or press harder, or deeper.

"I must end, my love," he said. He hardly recognized the hoarse voice that issued from him. "Forgive me. I must."

She turned her head, holding him as he heaved through his release. He buried his moans against her neck. Then he felt her answering tremors, the quick churn of her hips, the breathy gasps against his temple.

And he tasted the salt of her tears.

Then it was done. She moved away and he heard her fumbling for her clothing. He reached out and grabbed for her hands, missing, then grasping her wrists. With a quick jerk, he held her still. He conjured her face and stared where he imagined her eyes to be, looking into their depths to understand her. "Why did you weep?"

"I did not," she said.

"Let me light a candle so I may see the lie in your eyes."

"You're mistaken."

"I tasted the salt of your tears. Does our lovemaking bring you grief?"

"Nay." She touched his lips with her fingers. "Rest easy. It brings me joy, naught but joy. I was overcome; that is all. It is a womanly thing, I believe, weeping for joy."

She shivered.

"You're cold."

"Aye. Allow me to dress."

She shifted from his arms, and he felt rather than saw her draw on a cloak of distance along with her clothing. With a sigh, he searched cautiously across the chamber to the altar and struck the flint to light a candle. The one small halo of golden light fell across Diana.

"This is you," he said. "You are the huntress and I am surely the stag who pays homage." He found his clothing and pulled it on. "You know that you are probably with child."

"Or will be," she said softly.

He handed her a candle and wondered what she thought inside. Her expression was as shuttered as Richard's lodge windows had been. "I will see to you and the child. You have my oath on it," he said.

Her hair was a wild tangle of gold and brown. It cascaded across her shoulders and breasts. While she plaited her hair, he examined her face. Suddenly, he saw doubt and mayhap fear in her gentle eyes. He put out his hand and smoothed a few strands of hair from her brow. "And if it is a daughter, shall we name her Diana?"

Joan chose to leave the Roman chamber by the river way. If Nat was out and about this early, and found her, he would only see her come from the fields outside the castle, and she could say she had been searching for Basil.

How quickly the lie came to her.

Adam had taken the way through the crypt. As Joan stood on the river's edge, by the spot where Adam had gone swimming the first night, she looked up at the great towers of Ravenswood, now clear in the dawning light.

One of the reasons the Roman entrance was so hidden was the way the towers and walls were situated. Here, at this point where even the river's flow was sluggish, no one on the wall or in the towers could see her.

She stripped off her gown, draped her clothing over a bush, and waded into the shallows, but after her experience in the fish pond, she was loath to go much deeper than her knees. The water was icy cold and gooseflesh broke out on her arms and legs. Her nipples tightened. They ached from Adam's fingers, lips, and teeth. She lifted cold water to her breasts to soothe the ache.

Then she washed away the evidence of his lovemaking. She scrubbed her hands up and down the insides of her thighs, though she imagined it was too late.

The deed was done. More than done. Another reason she could never wed Oswald. A cold thought came to her. Wedding Adam did not assure her she and Nat would remain at Ravenswood. He swore he was here to claim the castle, but how was he planning on doing it without taking the lady as well?

Her skin broke out in gooseflesh. She climbed out of the shallows and used her shift to dry off. A bird swooped near her and she ducked, crying out, holding her gown before her.

It was a raven. It settled on a rock and turned its inky head in her direction. She drew on her gown, knotting the leather thong that acted as her belt.

The raven burst into flight. It rose overhead, into a sky now clear of clouds and filled with pink and gold streaks of dawn light.

As the raven soared down again, its wings in a tight V, she thought of Adam Quintin's device. Suddenly, she realized it *was* a raven. Why would Adam have a raven as his emblem? She stared up at the castle. The former lords, the de Marles, all used ravens on their banners. Their very name meant black bird. Was Adam somehow related to those former lords of Ravenswood?

Nat said he'd seen Adrian de Marle, son of Durand de Marle, in the woods. Then she laughed. She was growing as fanciful as Nat. No de Marle, whether Durand's son or a distant relation, would return to England under banishment. A man would have to be mad to take such a risk. Adam had simply done as others had before him— emulated an admired lord's device.

Adam stood in his tent and washed the scent of Joan away with great regret.

She would never know how much she looked like the Diana mosaic with her hair down, her slim white body standing in the same attitude as the goddess in the mosaic, one hand on the altar.

As Adam dried his face and hands, Hugh swept into the tent. Adam belted on his sword and slid his dagger into its sheath whilst Hugh paced the small space.

"Where are you going so finely garbed?" Hugh asked.

"To see the bishop. He's had an audience each morning with two or more of the suitors. This is my morning."

"We must leave this place," Hugh said.

"When I've not achieved my goals?"

"You cannot wed Mathilda. She'll make you miserable. No lands are worth the sacrifices you'll make to keep her happy and—"

"Hugh. Enough. Ravenswood is worth any sacrifice. There's no argument you may offer that will deter me."

"There are no ravens here."

Adam paused in the act of sheathing his dagger. "No ravens?"

"Aye. It is an ill omen. The ravens abandoned this castle with your father's banishment. I had it from the mews master."

"That's nonsense. They were captive birds."

"Still, no one has seen ravens here since your father left. I'll wager you any amount *you* have not seen a single raven since you arrived. Confess it."

Adam fastened his mantle with the V pin that no one but he knew was a raven, the symbol of the de Marle family. He would wear it beneath the bishop's nose. "You sound like an old woman. When I am lord here, I'll net dozens of ravens and fill the sky with the flutter of their wings."

" 'Tis an omen of sorts, I tell you, and you'll regret every day if you live with that woman."

"Not another word. I'll not be deterred."

Adam strode from his tent and across the bailey to the hall. The sky had brightened over the ramparts and he paused with one foot on the lowest step up to the hall. As he watched, the sun rose over the castle wall, bathing the stones in gold.

The longing, the fierce pangs of anger and desire for revenge that had swept through him each morning he'd been within the castle walls, did not rise to claw at him this time.

Instead, he thought of standing high over the river with Joan and watching a different rising, that of the moon. He thought there could be no one but she who would appreciate the sight as much as he.

He looked down at his foot on the step. Ravenswood was what he wanted, wasn't it? Then he looked over where the hunt master's cottage sat against the castle walls. A lord could do as he wished. And his first act as lord of Ravenswood Castle would be to wed the huntress.

Who would stand in his way? Not William Marshal. He would not care who shared the bed of Ravenswood's lord if that man could hold it for King Henry.

Adam presented himself in a timely manner before one of the bishop's clerics. The young man, who wore simple homespun robes, reminded him that the bishop had little Christian charity. Else it would be Ivo sitting here diligently writing the bishop's letters.

The man gathered up several documents and gestured for Adam to follow. They entered the bishop's chamber. Whatever emotions Adam had expected, they were swept away by the chamber's complete and utter contrast to what had been. The chamber was now that of a man who served God and the church and liked his pleasures. The room held tables for his clerks and a small shrine, as well as hunting boots and a long couch covered in fur robes.

The cleric announced him and then went to a great chest, hefted the lid, and deposited the parchments. Adam thought he would give his right hand to read the contents of those papers.

The bishop wore no homespun. Instead, he wore a fine robe of deep green samite trimmed in white fur. When Adam knelt, the bishop extended his holy ring for a kiss, one ring among others.

"Sit and have some wine." The bishop took a seat by the hearth.

Adam mused on a bishop who required poverty and chastity of his priests, but kept this luxurious chamber for himself.

"You smile," the bishop said. "What amuses you?"

Adam sought an excuse for his smile. "The cat." He pointed out one of the castle mousers, who stalked some corner creature.

"Ah. A necessary evil. Vermin themselves as far as I'm concerned."

Adam sat down and arranged his mantle so the bishop could see the jeweled dagger at his waist and the ribbons tied there.

"I am meeting with each suitor to make a few . . . shall we say, private inquiries."

"Ask me whatever you will."

The bishop was a large man, but not soft, and Adam assumed he spent less time on his knees praying than he did in the saddle hunting.

"It is simple. I want to know how many men you have at your disposal to defend this castle."

Adam shrugged. "I have as many as need be. I have

those on my manors who owe me their days, say one hundred men, most with their own horses. And I have my personal force, another one hundred or so that knows no daily limit as they have no fields to till. I have strong alliances in the north and in the Welsh marches."

The bishop took up a cup. He contemplated the wine inside. "And if another, say Roger Artois, wanted to usurp your personal forces, he need only pay higher wages?"

Adam crossed his arms on his chest and laughed. "Nay, my lord Bishop. No man may take my men from me with such a ploy. They are my men as much as any other lord's who has heard their oaths of fealty. My first requirement of any man who seeks a place in my service is just that. He must seek *me*. And swear to me. And honor that pledge."

"You dismissed a man at the fair."

Adam shrugged. "Not every man is perfect. Is every man who serves you, and through you, God, without sin?"

"And whom do your men serve through you?"

The question was asked. The bishop must seek a husband for Mathilda who would be loyal to the bishop's needs.

"My men serve whomever I serve."

Gravant set his cup down. "The history of England's kings will show you that not all have treated the Church as they should. Some have tried to use the Church to their own ends. Others have seen God as a partner, rather than the supreme being without whom they would not rule at all."

"We all must thank God for our blessings."

"A politic answer."

Adam waited in silence.

"England, and the Church, are ruled by a hierarchy of men, each with his own role to play, whether one is so high as a regent or archbishop or so low as a simple soldier or priest."

"Agreed." Adam nodded.

"It is necessary that each link in the chain be strongly joined to the one beside it."

"Agreed. Men serve best the man they know. It is his call to arms, not the distant figure of a king or pope, that rallies them to arms . . . or prayer."

"You understand." The bishop smiled. "And where will you deploy your arms when king and pope are at odds?"

"Let me be completely honest. I want the honor of Ravenswood. I want the power that accompanies this manor and its strategic location. I want to be lord of Ravenswood Manor. Nothing less will satisfy me, and for that, I would serve the devil himself."

The bishop's eyes widened. Adam held his breath. Had he overplayed his hand? At least the bishop would see nothing but truth in his manner and expression.

"And Lady Mathilda?"

"I doubt it is Lady Mathilda who truly draws any of these men. Mayhap the younger ones will tell you so, they may be dazzled by her beauty, but their fathers are not. They are dazzled by Ravenswood, nothing more."

"And an older man, such as yourself, can see beyond the lady to the real prize?"

Adam smiled. "An older man, such as myself, who has no baronial father, can see beyond the lady to the true prize."

Gravant stood up. "Our time is done. I have a holy office to perform."

Adam rose and went down on one knee. He kissed the bishop's ring. When Adam reached the door, he stood aside to allow a monk with the bishop's robes over his arms to enter. As the monk helped the bishop out of his fine green tunic, Adam said, "My lord Bishop?"

Gravant turned. "What is it?"

"If I am given the opportunity to serve as Ravenswood's lord, I can assure you that I will defend it to the death."

"Strong words."

"It is strength you want, is it not?"

The bishop's face twisted into a smile. Adam almost recoiled. If the man were not donning an ecclesiastic robe, Adam would have thought him more devil than servant of God at that moment.

Gravant gave a barely perceptible nod that was more dismissal than agreement.

Adam did not go down to the hall. Instead, he hid in a nearby privy. He listened until he heard the sound of the bishop and others going down the steps for Mass.

Silently, he opened the privy door, took three steps, and slipped into the bishop's quarters. He might never have such an opportunity again. No guard stood at the door, no clerk copied at the long oak table.

Adam looked around and went straight to the iron-bound chest where the cleric had deposited the bishop's documents. As quickly as possible, an ear alert for sounds of footsteps, Adam examined documents, ignoring the sealed ones.

One thought ran around and around in his mind like a hound chasing its tail. There was no one to go to Winchester for him if he found something of worth beyond Brian's Greek paper. Whether Adam went himself, or sent one of his men, he would forfeit the tournament.

But if he learned the name of Gravant's conspirator, it would be a triumph of sorts. He must depend on William Marshal to reward him.

Adam glanced around the chamber. He knew what he would ask for. He would ask William Marshal to lift his father's banishment. Even if his father chose to remain in Wales for the rest of his days, still, the de Marle name would be cleansed of the taint of King John's banishment.

Adam stripped a leather thong off a rolled parchment. For several moments, he stared down at the words without comprehension. He read and reread the ten or so sentences at the top of the document. Unable to believe, he touched each name listed.

He had found what William Marshal wanted.

The document—written so clearly even he, an indifferent scholar at the best of times, could understand it—was not in Greek, nor was it in Latin. It was written in Norman French—and signed in six different hands.

Six names. Six men who by signing took an oath to Prince Louis.

The flowery phrases, the promises of land, wealth, and favor at the top of the long page, promises made by a French prince, mattered not. It was the names that held Adam in thrall. He rolled the scroll and tied it as he had found it, the words committed to memory.

Each signer was the son of a wealthy and powerful baron, a son who now need not wait upon a father's death to attain wealth and power.

Nay, the men who had signed the document would receive their rewards quite soon—or soon if Louis fared better in England this time and defeated William Marshal.

Adam thought of his conversation with Christopher at their first meeting. He had stated the truth without realizing it, and there was a royal example of sons not wishing to wait for their own time. Both Richard and John had conspired against their father with other kings.

Every action of this Harvest Hunt and Tournament was mummery. None of the sons needed Mathilda. She was naught but an excuse to gather men and take a castle—nay, the castle was already taken. Had been from the moment the suitors had ridden in a few days ago.

Preparations for defending the castle need not be hidden, either. Sharpening weapons, tending horses, repairing armor constituted preparation for a tournament as much as for a battle.

Adam slit open every sealed document with icy determination lest he miss other important information. His wanton opening of the documents would be noticed, but could not be helped. When he had read everything, he looked around. Was it possible to conceal his true reason for opening the documents? If the bishop suspected his papers had been read by an outsider, everyone not on his list would be expelled from Ravenswood.

Adam knew he was an outsider.

He set a candle near the chest and looked around. There, on the table, lay the wax, the bishop's seal. Could he repair some of the documents to make them look undisturbed?

Not possible.

Adam stared at the hearth flames. Should he burn all of the documents? His heart raced as it did before battle. How could he conceal his time here, or make it look less suspicious?

Glancing about, Adam saw the fine jeweled cup the bishop drank from at their interview.

An audience at which the bishop had not asked Adam to sign for Louis's cause.

Perhaps six men out of ten was enough. Surely, six score men could hold Ravenswood. Gravant did not need to waste his time with men whose loyalty he might question.

Adam thought his time at Ravenswood might be very short. And what of de Harcourt? He'd not signed, either. Or perhaps he'd not been asked yet.

Would that make the bishop's true intent too obvious— dismissing the two most worthy bachelors in the land? And without flattering himself, Adam knew he and Brian were the best. Perhaps when the tournament was over, Mathilda would choose a husband from the bishop's group, and all others, the unsigned, would then have to ride out, leaving the castle manned by only those loyal to the bishop, with no one the wiser.

Adam made a painful decision. He must leave Ravenswood and ride to Winchester as quickly as possible, forfeiting all right to be inside the castle. John d'Erley needed these names and Adam could return with his men and lay siege to Ravenswood—if William Marshal chose him, that is.

Could a siege be avoided? Aye, if he could bring his men in by the Roman Way.

Timing was crucial. It would not do to have his men arrive while the tournament was in full swing. That would only ensure that every man was armed and of a fighting mind. Better to time it whilst they feasted, gathered in the hall, many of them drunk.

Adam tossed the bishop's papers in a haphazard way about the chest. He pocketed two rings and several fine chains from a velvet sack that lay in the bottom. A weighty purse of coins he tucked into his tunic. One coin he spun across the floor to lie winking in the firelight so only the blind could miss it.

Joan.

Joan could go to Winchester for him. He could remain in the castle with his full team of men, vanquishing all, collecting armor, horses, and weapons during the tournament. He could delay ransoming back the booty until after the tournament feast.

Joan could let his men in through the Roman Way. There need be no siege—just a quick surrounding of the hall while the feast raged. His men would appear like phantoms in the night and take control before ever the guards on the walls or at the hall doors knew what was happening.

With a new determination, Adam prized the gems from the bishop's goblet. A sound made him turn. Brian de Harcourt stood in the doorway.

Brian looked about the chamber, his gaze sweeping across the scattered papers, the coin, the goblet in Adam's hand.

241

Adam opened his mouth, but no words came out. Brian pulled the door softly closed.

Adam did not chase after him. Some inner voice told him Brian would say nothing of what he'd seen. He might use it at some future time, but he would call no guards to have Adam Quintin, thieving mercenary, arrested.

Adam's knees felt loose in their joints as he took the few steps to the private privy set aside for the lord's use. He tossed the jewels and coins into the black abyss. They would find their way to the moat and mayhap one day, a poor peasant would find them and benefit.

Chapter Twenty-four

Mathilda set a crooked stitch in her square of linen, a wreath of harebells the color of Adam Quintin's eyes. She worked the piece to annoy Hugh. The bishop paced and swore some very ungodly words, going again and again to his ransacked coffer. He had spent the hours after mass questioning servants about the theft of the gems and coins from his chamber.

"You must not fuss so," she said. "It happens all too often. Servants cannot be trusted these days."

"Indeed. The coins will probably be spent in the ale-house, but the gems will be found, I promise you. I sent my men to the village and they're searching every stall and hut."

Mathilda shivered to think of the manner in which the innocent would be treated. She changed the subject. "I do not think Joan Swan was pleased by Oswald's offer, do you?"

"I have told you 'tis foolhardy to allow women to decide

such matters. Men such as Oswald are hard to find. I insist you persuade her to the match or I shall be very displeased."

"I intend to decide my own matters; why should Joan not do the same?"

"In truth, Mathilda, Lady Claris and I discussed this very issue just an hour ago. We think 'tis time I told you who will be your husband."

She studied his face. It was set in stubborn lines. "Father wished me to choose."

"And have you?"

"I will before the tournament is over."

"And at the feast to follow, you'll announce your choice and it will be Francis de Coucy."

Mathilda choked on laughter. "Francis? I can safely say, my lord, that Francis will not be my choice."

Gravant leaned back in his chair. "And why not? He has the necessary wealth and stature."

"Any of the other suitors would be more palatable than that strutting boy."

Gravant leaned forward and snatched her hand. "You will wed whom I choose, boy or man, do you understand?"

Mathilda tried to twist her hand from his grasp, but he only tightened his fingers. "You're hurting me," she cried.

"You have no idea the hurt I can mete out if necessary. You will obey me. Play with the suitors all you wish, but when you stand up to announce your choice, it will be Francis you name."

"I will not."

"Shall we try another name? Del?"

Mathilda felt sick. Her heart missed a beat, then made up for it with a double-time rapping in her chest.

The bishop lightened his hold on her hand but did not release her. "Del is a servant in the wash house, is he not? He, too, was once a boy. And I believe he had your virginity whilst scarcely more than ten and six."

A flush heated Mathilda's face. "What nonsense," she managed to choke out.

"I've questioned the man, for man he is now, and he is quite willing to admit he had you often over the past two years."

"Then he will be lying."

"Oh? About which statement? That he had your virginity when he was ten and six or that he has had you often over the past two years?" Gravant let her hand go. He sat back in an indolent posture, a smile on his face. "Shall I question him again? For all his size, he's not very strong. It only took one splash of boiling water on his feet to make him confess he had been your lover. I have need only to *show* him a pot of water and he will swear to anything." The bishop leaned forward. "I believe he will be useless in the wash house after this."

"Do it. Say what you want. Bring in a legion of men." Mathilda leapt to her feet. "I don't care. Call me a whore. But I'll not wed Francis de Coucy."

The bishop stood up, too. "I believe I misjudged you." He strolled around the table and to the hearth. He contemplated the flames for a few moments. "You have a bit more steel than I expected, but we shall see how strong you are when I take you to Del. He's not far, merely over in the cells below the gatehouse where none of our fine guests can hear him. I shall simply pour boiling water on his feet until you agree to wed Francis. Did you know it takes very little time to wear away flesh from bone with boiling—"

Mathilda vomited on the furs by the bishop's desk.

"Ah. I see you will be touched by the man's sufferings."

"You're a fiend."

"Nay, Mathilda," Gravant said, stroking back the hair from her damp forehead. He handed her a cloth to wipe

245

her mouth. "I am no fiend. I am just a father who wishes to see his son well situated."

"Son?"

"Aye. Francis is my son. Old Lord de Coucy has no idea, but surely, you knew Lady Claris was once my mistress?"

Mathilda nodded, wiping her hands on the cloth. "Is she not still?"

"That is my business. All you need know is that the boy is mine and is impatient, as are all sons, to have what is due him. And the Church will hold Ravenswood through him."

More bile ran up Mathilda's throat. "And you would hurt Del to force me to wed Francis?"

"Oh, I'll be pleased to boil Del's whole body in the wash house if it becomes necessary."

"I shall tell everyone what you are about."

He smiled. "If anyone challenges my treatment of the man, I shall say he is our thief and needed persuasion to admit to it."

"Everyone knows Del is honest."

"Is he? Who will dispute my word? Not the real thief. Not you, now you know what else will happen to the man if you don't cooperate. So, kiss my ring and say you'll wed Francis. And take heart, his mother swears he can be taught."

With her knees shaking, Mathilda did as bidden. She kissed the ring and agreed.

"And Francis has taken quite a liking to Oswald Redhair. So while you are composing yourself to be an obedient wife to my son, see that Joan Swan reconciles herself to the man who will be Ravenswood's new hunt master."

Mathilda nodded. Her hands dampened with sweat.

"Fetch a woman to clean this mess," Gravant said. "And I see you are not wearing the ring I gave you, so fetch it."

New fear brought bile up her throat again. She saw herself bound in the dungeon, water, boiling hot, dripping over her feet. Her voice came out as a whisper. "I gave the ring away."

"What?" Gravant thundered and took a step toward her, fist upraised.

"I did not want it. I gave it away as a token," she said hastily, backing up, but the door blocked her flight.

Gravant reached her in two strides. He slapped her face. The blow knocked her sideways to the floor. "To whom did you give the ring?" he demanded.

"Adam Quintin."

"You get that ring and bring it here. I gave it to you and bade you wear it always. Had I known you could not abide by your word, I'd have boiled *your* toes, not Del's."

"I'll get it back, I swear it." Mathilda struggled to her feet. The door latch was slippery in her hands as she tried to lift it. Her cheek stung. Her teeth ached on the side where he'd struck her.

Adam stepped into the melee of hounds beside the kennels. The deployment of the dogs was as much an art as the deployment of troops for battle. The hunt strategies so resembled those of war that it represented preparation as much as practice at arms. He waded through the huntsmen with their coupled dogs being loaded onto carts, looking for Joan.

She stood near her father, looking up at him. She smiled, then turned to the hounds.

Every man was occupied with his duties. No one save Adam paid her any attention. It was only he who saw it. She held her hand out as if offering a coin, then fisted her fingers and turned them down. The row of coupled hounds froze, then sat on their haunches.

Joan spoke a few words to Nat, touching him gently on the sleeve. Nat smiled, nodded, and went to the row of hounds and gave their handlers some commands.

So, it was not magic between huntress and hounds that made them obey her in such an uncanny manner. Who knew of her hand signals? And why did she use them? To hide her part in the hunt lest other men be offended that a female worked the dogs?

Adam stood arrested by her loveliness. The headcovering she wore might hide her glorious hair, but it also emphasized the long line of her neck. He remembered kissing her throat, burying his face against her soft skin, and breathing in her scent as he spent himself.

A ripple of emotion ran through Adam. He loved Joan's body, that he could easily admit to himself, but the fact that he could no longer imagine riding away from Ravenswood without her gave him a pang of uncertainty about his goals.

He was sure he wanted his family's banishment lifted. He was sure he wished to wear his grandfather's sword and declare to all the world that he was a de Marle. But how necessary was Ravenswood in all his schemes?

How necessary was Joan?

How necessary was meat and drink for life?

As Joan walked among the hounds, he knew he wanted to see her just so even when her hair was gray.

Another ripple of sensation, much different from the protective one he felt for her, filled his body with unwanted desire. He took a deep breath and stood still until his unruly manhood decided to lie down like the proverbial sleeping dog.

Adam waited until Nat mounted up and led his horse to the fore of the army of men and dogs before navigating the crowded throng of men and carts to where Joan stood. "Joan?"

She kept her head down and bobbed a curtsy. "Sir Adam?"

"I have need to speak to you."

"Now? I fear—"

"It is very important. Mayhap we could go into the kennels? I'll wait a few moments before joining you."

She shifted her gaze to Nat and frowned. "We're about to leave."

"A moment. No more."

With a nod, she walked away. He admired her stride, the swing of her skirt, the way the soft wool draped her lush shape.

"How may I serve you?" she asked when he stepped into the empty kennels. She went to one of the great support beams and took down several leashes from a hook. She shook them out, eyes on her task. Her formality puzzled him until he saw Oswald loitering by the kennel doors.

"I need someone to take a message to Winchester for me," Adam said softly so no one but she could hear.

Her head jerked up. "What?"

"I need someone I can trust to take a message to Winchester. You would be back on the morrow."

She bit her lip and looked down at the leashes in her hand. Her long, elegant fingers smoothed the leather over her palm. "Do you not have many men here? Is not even one trustworthy to carry a message?"

It was a slap at mercenaries. Anger filled his voice when he spoke. "My men are trustworthy despite the fact they must earn daily wages. It is that I cannot spare them to the task."

Horns sounded. Huntsmen moved away from the kennel yard.

"And my father cannot spare me." She slung the leashes back on the hook and looked toward the kennel doors.

"Of course he can."

It was the wrong thing to say.

Her face settled into a blank mask. "Is that your assessment of my abilities or your opinion of women's tasks?"

"Neither." He raked his fingers through his hair. "It was a stupid thing to say. What I meant is that your father has a score of huntsmen to do his bidding. Can he not spare you to aid me?"

"Nay. He cannot." She walked past him.

He hooked her arm, gently, mindful of her injury at the fish pond. "I'll pay you."

"Money will not change my mind."

"Joan, I desperately need your help."

Her face softened, her straight brows lifting in question. "Desperately?"

"I wish I could make you understand."

She touched his hand. "What is so important?"

To his great relief, she could be reasonable, even when offended. "I cannot tell you, just as I could not tell one of my men that might carry the message."

"Then send one of them."

"I'll have to forfeit the tournament. I may as well go myself as send one of them." In truth, beyond a fear he should not leave the castle lest he lose it, he did not trust any of his men to do the task. If he said so, he would confirm all of Joan's feelings about mercenaries. Instead he said, "The bishop was very specific that each suitor must field twenty men. If I send even one, I will forfeit."

"Is that so? And what do you lose if you are not part of the bishop's tournament?"

"Possibly Ravenswood. I cannot chance it." This, at least, was part of the truth.

Her hand fell from his. "I'm sorry, but I cannot go to Winchester for you."

He watched her walk away, back straight, head high. Disappointment, bitter and thick, filled him as if he'd eaten rotten eels. He left the kennels, bumping into Oswald.

Adam strode to Douglas, who held his horse. "Ye'll no

like what's planned for ye," Douglas said. He patted Adam's saddle.

Draped across it was a green tunic. A quiver of arrows hung from the saddle. "What the devil?" he said.

Gravant strode to the center of the milling horses and men. His voice, deep and rich, captured everyone's attention. "We hunt bow and stable style as you all know. It suits the size of our party and will bring in a fat harvest of deer for the feast on the morrow."

"My least favorite hunting," Adam said to Douglas. "It is like shooting penned beasts."

The bishop continued, "Lest our suitors think this day is naught but a quiet ride to drive deer into lines of archers, we will vary the entertainment a bit. Each of the suitors is to don the green garb of an archer and take his duties."

Mathilda nudged her horse next to the bishop. "I shall award a ribbon to the suitor who brings down the most deer."

Adam and Hugh exchanged looks. "My lady," Hugh said, "might those who do not aspire to your hand also take part?"

"As you wish," Mathilda said, but she looked less than pleased.

As Douglas helped Adam exchange his tunic for the huntsman's green, Hugh convinced another archer to give up his garb and bow. Servants moved throughout the party distributing green hats. The archers chosen to give up their bows and quivers of arrows to a suitor looked disgruntled to be left behind.

The suitors rode out first, to be placed among other, experienced archers. The remaining members of the party would ride through the wooded hills and help drive the deer into the V of archers deployed in a strategic location. The archers spaced themselves within view of each other and the fewterers held leashed running hounds nearby to track and bring down any deer the archers shot but did not kill.

Oswald deployed as many archers and dogs as Nat. Joan, at her father's side, made a hand gesture Adam now recognized to settle a dog who did not like his post.

Joan rode with a bow across her back, and Adam wondered if she was skilled in its use. The archers were strung out across the two hills as if they were a giant pair of arms spread to embrace the deer the bishop's party would soon drive toward them. As one of the archers, Adam's task was to stand with his back to a tree, bow half drawn, the green of his clothing allowing him to blend with the forest colors.

The archers who made their living at this task were trained to stand for a long time, in silence, bow half drawn, waiting for the stag to come to them head-on.

The archer would hope the quarry ran at him and to the left. Such a route offered the best angle for shooting the beast. If the deer ran to the right, the hunter must turn his whole body and the movement alerted the deer to the hunter's position. Shooting head-on offered the worst shooting angle.

But as he waited, Adam's mind lingered, not on the hunt, but on Joan and her refusal to go to Winchester. If she did not go, there was no one else he trusted to send.

He mused on excuses for leaving Ravenswood that would not arouse the bishop's suspicions. His imagination failed him. In addition, Adam knew if he left, taking Ravenswood must happen from outside the walls. It would be impossible to approach the castle without being seen, and even if he used the Roman Way, it might be a long, bloody siege.

After the tournament, those inside would prepare for siege. There would be no more pretense they were suitors. Mathilda would be wed and the remaining men need only await their promised lands and favor from Louis.

How many other sons did Louis intend to seduce this time around? And once it was known how easily Ravenswood had been snatched from beneath William Marshal's nose, others might join the French prince. England might revert to a state of war.

The cry of the hounds and a blast of a horn told Adam the deer, with their usual perception, had not come through the valley of the two hills in the neat manner planned.

Hugh, not half a furlong away, grinned and shook his head. He pantomimed to Adam that his arms were tired and he would rather be drinking.

Adam returned Hugh's grin. Hugh might want to slip this duty and ride back to the castle for better entertainment there—and Adam could write down all he'd learned from the bishop's papers. Who cared for ribbons? The game was done.

Adam lowered his bow and headed toward Hugh. He heard a hiss and a thwack.

Hugh swayed a moment, then fell like a stone to the ground.

Chapter Twenty-five

"Hugh!" Adam swore and went down on his knee by his friend.

Hugh stared up at Adam in disbelief, one hand to his shoulder. "I'll have that man's balls for supper," he said.

Blood oozed around his wound. Adam drew his dagger. He sliced open Hugh's tunic and the linen shirt beneath. An arrow had passed straight through the fleshy part of his friend's shoulder.

"You have the devil's own luck—it missed the bone." Adam pulled off his green tunic and shirt. He slashed the shirt into long strips, and bound Hugh's wound, packing it well. A cacophony of shouts and snarling hounds told him the bishop's party had arrived.

Mathilda shrieked and half fell from her saddle. Adam found himself pushed away. Her hysterical, hand-wringing display allowed Adam time to pluck the arrow from where it had buried itself in the base of a tree.

He examined the faces of those who gathered around

Hugh. One archer, who had been a stone's throw from Adam, stood with his bow resting on the toe of his leather boot. He, alone, did not watch Mathilda and her women or the wounded man upon the ground. The archer's gaze was fixed on the arrow in Adam's hand.

Francis and Roger joined the milling crowd. Francis wormed his way behind Mathilda, a sulky look upon his face. He lifted a hand and touched the sores near his mouth. On the back of his glove was a mottled stain, shaped like a teardrop.

Roger Artois addressed Adam. "Do you remember Lord Stephen of Gloucester? He died in just such a way."

Adam remembered the baron. An archer trying to shoot straight on at a deer missed, nailing the next hunter along the trail instead.

Only this time, the deer had evaded the hunters, belying the need to shoot at all.

A hand touched Adam's arm. He turned around. It was Mathilda. She held a scrap of linen in her hand. She dabbed at his chest.

"Allow me, sir, you've a spot of blood here." The lady rose on tiptoe and scrubbed his shoulder. The men nearby hid grins behind their hands, save Francis, whose face looked blank, though flushed, each sore standing out in dark isolation.

"Please, I must speak with you, 'tis most urgent. Secretly," Mathilda whispered, swiping his biceps.

A sound behind them, more growl than groan, tore Adam's attention from her to Hugh. "Any time, my lady," Adam said, edging around her to go down on one knee by his friend.

"Should I lose my fortune, I shall not seek employment as an archer," Hugh said. The crowd laughed.

Joan and her father rode into the confusion. Mathilda fussed around Hugh like a nervous pup as Adam and Roger helped him to his feet.

"Leave off, woman," Hugh said when Mathilda reached for his arm.

Mathilda's face fell, but she did as bidden, backing away. She leaned over and lifted Adam's green tunic. She held it close to her chest. "Don't forget your promise," she said.

Joan turned abruptly away. Adam grew conscious of how the circumstances appeared, him standing half naked in the forest, his clothing in Mathilda's hands.

"May I have my tunic?" Adam asked. If he must, he would walk away without it, though the damage was done with Joan.

Mathilda draped the tunic across his hands, clasping them and leaning in. "Remember. I must see you."

Bishop Gravant and Brian de Harcourt entered the confusion.

"What happened here?" the bishop demanded.

Adam took the bishop's bridle that he might speak first. "One of these archers mistook a man for a deer. If they be blind, they should be set to tasks more worthy, such as holding thread for ladies." He held up the arrow.

The hunters laughed and the man who Adam suspected had loosed the arrow flushed as angry a red as his master.

"Whose arrow?" the bishop asked.

The man took a step forward and bowed.

Francis clapped a hand on the archer's shoulder. "A mere accident," he said.

Adam sobered. "An accident, you call it? An inch over and Hugh would be dead. I demand the man be disciplined."

"You overstep yourself. Is it not the hunt master's place to set the archers so they are not in such a straight line?" Francis asked.

Adam saw Joan's mount rear its head as she jerked the reins. Confusion crossed Nat's face.

The bishop looked over the gathering. "It is indeed the

hunt master's duty. Who placed this set of men?"

Nat opened his mouth, but Hugh answered. "I asked Oswald, Lord Roger's man, where I should stand. Oswald placed me, 'tis no fault of Nat Swan's."

Adam saw Oswald and Francis exchange a look. Oswald, who sat on a fat, spotted mare, shrugged.

The bishop frowned. "Oswald, what Quintin says is true, you imperiled a man's life. It was not well done. Now let us discover if there are any deer to be driven."

"I'll take you back to the keep," Adam said, hooking Hugh under the arm. The color ran from Hugh's face.

"Mayhap I was shot to ensure you were short a man for the tournament," Hugh said between his teeth.

"I saw Oswald and Francis holding a clandestine meeting the day of the fair. They might have plotted to eliminate someone of my party so I could not compete. Francis hasn't a chance on the field if I am fighting."

Hugh nodded. "No one has a chance if you compete. No one. It could be all of the suitors conniving through Francis."

Adam frowned. "Pray make no more than one man my enemy. I'll be watching not only my back but all sides as well. I'll be driven out of my wits." He spoke lightly, but meant what he said.

Was the shooting a deliberate act? Adam wondered.

Several of Adam's men helped Hugh into the saddle, but it was Adam who mounted behind his friend. They walked the horse, for the weight of two men was a burden to the hunting steed.

"Have you thought," Hugh said, "that the archer might have meant to kill you, but missed?"

Adam did not speak for several moments. "I did move rather unexpectedly. The devil take it, Hugh, I cannot have you suffer in my place."

"I'll have this paltry wound cauterized and even if I'm

as weak as a newborn calf, I'll be in the saddle and fighting at your side come tournament time."

"You are the best of friends," Adam said.

"I'll exact some payment for this, you know."

The horse faltered and jostled the riders. Hugh groaned and swayed.

Adam tightened his grip on his friend. "What payment?"

"I'll think of something. Mayhap I'll demand you name your firstborn son after me."

Adam thought of how many times he'd spilled his seed within his huntress. And if Hugh was right and someone wanted him dead, who would see to Joan and her child should his enemy succeed?

"Hugh, should Joan Swan come to you for help—"

"Help? What kind of help? Why would she come to me?"

"Just swear to me, Hugh, that if Joan should come to you for help, you will render all possible aid as if . . . as if it were I who did the asking."

Hugh's body rippled through a shrug. "I swear it, but I'm now so curious, I'm forgetting this shoulder hurts as if Lucifer held a brand to it."

Adam kicked his mount to a quicker pace. Hugh rarely complained.

When they reached the castle, he took Hugh to the lower level of the castle where the physician kept his herbs. As Hugh cursed while his bandages were removed, Adam cursed that he'd betrayed knowledge of the castle a mere tent-dwelling suitor wouldn't know.

Adam said a silent prayer for his friend. If the arrow had been meant to kill, it might have been dipped in ordure. Recovery from such a wound was impossible.

Mathilda arrived with a bevy of serving women behind her. Her eyes went wide when the physician thrust an iron among the hot coals of his brazier.

"My lady," Adam said, "you should not be here. This is a man's business."

Her eyes grew even rounder when the physician spat on the brand to test its heat.

"My lady, he would not want you to see him—see this," Adam insisted. "You did say you wanted to speak with me. The time is now."

She nodded and flitted from the physician's chamber, the servants scurrying after her.

Adam handed Hugh a piece of leather to bite on, then stepped out of the chamber to allow his friend privacy for his suffering.

Hugh's roar of pain echoed down the stone corridor. One squeal of anguish came from Adam's left. While searching for Mathilda, he noticed that the harvest at Ravenswood was fat. Every chamber held stores stacked to the roof. He found Mathilda in a chamber filled with racks of apples.

"He'll heal," Adam said with a fervent prayer the arrow had not been tainted.

"You need him to ride on the morrow. It will open his wound."

"Do you suggest I withdraw?"

She looked up at him. "It would be a useless endeavor, a woman suggesting such a thing to a man."

Adam knew 'twas folly to answer such an accusation. "What is it you want, my lady?"

"The ring I gave you." She gnawed a knuckle, her attention divided between him and the way to the physician's chamber.

"Why?"

"I made a grievous error in giving you the ring. I must have it back," she said.

Adam considered Mathilda. She looked far from lovely at this moment. Her headcovering was askew, and her right cheek looked bruised.

259

"I'm not sure I can find it," he said. "So many women give me gifts. I'm rather careless about such things."

Even in the dim light of the storeroom, it was obvious that her face paled.

"I'll be in grave difficulty if you cannot find it, sir."

He decided to test her need. "I'll search for it . . . later," he said vaguely.

She grabbed his tunic. Tears appeared in her eyes. "Please, I beg you. Search now."

"Why do you need the ring so badly?" he asked.

"The bishop needs it."

"The ring belongs to the bishop?" he asked, forcing himself to display surprise. "And why would the bishop give an important ring to you?"

She licked her lips, catching one tear in the process. "If I honor you with the truth, will you promise to keep it between just us?"

He contemplated the cobwebs in the corners, delaying to raise her anxiety another notch. "I suppose I can keep your secret. Of course, I may wish a favor of you one day."

"Anything."

Adam wagged his eyebrows. "I'm honored."

"Sir, that is, I . . . that is," she stammered. Her pale face flushed a blotchy red.

It intrigued him to see how unattractive she could become when something disturbed her placid world.

" 'Tis a jest, my lady. What I really want is simple information. Why did the bishop give you Prince Louis's ring?" It was best she know he recognized the ring for what it was.

Her look of relief amused him.

"Bishop Gravant did not wish to be seen to have Prince Louis's seal and thought it better a woman hold it."

"Why not give it to Lady Claris?"

"She is a gossiping, unfaithful creature—that is why.

And I could explain it away as a love token from the prince. I met him once, you know. He's very . . . compelling."

"And a love token is less treasonous than a ring to mark a document in Louis's name?" Adam touched her shoulder. She shivered, and he wondered if this was the first time she'd considered the significance of wearing the French prince's ring.

Adam believed Mathilda usually did what men told her. Selecting her husband must be a rare instance of defiance. And that defiance would crumble when faced with some physical retribution.

He touched her cheek. "He struck you, did he not?"

She nodded.

"And now, the bishop must need to seal some document, I suppose."

"I don't know why he wants it. He just demanded I produce it."

"Do you not fear I'll tell someone that the bishop is in league with the French prince?"

She cocked her head to the side, a studied posture he imagined she often used on men. It left him cold.

"Are not all of you here because you crave the rewards Louis will heap on you?"

So, she knew of the bishop's plot. "And you do not care if you serve an English king or a French one?"

She shrugged. "I'll serve whomever my husband serves."

Adam felt loath to cause her further distress, but it could not be helped. "I'm sorry, my lady. I'll not give you the ring."

She flew at him, fingers hooked like claws. "You will. You must. I'll see Joan weds Oswald Red-hair if you do not."

Adam thrust her hand away from his face. "What utter nonsense. Joan would not have such a man!"

"Nonsense?" She smiled, but the curve of her lips held

261

no joy. "Oswald asked the bishop for her, and I have agreed to persuade her. Now give me the ring or I'll do just that."

"You gave me the ring to bedevil the bishop and cause me grief because I betrayed my interest in Joan, did you not?" He wanted to wrap his hands around the woman's white neck.

"Aye. Everyone I've ever wanted has wanted Joan. And she is ugly! She is sun spotted and tall and skinny. And soon to be wed and gone from here!"

"Why do you want her gone so badly?"

"If she goes, I'll not need to see Brian and you and Hugh de Coleville stare at her every moment of every day." Her voice rose to a high shrill note.

"But Nat would need to leave Ravenswood as well."

"Why? He can stay in the kennels."

"Joan would never leave him."

"Then she's a fool. And if you don't give me the ring, I'll see that Oswald weds Joan in the next hour."

"You can't force someone to wed."

"Really? You think not?" Tears ran down Mathilda's cheeks, her nose ran. She wiped it clean with the back of her hand.

Adam knew it was misery that made her weep. He understood misery. "How can you force her to wed the man?" he managed to ask in calm and even tones.

"The bishop will find someone she cares for and torture him." Mathilda said it matter-of-factly.

"And whom did he torture for your compliance?"

Mathilda bowed her head. "Del from the wash house."

Adam remembered the laundress asking after the man. Adam pitied him.

He made a decision. "I'll do my best to see no harm comes to you or anyone you care for, but I'll not give you the ring. And I'll not lift a hand for you if you cause Joan any more grief."

"The bishop will be in a rage." Mathilda looked ill, her face white. Her shoulders slumped. "Adam?"

"Aye?" He took an apple and rolled it between his palms.

She watched his hands a moment. "We'll not make each other happy, but . . . if you would but give me the ring, I swear, I will choose you for my husband."

Chapter Twenty-six

Adam stared at Mathilda in surprise. There was a note of desperation in her voice. But Adam knew the bishop would never allow Mathilda to wed a man not on Louis's list.

He bowed and said, "I'll think on it."

The physician stepped into the hall. She grabbed Adam's sleeve. "Help me and I will reward you." She rose on tiptoe and kissed his lips. Never had a kiss left him so unmoved.

Adam watched Mathilda run down the hall. No one paid him any heed as he climbed the steps from the lower levels. Most of the men had not yet returned from the hunt. Only a few of the women were before the hearth, stitching and gossiping. Servants were preparing to feed the hunters. He saw his young page sitting with several others eating meat pies.

He called the boy from the group. "The man who directed you about my sword—had he a mark on the back of his hand?"

The boy's head bobbed agreement, while he struggled to swallow a mouthful of pie.

"Tell me about the mark."

" 'Ere it were." The boy traced a dirty fingertip on the back of his hand.

"Aye, more, lad. Tell me more. What made the mark?"

"Mayhap somethin' dripped on the leather? Or 'twere burned."

"Ah, so it was not a scar?"

"Nay, a mark on 'e's glove. 'Ere," the boy repeated.

So de Coucy had plotted trouble for Adam from the start. The page ran back to his company, and Adam headed for the bailey. There, he assessed the sea of tents. No other man or company could defeat him in the tournament, so if de Coucy held any hope for success, the competition must be eliminated.

Adam's thoughts were torn from de Coucy.

Joan rode into the bailey behind her father. Adam walked straight past her to his tent. He could not look at her, nor acknowledge her. He was too full of anger at de Coucy.

In his tent, Adam stripped and washed away the sweat and dirt of the hunt. He pulled on a black linen shirt and tunic and stood by his table, the sealed package in his hands. He slit it open and set out to write down all the names he'd seen on the scroll along with the terms and benefits offered in exchange for fealty to the French king.

The letter was twice its original length when finished. He wrote of Christopher's death, filled with grief for a man who might have died because of the color of his hair and beard.

Those who wanted Louis on the throne were already within the castle walls.

Twenty men accompanied each of the six signers of Gravant's document. One hundred and twenty men could hold a fortress such as Ravenswood. They could ride out and raid, raid and retreat to the fortress with impunity. Travel on the roads to Winchester, the west country, or Portsmouth would be impossible.

With a touch of dry mirth, Adam realized it was how the original de Marle had held the area in thrall for William the Conqueror.

Were he and Brian soon to be dismissed for some frivolous reason? Nay, he would not believe it. The bishop could not dispatch the two best tournament players in England without suspicion. He would have to let the thing go forward. After the feast, all those Gravant had not deemed worthy of signing would ride out.

Adam knew if he'd not been hired by William Marshal, he'd have ridden out of Ravenswood to learn along with the crown that Louis possessed the castle—unless he was dead. Then his men could be hired on by any of Gravant's recruits and they'd be glad of the work.

Where did Brian stand? Had he met with the bishop, and like Adam, been found questionable as an ally of Louis? Would Brian leave after the tournament, ignorant of the plot?

Adam contemplated the mark on the back of Francis's glove. That set his mind on Mathilda, who promised her hand if Adam returned the ring.

Ravenswood could be his for nothing more than turning over the ring. Adam shook his head. Mathilda deceived herself if she thought the bishop would allow her to choose her husband.

Weariness stalked Adam. His last full night of sleep seemed months before, not days. He leaned back in his chair and closed his aching eyes. He must earn Ravenswood himself.

Whatever plan he formed, he had no one to carry his

message to John d'Erley save himself. Even with a fast horse, he could not get to Winchester, seek audience with d'Erley, set out his plan to take the castle by stealth, have it considered, agreed to, and get back without suspicion falling on him like a pot of pitch poured over the battlements.

With regret, he thought of Joan's refusal to carry his message. If only he could remain at Ravenswood, see the tournament through, and be the person to let the men he'd stationed nearby into the castle through the Roman Way.

His men outnumbered the suitors' troops by at least one hundred. He thought of the many fewterers and huntsmen of Roger Artois's party. How many of them could or would wield a sword? Such men might shoot an arrow at a living target, but rarely wished to fight close in with a sword. 'Twas not their weapon.

Adam looked over his letter to William Marshal's man. Even if every one of Roger's hunting stable raised arms, Adam believed surprise would more than tip the scales.

Surprise from within.

As he finished his letter, he knew it to be a futile wish. Instead, he must ride openly up to Ravenswood's gates and lay siege—if William Marshal assigned him the honor at all.

John d'Erley's words, "A siege is to be avoided at all costs," tormented him. A siege seemed inevitable, and Adam knew he must admit failure.

Who would lay the siege? Would another be given the task, and later, the rewards if the castle eventually capitulated?

Regardless, Adam wrote all that might be helpful. He wrote of the full storerooms from a fat harvest, of the two good wells within the walls, and of the simple manner in which Gravant had taken one of England's finest castles. If necessary, Adam knew William Marshal would order those fine castle walls brought down to oust Gravant's men.

When Adam went to seal his letter, he saw the sheet of Greek writing from Brian de Harcourt's chest. He folded it around his letter to John d'Erley.

De Harcourt's parchment seemed less and less likely to have aught to do with anything, but as long as he could not read it, he must suspect it. He sealed the package and tucked it into his tunic.

He shook his head over the business. It would be far easier to give Mathilda the ring and wed her at the end of the week.

Joan, beautifully naked, hair tumbling down her back, visited his imagination. He began to laugh. He must wed no woman but Joan.

"I believe I would live in a hut in the woods with my huntress, if that was the only way to have her." He shot to his feet. "That is equal madness. Whatever else may happen, I must see the de Marle banishment lifted."

Saying the words reminded him of his duty, but a tinge of uncertainty tainted his resolve. "I am simply weary. I need sleep."

Douglas stuck his head into the tent. "Did ye call me?"

Adam shook his head. "Nay."

"Anything ye need?"

Adam considered his squire's grin. "Aye. Take a message to our lady, would you?" He drew a sheet of paper to him and penned two lines.

Upon reflection, I have decided to retain your token. It is precious, a reminder of all you mean to me. A

Adam sealed it and handed it off. With pity, he thought of Mathilda's reaction. And the bishop's.

He flung up the lid of his coffer and drew out his hauberk.

When Douglas returned, his eyes went round. "What're ye doing?" He hastened to buckle Adam's mail shirt.

"I'm off to Portsmouth," he lied.

"Whatever for?"

"A lady, my friend."

Douglas's face reflected his sour thoughts. "There's plenty of fine pickings in the village. Why must ye go to Portsmouth?"

Adam didn't answer.

Douglas shook his head and handed Adam his sword. "Ye'll not be back in time for the tournament. Ye'll be worth nothing and neither will yer horse." He tidied the table and angrily folded the bed furs. "And I so wanted to pick off that Roger Artois's horse right from under 'im. And what'm I to say if anyone asks after ye?"

"Exactly what I said, I'm in Portsmouth seeing a lady."

They walked to the stable together and Adam waited outside, impatient to be gone. He hoped Douglas would spread the story about that he rode to Portsmouth for physical pleasure, lest anyone suspect him of another destination.

Adam stood in the stable doors and stared up at the high stone towers of Ravenswood. The sun shone on the bishop's pennants. "They will come down," he promised.

Joan saw Adam by the stables. She lifted her hem and ran, heedless of what anyone might think. "Adam, may I speak to you?"

He nodded and led his horse behind them as they walked through the busy bailey. Only Oswald, directing a carter with straw for the kennels, paid them any attention.

Adam held up a hand to Joan; she fell silent in mid-sentence. He lifted a brow and stared at Oswald until the man turned away, scurrying like a rat into the kennels.

"Now, he is gone, what is it?" He tried to soften his tone.

"I've thought of nothing but our last conversation all through the hunt," Joan said. "It shames me that you asked me for help and I said no."

"Don't fret, Joan. Listen to me and listen well. There may be trouble here in a few days. I want you to take Nat and go away. Go anywhere, but not to Winchester or Portsmouth."

Her dark eyes grew wide. "Go away? What trouble?"

"Trust me. Trouble often accompanies a tournament. And this one, with Mathilda the prize at the end, just smells like trouble. I wish I could escort you to safety."

Her brows drew together. "I cannot leave Ravenswood. Not now. And I owe you an explanation"—she could not quite look him in the eye—"considering all that is between us. I owe you that at least."

"Come. You can tell me your tale as we walk. It will provide less amusement to Oswald." Adam mounted up and walked his horse toward the gates; Joan walked at his side, with one hand on the horse's bridle.

She looked up at Adam and said, "Nat is not so young as he used to be. Sometimes he makes mistakes. I fear if I leave him, he might anger the bishop, who is most intolerant—"

"You fear the bishop might dismiss Nat?"

"Aye, the bishop has been at Ravenswood for almost a year. He's a hard taskmaster, but lately, he has dismissed workers for no reason, turned off tenants as well.

"Nat has served all his days at Ravenswood, risen from a kennel man, his father a huntsmen here as well. He deserves to end his days here, not be driven off to look for work in his old age. I cannot leave his side."

"Is that why you signal the dogs?"

A pain, one that had throbbed dully for many months, eased; then alarm filled its place. "You noticed." She wrung her hands. "If you noticed, then—"

"Don't be afraid." He leaned down and touched her

shoulder, then withdrew as if remembering it was not appropriate to touch. "I believe only I have noticed your command of the dogs. I'm right, am I not?"

"Aye. I've needed the hand signals more and more, especially when the bishop is about and Nat is forgetful."

Adam smiled. "You mean he might be telling a story to one of his men and not see that the dog carters need an order to move the hounds out?"

She smiled back. "I have no signals for the carters."

"If the bishop were gone, you would not have this burden."

"The bishop *is* the burden. He has no kindness, no patience."

"I knew a priest once who was much like Nat. 'Tis but old age. We will all be there one day."

"Aye." They passed through the gate and over the drawbridge. When wood and paving stones gave way to the dirt road, she stopped and held his bridle, lest he ride out of her life without an explanation.

"The men know their business. No one bothers if Nat forgets something now and again. Their respect for him and their training allow them to just do as they should. We've all been in harmony for years. Now, Roger and Oswald are here. If Roger wins Mathilda, we must leave, but if another wins her, we could stay. But if the bishop finds fault—"

"And that's why you cannot leave." Adam dismounted. He stood by his mount, stroking the horse's neck. "Mathilda told me Oswald has asked for your hand. It would solve your problems."

"Never," she said. "Never will I wed the man. How could you think such a thing? The hounds don't trust him. Never. I will never wed him."

He watched her face. She met his gaze with wide, guileless eyes. She said naught of her feelings for him. When he left, he might not see her again if the bishop prevailed.

271

He longed to gather her in and kiss her breathless. And ask her why she gave the dogs as an objection to Oswald, but not him.

An idea bloomed in his mind. "What if I learned your signals? Would the hounds obey me?"

"Why would you want to?"

"If I knew the signals, and stood in your place, I could correct any vagueness of Nat's orders, and be here to take the tournament field. I could delay . . . certain events that might arise. Would you then go to Winchester for me and stay there until I called you back?"

"If you could command the hounds, I would go."

Her statement was so simple, so assured, he felt a knife edge of guilt that he could not tell her his true reason for sending her to Winchester.

He skimmed his fingers along her cheek. "You would do that? Help me?" he said.

"You would protect Nat."

It was not a question. "Aye, I would protect Nat for you." And Joan would be in Winchester out of harm's way if hostilities broke out before he could effect a solution to the army already in possession of Ravenswood.

He looped his horse's reins over the branch of a low bush near the castle road. He took her hand, held it briefly, then let it go, wishing he could take her into his arms, and express the gratitude that filled him. "Come, teach me the hand signals," he said instead.

She clapped her hands over her mouth and laughed. "Oh, you must have the hounds to do the teaching. They'll need to know you, learn your smell. See that I trust you."

"You do trust me, do you not?"

There was only a heartbeat of hesitation. But it was there. "How could I not?" she said. She turned away from him and rubbed his horse's nose. "You showed me the Diana chamber. Were you not offering me your trust then?"

They agreed to meet in the fields outside the castle in the first hour after Matins. She would leave at dawn with three of her father's huntsmen for protection and ride for Winchester if he was able to control the hounds.

"Will Nat object?" Adam asked.

She shook her head. "Nay. I'll tell him the truth, that I'm carrying a package for you and you are rewarding me handsomely."

Adam nodded. "Aye, remind him I paid his gaming debts to Lord Roger and that carrying my package will more than repay the favor. Tell him I'm paying you ten pounds and traveling expenses for the work."

"Oh, too much! Make it less, or he'll be suspicious."

"The amount of his gambling debts? And traveling expenses?"

"Perfect. Now, you must get some sleep. You may be out all night if the dogs prove leery of you."

She slid her hand down the horse's neck and across his fingers. He shivered. The gentle caress felt as if someone had drawn a silken cloth over his skin. His voice sounded thick when he spoke. "I'll want more than lessons when we meet."

Chapter Twenty-seven

Adam stood on the riverbank, near his swimming spot, where no guards on the ramparts could see him, and watched Joan come across the fields toward him with the stride of a woman who had no pretensions, who knew where she belonged, and with whom. Adam wished for such surety in his own life.

Behind her trotted a troop of hounds: greyhounds, a lymer, several alaunts, and running hounds.

They met on the riverbank, by a flat rock. She smiled, but did not touch him. Instead, she held her hands very stiff at her side, fingers together. The dogs sat like sentinels at a mystical gate, stiff and straight.

Joan turned from the dogs to where Adam stood. Dark clouds roiled across the sky, snuffing the meager light, casting him in shadow. Wind whipped her skirt and snapped her mantle against her legs. Something, turbulent as the storm that tossed the river water to a frothy mix, swept through her as well.

He put out his hand in a signal as ancient as any man had devised. She slid her fingertips across his warm palm. He pulled her close, then crushed her against him.

His mouth was as hungry as it had been the first time. She burrowed into his mantle for his warmth. *I love you,* she wanted to say, but held silent. He must say it first.

He ended it, setting her away with two firm hands on her shoulders, and turning toward the waiting dogs.

"I've brought the most important dogs," she said, trying to sound as efficient as possible lest he doubt her abilities. "These dogs lead the others. Most of my commands are hold and release orders. Sometimes Nat is telling a story or studying the flight of a hawk and forgets to release them. Then I do so with a signal."

"The huntsmen and fewterers don't know when to let them loose?"

"Oh, aye, but the huntsmen always look to Nat for their orders. But if the dogs go, the men go." She smiled and shrugged. "It is just so. Nat can fail to give the order, but the huntsmen will move if the dogs move."

And so Adam's lesson began. Within an hour, he had Joan's signals by heart. The hounds knew them already, so it was just a matter of teaching him. The hounds gave him their instant allegiance, perhaps because Joan's scent and his were so entwined.

A short while later, Joan pointed at the milling dogs, who now ran and frolicked by the water's edge. "Give them the signal to gather."

Adam did so. When one hound caught the signal, he woofed and the others drew around.

"Now release them," Joan said.

Instead, when she turned her head, he gave the signal for them to sit like statues. The dogs lined up and stared at her.

"Oh, dear. What's wrong?" Joan held his sleeve. "It was going so well."

"I guess we'll need to continue. We have a few hours more." But he couldn't help smiling.

"You're teasing me." She tucked a few strands of hair back into her plait. "That will not do."

"I wanted more time—for us." He tugged on the leather thong that held her hair. The wind whipped it loose in glorious disarray about her shoulders. Blood sang in his veins at the sight.

"You have as much time as you wish." She looked down, the leashes wrapped about her fist. "I could take the hounds home . . . then come back."

Adam sat on a rock at the river's edge and waited impatiently. He felt as if half the night was gone, precious hours he could never reclaim. Then he saw her.

A low mist lay on the fields and it parted before her in an eerie swirl. She looked like an ancient goddess in the silvery light. Coming to him for one purpose only—to lie in his arms.

He stood up slowly and waited for her. She walked straight into his embrace. Her cheeks were cold and he threw his mantle about her, drawing her to the spot where they could climb to the caves.

"See that stack of rock?" he asked.

"Oh, aye."

"If you climb it, you will come to the entrance of the Roman Way just about where the water has stained the rocks."

Joan looked where he pointed. "I see the mark."

"I doubt you will get lost once you have found the opening, and I've left the trapdoor in the crypt unlocked, should you ever need it. Come, we'll see if you can navigate your way up there."

"I cannot imagine why I would need to," she said.

The climb was easy once you knew the route. When they reached the top, Joan felt her stomach begin to dance

about. She had returned to make love with him. She'd tried
to deny it as she'd put the hounds to bed, but once she
crossed the field and saw him waiting, there seemed little
point in denial.

"I want you to promise to seek Hugh de Coleville
should you ever find yourself in danger."

"You are so solemn. What ails you?"

"A tournament melee is dangerous. Men as able as I
have fallen there."

"I'll not see the tournament—"

"Have you ever made love in the open air?" he asked
abruptly.

"Foolish question," she whispered as he drew her close.

"Aye. I should know, shouldn't I?" He kissed her forehead. "If you are with child, I will see to it, I promise."

Her belly churned a bit.

"You say nothing." He lifted her chin. "You surely
know that we cannot lie together as we have and not make
a babe."

"It will be as God wills."

"And will you take a mercenary to husband, if need
be?" His words were whispered across her lips, yet she felt
their import deep within her body.

Could she wed a mercenary? One who'd risen through
the very Flemish company that had orphaned her?

He lifted her chin. "Joan. Three men are responsible for
your family's deaths. Only three. Not a company. Not
every man who followed after them."

Her throat hurt. "I know you're right."

" 'Tis said you have one passion—the hatred of mercenaries."

Joan heard the urgent need in his voice to know her
heart. "That was true—once. Nat helped me make peace
with what happened. Nat and helping with the hounds.
But I remember sometimes. I cannot help it."

"Could you wed a mercenary?"

"Are you saying you'll want to wed me if I'm with child?"

"I will want you even if you are not."

How warm was his body, how strong his arms. She relaxed against him and knew he felt as aroused as she.

When he spoke, his breath was warm on her temple. "You may return from Winchester to find Roger or possibly Francis has been chosen by Mathilda. If so, if 'tis Roger, you might want to reconsider Oswald's proposal. It would protect Nat in a way I cannot. Yet, I ask if you will wed me."

She leaned back, looked up into Adam's face, and gave him only half an answer. "I cannot lie with Oswald."

It was an equivocation. Could she take Nat away from Ravenswood to one of Adam's manors? Should she wed Oswald to see Nat happy? Had she been lying to the bishop and herself when she'd said she would never wed the man?

Adam pulled her tightly against his body. "I know it is cold, but lie with me. Now. Here."

She stepped only as far away as necessary to reach for the laces at his throat. She stripped them open, slowly, and then rose on tiptoe to plant a kiss on the beat of his pulse. A soft sound penetrated the haze of his allure.

"It sounds like one of the dogs." She broke from Adam's embrace and clambered cautiously over a tumble of rocks. "Adam. Oh, my God. Adam, come."

She reached the dog where he was trapped, his paw wedged in a crevice. He lay in a puddle of water. "Oh, Basil," she whispered, releasing his foot. He crept into her lap.

Adam went down on his haunches at her side. "Is his paw broken?"

With a practiced hand, she ran her fingers along the dog's legs and paws. "Nay. No bones are broken. Look—"

She showed Adam a ragged piece of rope tied to his collar. "He's chewed through this."

"That answers the question of what happened to the dog. He must have run away."

"Nay, Adam. We do not use rope to tie our dogs, and they are not collared in the kennel. This was done to him by another."

Adam undid the rope and wrapped it about his fingers. "Why not just kill him? Why tie him up somewhere?"

Joan rubbed Basil's ears. "To discredit Nat."

"Then why not kill him?"

She shrugged. "To return him later and reap the praise . . . Oh God, this must be Oswald's work. He, alone, would benefit from finding Basil. He reported our trouble to the bishop, you know. It makes Nat look incompetent and him . . . oh, I hate Oswald. And to think he wants to wed me."

Adam took her hand. "I'm assuming you'll resist the man's allure."

She smiled and ducked her head. "Just thank God whoever did this has some mercy in him, and thank God for the rain as well, or Basil would be dead, caught here with no food. At least he had water to drink."

Joan looked at Adam over the lymer's ears. "Whether it was Oswald or another, someone did this to blame Nat."

Uncomfortable, Adam said. "I've already mentioned the dog's loss to Mathilda. When we spoke of Christopher."

"If I take Basil home, there will be a dozen questions to answer. I'll be endlessly delayed. But Nat must have this dog back."

She stroked Basil's nose. He licked at her fingers and gave a soft woof.

"I'll take him back." Adam combed her hair from her brow. "Let's get him up to the caves and dry him off."

Involving himself with the dog meant risking Nat's recognition again, but it could not be helped. "When you're gone," he said to Joan, "I'll simply go swimming and find him."

Adam carried Basil up the stony way to the caves. Once inside, he laid his mantle out and this time, instead of inviting Joan to lie there with him, he coaxed Basil to the center and scratched his ears until he settled, nose on his front paws.

Joan noticed the moon had set behind the trees. "We have no time," she said.

"No point in wasting it with sleep." Adam drew her close and kissed her.

His tunic served as a place for her to kneel when she had set aside her gown. Garbed only in her shift, she could feel the rising winds as they crept like fingers across the rocks.

She moaned in her throat when he pulled off his shirt and knelt before her.

"What man with wits would think you plain?" he asked, smoothing his fingers across her cheeks.

"I've freckles. I've a scar." She touched her temple.

" 'Tis a tiny mark. I have my own." He took her fingertips and kissed them, then drew them to his eyebrow.

"How did it happen?" she asked, tracing the fine shape of his bones from eyebrow to jaw.

"I challenged a mercenary for command of his men. He was a mean brute and used them ill. I knew if I treated them with respect, they would follow me to the death." He smiled. "And I confess, it helped that I paid them better."

She covered his hand and drew it to her breast. "Did you carve your mark in a woman's breast?"

"Answer that question yourself." He traced his V on her breast over and over.

" 'Tis strange, but when you touch me so, I feel it here." She cupped her hands over her mound.

"Sweet Joan. It is passion you feel."

He took her hands and placed them over the hard line of his manhood. "When you look at me thusly, I feel it here."

He shuddered when, without his urging, she caressed him from the warm fullness of his sack to the tip of his cock. When he could bear it no more, he undressed her. Soon, there was naught between them. He felt a throb of blood in his groin and when he put his hand to her breast, her heart beat with equal speed, rapid and hard.

He thrust his fingers into her hair and kissed her forehead, brows, and eyes again and again.

"I am afraid of what the morrow will bring. It's hard to leave my father in your care," she said, turning her face into his palm.

"I'll honor my promise to look after Nat. You've heard tales of me that are not true."

She traced a V on his chest.

"Once, I lay with a whore. She was not so very young and not so very pretty, but she made me laugh at a time when there was little laughter in my life. When we were finished with each other, and I took my leave, she begged me for a token. I had naught to leave behind, so I took up a stick and with the ashes of the fire, I wrote my V upon a scrap of my shirt.

"She held it to her breast and said she would treasure it. Some of the ash was transferred to her skin. To my great amusement, she flung open the shutters as I rode away and displayed her breasts, calling her adieus. My men saw the mark and have teased me ever since. Thus, through time and gossip, the legend has grown." He drew a V on her breast with the edge of his finger. "And if I could mark you so all would know you were mine, I would."

She wrapped her arms about his neck. She gently bit his lower lip.

"Kiss me everywhere," he said.

She hesitated for one heartbeat, unsure until she touched her lips to his chest. His answering moan emboldened her. In that moment, she felt like the goddess in the Roman chamber, in command of his body, able to bring him to his knees.

She pleasured him with her tongue, hunting through the crisp hair on his chest for his nipples, and stroking them hard. She kissed his shoulder, his throat, and finally his mouth with a hunger she had not known was possible. At the same time, she drew her nails down his hard belly to his manhood.

He lifted her, parting her legs that they might encircle his waist. She cried aloud at the feel of him sliding into her. Then she could only hold him, his breath panting hot and moist on her shoulder as he moved. Each powerful stroke of his body sent jolts of sensation through her.

Then he ended it, pushing into her, holding still, groaning her name. She cried out her ecstasy, then sagged in his arms. He eased her to the ground.

His breath was warm on her skin as he spoke. "There is a legend in these parts that the stag is saved from the boar by a huntress and from that moment, she owns his heart."

She rubbed her thumb on the scar through his eyebrow, then combed his black, thick hair off his face. "What does a man mean by such noble words?" She held him still by his hair, clasped at his nape.

Then she pulled him up and kissed him.

The feel of his hair sliding on her breasts puckered her nipples and she whispered a request. When he complied, his hair slid along her skin, warm and heavy, as much a caress as his lips closing on her nipples. He teased first one, then the other, licking fire across her heart.

"Diana, magic commander of the hunting hounds, I have found you at last, here at Ravenswood," Adam said, lifting his head from her breast and gazing into her eyes.

"Adam, rescuer of maidens in distress," she countered, attempting to mimic his light tone, but her voice cracked and went breathy, for he had bent his dark head again.

He dragged his tongue along her throat with agonizing slowness. She began to shake. His hands journeyed over the lines of her body, along her sides, over her stomach, down her thighs, across her mound. He never lingered, just stroked her and soothed her as she might an ailing hound.

"Diana—"

"I do not want to hear legends, Adam Quintin. Be still."

He stopped talking, but his body shifted subtly against her. Then he said, "But I know one you'll want to hear."

She could not help smiling.

"There was a stag who was rescued by a fair maiden named Diana, or was it Joan? I forget. So, the stag was taken deep into the forest and held captive there for a year until every wish was granted."

"I am not a fair maiden. And your tale makes no sense. Whose wishes were granted? The stag's or the maiden's?"

He laughed.

It did strange things to her body to feel his move so sharply against hers. He was all hard edges, a honed warrior, forged in battle. And she loved him.

"Joan, a woman should not point out the inconsistencies in a man's tale. A woman should just listen and marvel at his cleverness. To do otherwise would be to risk punishment."

"Punishment?"

"Aye. Like this." He rolled her over to lie atop him, cupping her buttocks, and pressing her down on his aroused body. Then he kissed her.

It was invitation, not subjugation.

It was a gift, not a punishment.

She accepted the offer, the light feathering of his lips on hers, the slow drag of his warm tongue after them. He kneaded her with his palms and she could not stifle the groans of pleasure he evoked with every subtle flex of his fingertips.

Her arm was still sore, weak, but she forced herself to embrace him as he did her, holding him close. Whatever fear she felt of him and who he was fled before the tide of his ardor. The scent of him, his skin, the taste of his mouth, the strength of his hands, washed all concern away.

The cave was quiet. Water dripped somewhere. The dog snuffled in his sleep. Adam breathed deeply, then shifted her to her side.

She stroked her fingers on the line of black hair that ran down his belly. "You are a lovely man," she said.

She bent over him and traveled the same path with her tongue. He held her head and arched in to her caress. When she sat back, he subsided, letting out a long sigh.

He opened his eyes and touched her cheek with the tips of his fingers. "Did I tell you the tale of the boar who met a huntress in the king's forest?"

"Nay, but I'm sure you will."

He pinched her nose lightly. "This huntress kept a respectable tongue in her mouth. And she met a wild boar. A magic boar."

"Of course it must be magic," she said.

"Aye. The huntress, cornered by the beast, commanded him to let her pass. He said that if she could answer a riddle, he would let her go without harm."

"Oh no. A riddle. I am hopeless at riddles."

He played with her hair. "The huntress agreed to try the riddle because she was an adventurous woman. The riddle the boar posed was this: What is it men truly want?"

She burst into laughter. But when Basil woke and woofed, startled from sleep, she lowered her voice to a whisper. The dog edged along the cave floor until he was lying against Adam's hip. She made to shift the dog, but Adam shook his head, and Basil fell asleep again, stretched out against Adam's flank.

"This is a sorry thing," she whispered.

"What is? My riddle or this hound, who is a much less appealing blanket than you?"

"Passing off the oldest of riddles as one of your own."

"Then answer it, if 'tis so simple. What is it men truly want?"

"Your riddle is an old one posed by an ugly witch to King Arthur. And it was, 'What do women really want?' "

He pulled on her hand so she leaned forward over him.

"Men. Women. 'Tis all the same." He wrapped a hand around her neck and held her for a kiss. "Answer it."

"What do men truly want? To have their own way." She whispered the words.

"Allow me my way," he said, rolling her over once, twice, her legs splayed open about his hips.

She lost her thoughts, driven like the beasts of the forest before the hunters, driven some place where sense was dormant and caution lost.

Joan watched Adam sleep. His face looked very young in the pale light of the breaking dawn—a noble face. Who was he?

She woke him. They walked to the edge of the rocky ledge and looked over the river. A faint gray light picked out the tops of trees. She must go to Winchester but did not know why.

They stood on the precipice, completely naked, hand in hand. The wind tightened her nipples and brought gooseflesh out on her arms and legs.

"I feel wanton to be standing here like this," Joan said.

"No one can see you, save me, and I don't think you wanton. I think you're the most desirable woman in the kingdom."

She shivered and laughed nervously.

"Let me warm you."

"I'm not cold. I'm afraid."

"Do you regret agreeing to help me?"

She shook her head, laying her hands on her breast. "Nay, never."

"Let me hold you. *Jesu.*" He backed away from Joan. Basil stood before him growling, snapping, inches from his manhood.

"Basil." She swept her hand out and the dog sat, tail wagging. "I offer you my humble apologies. I fear I gave the hand signal to guard without realizing it."

"Guard?"

"Aye, watch."

She crossed her hands on her breast. The dog rose and stood facing him. Unmoving.

He took a step toward his braies near her feet. The dog limped, baring his teeth, growling low in his throat. Adam hesitated, one hand out. "Will he—"

"Aye. He will attack you if you come any closer to me."

"*Jesu,*" he said softly. "Are all the hounds trained to guard you like this?"

"Almost all."

"Can you call him off?"

She swept her hand out, parallel to the floor, and the dog lay down, head on its paws.

"Teach me," Adam said, cupping her face, kissing her hard.

Chapter Twenty-eight

Joan buckled the straps of her saddlebags, which lay across the table. The light from the door was blocked and she looked up, expecting to see Nat. Instead, Mathilda stood there in the pink shades of dawn light, in glorious splendor, an ivory mantle set back over her shoulders to show a gown the color of Adam's eyes. Dozens of small braids and blue ribbons tied her hair up in a coronet about her head.

"My lady?" Joan curtsied.

"Where have you been?" Mathilda set her little foot on the stone floor as if she might soil her dainty leather shoe. Then her gaze went to the saddlebags. "Where are you going?"

Joan ignored the first question. "I am going to Winchester."

"I thought so. What of your duties?"

"I have no duties that prevent my going." Joan closed the saddlebags.

"You carry something for Adam Quintin, do you not?"

Joan silently cursed. It had taken much persuasion to get Nat's permission to leave. In fact, at first, he had been confused and alarmed. It was the prospect of the pennies she would earn that had finally reassured him.

Guilt that she was leaving Nat, even for a moment, settled on Joan like a mantle too heavy for her shoulders. Now, Joan regretted that she had not told him 'twas a secret.

"What are you carrying?" Mathilda persisted.

"It is not my place to say."

"You don't trust me." Mathilda spread her skirts out and sat across from her at the table. She lifted a cloth from the bread and butter Joan had laid out for Nat.

"It's not a matter of trust, my lady. It's a matter of the tale not being mine to share."

"At chapel, Brian said he would never trust Adam Quintin. You and I know Brian well, you more than I, but we do know *Brian's* word is spotless. If *he* doubts the value of Quintin, how can we then trust the man?"

"And how will you choose a husband from among these suitors if you rely on one of them to direct you? Brian is jealous."

"Is he?" Mathilda tore the heel from the bread and chewed it. "I do not believe him jealous. He is concerned that two women he knew as close friends might be taken in by a handsome face and fine figure. Have you forgotten Quintin's company is composed of mercenaries? Mercenaries killed your parents. Such men are a necessary evil, I grant you, and might have the strength to hold this place, but their leader may also be a treacherous beast."

"Then why did you not dismiss him at your love court?"

Mathilda smiled and smoothed her skirt. "Dismiss him? I intend to wed him."

Joan felt as if a knife had been thrust into her breast. She squeezed her fingers around the saddlebag straps lest she betray herself in some way. Her voice sounded too high when she spoke. "Why? You just said he's untrustworthy. A mere mercenary."

"He is also very, very handsome . . . and my desires are different from those of other women." She stood up, sweeping crumbs from her skirt. "In fact, he and I have struck a bargain."

"A bargain? When?" Joan's fingers jerked on the straps.

"After the hunt."

Joan stared at Mathilda, thunderstruck. After the hunt she had gifted Adam with her secrets, her trust, her body, her heart. "I don't believe it," she whispered.

"Then you're a fool. He's using you for his own purposes. Have you thought that Adam might be a traitor? That he might have sold his services to Prince Louis?"

The veil of joy from Joan's night with Adam was torn away like a scab from a wound. "You speak nonsense. William Marshal defeated Prince Louis."

"Did he? When is an ambitious prince ever defeated? Haven't you heard the gossip that someone here, one of these suitors, works for Louis, and so, against our king?"

Heat spread from the wound in Joan's breast, carved wider and deeper with every word Mathilda uttered.

"I've heard nothing of such things," Joan said.

"You've been cloistered like a nun in our kennels then, and I hold myself responsible. But you must understand what I am saying. Think, Joan. If you wanted to take a castle with stealth, from within, would you not send a man who could seduce others to him, both men and women?

"Think of how seductive is Adam Quintin. I'll wager he's had half the women's skirts about their heads in just these few days. The serving women trip over their feet for watching him. Tell me you've not been one so used."

Joan plucked at the buckles of her saddlebag. "I've not seen anyone fall on her face."

"Then you see only what you wish. Lady Claris says he has been quite free with his favors in her direction as well.

You do know what she means by that, do you not?"

"I'll not believe such a thing." Joan's throat went dry; her heart thudded uncomfortably in her chest.

"Can you, at least, believe the man is as seductive as Lucifer? Think of his handsome face, his—"

"Is there aught else you wanted?"

Mathilda stiffened at Joan's interruption. "Pray forgive me if I overstepped my bounds." She went to the door. "I have but one more thing to say. You are terribly innocent. You have lived in a world of simple animals. Don't be taken in by Adam's pretty face. Oh, and lest you disbelieve Lady Claris is his lover, she says he has terrible bruises on his ass."

"And you still want him?" Joan whispered.

"He'll not take lovers after we are wed." There was no triumph on Mathilda's face. Nay, Joan shrank from the pity she saw there.

Mathilda hesitated in the doorway, turned, and dashed back across the cottage. She enveloped Joan in a cloud of flowery perfume. "Oh, dear friend. We were friends once, were we not? I cannot see you hurt."

The embrace sent pain down Joan's arm and more through her heart. A heart shattered beyond repair, not with weapons, but with words. Nay, a single word.

Bruises.

Mathilda cupped her face as Adam had. Joan looked at the purity of Mathilda's complexion, the beauty of her golden hair, the perfection of her rose-red lips.

"I know how to control such a man, Joan, you do not. Think with your practical head, not your womanly heart. Do not be deceived. If 'tis true a traitor lies within these walls, he cannot take this castle or defend it later without an *army*. He must summon them. Is that what you carry, Joan? A summons?"

Mathilda kissed her cheek and drew away, closing the edges of her mantle over her gown. "Or, mayhap I misjudge him. Mayhap it is simply the missing jewels and coins from our lord bishop's quarters you carry." She held out her hand. "Come, give me the package. I'll open it, see what's in it, and if I'm wrong, I'll apologize to the man."

"I cannot," Joan said, her voice barely above a whisper.

"I could order you to do it."

Joan stood up. "I beg that you do not."

They faced each other and Joan held her breath. Refusal might mean dismissal.

Mathilda slowly dropped her hand. "As you wish." She left in a swirl of skirts.

Joan sat heavily at the table, the saddlebag before her. Mathilda thought her a fool. She had not said the word, but still, she had meant it. Was she a fool? Was Adam a traitor? A man who ruthlessly used her?

Something crackled and Joan looked down. Adam's package lay in her hands. She had pulled it from the bag without thinking. Should she have given the package to Mathilda?

Joan weighed the bundle of parchment tied with twine and sealed with a deeply incised V. She wondered if she could recognize guile. She knew beguilement. And how often had she been beguiled by a man in the past?

Once. Brian de Harcourt.

But she had not erred in her beliefs of what he felt for her. Brian had loved her.

Richard? A fleeting affection that was mostly on his side, and which had likely dissipated with every mile from Ravenswood he'd ridden.

Adam beguiled her. He filled her thoughts at every moment. And what did she know of him? Almost nothing. And yet, she had given herself with complete abandon.

A voice in her head said, "Nay, he has compassion, kindness."

Another voice, a kennel lad's, whispered, "His hair is

291

black. His tent is black. His clothes are black. He draws a bow left-handed."

Her stomach knotted, a feeling she'd experienced all too often since the coming of the suitors. She jumped to her feet. She paced, Adam's package in her hands.

The hounds trusted him.

Was Adam Prince Louis's man? Could a man who cared about a mere minstrel's fate also be a traitor?

By helping Adam, was she betraying her king? Nat set great store on one's loyalty and honor. His favorite stories were of the time William Marshal had hunted at Ravenswood. And William Marshal was the regent—loyal and dedicated to the Crown.

Why could Adam not tell her what he was about? He'd sworn an oath, he'd said.

To whom?

Was it possible to find him? Speak to him one more time? Would she be able to read his loyalties in his eyes or detect guile in his words?

He was swimming. So he could find Basil. Joan remembered the lymer lying so trustingly by Adam's side in the cave.

A terrible, aching thought twisted the dagger in her breast. Had Basil been stolen, not to discredit Nat, but instead, so she would be grateful to the finder? So she would then agree to carry a package of treasonous documents to Winchester?

She desperately wanted to weep. She crushed Adam's package to her breast and closed her eyes, saw him standing naked in the center of the Diana chamber, lighted by candles.

Desire and fear warred within her.

Bruises. One simple word to taunt her, make her doubt. But how could Lady Claris know he was injured unless—

A ferocious jealousy filled her. Was this how the dogs felt when they hunted? Ready to tear something apart?

Lord of the Hunt

As quickly as the fire of jealousy flared, it spent itself. She wanted only to weep, to drive off the visions now filling her mind. Adam with Lady Claris. Herself on her knees touching and learning him in intimate ways that would shame her to the day she died if he were treacherous.

Her eyes burned. "Oh, Adam. Why must you test me this way?" She tried to force away her fears with thoughts of him praying over the minstrel, of the hounds vying for his attention, of Basil curled, sleeping, at his side.

She clutched the package to her lips with a gasp. Adam knew her hand signals and why she used them. He knew every fear of her heart—every secret.

The hounds trusted him.

"I'll not listen to her. I'll not let Mathilda do this to me."

Joan turned the package end over end, kneading it, thinking of Nat. What shame would he endure if she was part of a conspiracy against the king?

He would suffer far more than he had when Brian's men had blackened her name at the alehouse. If she were imprisoned, he might die of shame. Worse, what if she were hanged?

She looked down. Adam's package lay in her hands, crumpled, twisted, the seal broken.

Hot stew from her morning meal rose in her throat. As if it burned her hands, she dropped the mutilated package to the table. It bloomed open like a flower in the summer sun.

Unable to control the urge, she spread the wrapping with the tips of her fingers. The center sheet, stiff new parchment, contained a list of names. The suitors—or some of them. She shifted it aside to the next page. 'Twas a well-creased sheet of paper, in Greek.

She remembered little of her childhood learning from her scholarly father, but a few words leapt off the page at her. The final sheet contained close writing. She saw only the last line. *Keep Joan Swan in Winchester.*

"Joan?"

She looked up.

Adam stood in the doorway. "Why are you still here? What did Mathilda want—" His gaze dropped to the table.

"Adam, I—"

He crossed the cottage and snatched up the papers. "You broke my seal?"

"Nay, it just . . . fell apart." She looked up into his eyes and read naught but disbelief.

"And Mathilda just happened to be here when it happened?" The heat of his words heaped anger onto her guilt.

"Nay, she saw nothing, indeed I have not really—"

"Not really what? Read it all yourself?"

She felt the burn of shame on her cheeks. "I only glanced at it." She ended on a whisper, for his face had gone hard, so devoid of expression it might be stone.

He thrust the papers into his tunic. "I thought I could trust you. Yet I leave you but an hour and find you reading that which is for the eyes of only one man."

"Adam, please, let me explain—"

He turned and strode away. She ran across the cottage to the door. He walked, head up, with long, angry strides toward his tent. Suddenly, he wheeled about and marched back to her.

She recoiled from the fierce expression on his face, backing into the cottage, suddenly afraid.

He walked across the threshold without breaking stride. He pointed his finger at her. "If you so much as say one word of what you read, you could cause good men to die. And if you ever reveal the Roman Way to the river, you shall rue the day."

Tears spilled onto her cheeks. She made no effort to

wipe them away. Words failed her, trapped in her throat.
Then he was gone.

She sank to her knees at the hearth. Misery filled her.
But as she stared at the flames, tears running over her
cheeks, she saw a broken leash hanging on a hook by the
mantle. A leash could be mended if one cared to do the
work. Could this rift with him be mended? Did she want
aught to do with a man who bedded Lady Claris? "Nay,"
she said, jerking the leash from the hook. "A man would
have to have less sense than a mongrel to want that
woman."

She found an awl to bore a new hole for the leash's
buckle. As she stabbed at the leather, she grew angry. How
dare Adam think her so perfidious she would break his
seal deliberately?

He dared because he knew more of her body than her
soul.

She dropped the awl and leash, wiped her tears, and
slipped her feet into the low boots she wore when hunting,
lacing them with sharp jerks of her hands. "I'll make him
see reason. I care nothing for what is in his parcel of papers."

She paused, one boot half laced. "Indeed, I saw naught
to make me believe him a traitor either."

Once, malicious, false gossip at the alehouse had caused
her untold pain. "This time, I'll defend myself, by myself,
to the very man who accuses me.

"I shall demand he tell me for whom he works—King
Henry or Prince Louis. If it be for King Henry, then I shall
tell him his letters opened"—she had a momentary pang
of guilt—"by my rough handling, not through some deliberate intention to read them. I shall tell him to trust me."

She latched the door and faced the black tent. Her stomach felt as if a thousand fleas leapt about in it. "And if he
says Prince Louis, I shall simply say . . . the same thing.
For it is the truth. I cannot believe he works against our

king." To herself, she wondered which truth she most feared to learn—that he conspired with Prince Louis or that he had made love to Lady Claris.

Adam shoved the seal ring and his package of letters far back into the crumbling mortar over the crypt door. How could he have made such a mistake about a woman?

He dusted off his hands, and left the crypt for the stable. A dog walked past him and, unthinking, he slapped his hand on his thigh, fingers stiff and together. The dog ignored him, continued on his way, marking the corner of the crypt wall.

It was how he felt—pissed on.

Something wet nosed his hand. He turned and saw Basil. And Nat behind him.

"Quintin, I just wanted to thank you again for finding old Basil." Nat grinned. "He's more son than work dog, he is. And I want to thank you for the money. For Joan going to Winchester. She's a good girl, isn't she?"

Nat's words penetrated Adam's fury.

"Well, we're off, aren't we?" Nat whistled and headed toward the kennels.

Basil gave a soft woof. Adam put his hand down, fingers together, and Basil went stiff on all fours, then sat, poised like a sentry awaiting an order.

Joan was a good girl.

She'd entrusted him with her secret hand signals, her worries. Her body. Her heart.

"Basil, I'm a fool. What does Joan care of kings and castles?" The dog did not move. "Off with you, now, I've some groveling to do." Adam gave the release signal and watched the old dog bound after Nat with a limping stride.

"Quintin?" The bishop's deacon stepped in front of him as he rounded his tent.

"Good day, Father." He veered around the man and kept walking.

The deacon hurried after him. "The bishop wishes a word, sir, before you gather your men for the tournament. Would you be so kind as to accompany me?"

Adam gritted his teeth, his eyes on Joan's cottage. "Can it wait? An hour?"

"I believe not." The deacon slid his hands up into his wide sleeves and raised his eyebrows. "The bishop insists. He's seeing to the security of the gatehouse. This way."

Weapons were stored in the gatehouse. Adam hesitated. Joan's cottage beckoned, but so did the opportunity to count crossbows and estimate numbers of quarrels.

He followed the deacon. They waited near the great stone gate as two carts pulled by oxen and stacked high with barrels of ale for the feast lumbered across the drawbridge.

The deacon opened a wooden door in the castle wall that Adam knew led in several directions, up to the wall walk, down to punishment cells and the guards' quarters, and finally, to a pair of storage rooms for weapons.

Adam felt a surge of satisfaction as the deacon flung open the door to one of the storage rooms and entered. Adam followed. He turned to close the door, and his world went black.

Chapter Twenty-nine

Joan saw the deacon and Adam walk toward the great gates. She hurried to catch them. She dodged two large carts of ale kegs, and ignored several women from the village who called her name. At the gatehouse, the deacon and Adam entered without challenge. Joan halted, unsure what to do. She must speak to Adam, but hesitated to ask for him of the guards.

"Joan? Why are you not with your father?" Oswald fell into step with her.

A wood-carver's stall drew her eye. "I wanted to have a last look over these wares," she lied and feigned interest in the carving of a small dog. It was a canny likeness and she wished for the pennies to buy it.

Oswald wore his hunting green. Two of his greyhounds sat at his heel while he waited for her. She examined several other carvings of birds while keeping the gatehouse door in view.

Carts and horsemen, servants and villagers passed back

and forth through the gate in preparation for the tournament. In the fields along the river, she could make out men who she assumed were squires or servants. They erected wooden barriers to mark a place for each suitor.

She saw splashes of bright color and realized each area flew a suitor's banner as each claimed his territory.

In the enclosures the men would regroup, rest, repair armor, and gloat over conquests.

Oswald showed no sign of leaving her. He stepped back to avoid splashing mud from a great cart piled with ale kegs, but he took up his post beside her when the lumbering oxen passed.

She glanced about the many stalls clustered near the gates, looking for an excuse to linger.

"Your father has annoyed the bishop," Oswald said.

"What?" She jerked her attention from the gatehouse to Oswald. His pale blue eyes watched her with a slight smile.

"A huntsmen came into the kennels and said he saw a stag with antlers of at least twenty tines. Your father questioned him closely as to the exact location of the beast and then went after it. Alas, his orders were to take deer for the feast."

"He'd not do such a thing," she said, but heard the doubt in her voice. Once she might have stated what Nat would do with complete assurance, now, she might be wrong.

"I'll be gathering my men in another hour for the deer hunt, but your father muttered something about this stag of legend and went off. The bishop was quite annoyed when he came to ask if he could join Nat's huntsmen. I, of course, assured him he was welcome in my party."

Joan dropped the carved dog in her hand. She left Oswald and walked to the kennel as quickly as she could without arousing suspicion. She refused to allow Oswald to see her agitation. Adam should have been in the kennel

299

with Nat. Instead, he was in the gatehouse, and she must find her father.

She interrupted two kennel lads in their sweeping. "Have you seen my father?"

"Nay," one said. The other shook his head.

She went through the stalls that separated the dogs. Basil lay on his bed rack, safe at home where he belonged. She knelt by the lymer and examined his paw.

Her mind seethed with questions. Had Adam taken Basil to curry her favor? Was Nat out in the hills chasing a legend?

With a final stroke to Basil's head, she rose and shook out her skirts. She looked over the ranks of dogs and saw the young lymer, Matthew, was missing. In the rows of hanging bows and quivers stood an empty hook. Her father's.

"If the bishop hunts with Oswald, if Nat fails to make the hunt, we are doomed."

She ran back to the cottage, ignoring Oswald, who called out her name. She threw off the traveling gown and pulled on her hunting green. Taking up her bow and quiver of arrows, she ran for the stable. There, she saddled a mare.

As she passed through the castle gates, she looked again at the gatehouse door. Was Adam still in there? She must explain herself to him. But first, she must find Nat and set him back on his duties.

Beyond the castle gates, Joan wove her way through the carters and servants who prepared for the next day's tournament. The massive numbers of men and horses filled her with dread. It looked as much as if a battle was to be fought in Ravenswood's fields as it did a mock challenge of arms.

As she cantered up into the hills, she wondered at the great amounts of venison the bishop wanted. It could not all be eaten at one day's feast. Were the suitors to linger?

She dreaded the thought. Dreaded the idea Mathilda intended to choose Adam. Just as her imagination shied from thoughts of Adam making love to Lady Claris, so her mind revolted from images of Mathilda and Adam entwined in a lover's embrace.

As she entered the area where the hunters drove deer, she saw only Mathilda and Adam in the lady's fine bed, the hangings let down to ensure privacy while they made love.

Joan knew the skill with which Adam made love. The thoughts brought a pain to her chest like no other.

Adam woke to find himself on the floor of a straw-strewn cell. His head throbbed. When he moved, chains rattled. Attached to his wrist was a wide iron manacle.

The cell door opened. Torchlight dazzled his eyes. Bishop Gravant stood in the open doorway. "You have proved a nuisance, Quintin."

Adam tried to rise, but found his chains prevented it.

"I shall not bandy words with you, Quintin. I want the ring."

To reveal the location of the ring was to reveal the location of the secret entrance through the crypt. He would be giving up more than just Louis's ring. Physical pain did not concern him. Honor did.

"I want Mathilda. When shall we arrange the exchange?" Adam tested the length of his chain. The bishop stood just beyond his reach.

"That simple? I give you Mathilda, you give me the ring?"

"That simple."

"This says you intend to keep the ring and refuse her bargain."

The bishop tossed something at Adam's feet. It was the note he'd sent Mathilda.

"If you read it, you know I did not refuse her. I simply

301

refused to give up the ring. I'm not a complete fool."

"How so?"

"What reason does she have to honor the bargain if I give up the ring? So, I hid it away."

"And if I say you can have Mathilda?"

Joan would cringe to hear them bargain over her lady. "I'll slip the ring on her finger as I wed her. You'll not get it sooner."

The bishop paced in the narrow corridor outside the cell for a few moments, then called for the guard who minded the cells. The guard unlocked Adam's manacle.

When the man retreated to his post, Gravant said, "I'm not a fool either. I'll want more than the ring to give her over to you. I've had wealth beyond your imaginings offered for Mathilda's hand. De Harcourt, alone, offers a king's ransom."

Adam assumed this further bargaining was simply to conceal how much the ring meant to the bishop.

"Let us be clear. I know de Harcourt's worth. We shared our prospective offers," he lied. "I know pound for pound what Mathilda is worth to him. But I agree you should be amply rewarded for turning over the jewel of England's heiresses to a nameless mercenary."

"What do you offer then? Beyond the ring, that is?"

"Whatever I need to. I'll not be outbid by the likes of Artois or de Harcourt." He rattled off a list of manors and stated a sum of silver de Harcourt and Artois could not hope to amass even if they put their fortunes together.

Gravant tapped his finger on his chin. "You can deliver that sum? When?"

"The day after I consummate the vows."

Gravant wrinkled his nose as if he had just noticed his surroundings. "I will hold you to this bargain. I shall perform the wedding ceremony, and if you do not put the ring on her finger upon the vows, one of my men will put a dagger between your ribs."

He turned away. Adam followed the bishop up from the punishment cells. The man's long robes dusted the stairs with every step.

Adam reflected on the bargain he'd made with the bishop. Adam's first thought, that the moment he said his vows and slid the ring on Mathilda's finger, he'd receive a dagger between the ribs anyway, or poison in his wedding wine during the feast, gave way to other ideas.

Did the bishop plan the consummation of the vows so he could collect not only the ring, but also Adam's bride offer?

And Mathilda, the widow, could wed again in a few days, to one of the suitors on the bishop's list, reaping another fortune for Gravant.

Adam imagined the second wedding would wait until after the departure of his men—with his body—whereupon the castle would be closed.

Thoughts of Joan trapped at Ravenswood brought an unholy chill to his vitals. Could he make amends suitable enough to persuade her to leave for Winchester? Or was it too late?

If she refused, he would go to Nat. Nat must take her away—perhaps ride into the hills to hunt and just keep going.

And if Joan refused to go to Winchester, Adam knew he must go himself—within the hour if any good were to come of it.

His steps carried him to the kennels.

Joan rode along the defile without seeing any sign of Nat. Confusion filled her. Why would her father be out here, chasing after a legend? And if he was not, where was he?

Her horse went down beneath her. She rolled away from the flailing hooves and lay stunned on her back, staring up at the blue sky overhead.

The horse thrashed until she regained her feet. An arrow

protruded from the mare's shoulder. She bolted.

Joan cried out and tried to regain her feet. But it was too late, the horse was gone. She knelt in the path and cursed the archer.

An arrow slapped into a nearby tree trunk. And another.

"Joan," called a voice, "stand where you are."

She froze in place.

Oswald came around a tree, dressed in green, a bow in his hands. "There must be a poacher about."

He tried to take her arm. She slipped out of his grasp.

"This is nonsense, Joan. Let me help you, you're limping." He put out his hand. "Perhaps it is Nat who shot the arrows."

"He doesn't come up here with a bow. He comes with his lymer or alone." Joan turned to run. "You're the only man I see with a bow."

"Except me," said Francis de Coucy. He stepped into her path and said to Oswald, "I told you she'd run after her father."

Adam saw Nat with three of his huntsmen in a friendly argument about the preference of ladies for a decorative lapdog over a dependable hunting dog.

Several of the running hounds jumped up against the partition walls and greeted Adam. He recognized many of them now and saw the individuality of their markings, the set of their ears, and the way they moved their heads.

Hugh strode into the kennel from the run, his arm swathed in a fanciful yellow cloth Adam imagined had come from Mathilda.

"Are you looking for Joan?" Hugh asked, putting out his hand for one of the dogs to sniff.

"Why?"

"You spend too much time here for one who is a rather indifferent hunter, and also for one who courts the lady."

"I thought you encouraged me to seek the huntress."

"She's kind, generous, lushly made," Hugh said softly. "She's well loved, or so I hear from gossip. She's not so lovely as Lady Mathilda, but still, she's quite pretty in her own way."

Hugh took Adam's arm and led him away from Nat and his huntsmen, out into the run. No dogs raced around the green space. A servant trimmed the grass along the fencing with long, slow sweeps of his scythe.

"Look, I've a confession to make," Hugh said. "And it's got to be made immediately. I fear if I fall in the tournament"— he touched his injured arm—"I'll die with the sin on my soul. I'm in love, and just thinking of the woman is a betrayal of you and our friendship."

Suddenly, the air around them went cold. Hugh loved Joan?

"I'm in love with Mathilda," Hugh said.

Adam stared at Hugh's craggy features. "The devil you say." But he read the truth in Hugh's eyes.

"Let me think," Adam said. He leaned on the fencing and watched the bustling activity centered on the next day's tournament: Men honed weapons; grooms polished hooves and plaited manes and tails; women stitched rents in caparisons and banners; two carts of ale kegs were being maneuvered alongside the steps up into the hall.

If he was to take the castle by stealth, he needed to be inside. If he went to Winchester, he, or William Marshal, must lay siege. Until his conversation with the bishop, he'd been sure only a siege would result if his team needed to forfeit the tournament. Now, he was not so sure. "Hugh," he said, "I think Mathilda will make you miserable, but I'll see the two of you wed if you but offer me one service. Consider it your penance."

"Anything."

"Take Joan and her father, if you can persuade him, to Winchester."

"You'll forfeit the tournament."

"You're not fit to ride, anyway. If you were injured, I'd never forgive myself. Now do as I ask. Now. This minute. I may forfeit, but I think I can still find a way to linger here." If the bishop really wanted his bribe and the ring, the man would need to contrive some way to allow Adam to stay, if only as a spectator.

And if Joan delivered his letter to John d'Erley, all might not be lost. "Go, find Joan, and persuade her to leave."

"I'd be happy to do so, but Joan's not here."

"Not here?" Adam rounded on his friend. "What do you mean?"

"I saw her ride off with her bow on her back." Hugh frowned. "If she's hunting, who knows when she might return?"

Adam strode past his friend into the kennels and grabbed one of the kennel lads by the sleeve. "Is your mistress hunting?" he asked.

The boy bobbed his head. "Aye. Oswald Red-hair spotted a stag with antlers this big." The boy stretched out his arms. " 'Tis said it's the one from the legends."

Adam swore. "Hugh, I've changed my mind. Stay here and go on as you should. If anyone asks for me, I'm . . . in the privy . . . or swimming. Make excuses for me—say whatever needs saying. As to Mathilda, tell her to prepare to leave at a moment's notice. And when I tell you to take her and go, do so without questions. She'll likely bedevil your days, but if you want her, have her."

"What of Joan? And Nat?"

Adam looked up at the towers of Ravenswood, then to the hills. "I'll see to Joan myself. And, aye, to Nat as well. Now, find Mathilda."

Hugh found Mathilda in her solar. He beckoned her from her circle of gossiping ladies. "I must speak to you."

She followed him from the solar. They climbed the steps

up to the battlements and stood looking over the far fields filled with men and horses preparing for the final tests between the suitors. Hugh wondered if Adam would ever take the field. He spotted Adam mounting Sinner and riding off toward the hills. Going after Joan, he suspected.

"You are very silent. Why did you need to speak to me?" Mathilda asked.

"Do you wish to wed me?"

"The bishop will not allow it."

Her voice was a breathy whisper.

"Will you trust me enough to run away with me?"

"I shall fetch my things."

He grabbed her sleeve as she turned toward the steps. "Not so hasty. I did not mean this instant. We'd get no farther than those encampments there." He pointed to the fields. He hoped the sentries standing nearby would think they were doing naught but discussing the tournament.

"Then when? My lord bishop will see me pledged and bedded ere you make a move, Hugh de Coleville."

"When the time is ripe, the way open, I will tell you. Just be prepared to go." He eyed her up and down. "And I want you just as you are. No encumbrances, no baggage, nothing. Just you."

"Shall we seal this bargain? Now?"

His heart beat a trifle faster. The throb in his shoulder intensified. Blood beat in his temples. And lower. "Now?"

"I want you this moment. Follow me."

He did so, thinking he was as trained to follow her as the hounds were trained to follow Nat Swan. She passed quickly down the steps to the lower levels. Servants bowed or curtsied to them as they wended their way to the physician's chamber.

The healer looked up and smiled.

"I want you to put a new poultice on Lord Hugh's wounds," Mathilda said.

Puzzled at what she intended, Hugh shrugged out of his

307

tunic and shirt and allowed the healer to remove his bandages and look over his wound.

Mathilda stood by, arms wrapped around her waist. Only the soft tap, tap of her small foot betrayed her impatience with the man's careful inspection.

When the bandages were set in place she said, "Now, I want you to go to the gatehouse and see to the wounds of a man called Del. Tell them you come in my name."

"Aye, my lady," the healer said. He picked up a basket and moved slowly about the room, gathering what he needed.

When the healer was gone, Mathilda shoved the man's table across the door to bar its way.

"A clever way to get me naked," Hugh said, one hand on his freshly bandaged shoulder.

"In truth, I thought less of your nakedness than I did of your wounds. I would not want to overtax you."

She put her hands on his hips "And you are not but half naked." She helped him remove the rest of his clothing and he helped her out of hers.

She was all gold in the light of the healer's many candles. Her perfume still reached him despite the hanging herbs and bowls of mysterious concoctions. His cock stood up as stiff and alert as a sentry on the ramparts.

Her hand was warm and soft when she wrapped it around him and began to stroke him.

"I've wanted you since I was ten and two," she said. "Since ever I first saw you."

"I've wanted you since . . . well . . ." She dropped onto her knees before him. "Since a few days ago." He gasped as she nipped his manhood. "As you wish. I have wanted you since almost as long."

She sighed in a whisper of warm breath on his skin. He pulled away lest he make a fool of himself and find release without offering her even a modicum of satisfaction.

She hopped onto the table and held out her arms,

spreading her legs. "You once asked me how many swords I've known. I think you must understand I've played the harlot since Richard died."

He slid into her and held her close against his chest. There was nothing to say.

"I was lonely, but 'tis no excuse for wantonness, is it?" she asked.

"Aye, it is, my love. And I've not been living in a monk's cell, myself. Hush and make no more confessions. The past is the past. Just know you'll polish only one sword from this moment on. Mine."

She moaned softly in her throat when he began to move. He sealed his avowal with quick hard strokes, showing her who was her master. The table thudded against the door with each thrust. But he spared no thoughts for detection, concentrated only on the end. It came with near painful intensity, the blood pulsing in his shoulder as much as in his groin. Her answering gasps filled him with intense satisfaction, but he allowed her only a moment to savor the small ripples he knew still coursed her body.

"Dress and prepare yourself. When I say we must go, we must go. There will be no time for contemplation or good-byes."

She smoothed her gown and slipped her feet into her tiny slippers. "Believe me when I say I shall be waiting for your signal. I cannot wait to bid this place adieu. What shall the signal be? Something secret? Shall you tap your nose? Hold up a certain number of fingers?"

He drew the support for his wounded arm over his head and settled the bright yellow cloth about his forearm. His shoulder throbbed with every movement. "You are ridiculous, my lady. Secret hand signals will never work. Who would think of such a thing? Nay, I shall simply say, 'Time to go.' "

Chapter Thirty

Joan stared at the boy suitor who stood with Oswald in the shelter of the trees. "Nat's not here?"

Oswald smiled. He touched her cheek. She jerked away. His smile became a frown.

"See, Oswald, she's a bitch in more ways than one. Now get her to the lodge."

Francis took her one arm, and Oswald the other.

"I don't understand."

"I told you she was stupid," Francis said to Oswald. To Joan he said, "One night with Oswald and you'll have to wed him." Francis pulled her along, and pain radiated from his fingers up to her shoulder.

"I want her to understand," Oswald said. His hands were more gentle, but she could not wrest herself from his grasp.

"Understand what?" she said. "That you are two fiends for hunting a woman?"

"I should have shot her through the throat to shut her

up," Francis said. "Of course, I imagine she'd be useless then. She'd not be sucking the marrow from anyone's bone after that, would she?"

Oswald clucked his tongue at Francis's crudity. "You're frightening her. You and I are simply going to spend the night together, my dear. Come morning, Francis will find us and report your seduction to his mother. She'll go to the bishop and insist we wed. You'll agree, of course, to save Nat the shame. Remember last time? How he suffered when you spent the night with Brian de Harcourt in the kennels? They still talk about it in the alehouse." Oswald jerked her to a halt. "I'll be wanting exactly what you gave de Harcourt."

"I'll be wanting the same, as well," Francis said.

Joan rolled her eyes up into her head, swayed, and collapsed.

Oswald yelped like a woman. Francis cursed and kicked her thigh. She stifled a gasp.

"Carry her," Francis ordered.

Joan sensed when Oswald bent over her. She opened her eyes, poked her fingers squarely into his, and leapt up. She dashed into the trees.

Adam went first to Joan's cottage. Her saddlebags lay open on the table. One pouch held bread and cheese, the other a clean shift. He pulled it out, held it to his face and breathed in her scent.

He imagined her pulling this soft garment over her head and revealing her lithe, young body for his pleasure.

And he had taken the first opportunity to crush her spirit and question her honor. Now, she was alone in the hills, hunting a legendary stag no one believed in.

Adam felt sure Oswald had used the legend as a ruse to lure Joan into the hills. Joan had only her bow. She had no dogs to guard her.

"Dogs." Adam walked quickly from the cottage, dodging a party of jugglers who performed for any who had leisure to watch.

"Nat," Adam called, "may I take Basil for a short hunt? I'm craving another meat pie."

Nat came toward him with a frown on his face. "I'd lend you Joan as well, but she's not to be found. It's not like the girl to disappear like this."

"I'll find her while I'm out then."

"Take Basil, and bless you." Nat plucked down a leash and collar for the lymer. "I don't like Joan out alone with all these suitors about."

Adam accepted Basil's leash and hurried to his tent.

"Nay, ye're not hunting again, are ye?" Douglas protested.

"I am. Now help me." Adam threw open his coffer. He drew out his hauberk.

"Ye'll no need that for hunting."

Adam shrugged into the heavy coat of mail. "I will for what I'm chasing."

Joan rubbed her sore arm. She crouched against a tree, halfway along the defile, in the exact place Hugh de Coleville had been shot. The forest looked dark and sinister, though the sky overhead was blue, outlining the tops of trees and the birds of prey who coursed the heavens.

She listened and recognized a few sounds, soft, distant sounds.

Oswald had a dog with him now. She knew it was Oswald who was tracking her. He'd shouted and sworn at her as she'd run away. Then he and Francis had stalked her.

Three times they'd shot arrows at her. At her back. Dangerously close. So close, she thought, a sob in her throat, so close they must have meant to kill.

Luckily, Francis cared nothing for the noise he made, swearing, crashing through underbrush. She had managed to evade them, and for a while, she'd thought they'd given up the hunt.

But, Oswald, at least, was back. Silently, this time, save for the telltale sounds only a hunter would recognize.

She worked her way along a barely perceptible deer path, trying to avoid him. But one could not hide from a scenting hound.

Her leg ached from the fall. She knelt behind a deadfall and readied her bow, but when she lifted it, the bow trembled. She stifled a cry of pain. She must have reinjured her arm in the fall.

The dog would find her. She stared at the weapon in her hand and knew she could not shoot a dog, even one of Oswald's undisciplined hounds.

She examined the surrounding trees. If she climbed one, she could avoid the attack of a dog. But she'd be ripe for picking off by Oswald. How had he gone from wanting to wed her to wanting her dead?

Was she mistaken about the arrows? Was it Francis who shot to kill, not Oswald? The horse had not been mortally wounded, and to do his job, Oswald needed to be very skilled. She felt sure it was Francis with the black heart.

And where was Nat? Was he home in the kennels?

The hound came closer, the subtle sounds he made so familiar, she wanted to weep. Even Oswald's horse moved slowly, cautiously.

"I'm such a fool," she whispered. "Why don't I just reveal myself and be done with it?"

Another part of her revolted. She braced herself to rise. To run though her leg throbbed.

But where could she go? Back to the castle where the bishop and Mathilda would simply support the man's claim on her?

To Adam? He despised her.

The thought of his anger, his hard face when he'd seen the open package raised a turmoil of emotion within her.

She could not tell where her anger at his precipitous accusation ended and her pain at his distrust began.

The hound was very close. And hunting silently. The horse came on behind it.

Evasion was useless. Oswald had surely given the dog something to scent. She hung her head and prayed Oswald did not intend to pursue his foolish plot.

She stood up and turned to face the faint line of the deer trail, visible to her, invisible to the casual wanderer. She set her shoulders square and lifted the bow. Though it trembled terribly, she kept it half drawn as an archer would in the hunt.

A dog appeared a furlong away on the trail. A huge gray horse coalesced from the shadows behind him.

"Basil. Adam." She lowered her bow, her knees weak.

Basil lifted his head and bayed. The horse broke into a canter. Moments later, the lymer was in her arms, licking her face, nudging her under her chin.

Adam sat in silence on his huge war horse, sword sheathed at his side, a long fighting dagger in his belt. He wore no mantle, his head was bare, his hair blown back from his brow by the wind.

Her throat went dry. No words would come. He was beautiful. And she feared him.

"What brought you out here?" he asked.

"Oswald told me Nat was after a stag—one only found in legends."

"Nat's in the kennels."

"Thank God." She thrust her arrow into the quiver and slung the bow across her back. "Either Oswald or Francis de Coucy shot my horse. And also shot at me."

"They must be mad."

"I think de Coucy is simply bad. Oswald? I don't understand what drives him. One moment, he is courting me, one moment aiming an arrow at my back.

"He intended to keep me at the hunting lodge all night,

then claim carnal knowledge of me in the morning. The two of them seem to think that would force me to wed Oswald."

Adam's face looked as though it were carved in stone. He settled his hand on his sword hilt. "I'm going to have to kill them both."

She walked away, Basil at her side.

"Where are you going?" he called.

"Home." She did not turn. "I'm perfectly safe with Basil."

"*Jesu*. From an arrow? In the back? *Mon Dieu*."

He swore a few other oaths, but they sounded strangely like the Welsh tongue to her. She stumbled. *Welsh*.

"You can't even walk straight. How will you get home? Must I rescue you every day of the week?"

His horse drew level with her. She looked up at him. "I believe it is I who have rescued you. Don't you have secrets to take to Winchester, Adrian?"

He jerked on his reins. The great warhorse stamped and blew air down its nostrils.

She backed away. "Don't answer that. Forget my hasty words. Of course you have secrets if you are Adrian de Marle. And I know you cannot trust me. I understand . . . I would not trust me either." Her throat felt thick, the forest around her grew blurry. Basil whimpered and nudged her hand with his nose.

Adam swung his leg over the front of his saddle and dismounted. "If you have guessed my name, then you must, at least, appreciate that everything at Ravenswood is not as it seems. My silence concerns the oath I took and for that reason alone, I cannot answer. If I could, I would."

"You would?"

He bent his head and kissed her. She wrapped her hand around his nape and kissed him back. Hard. His tongue was fever hot in her mouth.

"Will I ever see you again?" she asked.

"Am I going somewhere?"

"Winchester."

"I intended to ask your forgiveness in the hope you'd go for me."

She went down on one knee and hugged the lymer. "This is about who you are, isn't it?"

He nodded.

"One of your ancestors built Ravenswood, didn't he?"

"Aye," he said softly. "It is my grandfather's sword hanging in the hall. How did you guess?"

"Little things. Nat swore he saw Adrian de Marle, though I thought it was just another of his confusions. The Welsh curse just now. Is that not where your father settled? And you know a secret way into the castle. You lied about how you found it, didn't you?"

"It happened as I said, save that I was a child at the time."

"I suppose I can now understood how you can separate Ravenswood from Mathilda."

She put out her hand. He placed his, heavy in its gauntlet, on hers. "If you can but trust me, one more time, Adam, I will go to Winchester for you."

He swept her up into his embrace. He wanted to devour her, to shed his mail that he might know the feel of her soft breasts and thighs against his again. Her lips parted to his tongue and he savored the moaning sounds she made.

Her body went taut in his arms. "Dogs," she whispered, pulling away.

Adam lifted his head. He heard the sound, the distant bay of hunting hounds.

"Joan." He touched her shoulder. He drew her toward the shelter of a fallen pine, crouching low. "I believe we have become the quarry."

Her eyes widened. For a brief moment he thought she

might object, but instead, she lowered her eyes and nodded. Her lips formed one word.

Oswald. He must have returned with his pack.

Adam thought of the man hunting Joan. "Go back to the castle. I'll let him hunt me."

She shook her head so violently, her plait whipped across her shoulder. "You cannot run from the hounds. They'll bring down a horse as easily as they would a stag."

He bent his head at the image she painted. Her hand on his knee reminded him of how powerless she was alone. He cared for nothing save that she remain unharmed. He placed his lips near her ear and said. "If we're the quarry, we must behave as such, and evade the hunter. I'm sending Sinner back to the stables. If he returns riderless, perhaps my men will come after me."

"Adam, Basil cannot withstand a battle with a pack of dogs."

"Will he follow my horse, do you think?" He rose and drew the leash from his saddle.

"Aye. If he is leashed, he will go where the destrier goes."

He stroked the destrier's neck, speaking in the great horse's ear. He secured the leashed Basil and the reins to the saddle, then slapped the horse's rump. It pawed the ground, and cantered away, Basil at his heels.

When Adam turned toward the hunter, she made no demur. He did as the stag might, doubling back on their path. If the hounds were scenting hounds, they would have been given something of Joan's or his to aid their search. Adam crossed their path twice before turning and moving in the direction they needed to take, out of the defile.

If they did not leave it, the terrain would herd them. It would lead them to a trap as surely as if they were simple deer.

Adam listened. Wind riffled the leaves. A small animal scurried away in the undergrowth. No hounds gave voice.

He signaled to Joan they should go left, crossing their path again, but she shook her head.

She touched the bow she wore slung on her back and pointed, then tapped her arm with two fingers. He realized they were within two furlongs of the place where the archers in a hunt would be placed. This time, they would not be facing the quarry, their backs to the trees. This time, if there were archers, they would be concealed.

Concealment meant a narrow shooting angle. If they came at Oswald from his right, they would further lessen his chances of hitting them. Adam silently demonstrated to Joan that he wanted her bow. It was the same hunting bow most archers used. It was light and flexible to allow the hunter to stand for long periods of time waiting for the deer with the bow drawn.

Joan only had the five usual arrows a hunter carried. But she also had a dart. It was naught but a small spear, but Adam grinned, it was a weapon he knew well how to use.

They had his sword. He drew his dagger and pressed it into Joan's hand. She stared at it and shook her head, refusing to curl her fingers about the hilt. They warred for a few precious moments, pressing the dagger back and forth between them. In the end, Joan took the long blade in her hand.

He stroked a few strands away from her forehead and kissed her.

They moved up the hill, exposed for a few feet as the trees thinned. He heard the rush of water along a narrow cut where dirt and rocks had been eroded by the last storm. It was Joan who stepped into the water, moving carefully on the slippery rocks, just as a deer might to evade the hunter.

He followed, bow ready. As they headed higher, Adam realized he would follow Joan Swan anywhere. A spill of emotions, so often tangled in confusion within his head and breast, unknotted in a long skein of understanding. If Joan dwelt in a cottage in a village, a daub and wattle hut, or a castle, he would want her, want to lay his head beside hers at night.

Follow whatever path she forged.

All seemed clear as nothing had been clear before. The woman moving up the narrow ravine mattered beyond all else. Returning to Ravenswood without her became a thought that lodged like a dart within his breast.

The bay of a hound sounded below and east of them. Another took up its call. Joan signaled how far away she thought the dogs were, and he was startled to know they were so close. She quickened their pace.

Sweat broke out on his skin. At the top of the ravine, they hunkered down behind a straggly stand of pine. He wiped his hands dry on his tunic.

"Look." Her whisper was no louder than the sound of a breeze on his cheek.

There was an uncanny stillness to her. She knew the forest and knew how to wait, whereas he ached for movement. He forced himself to be still.

She skimmed a finger across the back of his gauntlet and pointed up. Atop the hill, no more than a bowshot away, stood a great stag. The many tines of its antlers were silhouetted against the sky—at least twenty.

Chapter Thirty-one

Adam blinked. He shook his head. Joan nodded and smiled. It seemed the stag of legend was no legend after all.

Joan touched Adam's sleeve and he tore his gaze from the huge beast. She gestured for him to follow her. She headed toward the stag. Adam understood. If they could follow the stag's trail well enough, silently enough not to startle the animal into flight, they might be able to confuse the dogs. And when their paths diverged, stag one way, human quarry another, the dogs might continue after the stag as was their habit.

A light rain began to fall.

The cries of the hounds were nearer now. A horn sounded.

She quickened her pace, moving like a deer across the wooded hill. Light, graceful, sure-footed. He felt clumsy as a boar, knowing he made too much noise. Where she avoided twigs, he bent or broke them. Where her foot avoided loose stones and dead branches, his found them all.

They followed the trail of the stag. He walked with his majestic head up, never looking left or right, as if he were leading them to safety.

Adam saw a dead fox. Insects crawled on its fur and snout. He held Joan still a moment, going down on one knee. He slit the animal's belly. He motioned for Joan to find cover; then he ran as lightly as possible up to the ridge of the defile. There, he rubbed the carcass judiciously along the trial. He wanted it to confuse the hounds.

He smeared the guts in muddy spots where it blended in color as well as in consistency. Last, he buried the carcass in a fallen tree trunk, deep in its soft, insect-riddled cavity, along with his tainted gauntlets.

As he took an angled route up the ridge for a better look over the countryside, he saw old, wooden fencing, hurdles, covered in vines, their staked tops leaning toward the downslope. The fence was deliberately planted to prevent the stag from escaping the hunters. Any stag who tried to leap it would be impaled. Joan had his dagger, so he drew his sword and slashed at the matted vines, separating the hurdles and squeezing through to the hill's summit.

Looking around from the cover of pine branches, he took a sharp breath. A man, garbed in green and leading a pair of scenting hounds and two alaunts, was not three furlongs from where Joan was hidden. The scenting hounds would find them. The alaunts would pull them down. The man was Oswald Red-hair.

To Adam's satisfaction, the dogs followed the stag's path. The question was, would they continue and then divert to the fox trail, or instead, find the human quarry?

When Oswald and the dogs were headed away from him, Adam left his tree. To his dismay, he had left distinguishable footprints. A knight's prints. Swearing, he knelt and unbuckled his spurs, suspending them by their straps on the arrow quiver, far enough apart so they did not clink against each other as he angled his way back to Joan.

She read the news on his face, for she mouthed one word, *Oswald*, and led off, crossing the stag's trail, but veering a bit now to take them away from the security of the animal's scent.

Adam tugged Joan's sleeve when they were back into the floor of the defile. She turned, continuing to weave through the tall pines. He raised his bow and gestured forward, then behind him. With a nod, she allowed him to lead.

He readied the bow. It was not his best weapon, but protecting Joan meant keeping the enemy, whoever it was, distant.

And he doubted not that there would be archers ahead. Oswald was herding Joan and him, driving them between the hurdles, forcing them to take the direction he willed.

"Alaunts," Adam whispered when he had the opportunity, though he realized she probably knew their voices.

Joan gripped his wrist. "Color?"

"One spotted, one gray with a mark here." He touched his shoulder.

A worried look came over her face. He understood. They were not her dogs. She could not hope to use her silent controls on them.

They continued along the valley, doubling and trebling their crossings of the stag's trail and their own.

A slight movement caught his eye. A man, hiding behind a tree, the same man who'd shot Hugh, stepped boldly into their path. Adam thrust Joan aside, too late. The archer was quick. She fell silently. Without thought, Adam loosed his shot.

The archer dropped to his knees with a strangled cry, the arrow in his throat. A gout of blood erupted from his mouth and he collapsed facedown.

Joan lay in the path, eyes wide, face white. The arrow protruded from her thigh.

Adam dragged her under the trees, one eye on the archer ahead. Were his fellows also lying in wait? Or was he a solitary assassin, planted to kill in secret?

The wound on Joan's thigh stained her gown. He took his dagger, flung away in Joan's fall, and slit the fabric around the smooth arrow shaft. The barbed head had not penetrated far.

He put his hand around her nape and drew her up. Her lips quivered as he pressed his hard against hers. At the same time, he jerked the arrow out, swallowing her cry. Tears appeared in her eyes; she looked as hunted as any deer who knows the hound is near.

With as much gentleness as he could muster, though he wanted to tear someone or something limb from limb for hurting her, he kissed her again. Then he considered the wound.

He wadded fabric from her gown and tied it tightly to the wound. Then he dragged the dead archer into the brush and concealed him. The dogs would not be fooled, but another archer or Oswald might miss the telltale signs. The bloody leaves and broken arrow he put under the body, scraping up any dirt that looked stained with blood.

Last, he shoved the archer's arrows into his own quiver. Their heads looked clean and well sharpened, not discolored with ordure.

Joan was waiting for him when he returned along the trail. She was standing now, a stout stick in her hand, one she'd cut with his dagger. The dagger was fisted in her hand, a weapon now, not just a burden she carried to please him.

Although she limped, she did not allow him to lead. This was her terrain, though he remembered it somewhat from childhood. He realized she was heading for a place along the valley where the stream fell into a slower waterway and hence on its sluggish, muddy way to the river.

Adam could hear it. But it was no longer a lethargic body of water. It was swollen with the rain.

All around them the gentle rain pattered on leaves and dampened the earth—making it impossible not to leave footprints.

The shoulders of Joan's green gown were dark with damp. And when they came to the bank, she plunged in to her knees with naught more than a hiss of breath. He could do no less.

The water ran with them and they were pushed along the waterway toward the river.

A horn sounded and Adam judged it came from the direction where the dead archer lay. The dogs would have an easier time tracking them now. The scent of Joan's blood would be strong. They moved slower.

Joan held up her hand for him to halt. She pointed to the bank, where rocks had fallen in to make a natural dam.

He helped her up and out of the water. Would the dogs have lost the scent for the distance they'd waded in water? Would Oswald see through their ruse and follow the stream?

The small stream rushed by them, filling the air with its sound. Any sound man might make, whether footstep or spoken word, would be drowned.

Joan shivered as she limped along the trail. He slid an arm beneath hers and helped take some of her weight. Her body was fever warm, her face flushed, from exertion he prayed.

An arrow thwacked into the trees ahead. They froze. He followed the angle of the shaft to see whence it had come. Uphill, to their right.

He dragged Joan behind a tree trunk, listening. Was it a questing shot? To force someone from cover?

Joan dropped her head to his chest. He stroked her hair

and back, holding his breath and waiting for the archer to make another move. How in tune Joan and he were, not needing to communicate beyond a look or hand gesture.

A man's voice penetrated the sylvan silence, until then broken by little more than the soft patter of rain. His words were indistinguishable but it was not the sound of a man commanding hounds.

Adam's heart thudded uncomfortably in his chest. Not from fear, from a need to put aside this game of hunted and hunter, to confront Oswald no matter how vicious his dogs might prove.

Someone laughed, though 'twas choked off immediately. Joan's head jerked up. She traced an F upon Adam's breast and he understood. Her ears were tuned to the forest sounds, tuned to listen for birdcalls, hound cries, or the call of an injured animal.

If she said 'twas Francis, then it was.

Adam put his mouth near Joan's ear. "It is time to take a stand."

Her eyes went wide; she shook her head.

Again, he whispered. "The forest you know. The hunt. But all hunts must end when the quarry and hunter confront each other."

Adam drew the bow. He stood up and walked slowly forward, using the trees for concealment. She followed, though he gestured for her to stay back. She stubbornly shook her head.

Francis came through the trees on a horse as nervous as Sinner. The horse backed and shifted when Francis raised his bow and shot.

Adam dropped to his knees and shot second. Francis's bolt went overhead; Adam's met its mark, impaling Francis through the shoulder, the same shoulder as Hugh, though this time, the arrow had not passed cleanly through.

Without a sound, Francis fell off his horse. Adam ran

to where the boy lay thrashing in the undergrowth.

Francis's face was white. So was Joan's when she arrived at their side. "Will he live?"

Adam raised his hand and she fell silent.

"Will I live?" Francis grabbed at Adam's hand. "Help me."

Adam slashed Francis's tunic around the arrow. He examined the wound and shook his head. The fall had buried the head of the arrow into the ground. The boy was pinned to the earth.

"I am sorry, Francis, your time is very short. If I move you, or pull this bolt . . . you'll bleed to death."

The boy gave a high-pitched wail. Joan crossed herself.

"You have little time, Francis, so make your confession now, or you'll go straight to hell."

Francis's eyes rolled with fear. He clutched at Adam's sleeve. "Nay, please."

Sweat broke out on the youth's face. Every sore stood out red against the pallor of his skin.

"Confess, Francis. You cannot go to God with these sins. Did you not try to kill Joan but a few hours ago?"

The boy began to cry.

"Why were you hunting us?" Adam asked, taking the boy's hand. "Come. Confess. Cleanse your soul before it departs."

"I'm going. I'm going, aren't I?" Francis clasped Adam's hand and squeezed.

"I'm weary of kneeling here. Either make your confession, or we'll leave you here, pinned to the ground for any animal who might want a taste of you."

"Adam!" Joan gasped.

"Silence, wench. This boy is dying and if he doesn't confess now, he'll burn."

Joan's expression went icy.

"Forgive me, for I have sinned," Francis whispered. "It was my mother who bade me kill you."

"Joan?"

"Nay, you, Quintin. The bishop insisted that Mathilda would pick me on the morrow, but Mathilda told my mother that when the bishop asked for a name, it would not be mine."

Francis groaned and lay back, panting. "My mother does not believe in leaving aught to chance. She's wanted you dead since first she saw you."

"Did you mistake Christopher for me?"

"Who's Christopher?" Tears gathered in Francis's eyes. He began to shake.

"The minstrel who drowned."

He nodded. "She was so angry at the mistake."

Adam unlaced Francis's undershirt, contriving to bump the arrow with his elbow.

Francis shrieked.

Joan struggled to her feet and limped to a lichen-covered boulder. She propped her hip against it and bowed her head.

Adam returned his attention to Francis who wept and clawed at his shoulder. Adam took his hand and held it still. "Continue your confession. During the fair, you met Oswald at the hunting lodge. Why?"

"Mother assessed the suitors when we arrived. She feared you or de Harcourt might capture Mathilda's heart. Women can be fools, you know."

"I know. They are impractical creatures needing guidance."

Joan made a small sound in her throat, but did not interrupt.

"Just as my mother thought. Even with the bishop's assurance that Mathilda would choose me, Mother thought you or de Harcourt should have an accident." Francis squeezed Adam's fingers. "She'll be angry you killed the archer who was to kill you. She liked him very much, I think."

327

Francis's voice grew stronger, so Adam nudged the arrow. Francis hissed in his breath and gasped. Tears stained his cheeks, but the color was returning to his face.

"And the old man? Ivo?" Adam asked.

"Ivo? That old meddler. He saw my mother in the bishop's bed. He chastised her at the fair. She bade me hit him with a piece of firewood." He gripped Adam's arm. "Forgive me, but she is my mother."

"So, he didn't die for any papers he wrote or saw?"

"Papers? Who cares about papers!" Francis looked bewildered. Adam suspected Lady Claris had had Ivo killed less for finding her with the bishop than for reading something he shouldn't—possibly the scroll with the suitors' names?

"Surely, your mother did not intend to kill all the suitors?"

The confusion cleared from Francis's face. "Nay, she planned at first to see that any men Mathilda favored were dismissed. She thought to show our lady how perfidious you could be. And she hoped I might do better than all of you in the games."

There was a pathetic, wistful manner to his speech.

"So, she contrived to make us appear unfaithful wretches. What made her turn to murder?"

Francis gripped his arm. "Say not that word. It was not my fault. I am sorry the minstrel died, but when Mathilda disappeared from the fair—"

"Disappeared?" Adam wondered where the woman had gone.

"Aye. She disappeared," Francis's voice choked on the words. "Mother was enraged. She knew Mathilda was not with de Harcourt. He never left the fair, nor did any others except you. Only you. We paid Mathilda's maid to—"

"Spy on her mistress?"

Francis nodded and closed his eyes. Adam tapped the

arrow and the boy moaned, clutching Adam's hand. Joan made a small, inarticulate sound of protest.

"What did the maid say?"

"She saw stains on Mathilda's clothes and marks on her thighs and—and she said her lady went missing sometimes. Times when only you could not be found."

Joan looked up at him. Her eyes glistened with tears. One spilled over and fell on her breast. Her hand went to her waist. Her gaze was so full of sorrow, Adam felt it within his breast as if a blade were twisting there.

He wanted to reassure her that he and Mathilda had never made love, but could not. He wanted to remind Joan that when he had disappeared, he was often with her.

"Mother knew the only way to ensure that Mathilda picked me was to . . . kill you."

"And since you were already hunting Joan for Oswald, killing me just fit the day's amusements."

"Where is he?" Francis's voice grew sulky. "This is his fault." He gasped, more from fear than pain. "Nay. This is Mother's fault."

Although Adam was sure he knew the answer, he asked the question anyway. "Why did the bishop want Mathilda to choose you?"

"I'm his son." Francis's voice dropped as if his end were truly nigh. "My mother wants Ravenswood for me. Lord Charles knows I'm not his son. He swears he'll leave me naught but an old quarry. One tin mine." He gripped Adam's hand and beckoned him close. "It is right the bishop see to me, is it not?"

Adam nodded. "Another son," he said aloud. To himself, he added, *Another son who wanted property before his time.*

Joan limped away into the lush greenery. Adam had but one more question to ask.

"Remember your immortal soul, young Francis. Answer this truthfully. By what means did Gravant intend to make

329

Mathilda choose you? And why didn't your mother believe in it?"

Francis clutched Adam's hand and closed his eyes. He did not speak for several moments, moments in which Adam thought Joan might be walking out of his life.

"There's a man in the dungeon Mathilda cares about. But my mother is not so sure Mathilda cares for anyone but herself."

The boy fell silent, sketching a shaky sign of the cross on his breast. He began a rambling discourse on his venial sins but Adam had no more time for them.

He leapt to his feet and ran into the trees after Joan. She had not walked far. Indeed, she leaned against a tree, back to him, her green gown striped with damp, her head down.

Certain that words would not be sufficient, he pulled her into his embrace.

"I love you, Joan Swan," he said softly. "But will you believe me?"

She braced the heels of her hands against his chest and shoved at him. "Let me go. You questioned that boy when he is near to dying—"

"He's no more dying than Hugh is. I had to make Francis believe in his death or he'd have told me nothing."

Still, she strained against his embrace. "Why did he need to tell you anything?"

"Because Christopher died in my place. That is reason enough."

Chapter Thirty-two

Adam bound Francis's feet with a twist of vines so he could do naught but hobble along. Then he marched the boy to the hunting lodge. Joan rode on Francis's horse, which had not run far. Her thigh wound throbbed. Her head did, too.

True to Adam's assessment, Francis no longer appeared near death. He had reverted to the behavior of a sulky boy. She was sure his wound needed tending, but she felt less sympathy for him now. He had murdered the minstrel, who'd done naught but bring joy to everyone's lives, and for nothing more than his resemblance to Adam.

She pulled the lodge door open to admit Francis and Adam. She laid a fire in the hearth and then tended Francis's wound as best she could, washing it and tying it up in strips of clean linen from her underdress while Adam secured him to the bed with rope he found in a chest.

Adam insisted on kneeling before her and lifting her skirt.

His hands were gentle as he removed the wrappings on her wound, now crusted with blood. It oozed a bit, but looked better than she'd expected. He gave her privacy as she pulled off her mantle and overgown, to remove the shredded remains of her underdress.

The woolen gown was scratchy against her skin but the linen underdress must serve for more bandages. Adam secured them for her, his hands gentle and warm on her skin.

Adam checked Francis's bonds. The boy jerked on his ropes. "You can't leave me here."

"Aye, I can." Adam grabbed Francis by the tunic, unheeding of his wound. "You left Christopher to drown. I have no sympathy for your minor discomforts."

In the road, Joan shut her mind to Francis's cries.

"I wonder where Oswald has gone," Joan said.

"To ground if he's not a fool. When I find him, I shall skin him with his own knives."

She shivered.

"Forgive me." He scooped her into his arms. He remembered carrying her back to Ravenswood another time. Only a few days ago, yet it felt like a lifetime. "I'm going to saddle a horse for you when we get back. You're coming to Winchester with me."

"Why?"

"At first, I wanted you to go to Winchester to carry my letters. Then I realized you would be safe there. I still believe that."

She laid her head on his shoulder. It was a trusting gesture.

"I never made love to Mathilda. When I disappeared I was often making love to you."

She nodded. "Of course. It seems I'm forever doubting you."

"I cannot allow the bishop to rule here. And anyone he chooses for Mathilda will allow the bishop to rule." It was but half the truth. It pained him to be bound by his oath.

"The bishop sides with Prince Louis, does he not? It is the reason you must send letters to Winchester. To alert them?"

He kissed her forehead. "You are a canny woman. Aye, the bishop sides with Louis. I haven't enough time to ride to Winchester and return in secret in time for the tournament, but I can return afterward and openly lay siege. You must come with me. I must know you are safe."

Joan sighed. "I wish I understood this need men have for a pile of stone. Men are so willing to die for *places*."

She watched a rueful smile twist his beautiful mouth. "Put that way, it sounds rather empty, does it not?"

"Staging a battle is not much different from a hunt—or a tournament. By the time you ride to Winchester and back, the tournament will have begun. Every man in the castle will be armed, ready, mounted," she said. "They will have little trouble shifting from a staged melee to a real one. And with you gone, the bishop will be suspicious. He'll be on guard."

Joan wriggled out of his arms. She stood in the path, her dark eyes blazing with indignation. "The bishop will win! Adam, you could take Ravenswood *tonight*. During Matins."

"I don't understand."

"Will not every man be in his cups, boasting, puffing himself up for the tournament on the morrow? There will be song and merriment.

"I've attended enough feasts to know that few will miss the opportunity to drink deeply of the bishop's wine. The women will retreat into the solar. And the bishop, who must maintain a semblance of piety, will attend Matins with his priests."

Adam nodded. "And during Matins, they will be separated from the soldiery."

"And you can surround the keep at that time—"

"With what army?" he interrupted.

"Mine."

Chapter Thirty-three

Adam carried Joan straight to her cottage. He placed her on the fur-covered couch and knelt at her side. He did as he had once wished, he drew a fur up to her chin and kissed her lips. "Are you sure? Do you truly believe your father is able?"

"Aye," she said, against his lips. "I'll take half the dogs, he can take the rest. We'll come a quarter of an hour after the bells have sounded for Matins."

She kissed him again and he left her. He went to the kennels first. There, sitting at a barrel, drinking ale with one of his men, was Oswald.

Adam drew his sword. The hiss of the blade from the scabbard sent Oswald stumbling to his feet.

"One would not suspect you had spent your day hunting a woman down like an animal."

Oswald held out his hands. "Nay, I swear, I was searching for her because Nat was concerned."

"Did you know we saw the legendary stag?"

His red hair flew as he violently shook his head.

"We did. If one draws a bow on it, 'tis said to be bad luck. I believe Francis de Coucy must have drawn his bow."

Oswald's throat bobbed as he swallowed, his eyes locked on the sword blade as Adam swept it back and forth through the air as if testing its weight.

"What is it you want?" Oswald asked.

"Order your huntsmen, fewterers, and kennel lads to join with Nat Swan's. Take yourself from Ravenswood this hour, on foot, or I will see you tried in William Marshal's court as an accomplice to an attempt to murder me—a valuable knight in service to the king—whereas you are but a worm who mistreats his dogs."

Oswald did as bidden. It pleased Adam to watch Oswald's men and lads congratulate themselves on their good fortune at joining Nat's company.

The rest depended on Joan—and Nat.

Adam approached the chapel just before the bells for Matins sounded.

He watched the pious hypocrisy of the bishop as he led in his clergy and a few other faithful. When everyone was inside, Adam gently set the bar in place. It would not hold them long, but the dogs would see to them anon.

With slow strides as if he might be drunk, Adam mounted the keep steps, carrying an earthen jug of ale. The guard gave him a cursory inspection, then ignored him.

Adam leaned his forearms on the step railings beside the man and drank steadily from his jug.

"Mon Dieu," the guard whispered.

Adam followed his gaze. *"Mon Dieu,* indeed," Adam whispered.

An army of dogs flowed in a silent stream across the bailey, coming, he knew, from the crypt. They moved silently across the cobbles, encircling the stone church.

Leading the pack was Joan. She clasped her hands across her breast and bowed her head. The dogs went on guard. Anyone who left the crypt would rue the day.

At the great gates, another army advanced from the kennels. This one led by Nat. Interspersed in Nat's army were the huntsmen, the fewterers, the kennel lads. They carried their bows loose in their hands as if returning from a hunt.

Although men on guard at the tents watched them, they did not perceive the threat. Several sat down and went back to work. Though the hour was late, dogs and huntsmen were a common enough sight.

As Nat's army advanced, men in black slipped from the tents around Adam's and joined the hunters. These were his men, his mercenaries.

The guard beside Adam took a step forward when Joan reached the steps. He drew his sword, speechless. Joan walked up the steps, the old lymer at her side. Adam lifted his jug and brought it down on the guard's head. He dropped like a stone.

At the door, Joan curtsied to Adam, and at the same time, gave the sign to guard.

Basil stood stiffly over the sentry.

With a nod to Joan, Adam pulled the hall doors open. Light and sound spilled around him. Joan swept her hand out and the dogs ran by her in a swift and beautiful phalanx. The lymers led.

The flow of dogs swept the perimeter of the hall.

The hunters were carried in on the tide. Every man and boy held his bow half drawn by the time he reached the hall doors. When Adam walked into the hall, several warriors had made a halfhearted effort to resist, but they were faced with a ring of archers and silent dogs.

A hush fell on the assembly. The women cowered back near the hearth. Adam nodded at Hugh, who stood at Mathilda's side. Hugh turned and spoke to the lady. The two slipped from the dais and into the throng of servants. They must fend for themselves.

Adam spoke with the same authority and force he used before any battle. "Choose," he said. "King Henry needs you."

No one moved. Roger Artois spat upon the floor.

Brian de Harcourt bowed and grinned. Moments later, his men had joined the huntsmen on the perimeter, but did not draw arms until Adam gave a sign anyone in the hall might recognize—clasping Brian's hand. With one long hiss, de Harcourt's men drew swords and daggers.

Confusion broke out. Women screamed. Men realized they were trapped by a force of more than one hundred— hounds. Some men drew their swords. Some acquiesced without a murmur when Joan and Adam gave the snarling dogs the signal to guard.

Those animals who were not trained, all of Oswald's and some of Nat's, milled and barked, frenzied in a way the others were not. They frightened more than the silent guard dogs.

Adam walked slowly to the dais and bowed to Lady Claris and the suitors by her side.

He took his grandfather's sword from the wall. "I take this castle in the name of King Henry," he proclaimed.

Lady Claris quivered with anger. "The bishop will see you hanged for this." But her eyes were not on Adam's face, they were on something over his shoulder.

Adam turned. Roger Artois was rushing him, sword drawn. Adam met him, his grandfather's sword comfortable in his hand.

Roger fought well, but with wild emotion. Adam fought with the same cold deliberation he'd used to work his way from a tuppence-a-day mercenary to a knight.

It was simple work to force the man back to the wall, for Roger fought without reason, slashing without control. Adam parried the blows. He wanted Roger alive.

The man gave a ferocious yell and lunged. Adam's sword slid down the length of Roger's blade so they were hilt to hilt. With practiced ease, Adam twisted his blade over until Roger screamed and dropped his weapon.

Hand to his wrist, Roger spat at Adam. Then he crumpled to the floor. Behind him, one of Nat's huntsmen stood with a grin. He dropped the length of wood he'd used to lay the man out.

"Bind him," Adam ordered. He surveyed the chamber. A few men made halfhearted efforts to fight. But the archers loosed a hail of arrow over their heads and many dropped their weapons.

A stinging blow caught Adam's wrist. He wheeled about and saw Lady Claris dashing away from the dais, an eating dagger in her hand. He reached out and snatched her gown by the back. Stitches tore open, but her gown held as he pulled her in close.

"You will pay for your sins," he said to her.

She snarled like a wild beast. Another kind of snarling joined hers. She went stiff in Adam's arms, heaving and gasping for air.

"She'll not move," Joan said, unleashing a pair of alaunts.

A shout at the hall door told Adam the chapel hounds had failed in their work. Gravant burst into the hall. Only a few men were with him. The bishop shouted for order.

No one obeyed. Those not intimidated by the snarling, barking dogs were held immobile by the archers.

Gravant strode through the hall, Oswald Red-hair at his side. Adam realized he should have escorted Oswald off Ravenswood Manor himself. While the bishop ordered the dogs and archers out, Oswald veered to the hearth and snatched down the Viking ax.

He came at Adam swinging. Oswald's blows rang against the metal of his grandfather's sword. The old sword could not sustain much more before it broke. Then a pack of dogs rushed through the tables. They surged like an ocean of flesh toward the hearth, silent, teeth bared. Oswald was engulfed.

Joan ran to Adam and buried her face against his mailed chest. "They were not my dogs. They didn't obey me."

It was Nat who stopped the dogs from savaging their master.

"Don't look," Adam warned Joan, pulling her away from the carnage of a man who mistreated his animals.

"Bind every man," Adam said to his men. "Take them to the dungeons, or the cells beneath the gatehouse. There they can remain until we sort out who is loyal to King Henry and who is not." He grabbed Douglas's arm. "Find a young man named Del while you're searching the cells. Take him to the physician and leave Roger and Lady Claris in his place. And this one"—Adam pointed to the bishop—"his rank demands he have a cell all his own."

Chapter Thirty-four

Adam took Joan to the Diana chamber for privacy; there was precious little of it in the keep.

She lighted all the candles and did as he had once done. She spread out her mantle and sat in the middle. This time, however, he did not go to her. He looked at the mosaic. "I'll be sorry when those corridors are blocked up, but it must be done."

"Will you fill this chamber?"

He smiled at her. "Only from here to the river. This is too precious a place to destroy."

"I suppose Hugh and Mathilda are wed by now," she said softly. "I'm glad they got away, and I hope they are happy, though I suspect he will need to keep an eye on her every day." Adam smiled at Joan. "And she on him."

How lovely Joan looked, her arms neatly folded about her knees, her hair tamed in its plait. He wanted the wild creature, but he loved this quiet, gentle woman, too.

"My father left Ravenswood for his own good reasons,

reasons I never understood, because they caused his banishment. I think I understand now." He touched the cold, mosaic tile of Diana's knee. "What use is a place such as this if you have no one to share it with?"

"Come here, Adrian."

"Can you love me as Adam? A simple man, a mercenary turned knight?"

"I have loved Adam since first I laid eyes on him in the forest, unhorsed by a boar."

He smiled. "And now?"

"I suppose I shall have to love Adrian as well. It is how you will present yourself in the morning to William Marshal's man, is it not?"

"I haven't decided. Revealing who I am may mean I leave here, leave England. The banishment extends to me and my brother."

"And you want to know if I can follow? Because of Nat?"

"Aye. I cannot promise I will be allowed to remain. I can ask it, but I cannot make a guarantee."

"You could continue as Adam Quintin."

"I could."

She sighed and reached behind her to let down her hair. It was as fascinating and arousing a process as any he knew.

"Well, Joan, what do you say?"

"I must think about it. I owe Nat my first allegiance. I cannot allow him to be harmed by my decision."

She remained seated but held out her arms. He went to her because he could not resist her. And she was pliant and giving, soon naked and ready. But as he made love to her, he wondered if it was for the last time.

When they had exhausted themselves and lay wrapped in his mantle, she slept. He did not.

The castle, secure now, might be his by right of battle, albeit the strangest one he'd ever taken part in with an

341

army composed mostly of animals, but would it be granted outright?

Joan stirred in his arms, burying her face against his chest. At the most, as Adam Quintin, he could expect the rights of a seneschal, or steward, of the manor.

He thought of how he wanted the name of de Marle restored to honor. It would not be true honor if he earned it under any name but that. Quintin needed to die.

"Joan," he said softly. She did not stir. "Can you love a lord's son? One who invaded the privacy of others, read their documents? All for the cause of a king, but, in truth, for his own cause as well?"

The entourage that rode into Ravenswood came slowly. There was a sizable guard, then several knights. One caught Adam's eye and he squeezed Joan's hand. " 'Tis Marshal, himself, come to see how I've acquitted myself."

"I must change this gown."

Adam resisted the tug of her hand. "You'll remain exactly as you are. They'll remain exactly as they are." He nodded to the three hounds that stood with her.

William Marshal climbed the keep steps slowly. Adam thought he must be at least seven decades old. His age showed in every line on his face. The role of regent to a boy king weighed heavily on the man.

"Welcome to Ravenswood." Adam bowed and stood aside.

"It went well, then?" Marshal asked.

"Aye, my lord. It went well." He followed William Marshal into the hall.

Everyone stood as the earl walked to the dais. When he sat, servants rushed to pour him wine. Adam waited respectfully to be called forward. When the earl had drunk his fill, he invited Adam to sit at his side.

"So, John d'Erley told me everything. I congratulate you on taking the castle without much effort. However, the lawyers tell me we cannot accuse Gravant of treason to our king on the evidence you sent along. His name is not mentioned anywhere. The document looks like what it is, an agreement between six noble sons and Prince Louis. We need some proof the Church is involved if we are to make Gravant squirm. We need something solid."

Adam grinned. "I think I have just the thing."

William Marshal made a great ceremony of releasing Bishop Gravant. He made flowery apologies for Adam's overzealous efforts on the king's behalf. Marshal invited Gravant to wash and garb himself and sit down to supper at the high table, as if he had no sins upon him.

Adam found it difficult to watch, but thought he hid his feelings as he must, playing the role of the lackey to the great William Marshal, fawning a bit, which earned him a grin from the earl, who knew Adam well.

Joan did not appear in the hall, but when the earl suggested they all attend Matins and that the bishop officiate, she walked in with Nat. They stood in the rear of the chapel, while Adam knelt for his prayers beside the great William Marshal and his squire, John d'Erley.

Gravant rushed through the service, but the bishop's haste suited Adam well. It was time to bring the man to his knees.

William Marshal spoke to the bishop in deep, sonorous tones when the clergy had sung the final notes of the service.

"Bishop Gravant, will you bless Adam Quintin for me? I must send him into battle again."

Gravant's face went stony, but he bowed his acquiescence and held up his hand. Adam walked to the fore of the chapel, to the spot where he remembered his mother lying after death, garbed in flowers.

He knelt before the bishop. The bishop made the sign of the cross over his head, then held out his hand. Adam gripped it tightly with both of his. He pressed his lips to the bishop's ring. At the same time, he jammed Prince Louis's ring on Gravant's smallest finger. Gravant grunted and struggled to snatch his hand away, but Adam held it fast.

"Why, my lord Bishop," Adam said, turning the bishop's hand to the blaze of candles on the altar, "what need have you for this ring I kissed when you have another that pledges your loyalties elsewhere?"

William Marshal came to Adam's side.

"What is the meaning of this?" Gravant asked.

Although Gravant jerked his hand, Adam held it fast. Light gleamed off the seal of the French prince.

"Ah, something solid, after all," said William Marshal.

Joan looked up from dosing Basil. She squealed and hid her dirty hands behind her. William Marshal and one of his men stood by the low boards of the kennel, Adam at their side.

"Is this the one?" Marshal said.

Adam grinned. "Aye. She's a beauty, isn't she? Loveliest thing in the kennel."

William Marshal laughed and Joan felt the heat sweep up her cheeks. She was far from lovely. Her hair was down, her gown streaked with dirt from caring for the dogs who'd injured themselves in the battle.

"My lord," she said, dropping into a low curtsey, but giving Adam a sharp glare.

"Adam has asked permission to wed you," William Marshal said. "My man has all the details." He bowed as if she were a fine lady and walked away. To Joan's shame, she thought she heard him laugh again.

Adam vaulted the low boards and put his arm about her waist. The man the earl had indicated pursed his lips. He wore a monk's robes and held them up as he neared them. She was sure he'd never before set foot in a kennel.

"The earl has granted Adam Quintin position as seneschal of Ravenswood Manor until such time as its fate is decided. And with that honor will come all right to rents, tithes, and so on. With the exception of that owed the king."

"You may go," Adam said and the man tiptoed from the kennel, his nose in the air.

"I see you are still Adam Quintin." Joan slipped from his embrace to pick up her bowl and cloth. She walked out of the kennel and discarded the water and vinegar she'd been using in the grassy space behind the building.

"I have you and Nat to consider now. I don't want to take a chance someone else might be given the honors here."

She stared at him. "You took over this castle with the minimum of bloodshed, you deserve to be reinstated here."

"And if Marshal will not lift the banishment?"

"Then you will go."

"Without you."

She gripped his hands. "Aye, without me, but I will always be here. You can ask again and again for Marshal's favor until he grants it. And while you wait, I shall be here."

"But not in my bed."

Joan studied his blue eyes, solemn now; there was no hint of joy in them. "I will mourn the loss of you each and every day, but I want to wed a man who knows who he is and what he wants. I want to tell our child, should there be one, what his name is."

Adam pulled his hands from hers and strode away.

Later that day, as Joan brushed Basil's coat, Edwina made an unexpected visit to the kennel.

"What happened between ye, Joan?" Edwina asked. "Quintin rode out with 'is men not an hour ago."

345

"I don't understand. He left?" Joan looked out across the bailey. The black pavilion was gone.

The pain was not so raw as it had been when Mathilda had paid her call. Nay, this pain was dull. She imagined it would last much longer than the other.

"Aye," Edwina said. "Adam turned William Marshal down, 'e did. Said 'e won't be seneschal 'ere, then he up and left."

Chapter Thirty-five

Joan and Nat stood before William Marshal after a day of hunting. She was pleased to hear England's greatest knight praise Nat's men and dogs.

A man Joan recognized as John d'Erley, Marshal's squire, strode up the center of the hall. "My lord," he called, "you must come to the castle gates."

William Marshal hesitated, but Joan surmised that the urgent tone in the man's voice convinced him to rise. At the foot of the hall steps, Marshal's mount waited.

To her surprise, servants were running toward the gate. She saw Edwina and Del, limping along with a stick, heading in that direction as well. The king's regent mounted the waiting horse.

Joan lifted her hem and ran along with a throng of curious people.

She could see nothing as she ran.

"Are we being invaded?" asked one woman, clutching her child in her arms.

"Nay," one of the kennel lads said. "They's not enough men fer that."

Joan kept her eyes on William Marshal, who did not rush to the gates, but trotted there at a leisurely pace, his squire beside him.

As they left the inner bailey for the outer, she saw through the gates a company of men spread out in a V.

Her eyes suddenly burned. She pressed a hand to her breast.

The waiting horses were caparisoned in black and gold. Their riders bore shields with a stylized V upon them. Their faces were concealed by their helms. They ranged themselves in disciplined ranks behind a knight on a huge gray destrier.

Adam.

There was no mistaking him for he wore no helm. He did wear a long black surcoat over his mail, a V embroidered in gold on his chest.

William Marshal walked his horse over the drawbridge to confront the party. The two knights faced each other.

Joan squeezed through the gathering throng. The guard at the gate, Thomas, put out his pike to shove back two boys and let her pass.

She stood in the shadows of the great stone arch, the portcullis, dangling over her head. It was cold in the shade and she shivered.

A gasp ran through the spectators when Adam drew his sword.

"My lord, I beg admittance to Ravenswood. Not as your agent, or your servant, but as its master."

Marshal circled his horse. "By what right do you make this claim?"

"By right of ancestry." He lifted the sword and touched the V on his chest with the hilt. "And by right of service to the king." He lowered the blade and bowed.

"Who are these ancestors by whom you make claim?"

"Four generations of de Marles."

Behind Joan, the crowd whispered the name of de Marle, passing it along from the front of the throng to the back. She clasped her hands tightly together. Her skin felt suddenly hot.

"Would you be Adrian de Marle . . . or Robert?"

"Robert serves God these days as a priest in Wales."

"And you serve me."

"Long and well, my lord."

Marshal looked at his squire. "How long?"

"Ten years, my lord, and two before that in King John's Flemish company."

"A long time," Marshal said. "Not so long as I have served the Crown, but a good start."

Adrian's men never moved. They sat on their huge horses, in their black and gold, as forbidding a force as ever Joan had seen. Yet, she did not feel afraid of the men. She only feared that Adrian's hopes might die a death here, never to be resurrected.

William Marshal and his squire, who had joined his master, spoke in low tones. Then Marshal nudged his horse forward. Adam walked his to meet the great man. They sat facing each other. Marshal put out his hand.

Adam surrendered the sword. Marshal examined it. "This is a fine weapon."

Joan saw the hilt was polished now, the old metal gleaming.

"That sword," Adam said, "belonged to my grandfather. It is a sword I have sworn to wear. But I cannot wear it as Adam Quintin. I can only wear it as Adrian de Marle, son of Durand de Marle."

Silence, save for the jingle of a harness, the cry of a child, reigned over the crowd.

Marshal extended the sword to Adam. "Wear it as is your right and enter this castle as its rightful heir."

Adam took the blade, studied it a moment, then thrust

it into its sheath. His men gave a short, abrupt shout of approval.

William Marshal wheeled his horse and addressed the castle people who filled the gate. "Know this man may ride in with impunity to rule and guide this manor until such time as another de Marle, Durand by name, should choose to reclaim his rights. Until that time, I do appoint his son, Adrian de Marle, as guardian of Ravenswood Manor and all its people. In King Henry's name I hereby lift King John's banishment."

The swell of murmuring became cheers. Men waved their hats. Someone shouted for ale. Another for wine.

Marshal smiled at Adam over his shoulder. "The lawyers can untie the knots when I return to Winchester. Shall we take up these fine folk on their offer? I've a thirst for an English ale, myself."

The crowd parted for him. He walked his horse back through the castle grounds. John d'Erley guided his horse aside and Adam cantered his forward as next in rank behind the king's regent. Adam's men fell into a line behind him.

When Adam reached the spot where Joan stood, he drew up his horse and put out his hand. She took it and kissed the back. "My lord Adrian," she said.

The words came forth as if reeds choked her throat. She curtsied deeply.

"Ride with me, Joan, and know you will be my lady."

The people pressed in. Hands reached out from the crowd and she was lifted and fairly tossed onto the saddle before him. He laughed and held her close, his arm tight about her waist.

She rode with him in his triumph. His father was reinstated, his right to be heir of Ravenswood restored. They rode with the crowd surging along at their side. The kennel lads called out to her and she waved, then snatched her hand back and tucked it against her chest.

"A goddess may wave to her subjects," he said, giving his own salute to Edwina. Beside her, Del raised his stick and shook it in the air.

"A goddess? A moment ago I was to be a lady."

"You are the goddess of the hunt here at Ravenswood. But as I shall be known from this day by my rightful name of Adrian de Marle, so shall I promise not to call you Diana. You are a great huntress in your own right and shall be naught but Joan—*my* Joan."

Joan sat between Edwina and Nat in the hall. Adrian sat at William Marshal's side. Despite his words in the bailey, she feared what he had become. The lord of Ravenswood. Or son of the lord. Whether his father cared to return mattered not.

Ale and wine flowed long and freely. The minstrels composed a song to Adrian's triumph over the bishop. They sang of the boy king and the kingdom's greatest knight.

She concentrated on her meal, quail roasted in rosemary. She concentrated on the conversation at her table. That of the increase in Nat's hunting stable and the long hours it would take to undo Oswald Red-hair's poor teaching.

A hand fell on her shoulder. When she looked up, it was Adrian.

"Would you come with me while I say a prayer for my mother's soul?"

They walked with decorous slowness through the hall, but when they reached the foot of the hall steps, they linked hands and ran to the crypt, passing the priest, who gave them a disapproving glare.

They dutifully said prayers for Adrian's mother.

"He'll think we're blaspheming down here," Joan whispered as Adrian unlocked the trapdoor and lifted the section of floor.

They ran the length of the corridors to the Diana cham-

ber and there, she leapt into his arms and kissed him
soundly. "My Adrian," she said, testing his name on her
lips. "I love you."

"My Joan," he said. "My huntress. Beautiful as any
goddess and worthy of the name."

Joan offered Adrian her back and he unlaced her gown,
sliding the soft wool off her shoulders. He kissed her warm
skin, shifting her plait out of his way.

"I love the way you smell . . . and taste." He tugged her
gown down her hips and let it pool at her feet.

When he wrapped his arms about her waist, she leaned
her head back. "You're wearing too many clothes," she
said.

"Is that what you want? My clothes off?" He nuzzled
her neck.

"Did you not ask me once what women really want?"

"I believe *my* riddle was what do *men* really want?"

Joan captured his hand and clasped it to her breast.
"The answer is the same, whether man or woman. Each
wants his or her own way. Now, off with your clothes,"
she said.

He seemed unable to remove any article of clothing
without her help, complaining of some weakness in his
hands from fighting with his grandfather's sword. She
smiled and knew it was but a game he played.

It was she with the bandage about her thigh.

"You realize," he said as she straddled his leg to pull
off one of his high hunting boots. "I shall ever remember
this view of you."

She whipped around and clasped the boot to her chest,
then laughed. The sound echoed around them.

She set the boot down and picked up her shift. She held
it in front of her, suddenly flooded with desire, and equally
with a need to know the answer to one last question.

"How did Lady Claris know you had bruises on your—"

He threw back his head and laughed. She heaved his boot at him. He caught it. "I imagine every woman knows what my ass looks like. After the wrestling, we suitors stripped for any and all who chose to watch us bathe that day. Only my innocent Joan was absent from the ramparts."

"Is that what you think? I am innocent?"

"Innocent of guile and perfidious behavior, aye. I must say I cannot imagine you eyeing naked suitors from the castle walls." His throat went thick. "How different this could have turned out."

She knelt between his spread thighs, helping him off with the rest of his clothes. He lay on his back, knees raised.

She made a small cushion of his linen shirt and put it under his head. Then she set her palms on his spread thighs and he felt the desire to pull her down.

"When you were sitting at table, I thought, 'This is a noble's son.' And I was right." She leaned over and kissed him where his thigh and hip joined.

He closed his eyes, buried his hands in the brown and gold sheet of her hair, and felt his heart stutter in his chest. Her tongue was warm and gentle across his skin; her hands were not so gentle.

"Joan. I pray that you have the same want as I," he whispered. He drew her up and astride him.

She rocked gently. He arched beneath her. When he settled, she did it again. "You stir madness," he whispered.

Joan reveled in the sensations of his aroused body deep within her. She understood his madness. It brewed within her as well. She took up his hand and placed it over her breast. He cupped and weighed her, explored her shape, lifted his head, and kissed the swollen peak.

Then he wrapped his arms around her hips, buried his face between her breasts, and breathed fire on her skin.

She was supported in the cradle of his raised legs.

"Adrian," she said, "I remember thinking, the first time you entered me, that no possible moment could succeed it for joy. I was wrong. Each of these moments holds its own most perfect happiness."

"Joan." He pressed his lips to hers. He rolled her over. "Let it be as it was that first time." He stroked into her, deeply, slowly, hoping he could hold back for her.

She was sweet, hot silk about his manhood. There was nothing but her in that moment, no other wants or desires but feeling the slick slide of his body into hers.

He recognized her end in the sudden buck of her hips, the gasp, the clutch of her fingers on his back. He rode her storm, reveled in the throes of her passion, and knew her wants and his were the same.

They came out of the crypt, hand in hand, a few hours later to the soft, golden glow of the setting sun. Brian de Harcourt stood by the chapel with his horse, arms crossed on his chest.

"Were you praying for your mother's soul?" Brian asked.

"So, you heard I've changed my name."

"It explains many things." Brian took Joan's hand and lifted it to his lips, then addressed Adrian. "I came to thank you for taking my part when the suitors were examined. If not for your assurance that I'd not signed Prince Louis's pledge, I might be a banished lord myself. Or hanged, as Francis surely will be. What will become of Lady Claris?"

"I expect she'll be exiled to France along with the bishop and the other suitors," Adrian said.

"The death of her son might be a greater punishment than anything else." Joan covered Brian's hand with hers. "Are you staying?"

Adrian growled, but Brian and Joan ignored him.

"I must find another way to satisfy my father. He expects me to increase the de Harcourt wealth. Ravenswood stood to be a great jewel in our crown."

"I hope you'll return one day," she said.

Not too soon, Adrian replied silently. "Wait here, Brian, I have something for you."

Adrian went back into the crypt. He groped over the door and withdrew the sheet of Greek purloined from Brian's chest.

When he stepped back into the sunshine, Joan stood in the circle of Brian's arms. The heat of jealousy swept through Adrian, but he clamped it down. Joan would be his wife. Brian would ride away.

Adrian cleared his throat and the couple stepped apart.

Brian grinned and lifted his shoulders. "You cannot blame me for a final embrace."

"I took this from you," Adrian said without preamble. "In my search for the bishop's plot, I did many things of which I am not proud, including searching your tent. As I could not read this, I suspected it."

Brian unfolded the sheet of vellum. "It's an old letter of Richard's. I kept it for no good purpose, save it was from him."

Joan looked at the letter, then up at Brian. "What does it say?"

"You read it," Brian said, putting it into her hands.

"You read Greek?" Adrian asked, incredulous.

Joan examined the paper. "Not well. Mathilda insisted on learning along with Richard. Her father indulged her, though he thought it a useless activity. He did not know they employed it to send each other messages he could not read. As for me, I learned from my father. He studied Greek literature, particularly in the field of philosophy."

"Mathilda could have read this to me?" Adrian was stung that he'd thought Mathilda's head filled with naught but air.

"Aye." Joan took the page. "I can read but a word here

355

or there. See—" She touched several words with the tip of her finger. "This is 'father.' Repeated over and over."

"It is mostly a tirade on Richard's dissatisfaction with his father," Brian said, looking up at Adrian. "And the rest is about his love of Joan."

Her cheeks colored. Adrian shook his head. "Well, I do feel the fool."

Brian folded the letter and tucked it into his tunic. He turned to Joan. After a moment's hesitation, she threw her arms around the warrior and kissed him hard—on the cheek. "Go with God," she said.

Brian walked to his horse, mounted up, raised a hand in farewell, and cantered off.

"I do so hope he finds what he is looking for," she said, encircling Adrian's waist.

"A great manor to conquer and add like a jewel to the de Harcourt crown?"

She squeezed him. "What is it men really want, Adrian?"

"Their own way?" he asked, grinning.

"Nay, I think they really want what women want."

"Aye. Their own way."

"Love, Adrian. Love."

He took her to the chapel and led her to the niche dedicated to the Virgin Mary. "I once prayed to this lady that I might be worthy. At the time, I thought I wanted to be worthy of this place, of rule. As I hunted for Marshal's traitor, I realized I was not defined by my name, but by the things I did. Whilst here, I have alternately been a soldier, a thief, a liar, a—"

"Lover," she said. "Do not be so harsh upon yourself."

He took her hand. "I think the Virgin granted my wish, but in a way I hadn't planned. It is of you, Joan Swan, I wish to be worthy, not my name."

"You are." She kissed his fingers, entwined with hers.

Adrian brought Joan a cushion and knelt at her side. He clasped her hands between his.

He looked up at the Madonna. "I want to thank her for sending you to me in the forest. My life was changed from that moment."

"Thank her for the hounds. It was they who saved your life."

"You brought them into the forest."

"You wielded the sword."

"Joan, you're forgetting the answer to the riddle. I want my way. If I say you saved and changed my life, then it must be so."

"Have your way." Joan bent her head and kissed his fingers. "But just this once."

When they emerged from the chapel, they saw at least a dozen carters loading the forfeit belongings of the suitors into William Marshal's wagons, destined for the royal vaults.

Outside Joan's cottage, Nat sat on a bench, eyes closed, head back, three hounds by his feet. Joan and Adam laughed when they both lifted their hands at the same time, in the same signal. The dogs rose and bounded toward them.

They changed direction after a few strides to chase a pair of birds who landed where a black tent once stood.

The birds were ravens.

Ann Lawrence
Lord Of The Mist

As he kneels in the darkened chapel by his wife's lifeless body, he knows the babe she has birthed cannot be his. Then the scent of spring—blossoms, wet leaves, damp earth—precedes an alluring woman into the chapel. As she honors his dead wife with garlands, she seems to bring him fresh hope, just as she nourishes the little girl his wife has left behind.

Even though this woman is not his, can it be wrong to reach out for life, for love? He cannot deny his longing for her lush kiss, cannot ignore her urge to turn away from yesterday's sorrows and embrace tomorrow's sweetness.

Lord of
The Keep
Ann Lawrence

He has but to raise a brow and all accede to his wishes; Gilles d'Argent alone rules Hawkwatch Castle. The formidable baron considers love to be a jongleur's game—till he meets the beguiling Emma. With hair spun of gold and eyes filled with intelligence, she binds him to her. Her innocence stolen away in the blush of youth, Emma Aethelwin no longer believes in love. Reconciled to her life as a penniless weaver, she little expects to snare the attention of Gilles d'Argent. At first Emma denies the tenderness of the warrior's words and the passion he stirs within her. But as desire weaves a tangible web around them, the resulting pattern tells a tale of love, and she dares to dream that she can be the lady of his heart as he is the master of hers.

___52351-5 $5.99 US/$6.99 CAN